What readers are saying:

'I couldn't turn the pages fast enough'

'Absolutely brilliant. **Couldn't put this book down**.
Right from the very start you are **gripped**'

'A **chilling** tale of friendships, deceit, manipulation and
secrets that had me **hooked** in from the very first page'
'**Such a gripping story** that I read the rest of the
book in one sitting. **I just had to know what
was going to happen**'

'An **intense, chilling read** that kept me
gripped throughout'

'Heidi Perks writes with an instinctive knowledge
of how to keep the reader **enthralled**'

'**Brilliant** book to have for **summer reading**'

'This is a taut thriller that reads **like a TV drama**
in-the-making. It'll make you wary of those
around you, past and present'

NOW YOU SEE HER

Heidi Perks worked as a marketing director for a financial company before leaving to become a full-time mother and writer. She is a voracious reader of crime and thrillers and endlessly interested in what makes people tick. Heidi lives in Bournemouth with her family.

Praise for NOW YOU SEE HER

'A gripping tale of friendship and deceit, where nothing is what it seems' Laura Marshall, author of *Friend Request*

'Believe us when we say this novel is the real deal. *****'
Heat Magazine

'Totally hooked from the first page. Such an accomplished thriller!' Amy Lloyd, author of *The Innocent Wife*

NOW YOU SEE HER

HEIDI PERKS

arrow books

5 7 9 10 8 6 4

Arrow Books
20 Vauxhall Bridge Road
London SW1V 2SA

Arrow is part of the Penguin Random House group
of companies whose addresses can be found
at global.penguinrandomhouse.com

Penguin
Random House
UK

First published in Great Britain by Century in 2018
First published in paperback in Great Britain
by Arrow Books in 2019

www.penguin.co.uk

A CIP catalogue record for this book is available from
the British Library.

ISBN 9781787460775

Typeset in 10.56/15.95 pt Palatino
by Integra Software Services Pvt. Ltd, Pondhicherry

Printed and bound in Great Britain by Clays Ltd, Elcograf S.p.A.

For Bethany and Joseph
Dream big and believe in yourselves

NOW

'My name is Charlotte Reynolds.' I lean forward as I speak into the tape recorder, though I'm not sure why. Maybe it just feels imperative that I at least get my name across clearly. Reaching out for the glass in front of me I grip it between my fingertips, pushing it slowly in anticlockwise circles, watching the water inside it ripple into tiny ridges. I don't even realise I'm holding my breath until I let it out in a large puff.

The clock on the otherwise bare white wall flashes 21:16 in bright red lights. My children will be in bed by now. Tom said he will stay the night and sleep in the spare room. 'Don't worry,' he told me when I called him earlier. 'I won't go anywhere until you're home.' This isn't what I'm worrying about but I don't say as much.

Home feels so far away from this airless whitewashed room with its three chairs and desk and the tape recorder balanced on one end of it, and I wonder how long I will be here. How long can they keep me before they decide what comes next? Ever since the fete I have dreaded leaving my children. I'd do anything to be tucking them into their beds right now so I can breathe in their familiar smells, read them that one more story they always beg for.

'They're not holding you there, are they?' Tom had asked me on the phone.

'No, they just want to ask me a few questions.' I brushed off the fact I was in a police station as if it were nothing. I didn't tell Tom that the detective had asked if I wanted someone to be with me, that I'd refused and had assured her as breezily as I could that I didn't need anyone as I'd happily tell her what I knew.

My fingers begin to tingle and I pull them away from the glass and hold them under the table, squeezing them tightly, willing the blood to rush back in.

'So, Charlotte,' the detective starts in a slow drawl. She has asked me if she can use my first name but hasn't offered me the privilege in return. I know her name is Suzanne because she said as much into the tape, but I expect she knows I won't call her that. Not when she introduced herself as Detective Inspector Rawlings. It's a small point but it reinforces who is in control.

My breath sticks tightly in my throat as I wait for her to ask me what I was doing there tonight. In many ways the truth would be the easy option. I wonder if I tell her she'd let me leave now so I can go home to my children.

The detective is interrupted by a knock on the door and she looks up as a police officer pokes her head into the room. 'DCI Hayes is on his way from Dorset,' the officer says. 'ETA three hours.'

Rawlings nods her thanks and the door closes again. Hayes is the Senior Investigating Officer in what has become the Alice Hodder case. He has become a constant fixture in my life over the last two weeks and I wonder if this means I will be kept here until he arrives because I assume he will want to speak to me. The thought that I could be cooped inside this room for another three hours makes the walls close in deeper. I don't remember ever feeling claustrophobic but right now the sense of being trapped makes me feel light-headed and my eyes flicker as they try to adjust again.

'Are you OK?' DI Rawlings asks. Her words sound rough. They give the impression it would annoy her if I weren't. She has dyed blonde hair scraped back into a tight bun, which shows the black of her roots. She looks young, no more than thirty, and has plastered too much bright red lipstick on to her very full lips.

I hold a hand against my mouth and hope the feeling of nausea will pass. I nod and reach for the glass of water to take a sip. 'Yes,' I say. 'Thank you, I'll be OK. I just feel a little sick.'

DI Rawlings purses her red lips and sits back in her chair. She's in no rush. She may want it to appear that the evening's events have disturbed her plans but her pregnant pauses betray she has nothing better to do.

'So,' she starts again and asks her first question but it isn't the one I'm expecting. 'Let's begin by you telling me what happened thirteen days ago,' she says instead. 'The day of the fete.'

Charlotte's story

BEFORE

Charlotte

At dead on ten o'clock on Saturday morning the doorbell rang and I knew it would be Harriet because she was never a minute late. I emerged from the bathroom, still in my pyjamas, as the bell rang a second time. Flicking back the curtains to be sure it was them, I saw Harriet hovering on the doorstep, her arm tightly gripped around her daughter's shoulder. Her head hung low as she spoke to Alice. The little girl beside her nodded as she turned and nestled her head into her mother's waist.

My own children's screams erupted from downstairs. The two girls' voices battled to be heard over one another. Evie was now drowning out Molly with a constant, piercing whine and, as I ran down the stairs, I could just make out Molly crying at her younger sister to shut up.

'Will you both stop shouting,' I yelled as I reached the bottom. My eldest, Jack, sat obliviously in the playroom, earphones on, zoned into a game on the iPad that I wished Tom had never bought him. How I sometimes envied Jack's ability to shut himself into his own world. I picked Evie off the floor, wiping a hand across her damp face and rubbing at the Marmite smeared upwards from both corners of her mouth. 'You look like the Joker.'

Evie stared back at me. At three she was still suffering from the terrible twos. She had at least thankfully stopped bawling and was now kicking one foot against the other. 'Come on, let's play nicely for Alice's sake,' I said as I opened the door.

'Hi Harriet, how are you doing?' I crouched down next to Alice and smiled at the little girl who continued to bury her head into her mum's skirt. 'Are you looking forward to the school fete today, Alice?'

I didn't expect an answer, but I ploughed on regardless. Besides, once Molly took her under her wing, Alice would happily follow her around like a puppy. In turn my six-year-old would have an air of smug superiority because finally a younger child was looking up to her.

'Thank you again for today,' Harriet said as I straightened up.

I leaned forward and kissed her cheek. 'It's a pleasure. You know it is. I've lost count of the amount of times I've begged you to let me have Alice for you,' I grinned.

Harriet's right hand played with the seam of her skirt, balling it up then pressing it down flat, and for a moment I couldn't take my eyes off it. I expected her to be apprehensive, I'd even thought she might have cancelled.

'But with four of them, are you sure—' she started.

'Harriet,' I cut her off. 'I'm more than happy to take Alice to the fete. Please don't worry about it.'

Harriet nodded. 'I've already put sun cream on her.'

'Oh. That's good.' That meant I now had to find sun cream for my own. Did I have any?

'Well, it's so hot and I don't want her burning … ' she drifted off, shifting her weight from one foot to the other.

'You are looking forward to your course today, aren't you?' I asked. 'Only you don't look like you are. You should be, it's exactly what you need.'

Harriet shrugged and looked at me blankly. 'It's book-keeping,' she said.

'I know, but it's what you want to do. It's great that you're planning your future.'

I meant it, even though I'd originally turned my nose up at the fact it was bookkeeping. I'd tried to convince Harriet to do a gardening course instead because she would make a brilliant gardener. I could picture her running around town with her own little van and told her I'd even design a website for her. Harriet had looked as if she was mulling the idea over but eventually said that gardening didn't pay as much.

'You could do my garden for me,' I'd said. 'I need someone to come and give me some new ideas. I would—' I stopped abruptly because I'd been about to say I'd pay her more than the going rate but I knew my good intentions weren't always taken in the right way when it came to money.

'How about teaching?' I'd said instead. 'You know how wonderful you'd be. Just look at the way you were with Jack when I first met you.'

'I'd have to train to be a teacher and that won't get me a job this September,' she'd replied and averted her gaze. I knew her well enough to know when to stop.

'Then bookkeeping it is,' I'd said, smiling, 'and you'll be great at that too.' Even if it wasn't what I'd do, at least Harriet was thinking about a time past September when Alice started school and she could concentrate on something for herself. I had another two long years until Evie started and I could get back some semblance of a career instead of two days a week working for the twenty-something upstart who'd once reported to me.

'Oh, I haven't packed a picnic or anything,' Harriet said suddenly.

'I'm not bothering with picnics.' I brushed a hand through the air. 'We can get something there. The PTA invest more in food stalls than anything else,' I joked.

'Right.' Harriet nodded her head but didn't smile, after a moment adding, 'Let me get you some money.'

'No,' I said firmly, hopefully not too sharply. 'No need, let me do it.'

'But it's not a problem.'

'I know it isn't,' I smiled. 'But please, let me do this, Harriet. The girls are excited Alice is joining us and we're going to have a great day. Please don't worry about her,' I said again, holding my hand out towards Alice, though she didn't take it.

Harriet bent down and pulled her daughter in for a hug and I watched the little girl melt into her mother's chest. I took a step back feeling like I should give them some space. There was such a tight bond between Harriet and her daughter that felt so much more raw than anything I had with my children, but I also knew what a big deal today was for her. Because, despite Alice being four, Harriet had never left her daughter with anyone before today.

I'd been thrilled when I'd first left Evie overnight with my friend Audrey, and she'd been barely two months old. I'd had to coax Tom into coming to the pub with me and even though we were home by nine-thirty and I had crashed out on the sofa half an hour later it was worth it for a night of undisturbed sleep.

'I love you,' Harriet whispered into Alice's hair. 'I love you so much. Be a good girl, won't you? And stay safe.' She lingered in the hug, her arms pressing tighter around her daughter. When she pulled back she took hold of Alice's face in her hands and gently pressed her lips against her daughter's nose.

I waited awkwardly on the step for Harriet to eventually pull herself up. 'Do you want to go and play with Molly in her bedroom before we go to the fete?' I asked Alice, then turned to Harriet. 'Do you still want me to drop her back at your house at five?'

Harriet nodded. 'Yes, thank you,' she said, making no move to leave.

'Please stop thanking me,' I smiled. 'I'm your best friend, it's what I'm here for.' Besides, I wanted to have Alice for her; Harriet had been there for me enough times over the last two years. 'You know you can trust me,' I added.

But then maybe we were a little more on edge than usual since a boy had been taken from the park last October. He was nine – the same age as Jack had been at the time – and it happened only the other side of Dorset. Close enough for us all to feel the threat, and still no one had any idea why he'd been taken or what had happened to him.

I reached out and took hold of my friend's arm. 'Don't worry,' I said, 'I'll take good care of her.' And eventually Harriet stepped off my doorstep and I took Alice's hand and brought her into the hallway.

'You've got my number if you need me,' Harriet said.

'I'll call if there's a problem. But there won't be,' I added.

'Brian's fishing; he has his phone with him but he rarely answers it.'

'OK, well I'll get hold of you if need be,' I said. I didn't have Brian's number anyway; there was no reason for me to. I wanted Harriet to hurry up and go. I was conscious I was still in my pyjamas and could see Ray from the house opposite staring as he mowed his front lawn in painfully slow stripes. 'Harriet, you'll be late,' I said, deciding I needed to be firm with her now or I'd find her dithering on my doorstep for the rest of the day.

When Harriet eventually left I closed the door and took a deep breath. There was a time when I would have called out to Tom that Ray was watching me and we would laugh about it. It was at the oddest times that it struck me I had no one to share those moments with since we'd separated.

'Ray caught me wearing my pyjamas,' I said, grinning at Jack as he emerged from the playroom.

My son stared at me. 'Can you get me a juice?'

I sighed. 'No, Jack. You're ten. You can get your own juice and can you say hello to Alice, please?'

Jack looked at Alice as if he had never seen her before. 'Hello Alice,' he said before disappearing into the kitchen.

'Well that's as good as it gets, I'm afraid.' I smiled at Alice who had already taken Molly's hand and was being led up the stairs. 'Everyone, I'm going to have a shower and then we'll get ready for the fete,' I called out, but my words were met with silence.

When I reached the bedroom my mobile was ringing and Tom's number flashed up on the screen. 'We agreed seven p.m.,' I said when I'd answered the phone.

'What?' he shouted over the noise of traffic.

I sighed and muttered under my breath for him to put the damn car roof up. I spoke louder. 'I said seven p.m. I assume you've forgotten what time you were coming to sit with the kids tonight?' Even though I'd only told him yesterday.

'Actually I just wanted to check you definitely still need me.'

I closed my eyes and gritted my teeth. 'Yes, Tom, I'm still planning to go out.' I didn't ask him often; I didn't go out enough to have to. In the two years since we'd separated I had gradually realised I didn't need to show him I was still having fun, and most of the time I wasn't anyway. Now I was comfortable enough in my single life to only go out when I wanted to. Though, if I were being honest, I didn't really fancy drinks with the neighbours tonight but I wasn't going to give Tom the satisfaction of letting me down at the last minute.

'It's just something's come up with work. I don't have to go but it would look better if I'm there.'

I rubbed my hand over my eyes and silently screamed. I knew what my night would be like: awkward conversation over too much wine with neighbours who I had little in common with. Yet I felt I should go. Not only had I promised them, but I'd let them down the last time they had a drinks party and probably the time before that.

'You told me you were free,' I said flatly.

'I know, and I'll still come over if you really need me. It's just that—'

'Oh, Tom,' I sighed.

'I'm not backing out if you still want me. I was just checking you definitely want to go, that's all. You never usually want to.'

'Yes, I want to go,' I snapped, hating that he still knew me so well. I wouldn't get this hassle if I used a babysitter but I knew the kids loved having him over.

'OK, OK, I'll be there,' he said. 'Seven o'clock.'

'Thank you. And come on your own,' I said, before I could help myself. I knew he would never bring his new girlfriend; he hadn't even introduced her to the children yet.

'Charlotte,' he said. 'You know you don't have to say that.'

'I'm just checking,' I said sharply before putting the phone down and feeling irritatingly guilty. I didn't have to say that because, despite the way he still annoyed me, I couldn't fault Tom's parenting. And we muddled through surprisingly well.

As I turned on the shower I tried not to think about why I was rattled by his latest relationship news. It wasn't as if I wanted him back. Fifteen years of marriage hadn't ended on a whim; by then we had gradually grown too far apart. Maybe I just didn't like change, I thought, stepping into the shower. Maybe I had got too comfortable with the easy flow of my life.

The ten-minute drive to the school took us through our village of Chiddenford towards the outskirts where the small village green and quaint little shops made way for expansive areas of countryside. St Mary's School grounds

15

rivalled those of some private schools. On the opposite side of the road to the school sat its impressive field, which backed on to parkland.

It was here that I first met Harriet, five years ago, when she was working as a teaching assistant. I'd always thought she'd end up sending Alice to the school, but the drive from their house was a nightmare. It was a shame because it would have helped Alice's confidence having Molly two years above.

It must have been well past midday by the time we finally arrived at the fete, joining the long snake of cars as they approached the corner of the field that had been cordoned off as a makeshift car park.

Underneath the brightly coloured bunting strung across the entrance, Gail Turner was waving cars through as if she ran the school rather than just the PTA. When she saw me she gestured at me to wind down my window, her white teeth flashing brightly in the sun. 'Hello, lovely, how lucky are we with the weather?' she called through my open window. 'I feel like I've been personally blessed.'

'Very lucky, Gail,' I said. 'Can I park anywhere?' Four-by-fours and people carriers like mine were already squeezing into tight spaces they'd be unlikely to get out of easily. 'Why's it so busy?'

'My marketing probably,' she beamed. 'I tried to speak to as many parents as possible to make sure they were coming.'

'So where can I park?' I asked her, flashing my own patient smile back.

'Hold on, my lovely, let me see if I can find you a VIP space.' She turned away from the window and I rolled my eyes at Jack who sat beside me. When Gail turned back she pointed at a spot at the far end. 'Go over there,' she smiled. 'No one will block you in.'

'Thanks, Gail,' I said as I slowly pulled away. Being friends with her had some advantages.

It was the hottest day on record for May, the DJ on the radio had said that morning. As I climbed out of the car, the pink sundress I'd plucked from the wardrobe was already starting to cut into the skin under my arms and I regretted not wearing flip-flops. Lifting my hair up I tied it into a ponytail and rifled through my bag for my sunglasses, rubbing at a scratch on one of the lenses before putting them on, promising myself I'd look for the case when I got home. 'Hundred-and-fifty-pound Oakley sunglasses should not be shoved to the bottom of your bag,' Audrey had once sighed, and I agreed with her but still I had no idea where the case was.

'Mummy? I need the toilet,' Evie cried as soon as we made it into the field.

'Oh, Evie, you have to be kidding,' I muttered, grabbing my dress out of her hands. 'And please don't tug on my clothes, darling.' I pulled the top of my dress back up and looked down to see if she'd revealed my bra. 'I've asked you not to do that.'

'But I need to go. I can go on my own.'

'No, Evie, you really can't,' I sighed. 'You are only three years old.'

'I can go with Jack.'

I turned back to Jack who was dawdling behind me, his head still stuck in his iPad, brow furrowed in deep concentration as he fought dragons. Jack was ten now and had accomplished major skills in flicking and tapping and swiping anything that posed a threat. I knew I should make him spend less time on gadgets. I'd even been told it wasn't conducive to the much-needed improvement of his social skills but despite all that I also knew my son was happiest when he was in his own private world.

He looked so much like Tom, with his thick, dark hair and the way his eyes scrunched up when he was trying hard. I smiled at him, even though he remained completely oblivious, and when I turned back to Evie I realised I'd lost sight of the other two. 'Where are Molly and Alice? They were both right here. Evie?' I cried. 'Where have Molly and Alice gone?'

Evie pointed a chubby finger towards the cake stall. 'Over there.'

I let out a breath as I saw them idly staring at the sugar-topped fairy cakes that had been delivered in hundreds by the mums. My daughter had a hand grasped tightly around Alice's arm and was talking at her and pointing out cakes as if she were about to reach out and pinch one.

'Girls! Stay with me,' I called. Streams of people wove in and out of the stalls and Molly and Alice were momentarily lost behind a family – a large father with a T-shirt that read 'Los Pollos Chicken', and his equally large wife stuffing a doughnut into her mouth. I edged towards the cake stall, peering between the legs of the kids trawling behind the couple.

'Molly! Come back here, now.' The two girls finally appeared. Meanwhile, Evie was bouncing from one foot to the other and tugging on my dress again.

'When can we get candyfloss?' Molly asked. 'I'm starved.'

'And I really, really need the toilet now, Mummy,' Evie shouted, stamping a little pink shoe into the grass. 'Urrrgh, I've got mud all over my feet,' she cried, shaking her foot and kicking me in the leg.

'It's a bit of soil, and I did tell you those shoes weren't the most practical footwear for a field,' I said, wiping the dirt from her foot and my shin. 'And try and watch what you're doing, Evie. You hurt Mummy.'

'I'm dirty,' Evie screamed, falling into a pile on the ground. 'I need the toilet.' I looked around me, praying no one was watching. A couple of mums glanced in my direction but turned away again quickly. I could feel the heat spreading rapidly to my cheeks as I decided whether to walk away and leave her writhing on the ground or pick her up and give in just to save face.

'Oh Evie,' I sighed. 'We'll go behind that tree.' I waved my hand towards the side of the field.

Evie's eyes lit up.

'But do it subtly. Try not to draw attention to us,' I said as I pulled her over to the tree. 'And then we can go and get candyfloss,' I called to the others behind me. 'And we can find the bouncy castles too – would everyone like that?' I asked, but if they answered I didn't hear them above the noise of the crowd.

Despite the start of a niggling headache, I ordered myself a coffee from the candyfloss stall. It felt inappropriate to get a glass of Pimm's when I had four children to watch and coffee was almost the next best thing. I looked around and waved at friends I spotted in the distance. Audrey tottered across the field, wearing ridiculously high-heeled sandals. Her hair was piled high on her head, a shawl draped over her shoulders, and a long satin skirt swished behind her as she walked. Audrey was completely not dressed for either the weather or a school fete but she didn't care. She waved back at me, grinning and gesturing at all the children huddled beside me with a look of mock horror. I shrugged as if I couldn't care less that I was on my own with so many children to look after.

I saw Karen and smiled to myself as she stood outside the beer tent waving her arms dramatically, no doubt desperate to get the attention of her husband who'd most likely tried to hide but would never get away with it for long.

'So the bouncy castles next?' I asked, when each of the kids were happily picking at the sticky pink floss. We began walking towards the furthest side of the field where I could make out the tip of an inflatable slide. 'Look how big that one is.'

'I want to go on that one instead.' Molly's eyes widened as she pointed to a huge inflatable that stretched back to the very edge of the field. It was bright green with inflatable palm trees swaying on the top and the words 'Jungle Run' plastered down the side. Molly ran over to look inside its mesh windows, and for once Jack was close at her heels.

'It's awesome,' she cried. 'Come and have a look, Alice.' Obligingly, Alice ambled over behind her and peered through the window. My heart went out to Alice, as it often did, seemingly happy to go along with whatever the others decided, but sometimes I wished she would speak up and say what *she* wanted to do. I rarely knew if she was happy or simply didn't have the confidence to say otherwise.

'Can we go on, Mum?' Jack asked.

'Yes, of course you can.' It was the kind of thing I would have loved as a child, and would have revelled in dragging my sister through.

Alice pulled back and looked up at me.

'You don't have to go on it if you don't want to,' I said.

'Of course you want to, don't you, Alice?' Molly piped up.

'Molly, she can make up her own mind.' I pulled out my purse to count out change. 'Would you rather stay with me?' I said to Alice.

'I'm not going,' Evie interrupted. 'I'm going on the slide.'

'Would you like to go on the slide with Evie?'

'No, I'll go with Molly,' she said quietly, and I realised those were the first words she'd said to me all day.

'Right, well stick together all of you. And Jack, watch out for the girls, won't you?' I called to him, though I doubted he heard me. He was already halfway up the side of the Jungle Run.

I passed the money to a mum I didn't recognise and, when I looked back, they were already out of sight.

'Come on, Mummy.' Evie tugged at my dress again.

'Five minutes, Evie,' I said. 'They've got five minutes on this and then we'll go on the slide.' I needed to sit down in the shade. My head was starting to thump and the coffee wasn't making it any better. 'Let's go and watch that magic show being set up and then I promise you can go on it.'

Evie was absorbed in watching the magician, which meant she was momentarily silent. I pulled my phone out of my bag as a matter of habit and checked my messages, reading a text from my neighbour about the drinks party that night, asking everyone to come round the back so we didn't disturb the baby.

I looked at my emails and pressed a link that took me to Facebook, reading some inane quiz and then scrolling through posts, getting caught up in everyone else's lives.

I glanced over and saw the children tumbling down the small slide at the end of the Jungle Run and then running around the back again before I or anyone else had the chance to tell them their time was up. I commented on a picture of a friend's holiday and updated my status that I was enjoying the hot weather at the school fete.

When I eventually got up and told Evie she could go on the slide, we went back to the Jungle Run, laughing as Jack hurled himself over the edge at the end and fell on to his back at the bottom.

'That was awesome,' he cried, picking himself up and coming to stand next to me.

I threw an arm over his shoulder and pulled him in for a hug and for once I didn't feel him tense. 'I'm glad you enjoyed it. Where are the girls?'

Jack shrugged.

'Oh Jack, I told you to look out for them.'

'They should have kept up with me,' he said smugly.

We watched Molly throw herself over the top of the slide and plummet down. 'Ha, I beat you by a mile,' Jack laughed.

'That's because you pushed me at the start. Mummy, Jack hurt my arm.'

'You'll be fine,' I said, rubbing her elbow. 'Where's Alice?'

'I thought she was behind me.'

'Well she isn't, Molly; she's probably stuck somewhere and she might be scared. One of you'll have to go in again.'

'I'll go,' Jack said, already sprinting around the side, eager for another turn.

'Me too.' Molly disappeared just as quickly, both of them out of sight again. I waited. I glanced around the field, marvelling at the amount of people, noticing Audrey again but she was too far away to call out to. I needed to ask her if she could take Jack to football for me on Monday, so I had to try and catch up with her at some point.

Jack appeared over the tip of the slide again. 'She's not in there,' he called, throwing himself over the edge and landing at my feet.

'What do you mean, she's not in there? Of course she's in there.'

He shrugged. 'I couldn't see her. I went all the way through, and she wasn't in there.'

'Molly? Did you see Alice?' I called out to Molly who had now appeared at the end too. Molly shook her head. 'Well, she has to be. She can't have just disappeared. You'll have to go on again, Jack,' I said, pushing him around the back. 'And this time make sure you find her.'

Harriet

Harriet was told to switch off her phone at the start of the course. She looked around the room and wondered why no one else seemed reluctant as they clicked off their mobiles and carelessly tossed them into bags and pockets. Surely there were others there who had children?

Of course Harriet knew it was unusual that her internal reaction to turning off her phone bordered on neurotic. But I have never left my daughter with anyone before, she protested silently. How can you possibly expect me not to be contactable when someone else has Alice?

In the end she decided to switch her phone on to silent and balance it carefully on top of her handbag so she would catch it flashing if anyone called or texted. With the decision came a tiny burst of relief that she had overcome the problem. She pulled out her pad and placed it in front of her so she could take notes.

As she listened to the teacher, Yvonne, making her introductions to the world of bookkeeping, Harriet considered that maybe she should have listened to Charlotte and done something she was interested in. Her friend was right after all; Harriet would make a good teacher and it'd be nice to put her English degree to better use. But this is about the money, she reminded herself as she tried to focus.

The minutes slowly ticked into hours and by early afternoon Harriet felt like she'd been folded into that small room for most of her life. The room was incredibly stuffy, filled with too many people, making it difficult to breathe. Fanning herself with her notebook, she wished Yvonne would open a window but the woman seemed oblivious to her mounting discomfort. Now Harriet's right leg was cramping and, even though they were surely due another break soon, she wondered if she could escape to the toilet and dampen her forehead with cold water. Then she could check her phone again too. It had somehow slipped into her bag and, without making a fuss of looking for it, she couldn't easily see if there were any missed calls.

Making a snap decision, Harriet picked up her handbag and squeezed past the people at the next table. Keeping her head down, she left the room for the bright, airy corridor beyond. Already she felt herself breathing more easily.

'You had enough too?' a voice rang out from behind her.

Harriet turned round to see a young girl from the course had followed her out.

'Sorry?'

'I'm done with it in there. It's too hot, isn't it?'

'Yes it is.'

'And too dull.' The girl sniggered. 'So I'm leaving.' She stared at Harriet, her gaze drifting towards her mouth.

Harriet brushed a hand across her mouth self-consciously but the girl continued to stare under thick false eyelashes, barely blinking.

'I can't listen to that woman, Yvette, for one more minute,' the girl carried on.

'Yvonne,' Harriet said before she could stop herself.

'Right,' she shrugged. 'You should leave too – unless you're enjoying it, of course.' The corners of her mouth twitched up.

No, Harriet wasn't enjoying it but she also knew she could never leave. She couldn't possibly walk out before it had finished.

With one last smirk the girl trotted off down the corridor, disappearing round the corner, and Harriet slipped into the toilets.

Letting out a deep breath as she ran cold water over her wrists, Harriet stared at her reflection in the mirror. Her cheeks were red from the heat and her neck was blotchy. Her hair was escaping from its bun, and as she scraped it back she caught sight of the grey strands glistening at her hairline.

Harriet frowned. At thirty-nine, she was ageing fast – though it was not as if she did much to help herself. She didn't wear make-up and her haircut was shapeless. Charlotte was always suggesting places to get it trimmed but thirty-five pounds seemed far too excessive. Though maybe a bit of mascara would highlight the fact she had eyelashes and make her look less tired. And her clothes did nothing for her. Her entire wardrobe was grey or dark brown. She'd borrowed one of Charlotte's bright-pink scarves once, winding it round her neck to keep the chill out at the park, and she couldn't believe the difference it made.

Once she had cooled down, Harriet grabbed the phone out of her bag and tapped the button to light up the screen. When nothing happened she pressed the side button to turn it on but the screen remained black.

'Come on,' she muttered, her stomach clenching by reflex. She pressed it again and again, but nothing came on. The phone must have run out of battery, but she didn't know how. She'd plugged it in the night before, as she always did when she went to bed. Harriet remembered doing so because she knew she needed it today more than ever.

Maybe she had forgotten.

No, she definitely didn't forget. She'd made a point of charging it, just before making a cup of tea to take to bed. She remembered because she'd checked it again on her way out of the kitchen. Yet somehow the phone was dead.

Harriet threw it back into her bag. Now she had no idea what was going on at the fete and no one had any way of telling her. And suddenly the stupidity of the phone's lack of battery made her want to burst into tears.

She gulped back a sob. It pained her to be away from Alice. It made her heart burn, but no one understood that. So Harriet had learned to play down how much she wanted to hold on to her daughter, how she hated the thought of letting her out of her sight. She saw the way Charlotte's friends glanced at each other when she admitted she'd never been away from Brian or Alice overnight.

'She'd cope without you,' Charlotte would say. 'Doesn't Brian want you all to himself for the odd night?' Harriet tried imagining what Brian would say if she ever suggested it. He'd probably be thrilled at the idea.

'Or leave her with Brian and come away with the girls instead?' Charlotte had persisted.

She couldn't see herself doing either so mostly she never let on how she felt because she despised the fact she was like this in the first place. No one would know what it took to leave Alice with Charlotte today. But Charlotte had been thrilled she had asked her so Harriet hadn't told her there was no one else to ask.

'You have to let them go one day,' a woman in a shop once said to her. 'One day they grow their wings and just fly away. Like a butterfly,' she added, flapping her arms in the air. Harriet resisted the urge to slap them back down.

Alice would want to fly away one day, just like she had. Her own mum had held on to her too much, so Harriet was well aware how destructive it could be. She'd promised herself not to be like that with her own children and yet here she was. Somewhere along the line she had become the mother she didn't want to be.

Harriet should forget the phone and go back into the room and suffer through the rest of the course. It didn't matter, she told her reflection. It was only another – she checked her watch – two hours at most, and she'd be home at four-thirty p.m. as planned.

Or she could slip away like that young girl had.

Harriet tapped her fingers against the basin. She really needed to be able to make simple decisions.

Charlotte

As I peered through the mesh window of the Jungle Run, all I saw were screaming children tumbling over each other, barely realising they were stepping on others in their excitement. Alice could be crouching in a corner and most of the kids wouldn't give her a second glance. I had to go on it myself – I couldn't rely on Jack to search for her properly.

'Come on, girls,' I said, trying to keep my voice even. 'Let's go and see where Alice has got to.' I grabbed the girls' hands and as we ran to the back of the Jungle Run it crossed my mind I wouldn't have been worried if it were any of my children. They were prone to hiding from me or wandering off. But Alice? I couldn't imagine her doing either. There was something so fragile about her that wasn't like any other child I knew. And there was something so unthinkable about losing someone else's child.

Five metres from the back of the run was the fence that separated the field from the parkland, and in the distance a line of trees partly hid the golf course beyond. I slipped off my shoes and, holding them in one hand, crawled through the Jungle Run, both girls close at my heels.

I called Alice's name as we clambered over ramps and scrambled through tunnels, looking at every child we passed, hoping to see a flash of her red dress.

'Where could she have gone?' I called out to Jack who was waiting at the end. He shrugged in response as I inelegantly swung a leg over the final slide and pushed myself down, holding my hands out to Evie who was giggling behind me, lost in a bubble of excitement that I had crawled through with her.

'God, this is ridiculous.' I looked around me, slipping my shoes back on and turning to the children. 'Did she say anything about wanting to go anywhere else? Did she mention the magician maybe?' I hadn't seen her come into the tent but she could have wandered off in the wrong direction and got lost. 'Surely I would have seen her,' I murmured to none of them in particular.

'Molly, did you actually see her get on this thing?' I asked, my voice rising an octave as I gestured behind us at the inflatable.

'I think so.'

'You think so?'

'Well ... ' She paused. 'I think she came on after me.'

'But you don't know for sure?' I said, trying my hardest not to shout.

Molly shook her head. I went over to the woman who had taken my money and was now talking to another mum about the cake stall. 'A little girl came on this with my children,' I interrupted. 'About ten minutes ago now, but there's no sign of her.'

'Oh?' I doubted she'd noticed which children were getting on and off. She'd barely lifted her head when I'd placed the coins in her outstretched hand. 'Sorry, I don't know,' she said. 'What does she look like?'

'About this high.' My hand hovered at the top of Molly's head. Alice was tall for her age. 'She's only four, though; she's wearing a red dress with a white belt.'

The woman shook her head as her friend stared at me blankly. 'No, sorry,' she said. 'I don't remember seeing her. I'll keep a lookout, though.'

'Oh God.' I felt sick. This couldn't be happening.

'What do we do?' Jack looked at me, biting the edge of his thumbnail as he waited for an answer. He wasn't worried; why would he be? He assumed I'd sort out the problem and then, when we found Alice, we'd move on to the next activity.

'We start looking for her.' I took hold of the girls' hands again. 'We'll search the whole field. She has to be here somewhere.' But my pulse raced a little faster as we started walking, Jack close behind us, weaving through the crowds across the field, back towards the car park. And the more time that passed, the quicker it beat.

We stopped at every stall, looked under trestle tables, between the long legs of the adults, all of us calling Alice's name with varying degrees of panic. Past Hook-A-Duck and the football shoot-out, the lines of dads cheering when one of them missed. The tombola, the cake stall again. As we passed each one the grip on my daughters' hands tightened, my head constantly swivelling round to check Jack was following.

'Have you seen a little girl?' I stopped just past the cake stall and called out to a mum from Molly's year who was running the toy stand. My voice was louder than I intended. 'Blonde hair to here.' I pointed to just below my shoulder. 'Red dress.'

Her expression was grim as she shook her head. 'Where have you looked?'

'Everywhere,' I cried out in a tight breath.

For a moment I couldn't move. My hands started to tremble; I didn't realise how tightly I was gripping on to my girls until Molly yelped as she tried to pull away. I needed to do something, but what? Put out an announcement? Call the police? I'd lost track of how long it had been since I'd seen her. Didn't every second count in these situations?

'Why don't you see if you can put a tannoy out?' the mum asked as if reading my thoughts.

I stared back at her, not knowing how to answer. The truth was I didn't want to. Because as soon as I did I was admitting this was serious. I was admitting I had lost a child. And someone else's child at that.

'Charlotte?' A hand clasped my shoulder and I turned, coming face to face with Audrey.

'Oh God, Aud.' I dropped the girls' hands and clamped my own over my mouth. 'I've lost Alice. I can't find her anywhere.'

'OK,' she said calmly, automatically looking about. 'Don't panic, she's going to be around somewhere.'

'What do I do? I've been round the whole field.' I needed Audrey to tell me. Needed her to fix it in the no-nonsense way she's so good at.

'We'll find someone in charge,' she said. 'Maybe they can close down all the exits.' She looked over towards the car park and I followed her gaze. Streams of cars continued to meander in. The fete was getting busier.

'Who?' There was no one in charge. I'd not once seen the headmaster, Mr Harrison, with his loudspeaker. He was supposed to be here today; he always attended the fete. But no one was acting as security or even watching the gates to the car park or the perimeters of the field apart from Gail. Alice could have got out in any one of four directions had she wanted to. Is that what she had done at the back of the inflatable? Had she, for whatever reason, climbed over the fence and headed towards the golf course?

'We've lost a little girl,' Audrey called out to anyone who would listen. 'We need everyone to look for her.' She turned to me. 'Maybe we should call the police.'

I shook my head as a couple of other mums came up to us. 'Are you OK, Charlotte?' one asked. 'Who have you lost?'

'My friend's daughter,' I cried. My hands pressed into the sides of my face, fingers stretching to cover my eyes. 'Alice. Her name is Alice. She's only four. Oh God, this isn't happening.'

'It's OK,' she said as she took hold of my arms and eventually prised my hands away. 'Everyone can help look. Don't worry, we'll find her. How long has it been?'

'I don't know,' I said, my heart beating rapidly as I tried to think how long it was since I'd last seen her. 'Maybe about twenty minutes.'

'Twenty minutes?' the mum said

'OK,' Audrey interjected. 'I'm calling the police.'

The news of a missing child spread rapidly. A Chinese whisper passed through the crowd, kicking up a burst of activity as everyone looked around them. The threat of danger, an unspoken murmur of excitement that everyone had a role in finding her, no doubt wanting to be the one who could call out that she was hiding beneath their stall.

I doubted any of them were imagining the worst. Children get lost and it was never long before they were found and the terrified parents gushed their thanks to the person who happened to be the lucky one to come across them.

In a daze I let Audrey lead us to the edge of the field by the car park, where she had agreed to meet the police.

I rested my back against the fence, the glare of sunlight pounding down on us. People in front of me were beginning to blur and, as my eyes flickered to refocus, a wave of nausea surged through me.

'Drink some water.' Audrey pressed a bottle into my hand and I took a large gulp. 'And for God's sake move into the shade. You look as if you're about to faint,' she said as she nudged me towards a tree. 'Alice will turn up,' she went on. 'She's just run off and got lost.'

'I hope you're right.' After all, nothing awful happened in Chiddenford. Not in a sleepy Dorset village. 'But I just don't think Alice would run off.'

'All kids do from time to time,' Aud said. 'Alice is no different to any other four-year-old.'

But you don't know Alice, I thought. Alice is different. Audrey had never taken the time to get to know Alice, most likely because she'd never got a word out of her. She'd never really taken the time to get to know Harriet either.

'I should call Harriet,' I said as she ushered my children to a patch of grass where they obediently sat down.

'Talk me through what happened again.'

'I don't know what happened. Alice just vanished. She went round the back of the inflatable and never came off it. What do I tell Harriet?' I took another sip from the bottle. 'I can't tell her I've lost her daughter, Aud,' I cried.

'You need to try and keep calm,' she said, taking hold of my arms and pulling me round so I was facing her. 'Breathe slowly. Come on. One, two … ' She started counting slowly and I fell into her rhythm. 'Alice will be found soon, I know she will, so there's no point worrying Harriet yet. And besides –' her gaze drifted over my shoulder '– the police are here.'

Audrey nodded towards the road and I turned to watch the marked car pull up alongside the field next to the entrance to the car park. Two uniformed officers got out and as they walked towards us the graveness of the situation smacked me once more. Now it was official. Alice was missing.

PC Fielding introduced himself and his female colleague, PC Shaw. They asked if I needed to sit but I shook my head. I just wanted them to get on with what they'd come for.

'Can you tell us what happened, Charlotte?' PC Fielding asked.

'The children were excited to go on the Jungle Run,' I told him, pointing to the furthest edge of the field at the large inflatable. 'Well, not my youngest, Evie, she wanted to go on the slide, but the other three went,' I said, though I knew Alice hadn't been excited.

'And you saw all three get on?'

I shook my head. 'They ran round the back of it quickly and you can't actually see the start of the run.'

'So you didn't go round and check?' he asked, one eyebrow slightly raised as he peered at me over the thick black rim of his glasses.

'No.' My breath felt tight. 'I didn't check,' I said. 'I assumed they had because they were begging to go on it.'

The policeman nodded and made a note on his pad. I reached my hand to my throat, scratching at the heat that began to prick my skin. 'Obviously now I wish I had,' I went on. 'But I didn't think I needed to because as far as I knew there was nowhere else for them to go … ' I trailed off. Of course I wished I had now. I wished to God I'd never let them go on it in the first place.

'And what did you do next?' he asked, nodding to PC Shaw who wandered off and began speaking into her radio.

'I sat down in the shade with my youngest, Evie. She didn't want to go on the Jungle Run and I had a headache,' I told him, watching the policewoman and wondering what she was saying and to whom.

'And could you see this Jungle Run from where you were sitting?'

'Yes, I could see the end of it. I had my eye on it the whole time,' I said, nodding to convey more certainty than I actually felt.

'And did you see them at all after they'd run around the back of it?'

'I – I did,' I faltered. 'I saw them coming off and running around again.'

'All of them?' He looked up from his pad.

'I saw Jack first,' I told him, remembering my son grinning from ear to ear, because I'd felt a surge of happiness that he was enjoying himself. 'And then Molly.' Her mouth had formed a wide O as she fell down the slide, her bunches flying into the air behind her.

'And Alice?' he asked, with a hint of impatience.

I paused. I'd thought I'd seen her at the time. Or maybe I just assumed I had. I couldn't actually remember her dropping down the slide like the others. 'I thought so,' I said, then added, 'I can't say for sure, though.'

'So when did you notice Alice definitely wasn't there?'

'When my two came off. They said she wasn't with them and they couldn't remember if she got on.' I looked over at my children, already dreading the moment the police would want to question them.

'What about her shoes?' This came from PC Shaw who was walking back towards us.

'What do you mean?'

'Well, don't kids usually take off their shoes to go on inflatables? Were Alice's still there?'

'Oh.' I paused and tried to think. 'I don't know. I didn't see.' I didn't even notice my own children taking off their shoes or putting them back on again.

'You'd better go and check,' PC Fielding said and Shaw nodded, walking off briskly in the direction of the inflatable.

My heart was beating so hard it rang through my ears. I was sure he must be able to hear it too. I looked over at Audrey and the kids, then back at him. Why wasn't he promising me she'd be found soon instead of asking me more questions? Now they were about Harriet and Brian and he needed me to give him their phone numbers.

I fumbled through my bag for my phone and pulled it out, scrolling until I found Harriet's number. There was no point in looking for Brian's. I'd never had it but I made a pretence of checking anyway.

I described Alice's red dress with its white belt and the little birds embroidered onto the top that I'd seen her wear so often. It was getting shorter against her growing legs but it was obviously one of her favourites. I told him she had a plain white T-shirt and white ankle socks and light blue shoes with a Velcro strap. The shoes had tiny stars pinpricked into a pattern on the toes. I was relieved I could so accurately remember what she was wearing.

I told him Alice was roughly the same height as Molly, with blonde, wavy hair to just below her shoulders. She didn't have any clips in it and wasn't wearing a hairband. I scrolled through the photos on my phone to see if I had any of her, but I didn't, and even though the image of Alice was as clear in my head as if she was standing right next to me, I wasn't sure how well I'd managed to get it across.

'We need to be out there looking,' I said. 'She could be anywhere by now.'

'Don't worry, there'll be officers already searching,' PC Fielding said. 'Where are the parents?'

'Her mum is on a course in a hotel.' I couldn't tell him which one. There were a number of small hotels scattered along the coast and I'd never thought to ask Harriet.

'And Dad?'

'Fishing. He goes every Saturday morning.'

'Do you know where?'

I shook my head. Fishing was as much as I knew.

'OK.' He beckoned to PC Shaw who was returning across the field. 'We need to get hold of the parents. Find anything?'

She shook her head as she reached us. 'No shoes, and the woman running it says none have been left behind.'

PC Fielding looked at me blankly. He didn't have to tell me what he was thinking: the mood was heavy with the sense of my incompetency. 'So, very possibly she didn't get on in the first place,' he said.

I joined Audrey and my children while PC Shaw tried to call Harriet. I stared at the woman's back as she paced away from us, straining to hear if the call had connected, imagining my friend on the other end listening to the officer telling her that her daughter was missing.

'You're shaking,' Audrey said. 'Sit down. I'll go and get you another bottle of water.'

I shook my head. 'No, don't go anywhere.' A ball of bile lodged in my throat and I desperately didn't want Audrey to leave me.

'Alice is going to be fine. You know that, don't you? They're out there, like the officer told you, and they're going to find her.'

'Only what if they don't?' I cried. 'What if it's the same guy who took that little Mason last year? And we don't find her, and we don't know what's happened. Jesus!' I sobbed, feeling Audrey's arms grab on to me as my legs buckled. She reached for my elbows and pulled me into her. 'I couldn't live with that. I couldn't live with myself if she never comes back.'

'Don't,' she said. 'Don't do that. She will be found. This has nothing to do with what happened to Mason. Alice just wandered off and got lost. No one's taken her, for God's sake. If that happened someone here would have seen something.'

'We can't get hold of the mum,' PC Fielding said as he walked back. 'I need to ask some more questions, if you don't mind, but I'd like to go over there with you to this Jungle Run, if that's OK?'

While Audrey stayed with the children I followed the officer across the field. Now he wanted to know more about Alice's family – asking me again if Harriet and Brian were still together, which I confirmed they were. Did any grandparents live nearby? I told him they didn't and the questions stopped when we reached the Jungle Run, where a couple of policemen were hovering around the back.

'There's no gap or gate in the fence,' one said, walking to meet us. 'The other side of the trees is the golf course and the car park to the golf club, which is pretty busy.'

'Any CCTV?'

'That's being checked out.'

'Good.' PC Fielding nodded, looking around. The crowds had clustered into small groups huddled by stalls, those nearby watching the commotion around the inflatable with undisguised interest. 'She could have slipped off in any direction,' he murmured. 'Any luck getting hold of the parents yet?' he said, turning back to PC Shaw who shook her head.

Alice wouldn't do that, I wanted to say, but I held my breath as I waited for him to decide what to do next. She wasn't the type of child to just slip off. But if I was right then what that meant didn't bear thinking about.

Harriet

Harriet drove home, all the time wondering if she'd done the right thing. She hadn't told anyone she was leaving the course, but as soon as she'd walked into the fresh air of the car park she was relieved to be out of the hotel. After a twenty-minute journey home she could plug in her phone again.

The roads were clear, the drive passed quickly, but as soon as she turned on to her street, her foot slammed hard on the brake. Blue lights flashed ahead and, even though the road was long and lined with cars on either side, she knew the bursts of light were directly outside her house because they were immediately in front of her neighbour's wretched caravan.

Cautiously she eased her foot on to the accelerator until she was forced to stop again to let a car pass. 'Come on,' she muttered, craning her neck to see if she could spot anyone outside the house. Her fingers drummed impatiently on the wheel. The other car slowly trundled by. She could feel her heart palpitating and pressed a hand against her chest. One. Two. Another missed beat.

Eventually Harriet pulled into the small space between the police car and Brian's silver Honda and saw her husband standing in the front garden, one hand clutching tightly on to his fishing rods, the other roughly rubbing his stubbly chin.

A policewoman stood on the grass beside him. Harriet could see her lips moving but her face was impassive. She held up both her hands and indicated with one towards the house, but Brian stayed stubbornly rooted to the spot.

Now Harriet could only see the back of his head, but he was shaking it and had raised it high, looking up to the sky, his shoulders clenched tight.

Harriet didn't move. She didn't want to get out of the car. Not right then. She could hear her breaths filling the silence, too deep, too fast, but as soon as she stepped out she'd have to listen to what Brian had been told. She didn't need to see her husband's face to know the policewoman had told him something bad. Just the way his body was arched, taut with tension, she knew.

Harriet's fingers shook against the key as she slowly turned it and the engine cut out, the policewoman and Brian turning to look at her. Still she didn't move.

Brian mouthed her name, as if it suddenly dawned on him that whatever he had just learned he was going to have to pass on to his wife. His eyes were wide with fear as he stared at her, before he cautiously walked down the garden path towards the gate, trailing his fishing rods behind him.

Harriet shook her head at him from behind the safety of the glass. Don't say it, don't you dare say it, because if you don't then I don't have to hear it.

The day she'd turned up at the hospital and saw her mum's empty bed, she'd run from the ward and huddled in the corridor with her hands clamped over her ears. She knew her mum had passed away; it was inevitable. Harriet had been told to expect it for weeks but still she didn't want to know it had finally happened. And she figured if no one actually told her then she just might be able to believe her mum was still alive.

Harriet hadn't taken her eyes off Brian, yet the click of the car door still startled her when he opened it.

She closed her eyes. 'What's happened?'

'Come out, my love.' His voice was lifeless but unnervingly calm. 'Please come out of the car.'

'Tell me what's happened. What is she doing here?' Harriet nodded towards the policewoman.

'Let's go inside,' he said, holding out his free hand.

'No. Tell me now.'

'Mrs Hodder?' The policewoman appeared by his side. 'I think we should go into the house.'

'I don't want to,' Harriet cried, but she took Brian's hand and allowed him to pull her out of the car.

He gripped on to her tightly, brushing his thumb across the top of her hand. 'Darling, I really think we should just go inside,' he said, managing to get her into the front garden before Harriet stopped. Her legs felt like they would give way beneath her if she carried on.

'Will one of you just tell me what's happened?'

The policewoman stopped beside her. She had a pudgy face and small eyes that flicked nervously between her and Brian. Harriet looked up at her husband. Over the years she had learned to read him well. She knew every expression by heart. She'd learned to tell when something was worrying him before he even opened his mouth, but never more so than in that moment.

'Mrs Hodder.' The policewoman cleared her throat as she spoke again. 'I'm afraid we have some bad news. Mrs Charlotte Reynolds has reported that—'

'Alice is missing,' Brian interrupted, throwing the words out. Harriet could almost see the letters spilling out of his mouth, reshaping in the air, making no sense. Then slowly her husband's words trickled down until one by one they landed on her.

'No.' Harriet's voice was a whisper. 'No, don't say that.' She shook her head almost manically even though her body was so tense it pained her to move.

'Let's go into the house,' Brian said quietly.

'Alice,' Harriet said, looking about as if she might find her in the garden and all of this was some sick joke. 'Alice!' she cried her name, this time in an ear-splitting wail, and with it her legs buckled and she fell to the ground. To anyone watching it looked like the air had been sucked out of her in one breath as she crumpled into a ball on the hard concrete of her front path.

'It's OK, Mrs Hodder,' the policewoman was saying.

Of course it's not OK, a voice screamed inside her head. How could it possibly be OK?

Brian's precious fishing rods clanked against the path as he threw them down, looking from the policewoman to his wife, his face startled and searching for one of them to tell him what to do. He didn't know whether to drag Harriet into the house or leave her there to punch the ground as she had started doing.

'What happened?' she cried. 'What happened?'

'I really think we should get inside,' Brian urged, looping his arms under his wife's and pulling her up and into his chest. Harriet allowed herself to sink into him; his arms swallowed her up as he tugged her along the path. With one hand he searched for a key in his back pocket and fumbled it into the lock. 'This is Officer Shaw and she's going to tell us,' he told her.

The Hodders' house was unfailingly dark. Despite the bright afternoon, Brian needed to switch on a light in the hallway. The door to the kitchen at the far end was closed as was the one on the right, making the small hallway even pokier.

Brian opened the door on the right, gently manoeuvring Harriet into their neat, square living room and on to the sofa. PC Shaw followed them, and even with only the three of them it felt cramped.

'Will someone just tell me what happened?' Harriet said.

The policewoman sat in the armchair and shuffled to its edge so she could face Harriet and Brian who were now side by side on the sofa. 'Your friend, Mrs Reynolds, was looking after your daughter today?'

Harriet nodded, feeling her husband wriggle awkwardly next to her. Out of the corner of her eye she could see him looking at her quizzically but she kept her focus on PC Shaw who had paused momentarily, distracted by Brian's jerky movements. 'I am so sorry.' She turned back to Harriet. 'I know how difficult this must be for you to hear, but Alice has disappeared from the school fete. We have officers looking and—'

'When? When did she disappear?' Harriet asked.

'We received the call at one-fifty p.m.'

'And what happened?' Harriet demanded. She felt her hand shaking inside Brian's tight grasp.

PC Shaw inhaled loudly through her nose, and didn't appear to exhale. 'Your daughter had gone on an inflatable. She'd run round the back and that was the last Mrs Reynolds saw of her.'

'I don't understand,' Brian said. 'You mean like a bouncy castle? What was she doing round the back of it? Alice wouldn't do that.'

'No, it wasn't a bouncy castle. It's called a Jungle Run,' the policewoman said. 'It's an inflatable obstacle course.'

'But Alice hates anything like that.' Brian shook his head. His grip on Harriet's hand tightened. 'She's never been on such a thing. Why would she go on one today?'

PC Shaw pressed her lips flatly together. It was obvious she couldn't answer his question.

Brian continued to stare at her. 'She probably got scared,' he cried. 'She'd have hated it.' Harriet felt his shoulders rise and dip with his deep breaths. 'But maybe that's a good thing?' he said. 'It means she probably ran off rather than that someone took her?'

'We are trying to ascertain what happened, Mr Hodder.'

'And Charlotte?' he asked, his gaze drifting over to Harriet and then back to PC Shaw. 'Where was she when all this happened? When she was supposed to be looking after our daughter. I mean, how did Alice even manage to go anywhere without her seeing? She should have had her eyes on her the whole time.' Harriet could almost feel his rising panic; his breaths had become more rapid. The thought of a mother not watching a child – it was all too close to home for Brian.

'Mrs Reynolds couldn't see the back of it from where she was,' the officer said. 'And when Alice didn't come off, they searched the fields and then raised the alarm. I believe she did everything she could to—'

'To what?' Brian cried out. PC Shaw dropped her eyes. 'She did everything she could to look for her, is that what

51

you were about to say? She should never have lost her in the first place.' He slumped back into the sofa, taking his arms away from Harriet and cradling his head in his hands.

'I'm sorry,' the policewoman said. 'I didn't mean to upset you, Mr Hodder. The area is being thoroughly searched and everything is being done to ensure Alice is brought home safely.' She paused, her eyes flicking nervously between the two of them again, making Harriet think the officer didn't believe her own words. 'We are doing everything we can,' she said more quietly.

Brian's body was hard and heavy and uncomfortably close against Harriet. She could feel the tightness of his muscles. Fear seeped out of him and bled into her until she wanted to move away so she didn't have to feel it. Every so often his eyes glanced towards her. She knew there was something he needed to get off his chest.

Instead he placed his right hand over her knee and said, 'They'll find her, my love. They will. They have to.' His hand squeezed her and he eventually turned back to the policewoman. 'Oh God, you don't think it's the same guy, do you?' he asked suddenly. 'The one who took that little boy?' Harriet felt the pressure of his hand harden against her leg. She tried to move away from him. She couldn't bear that he was asking this already. Her left hand gripped the leather cushion beneath her until the pressure was so much that she had to let go.

PC Shaw drew in another deep breath. There was already too little air left in the room to go around.

'We don't know, Mr Hodder. At this stage we are still assuming Alice has wandered off from the fete by her own will.' She gave a thin-lipped smile and dropped her gaze so she was no longer looking either of them in the eye.

'Do you really think that?' He inched forward until he was perched on the edge of the sofa. 'Or are you already linking this to Mason Harbridge? Because seven months on and no one has any clue what happened to him. How can you tell me it's not the same man that's taken Alice?'

Harriet saw flashes of little Mason, the boy the press had described as having vanished into thin air. 'I'm going to be sick,' she cried and rushed from the room and into the kitchen, where she leaned over the sink and retched.

Any moment Brian would be right behind her, rubbing her back in an attempt to soothe her. She wiped a hand across her mouth and rinsed it under the tap. She wanted to be left alone, just for a bit, before he started asking questions she didn't want the answers to.

'Just a moment, Mr Hodder.' PC Shaw's voice murmured through the open door of the living room, obviously stopping him on his way out. Their voices were low but once Harriet turned off the running water she could just make out what they were saying. 'I know this is a shock for you.'

'It is.'

'How well do you know Charlotte Reynolds?'

There was a pause. 'Personally, not well.'

'Is she a good friend?'

'Well, clearly not.'

'I mean, are she and your wife close?'

Harriet waited for him to answer and eventually he spoke. 'Yes,' he said. 'I suppose they are.'

NOW

There's a loud intake of breath as DI Rawlings rocks back and forth in her chair. It's not hard to forget we aren't on the same side, as much as she continues to reassure me I'm being helpful.

Yes, I know how horrendous it was, I want to say to her. You don't need to tell me that.

Yet we are all aware it's become so much worse.

'Tell me more about your friendship with Harriet,' she says. 'How did you first meet?'

'Harriet was working at St Mary's School,' I say. My mouth feels dry and I sip the last drop of water from the glass, hoping she might offer me more. She told me I can take breaks but I haven't yet found the courage to ask.

'The school where your children go?' she asks. 'The same school that held the fete?'

'Yes. Before Harriet had Alice she worked there part time as a teaching assistant.' I tell her I had been called into the school because there had been an issue with Jack but I resist the urge to say it wasn't anything my son had done. 'I'd seen Harriet around before then, but that was the first time we'd spoken.'

An image of Harriet flittering nervously across the playground pops into my head and I can hear Audrey's voice saying, 'She scuttles around like a mouse.' I may have sniggered because, as always, Aud's observation was spot on, but I also felt something else as I watched her. Pity, perhaps?

'She's probably just shy,' I'd muttered, looking back at Jack's small head. Another note had circulated about lice and Jack had already had them four times. I wasn't prepared to accept a fifth. 'Or she doesn't want to be bothered by any of the parents.'

'Hmm. She's a little odd,' Audrey said. 'She doesn't look anyone in the eye.'

At that I'd glanced up to see Harriet darting into the main building and wondered what she must have made of us mums all huddled in a group, heads close together as we gossiped and laughed loudly. We were a pack and most of us took comfort from that even if we didn't say it aloud.

I didn't tell the detective any of this. Instead I told her that Harriet had been honest and open with me and very easy to talk to. As she relayed her concerns for Jack, I had watched her fingers playing with the seams of her A-line skirt. Her fingernails were bitten low; a hard nub of dry skin clutched on to her thumbnail. At one point I had focused on that, willing her to stop talking about my son with unsettling accuracy for fear I would start crying.

'Mrs Reynolds?' Harriet had said softly. 'If you think I've got this wrong, then please tell me.'

I shook my head. 'No, you haven't got it wrong,' I said. She had been the first person to get it so very right, to see Jack for the little boy he was.

'He's very bright,' she went on. 'Academically he's streets ahead but socially he doesn't always cope with things as well as he should at this age.'

'I know,' I nodded.

'There are assessments we can look into, help we can get.'

'I don't want any labels,' I said. 'I'm not embarrassed but—'

'It's OK, Mrs Reynolds, you don't have to make any decisions right now, and you certainly don't need to worry about considering a different school if you don't want to.'

I tell the detective that she was a wonderful teaching assistant. 'She was so caring about the children,' I say. 'She gave me time. We talked and I realised we had things in common.'

'What do you have in common?' It's not the first time I've been asked this.

'At first it was our pasts,' I say. 'We spoke about—' I stop abruptly. I was about to say we'd spoken about our fathers, that we had shared confidences. Even though the meeting had started off about Jack, I'd somehow veered into the course of my own childhood and shared with Harriet the story of my father. Well, some of it. At least, I told her more than I had anyone else. I told her how he'd walked out on us when I was still a child.

But then Harriet told me hers had died when she was five and I immediately felt a pang of guilt because surely that was so much worse than what I had gone through?

'It was years ago,' she said as she pressed her hand into mine. 'Please don't feel bad.'

But despite her smile and the way she looked at me so assuredly, I had seen a glimmer of tears in her eyes and knew she was just trying to convey that I hadn't upset her. Deep down I could sense she was still hurting at the loss and even then, right at the start of our friendship, I'd felt guilty.

'Time is a great healer, isn't it?' Harriet said. 'Don't they say that?'

'They do, but I'm not entirely sure I agree,' I mumbled.

'No,' she smiled. 'I'm not sure I do either.'

It was only after the briefest of pauses that I found myself asking her to join me and my mum friends for coffee the following week. Harriet looked taken aback and I assumed she would turn me down.

But instead she thanked me and told me she'd love to and while I smiled at her and said that was wonderful I immediately wondered if I'd been too hasty with my invite. The other mums wouldn't like that they couldn't talk freely about the school, and Harriet would be my responsibility and I didn't think I needed any more of those.

When I told Audrey what I'd done, she raised an eyebrow.

'Give her a chance, I think you'll like her,' I said. 'Besides, she doesn't know anyone else in the area.'

Harriet hadn't any other friends, I realised early on. Tom called her another of my pet projects, which had dispro- portionately annoyed me, but there was something about Harriet that made me want to take her under my wing. I decided I could help her. First step – she needed to meet more people.

'Harriet had only moved to Dorset a few months earlier,' I tell DI Rawlings now. 'I wanted her to feel welcome.'

'And how did she settle into your group?' the detective asks me.

'Well.' I pause. 'She didn't really. Whenever she came along she always looked uncomfortable so in the end I stopped inviting her. I didn't want her to feel awkward when it obviously wasn't her thing.'

DI Rawlings's eyebrows flicker upwards and I fidget on my hard seat. 'I knew she didn't want to be there,' I protest. 'I knew she wasn't that keen on some of them.'

'But you carried on your friendship with Harriet?'

'Yes, although not so much at the start. I still chatted to her whenever I saw her but it wasn't until she had Alice and I had Evie that we started meeting up regularly. By then all my other friends had school-age children and were doing different things with their days. Harriet and I kept each other company.'

Harriet stopped me from going crazy. She became a friend at a time when I needed someone like her more than ever. When everyone else I knew could go back to work or to the gym or spend hours in coffee shops without feeling drained from a night of no sleep and very quickly forgot what it was like to have a newborn.

'I wasn't happy after Evie was born and Harriet was a good listener,' I say. 'On top of that my marriage was struggling and I used to offload on to her.' Much more so than Audrey back then, as Harriet had always been so keen to help.

'So you became close. You shared things?' DI Rawlings asks.

'We talked as friends do.'

'Would you consider yourself best friends?'

'She's one of my best friends, yes,' I say, thinking of Aud and how the two of them couldn't be more different. But don't friends play different roles in our lives?

'How would Harriet answer that?' she asks.

Harriet would say I'm her only friend.

'She'd say the same,' I tell her.

I imagine what Rawlings must be thinking but she doesn't ask the question that hangs on the edge of her lips.

What would Harriet say now?

BEFORE

Harriet

Brian and PC Shaw's murmured voices blended into the background as Harriet stared at her back garden through the kitchen window. She'd always loved the garden. It was nothing like Charlotte's – it didn't have space for a wooden climbing frame and double swings, or a fourteen-foot trampoline and playhouse. But previously she had only ever known a life of living in flats and making do with strips of balconies.

The garden was the only thing Harriet had liked about the house when they first moved in. Five years ago, when Brian had pulled up outside the thin semi he'd bought for them, her heart had plummeted. Their move to Dorset had been sold to her as her dream – the house on the coast, where Harriet had imagined opening the windows in the morning and smelling the sea air. Hearing the squawk of

61

seagulls circling overhead, maybe even glimpsing the water from a bedroom window.

Harriet hadn't actually wanted to leave Kent but it was Brian's portrayal of life in Dorset that finally persuaded her. It was, after all, what she'd always wished for as a child. So as they followed the removal van south-west, Harriet warmed to the idea enough to allow herself to get a little excited.

Besides, it was their chance to start afresh. Brian was trying to put the past behind them. He'd procured a new job in Dorset and found them a house. Her husband was making an effort so the least she could do was try and put her heart into it too, and on the drive down Harriet considered that relocating her whole life might not be such a bad idea. So she'd have no friends and would have to find another job but maybe none of that really mattered. And if it meant them being together in her house by the sea then it had to be worth it.

When they'd stopped outside the house, Harriet thought the removal company had made a mistake. They'd turned off from the coast road at least ten minutes earlier. She couldn't even walk to the beach from where they sat in the parked car, let alone see it. She'd peered up to the house and back to Brian, who'd unclicked his seat belt and was beaming at her.

The house was nothing like the picture in her head – the one with its large windows and wooden shutters. All the houses on this road looked like they had been squeezed in and no one had bothered finishing them. The house itself looked embarrassed by its appearance, with its peeling paint and roof tiles stained with yellow moss.

Brian squeezed her hand. 'This is it. The next chapter in our life together. What do you think?'

It crossed her mind her husband must have known this wouldn't be the house she'd dreamed of. But then she looked at his face and immediately felt a rush of guilt, pushing aside her worries that he was still upset with her and telling him she loved it.

She didn't.

Brian led her inside and showed her each of the rooms while Harriet held back the urge to scream. Everywhere was so cramped and dark. She wanted to rip down the walls of the characterless, square rooms just to let the sunlight in.

Yet the house was still bigger than what she'd grown up in. As a child Harriet had lived with her mum in a two-bed, first-floor flat that overlooked a concrete park. The flat could have tucked quite nicely inside the semi twice over. So she knew she shouldn't have anything to complain about, but she couldn't shake the feeling that she'd never be happy here.

The back garden was her haven, though, kept immaculately by its previous owners. Harriet soon learned the names of all the flowers that ran up the left-hand side along the fence that still needed repairing. It had blown inwards during the winter winds and Brian was adamant it was the responsibility of the neighbour, though she knew he would end up repairing it rather than get embroiled in a disagreement with him.

Then once Alice was born Harriet began taking her first coffee of the day on the patio bench while her daughter played in the sandpit at the far end of the garden. 'I've made you a sand pie, Mummy,' her little girl would call out.

'Wonderful, darling, I'll enjoy that with my coffee.'

'Do you want a blueberry on top?'

'Oh, yes please.'

Then Alice would totter across the grass, fixed concentration on the pile of sand, making sure it reached her mum in one piece. And Harriet would take the pie and pretend to eat it, rubbing her tummy as she laughed.

The memory hit Harriet with a surge of dread that made her double over at the kitchen sink. She could see her baby so clearly – and yet she was gone.

PC Shaw's voice broke her thoughts and the image of Alice fractured into a thousand pieces before dissolving completely.

'Mrs Hodder, are you OK?' the policewoman persisted.

Harriet turned to see the woman waving a photo of Alice that Brian had plucked out of an album. She took the photo and traced a finger over her daughter's face.

'This isn't a good picture of her. She wasn't happy here.' Harriet remembered that Alice had dropped her ice cream and Brian had stopped Harriet from getting her another one. Alice had to be persuaded to smile for the camera, which meant her eyes weren't sparkling like they usually were.

'Well, we just need one to circulate. Is it a good likeness of your daughter?'

Harriet nodded. 'Yes, but—' She was about to say she'd prefer to find a better one when the doorbell rang. She looked nervously at the officer and then through to the hallway, where Brian was already emerging from the living room.

'I expect it's Angela Baker,' the officer said. 'She'll be your FLO. Family Liaison Officer,' she added when Harriet looked blank.

Brian opened the door, stepping aside to let the visitor in. The woman introduced herself as Detective Constable Angela Baker, telling Brian he could call her Angela, a fact she repeated when she came into the kitchen and saw Harriet.

Angela had a sensible, neat brown bob of hair that didn't move when the rest of her did. She wore a grey suede skirt, flat brown shoes, and a cardigan that she took off and carefully laid over the back of a kitchen chair. 'I'm here for you both,' she explained. 'You can ask me anything and I'll be your main point of contact so it doesn't get too confusing for you.' She smiled again. 'Maybe I can start by making us all a cup of tea?' Angela gestured to the kettle. 'And we can go through everything that will help us find your daughter as soon as possible. Will you come and sit down?'

Harriet obligingly sat at the table, watching PC Shaw who had murmured a goodbye and was leaving the kitchen. She wondered what the arrival of a new detective meant for them. Meanwhile Brian had insisted he would make a cup of tea for everyone as he pulled out a chair for Angela.

'Thank you very much, Brian,' she smiled at him, and Harriet immediately wondered if she shouldn't have been so ready to let their new guest make the drinks but at the same time she had no desire to do it.

'So you're a detective?' Brian asked her.

'I am,' she said. 'I'm here to update you on progress and if there's anything you need you can ask me. We find families prefer having one person to speak to, someone they can get to know.'

'But ultimately you're a detective?' Brian asked again.

'Yes. I'll be liaising with the officers who are looking for Alice,' she said.

Harriet knew that wasn't what Brian meant but he didn't respond as he dropped teabags into mugs and took the milk from the fridge, giving the bottle a little shake as he did by habit before carefully pouring it in. They both knew Angela was also there to gather information from inside their four walls that could be fed back to the officers at the station.

'I don't feel like we know anything,' he said when the tea was made and he carefully placed mugs in front of Angela and Harriet. 'PC Shaw didn't tell us much. We don't even know who's looking for Alice.'

Brian always had a light tan on his face and his cheeks usually wore a ruddy tinge above his neatly trimmed stubble, but right then they were drained of colour. Harriet was grateful for him making conversation. If she opened her mouth she was afraid she might break down again and that wouldn't get them anywhere.

'Well, right now there are many officers looking for her,' Angela said as Brian pulled out a chair and joined them at the table.

'Where are they looking?' he asked. 'How many people have you got out there?'

'As many as we have. We're treating your daughter's disappearance as the highest priority.'

'Will you find her?' he asked, his words cracking as they left his mouth.

'We will,' Angela replied and she looked so certain that for a moment Harriet believed they would.

'But you haven't found the other one,' Brian continued. 'He's still missing after months.'

'There's no reason to think that the two cases have anything to do with each other at this stage.'

'But they might,' he persisted. 'That kid went missing exactly like Alice, so of course they could be linked.'

'Mason,' Harriet said quietly. 'His name is Mason.'

They both paused and glanced at her. It felt like they'd both forgotten she was there. Angela's features softened even further, looking at Harriet with what she hoped wasn't pity. But Mason Harbridge wasn't just a kid; he was a boy with a name and a mother who publicly fell to pieces. Harriet knew everything about the case, having pored over the news, becoming obsessed with the story as it unfolded bit by bit. The fact he had gone missing from a village like theirs in Dorset made it feel so close to home.

More than once fingers had been pointed at the parents, but Harriet didn't believe they were involved. Her heart went out to them when she saw the press invading their lives, exposing everything about their family for the world to see. No one thought that seven months would pass and there'd still be no news of little Mason.

'Like I said, there's nothing at all linking Alice's disappearance to Mason's,' Angela was saying. 'As far as we know at this stage, your daughter walked away from the fete of her own volition and is lost.'

'I just can't believe no one saw anything,' Brian cried, shaking his head as he pushed himself back in his chair. 'There must have been crowds of people there.' He looked from Angela to Harriet. 'I don't get it,' he said. 'I don't get it at all.' He stood up and walked to the sink, holding his hands together in front of his lips as if in prayer. 'God, I mean why, Harriet?'

'Why what?' she asked, although she knew exactly what he meant.

'You know what I mean,' he said, turning round. 'Why was Alice with Charlotte? Why wasn't she with you? Where were you?'

Harriet bit her bottom lip. She felt Angela's eyes on her.

'I was on a course,' she said.

'A course? What do you mean, a course?' He took his hands and rested them on the counter either side of him as if he was trying to steady himself. 'Harriet,' he said again, 'what course are you talking about?'

'A bookkeeping course,' she said finally.

He stared at her, his whole body frozen, until his lips eventually moved but without making a sound. When they did, his voice was soft. 'I knew nothing about a book-keeping course,' he said. 'You never mentioned it to me.'

'I did,' Harriet said slowly, keeping eye contact with him. 'I told you about it last week.'

Brian's eyebrows furrowed deeper as he came back to the table and sat down again. She could sense his confusion but she also wanted to remind him that none of this mattered.

'No, my love,' he said as he held out his hands to her, palms upturned on the table. 'No, you definitely didn't.' Harriet lowered her hands into his as his fingers curled around them. 'But it's not relevant right now, is it? Finding Alice is paramount.' He turned back to Angela. 'I want to be out there looking for my daughter,' he said. 'I feel useless sitting here.'

'I understand your need to be out there, but honestly this is the best place you can be right now. So, Harriet,' she said, 'tell me about Charlotte. Do you leave Alice with her often?'

'No,' Harriet said. 'I've never done it before.' Her hands felt hot and sticky as she pulled them away from Brian's and ran them down the front of her skirt.

'So who would you usually leave her with?'

'I've never left Alice with anyone.'

'Never? And your daughter's four?' Angela looked surprised. It was a reaction Harriet was used to.

'Harriet doesn't have any need to leave Alice with anyone,' Brian interjected. 'She's a full-time mother.'

Angela gave Brian an inquisitive look but she didn't respond. Harriet presumed that if Angela had children herself then she probably left them a lot, especially with such a demanding job.

'But today you needed someone to look after her?' Angela asked. 'Was Charlotte your first choice?'

'Yes,' Harriet said. She didn't add that her friend was her only choice.

'So is Alice happy with Charlotte? Does she know her well?'

'She's known her since she was born,' Harriet said. 'I met Charlotte before I was pregnant.'

'And, Brian,' Angela turned to face him. 'You were fishing today? Where do you go?'

'Chesil Beach,' he said. 'But why do you need to know this? Surely I'm not under any suspicion?'

'No, you're not. It's just crucial we build up a complete picture of everyone close to Alice. But Chesil Beach is a lovely spot,' Angela said. 'My dad always went there. He said there was nothing better than sitting alone on the beach with a bottle of beer and a fishing rod. Do you go alone?'

'Yes. And I don't drink.'

'My father used to go out on a boat too. There's a lovely spot just past—'

'I never go on boats. I don't leave the beach. But if you need the name of someone to verify I was there you can ask Ken Harris,' Brian said. 'He was out on his boat today. He would have seen me.'

Her husband had never mentioned anyone he fished with before. She'd always presumed he kept himself to himself.

'Thank you, Brian,' Angela smiled. 'And I'd like some details about your course too if that's OK, Harriet?'

Harriet nodded and stood up to get the enrolment papers from her handbag.

'And I wonder if you wouldn't mind getting me Alice's toothbrush too?' Angela said as she jotted notes on her pad.

'What?' Harriet stopped still and turned to look at Angela.

'Her toothbrush. It's just standard procedure so I have something of hers.'

'Oh Christ,' Brian cried, pressing the palms of his hands against the table and pushing his chair back so it screeched across the floor. 'You're thinking this already?'

Harriet slid out of the room, up the stairs, and into the bathroom where she could no longer hear Brian talking to Angela. Her hands shook as she clutched the basin. She knew they wanted Alice's toothbrush for DNA. That meant they were already thinking the worst – that they would find a body instead of her daughter.

Alice's princess toothbrush slipped through Harriet's fingers as she reached out to take it, tumbling into the basin.

The two remaining ones didn't look right on their own. His navy pristine brush and hers with its bristles sticking out in every direction. She grabbed Alice's brush and stuck it back in the pot. Angela could have a new one, an untouched one from the drawer. There were two still boxed in there, she saw, as she opened the drawer and ran her fingers over the hard plastic.

'What are you doing?'

Harriet looked up and saw two faces in the mirror. Hers was wet with tears that streamed down her cheeks in rivers. She hadn't even noticed she had been crying. Brian's reflection loomed over her shoulder as he placed his hands on her arms and turned her around to face him. Wiping away her tears with one stroke of his thumbs, he left a trail of dampness across her cheeks.

'They need the toothbrush, Harriet,' he said and reached over her to pluck it out of the pot and take it back down to Angela.

Harriet stared at the empty space he left behind, wondering how he was able to function so easily. A carelessly picked photo that was probably the first one he came across and now he was readily handing over their daughter's toothbrush. But Brian was good at holding it together. He was only doing what was necessary to help the police find their daughter and meanwhile Harriet was left replaying the memory of Alice brushing her teeth that morning.

'Finished, Mummy,' she had said, automatically opening her mouth wide for her mum to check.

'Gorgeous,' Harriet had told her. 'The tooth fairies will be pleased with how sparkly they are.'

A fresh wave of tears left Harriet clinging on to the basin again as if it were the only thing holding her up, until eventually Brian reappeared in the bathroom and prised her hands away, leading her back down to the kitchen where Angela was patiently waiting.

'I need to know what she was doing when our daughter went missing,' Brian demanded as he ushered Harriet into a seat and sat down next to her. 'I want to know what Charlotte was doing because she obviously wasn't watching Alice.'

'You're bound to have plenty of questions,' Angela said. 'I can't answer that myself. Not entirely, Brian.'

'Where did she go? She can't have been by the inflatable or else she would have seen where Alice went.'

'I believe she was waiting in a tent right next to it with her youngest daughter,' Angela said.

'So not looking,' Brian went on. 'Not watching my daughter, like I said. She was probably on her phone. You see it all the time – mothers ignoring their children while their faces are stuck elsewhere. Half the time they have no idea where their kids even are. This is why I don't understand it, Harriet. I don't understand why you asked her to watch Alice. You always say she's wrapped up in herself, that she lets her children run feral.'

'No,' Harriet said, aghast, 'I never said that.'

'I'm sure you did.'

'That's not true,' she argued. Charlotte's children weren't feral; they were boisterous, full of life and energy. Feral wasn't a word she would ever use.

'You told me once you wouldn't trust her with Alice.' He looked at her pointedly. 'That her head's not in the right place.'

'No,' Harriet cried, a flush of embarrassment heating her face. 'I never said that.' She could feel Angela looking at her intensely as Harriet tried to recall a time when she might have said something that Brian had misconstrued, but even if she had, she wouldn't have meant it.

Brian picked up his mug and took a swig of his tea, grimacing as he placed the mug back down. It must have turned cold by now. 'I'd just never have expected you to leave Alice with her,' he said.

'There's a few more things I really need to ask you both,' Angela said, and Brian nodded for her to go on. 'Let's start with families. Alice's grandparents, aunts, uncles.'

'There aren't many,' Brian replied. 'My dad died fifteen years ago and my mother—' He broke off and straightened his shoulders. 'My mother left when I was young. I don't see her. Harriet's parents are both dead.'

'Siblings?'

'Neither of us have any,' he answered.

'So your mother, Brian?' Angela asked. 'When was the last time you saw her?'

He shrugged. 'Years ago, I'm not sure exactly.'

Harriet watched her husband attempting to pass off his mother's abandonment. She remembered when he'd last seen her and she knew Brian did too. It was nearly eight years ago. He'd taken Harriet to meet her a month after they'd started seeing each other.

'And does she know where you live or know about Alice? Could there be any reason for her to come looking for her granddaughter?'

'I doubt she even knows she has one.'

'You doubt? Do you think she might?' Angela asked.

'She doesn't know,' Brian said. 'I wouldn't have thought.' He looked away and Harriet wondered if maybe he had once told his mother about Alice. She could imagine the lack of reaction he'd have got if he had.

Angela continued to ask about other family and close friends, but it was clear their circles were painfully small. Harriet told her that she didn't keep in touch with past colleagues; she saw some of the mothers very occasionally but only because they were friends of Charlotte's. It was sadly obvious there was only one person in her life who she saw regularly and that was the person who had just lost her daughter.

Brian's life was no more interesting. He left the house at eight every morning to go to work at the insurance company he had been at for five years. He was back in the house by five-thirty without fail. He didn't do drinks, or Christmas parties, or attend celebrations, and wasn't remotely fussed that he had no one he could call a true friend.

Every Saturday Brian went fishing. He left early and came back at some point in the afternoon and until today had never mentioned anyone he met there by name.

Later Angela spoke of an appeal, which would most likely go ahead the following morning and appear on all the major news channels. They also discussed the possibility of Harriet and Brian meeting up with Charlotte.

'I can't do that,' Harriet said. The thought of sitting opposite her and seeing the guilt slashed across Charlotte's face drove a knife through her stomach.

'That's fine,' Angela told her. 'You don't have to if you're not ready.'

'You'll feel differently soon,' Brian said. She ignored his comment – she knew she wouldn't change her mind.

But while thoughts of Charlotte and the appeal spun in her head, it was the idea of spending a night without Alice in the bedroom next to her that gnawed deeply. How would she get through it? How would Harriet function during every second that Alice wasn't with her? Life without her baby girl was not a possibility.

All she could see was her daughter's face, pale and frightened. 'Mummy? Where are you?'

Harriet was trapped. Inside her own body and inside their house with no idea what she should be doing for her daughter. Sheer frustration ripped through her like lightning, jolting her upright and on to her feet, unleashing from within her a raw, guttural scream.

Brian leaped out of his chair and to his wife's side, holding her tightly in his arms, hushing her and telling her it would all be OK. 'This is all Charlotte's fault,' he hissed to Angela. 'After all, this isn't the first child she's lost.'

Charlotte

At seven o'clock on Saturday evening I had a call from Detective Chief Inspector Hayes. He phoned to say Harriet wanted to see me, despite telling me earlier she was refusing to.

'Of course I'll go,' I said, when he asked if I was prepared to see them at their house, even though I'd been through every possible scenario of meeting Harriet and none of them came out well. 'I'll just need to get someone to look after the children.'

'Of course,' he said. 'I can send an officer round.'

'No, there's no need,' I said. A policeman babysitting the children would only frighten them. 'I can be there in an hour if that's OK,' I told him and hung up. I'd called Tom as soon as I got back to the house after the fete so I knew he'd come over when I needed him to.

*

I'd already met DCI Hayes that afternoon. Audrey had insisted I should leave the fete and she'd drive me and the children back in my car. I'd stared out of the car window as she shunted the gears into reverse, muttering under her breath that she 'wouldn't be able to get out of the sodding car park'.

'I shouldn't be leaving,' I said. 'I should be searching with everyone else.' Makeshift groups of parents were forming in clumps on the field despite police requests for them not to get involved.

'No, you need to be with your children,' she said. 'They need you more than ever right now and this isn't a place for them to stay.'

I knew she was right but as Audrey negotiated her way between the parked cars I felt as empty as the extra car seat wedged behind me. The space between Molly and Evie was a gaping reminder that I'd not only lost Alice but I was now walking away from her too.

We drove out of the car park, turning the corner with the field on our right. The tips of the inflatable palm trees on the Jungle Run, visible at the furthest edge of the field, were no longer swaying. No one would have let their children on it now, even if it hadn't become a crime scene.

'And there are enough people out there,' Aud continued. 'The police don't even want them looking. Look at this place,' she said in a whisper. 'No one must want their children here now.' Two more police cars passed us, their blue lights silently flashing. I watched them in my side mirror as they pulled over.

Hayes arrived at my house at four-thirty p.m. That was when he told me Harriet was refusing to see me.

'I've tried calling her,' I said. 'I tried as soon as I got home but her mobile must be switched off.' I picked up my phone and stared at its screen, a photo of my children smiling back at me. I'd tried Harriet a number of times. Each time I held my breath until her voicemail kicked in and I could hang up, able to breathe again.

'She must have questions,' I said to the detective. 'She must want to hear from me what happened. I know I'd want to.' I'd want to scream at me if I were her, pound fists against my chest until I broke down. Demand an explanation, beg me to find her daughter or to turn back time and change what happened.

'Everyone's different,' he said and I nodded because it couldn't have been more true.

When Hayes phoned again at seven p.m. I was in the middle of undressing the girls and running them a bath. I finished the short call, turned off the water and dialled Tom's mobile.

'Any news?' he asked as he picked up.

'Not yet,' I told him.

'Oh, Charlotte. Are you sure there's still nothing I can do?'

'Actually, there is. I need to go and see Harriet. Can you come and sit with the children?'

'Yes, of course. How is Harriet?'

'I haven't spoken to her yet. When can you get here?'

'I don't know, um, half an hour?'

'That's fine,' I said.

'So you've heard nothing about Alice at all?' he asked again.

'No, nothing.'

'It's been on TV. I've just seen it on the news.'

'God,' I sighed. I'd already had two calls from journalists, but as DCI Hayes advised me, I told them both I had no comment.

'I'm sorry, Charlotte – I don't know what to say.'

'Don't say anything. Just come round so I can get over there.'

I sat on the edge of my bed and waited for Tom as the bath water slowly went cold in the room next to me. My phone flashed again with another text message from a class mum. 'Is there any news? Is there anything I can do to help?' I picked up the phone and threw it behind me. Sooner or later I was going to have to respond to all the messages I'd had since I'd left the fete but I couldn't do anything until I'd got through this evening. With the curtains pulled, I was in semi-darkness as I brooded over one question: What the hell do I say to Harriet?

I would have to look both her and Brian in the eye and tell them I had nothing that could make it any easier. No explanation, no excuses. Not even one suggestion that might bring them relief. They'd ask me what happened to Alice and I'd have to confess I didn't have a clue.

She ran behind the Jungle Run with Molly.

Then what? they'd ask.

I don't know. I just don't know what happened to your daughter.

Molly and Jack had told me they'd taken their shoes off behind the inflatable, but that in their excitement neither of them had stopped to help Alice, waited for her, or even noticed whether she'd got on. 'You're ten, Jack,' I'd cried earlier. 'Why didn't you check the girls were safely on it like I asked you to?'

Jack looked at me with a doleful expression. I knew I couldn't expect my son to consider other children. Why did I presume he would do it then? Jack has a heart of gold but he's the last kid you give responsibility to.

'Molly,' I turned on my daughter. 'She was running after you. Why didn't you help her on? What did you do – literally race on after Jack and forget she was even there?' I knew I shouldn't transfer my guilt on to them but still the words spilled out of my mouth.

Molly's eyes filled with tears. 'I'm sorry, Mummy,' she cried.

I pulled her to me and said that no, I was sorry. This was not her fault. 'I'm not saying you did anything wrong,' I told her, though of course I had implied it.

There was only one person whose fault this was. Who had lost herself in texts and Facebook and maybe looked up occasionally but never enough to spot Alice. I knew deep down I hadn't seen her tumble down the slide. It was only ever my two I'd spotted from the shade of the tent.

Which meant, as PC Fielding said, she'd most likely never got on the run in the first place.

As soon as Tom arrived, I kissed the children goodnight and told them I'd see them in the morning. Then I tried leaving the house before we could get into a conversation but he stopped me before I got to the front door.

'Are you OK?' he asked.

I shook my head, pressing my fingernails into my palms so I didn't start crying. 'Of course not, but I don't want to talk about it.'

'It was headlines on the news.' Tom rubbed his hands together uneasily. 'To be expected, I suppose.'

'Yes, well it would be. Something like this—' I stopped. 'I really just need to go, Tom.'

He nodded and I knew there was something else he had to tell me but I opened the front door, not wanting to give him the chance. 'I just saw Chris Lawson as I was coming up the drive,' he said. 'He told me they'd called off their drinks party tonight.'

'I really couldn't care less if they have or not.'

'No, I know, I'm just saying. They're still your friends and neighbours. They want to support you.' I stepped into the front garden and he took a step too.

'Where are you going with this, Tom?' I knew him well enough to tell there was something else he wanted to say.

'I just—' Tom paused and ran a hand through his hair, making it stick up in tufts on the top of his head. 'Chris mentioned some things have been said on the internet, that's all. I don't want you suddenly coming across them.'

'What kind of things?'

'Stupid people with nothing better to do, that's all. Not your friends. Not anyone who knows you, Charl.'

'What kind of things?' I asked again, feeling my throat burn with dread.

'Just … ' He sighed ruefully. 'What were you doing when she went missing? How come our kids are OK?'

I took a step back, as if he'd slapped me.

'Oh, Charlotte,' he said, reaching out and taking hold of my arms.

'I can't do this now,' I cried, jerking myself out of reach.

'I'm sorry.' Tom gaped at me as if he were hurt or worried, or maybe even both. 'I should never have said anything.'

'Well it's too late now, isn't it?' I snapped and ran to the car before he could utter another word.

I'd rarely been to Harriet's house because she always preferred coming to mine. She'd often sit at my kitchen island and run her hands gently across its oak surface as if it were made of the most precious wood.

'Harriet, you don't need to worry,' I once laughed as she carefully placed her coffee mug down, checking for rings under it when I hadn't given her a coaster.

'Habit,' she murmured, smiling sheepishly.

'Well, I'm not worried about stains,' I told her. 'The kids make plenty of those.' But still she would swipe her hand across the surface and tell me everything she loved about my home, while inside I was begging her to stop.

In contrast Harriet's house was small and unbearably dark. The first time I visited she apologised for its lack of light, leading me quickly to the kitchen at the back.

'Don't be silly, it's lovely,' I told her. 'I can't believe you painted all this yourself.'

'Well, there isn't much to paint, really. It's not very big,' she said. 'Not like your beautiful home.'

The next time Harriet was at mine I found myself pointing out the chipped skirting board, the table that needed fixing, and the crack that ran along the length of the living-room ceiling.

I made things up too. Little harmless stories to show the perfect life she thought I had wasn't really that perfect. I complained that Tom was always working too hard and I never saw him, how I hated my job some days and wished I could leave. I told her she was so lucky to be married to Brian who was always home by five-thirty p.m. so they could have tea as a family.

I wasn't lying when I told her dinner wasn't an enjoyable experience in our house. None of the children liked the same food and most nights I ended up giving them fish fingers or pizza because they were the only meals none of them complained about. But I omitted to tell her Tom only added to the suffering at mealtimes so it was easier for me to endure them alone. I didn't say that the idea of him walking in the door at five-thirty p.m. every night without fail would actually be my idea of hell.

But Harriet seemed to be placated when she said, 'Yes, I'm very lucky that Brian never works late.'

I turned off the main road out of town to where the houses were packed much more tightly together. 'Crammed in,' Tom would say. Even at that time of night, Harriet's street was busy. I was forced to drive past the house to find a tight parking space between two dropped kerbs on the other side of the road.

There were a handful of journalists hanging outside Harriet's front garden so I'd been given the number of the liaison officer to call when I arrived who would come out to meet me. I looked back at the house, its windows blackened by pulled curtains. The thought of them sitting inside, engulfed in a misery that I had created, made me want to restart the engine and turn around. But I didn't have that luxury. Swallowing the lump lodged in my throat, I tapped out the number and told the woman who answered, Angela, that I was there.

An agonising fug hung in the air of their living room. Inside the boxed walls of the small room, its stuffiness did nothing to suppress a shiver running the length of my spine as I went in. 'Someone has stepped on your grave,' Tom would have said.

Their Family Liaison Officer, Angela, manoeuvred me towards the remaining empty seat, which was an armchair in the corner of the room that faced the sofa. On that, Harriet and Brian were glued together. In his lap Brian had his hands protectively wrapped around one of Harriet's. His fingers played, pressing into her hand, splaying them and then scrunching like a nervous child.

As I stumbled across the room and awkwardly perched in the seat, Brian's eyes followed me. His body was curved around Harriet's, a defensive wall to keep her safe and shield her from me. Inside his enclosure, Harriet was deathly immobile. Her glassy eyes stared out of the window and didn't once venture in my direction.

The silence was as cold as the atmosphere until Angela broke it. 'Can I get you a cup of tea, Mrs Reynolds?' she asked.

I shook my head. 'No thank you.' My voice was little more than a whisper. I made a point of looking past Brian to Harriet but she didn't peel her eyes away from the window.

'Maybe it would help if you could tell Harriet and Brian what happened,' Angela said softly. 'What was going on when Alice went on to the Jungle Run.'

I nodded. I could sense Harriet and Brian both tensing and my own muscles ached as I hunched uncomfortably in the chair. I had no idea how to start.

'I, um—' I broke off and swallowed loudly, inhaling a large gulp of air that hissed through my teeth. 'I'm sorry,' I said. 'I know nothing I say will mean anything.' I paused again. Brian's eyes continued to bore into me as if he could see right through my skin, but still Harriet wouldn't look over.

The skirt of my dress was damp beneath me. I shifted on the leather chair, the wetness of my thighs making it squeak, though any extra embarrassment wouldn't show on my already blotched face.

'I'm sorry,' I started again.

'Sorry is not going to bring back our daughter,' Brian interrupted, his voice quietly controlled. 'So we don't want to hear your apologies. What we want to know is what happened today. How you lost Alice.' His fingers continued to unfurl and then clamp back around Harriet's hand. Beside him she took a deep breath.

Brian leaned forward, moving his weight towards the edge of the sofa. I could see his eyes more clearly now, red lines creeping out from the edges. He might have been crying but now they just made him look angry.

'What happened?' he growled. 'Because we need to know how you lost our daughter.'

I felt my breath stagger in my chest. 'I'm so sorry, Brian. I don't know what happened.'

'You don't know?' He gave a short laugh, one of his hands flinging into the air, which made Harriet jump. Brian moved his body, wrapping himself around Harriet more tightly, and despite how awful I felt for him I wished he would get out of the way so I could see my friend.

'I don't mean it like that,' I said. 'It's just that everything happened so quickly. It was a split second. Alice went round to the back of the inflatable with Molly and Jack, but then she didn't—' The words caught in my throat, making me gulp down another large breath. 'She didn't come off it. And as soon as I knew that, I went on it looking for her myself. The others came with me, but,' I shook my head, 'she wasn't there.' I knew I sounded too shrill and my excuses hung awkwardly in the air as I waited for Brian to answer.

But it was Harriet who spoke, her voice rupturing into the room like it had no place being there. 'How long had she been gone before you noticed?' Still she continued to stare out of the window. It was a question I'd expected.

'I think it was maybe five minutes,' I said quietly, willing her to look at me around her husband's shoulder. I inched forward in the seat, the squeak of leather making another unpleasant noise. My hand flinched as if it wanted to reach out for her, but almost by instinct she withdrew further into the sofa. Eventually she turned her head and found my eyes.

'Five minutes doesn't seem very long,' she said. 'She can't have gone far in five minutes.'

'I – well, maybe it was a little longer. I'm not sure exactly but it wasn't long, I promise you.'

Harriet turned away again, staring out of the window once more.

'I don't know where she went, I'm so sorry,' I said. 'We looked everywhere and—'

'And what exactly were you doing?' In contrast to the softness of Harriet's voice, Brian's was fiercely powerful. 'When she went missing, what were you actually doing that meant you weren't watching my daughter?'

'I was waiting for them at the front.'

'But I want to know what you were doing,' he said. 'Because it wasn't what you should have been.'

'I was with Evie,' I said. 'I was just waiting.'

'Were you on your phone?' he barked. 'Did you get distracted?'

'I, erm, well I looked at my phone, but only for a moment. I was still keeping an eye on the children and—' I stopped. Of course I hadn't kept an eye on the children or none of us would be here. Alice would be asleep in her bed upstairs.

'But you weren't watching her, were you?' Brian's words felt like they had been screamed out at me but in reality they weren't. They were tense but quiet as they hissed through his teeth. He'd moved forwards until he was almost hanging off the sofa. His face was now only inches from mine and, as much as I wanted to recoil, I couldn't move. 'And you didn't see a thing,' he said, and all I could do was shake my head again, while the tears now sprang out of my eyes and slid down my cheeks. His gaze was drawn to them trickling down and I rubbed at them roughly with the back of my hand. He looked like he was about to comment when Harriet's voice spoke timidly from behind him.

'How was she?'

Brian inhaled a large breath of air through his flared nostrils.

'Sorry?' I leaned to one side so I could see past Brian.

'How was Alice? Was she happy?'

'Yes, she was perfectly happy.' I tried a weak smile. I knew Brian had every right to be there but how I wished I could take hold of Harriet's hand and speak to her alone. Just her and me. 'She was playing with Molly,' I said. 'She seemed absolutely fine. She wasn't upset about anything.'

'What did she have to eat?' Harriet asked.

Brian swung around to look at her. 'What did she have to eat?' he repeated.

'Yes,' she said quietly, her gaze drifting up to meet his. 'I want to know what Alice ate at the fete. Before she—' Harriet stopped.

'She had some candyfloss,' I said quickly. The tears continued to run down my face. I stopped bothering to wipe them away as I remembered how carefully Alice had picked at her floss.

'Oh!' Harriet threw her hand to her mouth. 'She's never had candyfloss before.'

My heart plummeted. Harriet's eyes were wide and wet with tears. I wanted to tell her that Alice enjoyed it, I was sure she would want to know that, but already Brian was speaking again.

'You mean you didn't get round to giving her lunch,' he snapped but he was cut off by the sound of an eerie wail, painfully long, filling the room with suffering.

Harriet slumped forward, her hands gripped tightly either side of her head. 'I can't bear this any more. Get out, Charlotte!' she screamed. 'I need you to go. Please, just get out of the house.'

Brian immediately grabbed her rocking body in his arms, whispering words I couldn't hear. 'Please just leave, Charlotte,' she sobbed.

I stood up, my legs shaking. I couldn't bear this any more either.

In the doorway Angela held out a hand as she stood to one side. Numbly I edged towards her. 'I'm so sorry,' I whispered, tears now cascading down my cheeks.

'Don't tell me you're sorry again,' Brian said over his wife's head. His cheeks were blotched in patches of fiery red. 'You can go back to your children now. You managed to take them home safely.'

'I think you'd better go,' Angela said as she took my hand and led me into the hallway.

'I'm going to do everything I can,' I sobbed. 'I'll do whatever it takes to get Alice back. Can you tell them that? I'll do anything.'

NOW

'And you hadn't heard from Harriet at all after that evening?' DI Rawlings asks. 'Since you went to their house?'

'That's right.'

'Not until this morning,' she says. 'Thirteen days later.'

'No.' I feel my chest getting tighter. 'Not until she called me today.'

I can feel the floor start to soften beneath me and the air feels heavier. I expect her to ask me more about the call, but she doesn't and I realise there's no point me trying to second-guess her.

'You said you would have liked the chance to talk to Harriet on her own. Why was that?'

I shift positions in the hard plastic chair. 'I guess it was because it's Harriet who's my friend and I didn't know Brian. I wanted to talk to Harriet and—' I break off and slump back in the seat, looking up at the clock. Its bright-red digits blur in front of me.

'I wanted the chance to tell her on her own just how dreadful I felt,' I admit eventually. 'I hoped that if I could talk to Harriet, just the two of us the way we used to, then I could get her to see I hadn't done anything wrong, like Brian was implying. Yes, I'd let them out of my sight and I wished more than anything I hadn't, but I was still there, I was metres away, and Alice really did just vanish. I wanted Harriet to understand I was looking after her like I promised I would, only—' Tears prick at my eyes. 'Only I also knew I wasn't.'

DI Rawlings looks at me, confused.

'If I was looking after her properly then she wouldn't have disappeared,' I say. 'But I also knew I didn't do anything any other parent wouldn't have done. Yet no one else saw it like that. Already I was being blamed. People saying I was irresponsible.' I wipe my eyes with the back of my hand.

'Who was blaming you?' DI Rawlings asks as she pulls a tissue sharply out of a box and passes it across the table. I take it from her and dab my eyes, keeping the tissue scrunched in my hand.

'Friends. Strangers,' I say. 'Everyone jumps on the bandwagon, don't they? They think it's their right to comment on what I'm like as a mother even if they've never heard of me before.'

'The power of the internet,' Rawlings states.

'It was the people I think of as my friends, though; they're the ones whose reactions sting the most. In the days after the fete, their silence became deafening.'

'And Harriet's reaction must have been difficult to handle too?' the detective asks, sharply turning the conversation as if I have no right to feel sorry for myself. 'Her silence must have left you wondering what she was thinking?'

'It did. I wanted her to shout at me and tell me she hated me, but she didn't and that made it worse. Harriet refused to see me again.' I look DI Rawlings in the eye. 'And that was so much harder,' I admit. 'I watched her crumbling in that living room and there was nothing I could do to make it better.' Tears are now flowing down my face and, as much as I wipe them away, more keep coming.

'But Brian was more forthright?' she says. 'Is that the reaction you expected from him?'

'I didn't know what to expect. I hadn't met him many times, and much fewer in recent years.' I always suspected Harriet felt like she couldn't bring Brian along after Tom and I had split up, even though I'd attempted to assure her he was welcome.

'So even though you became such good friends with Harriet, you never got to know her husband?' DI Rawlings asks, leaning forward in her seat. Her eyes are unnervingly still as she stares at me.

'No. Our friendship didn't involve him or my ex-husband when we were together.'

'That's unusual.' She continues to look me straight in the eye as she lays her hands out flat on the desk in front of her. 'Don't you think?'

I open my mouth to respond that I didn't think it was but instead I say, 'Actually, can we take a break now, please? I'd like to use the toilet.'

'Of course.' DI Rawlings pushes her chair back and gestures towards the door. 'And help yourself to a tea or coffee too,' she adds and for a moment I am grateful for her kindness. It isn't until I walk out of the room I realise she's really just telling me there's still much more she wants to know.

BEFORE

Harriet

That first night Harriet did not sleep, or if she did it was only minutes before she woke, soaked in sweat and disturbed by images she couldn't shake.

She lay on top of the covers throughout the interminable dark hours, staring at the ceiling, all the time thinking of Alice's empty room next to hers. Not one night had passed when she hadn't tucked her daughter into bed, kissed her goodnight, crept in to check on her when she went to bed herself. It was no surprise she couldn't sleep.

Earlier in the evening, while Brian was still downstairs, Angela had come up to Harriet's bedroom, offering to call her doctor to see if he could bring some sleeping tablets. Harriet shook her head vigorously. No, she definitely did not want pills. She would rather be awake all night torturing herself than knocked out, miles away from reality.

'Thank you for staying so late,' she said to Angela, grateful she was still there.

'Of course.' Angela brushed off her gratitude. It was her job after all, Harriet thought sadly, but still she was comforted by her presence in the house. It took her mind off Brian pacing the floorboards below.

'I promised Alice I'd always keep her safe,' Harriet said quietly. 'But I haven't been able to, have I?'

Angela leaned over and touched her arm. 'Try not to do this, Harriet. This is not your fault.' Harriet wondered if Angela would tell Brian that too because she could feel his blame hovering over her, his confusion that she'd left Alice with Charlotte. He knew Harriet would never have let Alice out of her sight.

Were her anxieties about Alice innate? she wondered. Would Harriet have been a different kind of mother if her dad had still been there, smoothing the path of parenting for her mum? With only her mother to learn from was it any wonder she'd become overly protective too?

'I see flashes of Alice's face.' Tears slid down Harriet's cheeks, pooling uncomfortably in the crook of her neck, but she made no move to wipe them away.

'Guilt is a very destructive thing,' Angela said. 'You mustn't let it take hold. You couldn't have changed what happened. No one can foresee something like this.'

Something like the fact my daughter is gone, Harriet thought. No matter what Angela said, the guilt would continue to bury itself deep into her skin, itching away until one day soon she would be driven mad with it. She was sure of that.

But when Harriet wasn't thinking of Alice, unwanted thoughts of Charlotte filled her head. Charlotte in her warm, large bed in the cosy bedroom with the deep-teal walls and fluffy cushions lined up along the pillows. She wondered how Charlotte felt knowing her own children were safely asleep in the rooms surrounding hers, whether she derived comfort from that even if she wouldn't admit it.

Charlotte's friends would rally around her. They would line up outside her house with warm casseroles in Le Creuset dishes and Tupperware boxes of homemade muffins. It was no surprise Charlotte had so many friends, but it widened the trench between them now. That Harriet had not received one call from a worried friend was evidence. Angela must have noticed she had no one else in her life.

She wondered what Angela thought of Charlotte. Did she feel sorry for her? Harriet knew her tears were real but she couldn't bear to look at them. If she'd looked into Charlotte's eyes she would have seen her pain and she couldn't bear to take that on too. 'Charlotte feels guilty,' Harriet murmured to Angela. 'I can't tell her not to.'

'Of course you can't, no one expects you to.'

'Do you think she wasn't watching the children properly?'

'I'm sure she was,' Angela said. 'But she could never have expected something this awful to happen.'

Harriet rolled over on her bed. She hated to think that Charlotte hadn't been looking after her daughter, yet none of that really mattered any more. Nothing but Alice's safety mattered.

'Brian said something earlier,' Angela said. 'Something about this not being the first child she's lost.'

Harriet inhaled a deep breath and shook her head as she nestled into the pillow. 'It was nothing like that,' she said and, despite everything else she was feeling, Harriet was still ashamed that she had betrayed Charlotte by telling Brian.

How she wished she hadn't listened to Brian about Charlotte coming to the house. It wasn't a good idea like he'd insisted it would be. If he did it again she would have to refuse. There was no way she could bring herself to see or speak to Charlotte.

Angela eventually left and, when Brian came up to the bedroom, he found Harriet lying in semi-darkness. The only light that filtered into the room was from the moon, slicing through the small gaps in the blinds. Harriet preferred it that way. Suddenly the ceiling light flooded the room with its harsh white bulb as Brian flicked it on and slumped on to the edge of the bed.

Neither of them spoke until he got back up and paced to the window where he peered through the slatted blinds on to the street below. 'The journalists are still outside,' he said. 'Is there nothing I can do to get rid of them?'

Harriet didn't answer.

'There are two of them hanging about outside our wall. What the hell do they think they're going to get doing that? She told them we had nothing to say. They just want to look at us, like we're animals.'

Harriet buried herself deeper into the covers, hoping he would either turn off the light and get into bed or preferably go back downstairs. She didn't want to talk.

Brian remained a while longer and then let the slats ping back, running a hand through his hair that now sprang out wildly from his scalp. Then he strode out of the bedroom, leaving the light on, and went into the bathroom. Every sound he made echoed harshly through the walls. Harriet held her hands over her ears but could still hear the splash of him urinating into the toilet, the toilet flushing, taps being turned on, water violently splattering into the basin.

'Why didn't you tell me about the course?' Brian reappeared in the doorway.

Harriet held her breath until her throat burned. She didn't want to have this conversation. 'I thought I had.'

'You definitely didn't. I would have remembered something like that. Why a bookkeeping course of all things?'

'So I could do something when Alice starts school,' she said. If he went on to ask why, she would tell him she knew they could do with the money. She'd seen the red bills hidden in his bedside drawer in the hope she wouldn't come across them.

'Did Charlotte put you up to it? Tell you that you needed to earn some extra money?'

'No. Charlotte never—'

'Is it because she's a career woman?'

'She works two days a week.'

'But that's still not a full-time mother,' he said. 'And you know that's what you want to be, my love. She's trying to do both and be good at it and you know you can't do that,' he went on, his voice rising higher. 'Christ, we both know that now, don't we?' he cried.

'Brian,' Harriet pleaded. 'Stop it, please.' She couldn't deal with this. Not now. Not tonight. Surely he must see that? 'The course had nothing to do with Charlotte.'

'I worry,' he said evenly. 'That it's happening again, Harriet. You – you trust people too easily.'

'I don't, Brian,' she said in no more than a whisper.

'Just promise me you'll forget about this bookkeeping idea,' he said, sinking down on to the bed beside her. 'You must know how it makes me so uneasy that you're even considering it.'

'I'll forget about it,' she told him. It's not like she ever believed it was a real possibility anyway.

'I care about you,' he said, shuffling closer to her. 'You know that, don't you? You know I'm only thinking of you. After what happened before – well, I just worry we'll go down that path again.'

Harriet sighed inwardly. How many times would he bring up the same thing?

'I hate to ask,' he said, looking at her with angst. 'But you have been taking your medication lately, haven't you?'

Harriet pushed herself up and stared at her husband.

'Oh, Harriet.' Brian closed his eyes and took a deep breath, carefully trying not to sigh out loud as he exhaled. 'Your medication. The tablets the doctor gave you two weeks ago. I had a horrible feeling you'd stopped. Please tell me you haven't?'

'Brian, I don't know what you're talking about. I don't have any medication.'

'OK, OK,' he said calmly, holding his hands in the air as if he didn't want a fight. 'Don't worry about it now. I'm sure it's not important.'

'Of course it's not important,' she said, 'because there isn't any medication to take.'

Brian smiled patiently. 'We don't have to think about it tonight. It just worried me, that's all, that you think you'd told me your plans and you clearly hadn't. But like you say, it doesn't matter right now, not with everything else going on. We'll talk about it in the morning.' He stood up and ran his hands down his shirt. 'You need to sleep.' And he walked out of the room, leaving the light on, and down the stairs before she could say any more.

Charlotte

I barely slept and, when I did fall into a confused mess of dreams, I was woken at six a.m. on Sunday morning by a piercing scream. I flung myself out of bed and raced into Molly's room where, the night before, Tom had laid mattresses on the floor for Jack and Evie to sleep on.

When I'd got home from Harriet's house I'd looked in on my sleeping children, my heart filled with love and grief.

'Thank you, Tom,' I whispered.

'For what?'

'I don't know, just being here. Looking after them.'

'Of course I'm going to, I'm here for all of you,' he said. 'Anyway, they wanted to be together. Evie said she was scared and I found Jack hovering on the landing not knowing what to do with himself, so I told him to go in with the girls. By the way, he could do with some new pyjamas. The ones he's in are skimming the top of his ankles.'

I didn't respond like I usually would have. How Tom thought pyjamas were a priority right now was beyond me, but I persuaded myself to let it go.

Evie was still screaming when I crawled onto her mattress first thing on Sunday and pulled her in for a hug. 'What is it, Evie?' I whispered. 'Mummy's here, what's happened? Did you have a nasty dream?'

'A bad man was coming to get me,' she sobbed. 'I was scared.'

'Shhh. There's no bad man,' I said, though by then I was certain there was and he'd been metres away from my children.

'What's happened to Alice?' she asked.

I put a finger to my lips and gestured towards her sleeping siblings. Molly stirred and rolled over but didn't wake. 'I don't know, honey, but the policemen are doing everything they can to bring her home.'

'Will she come back today?'

'I don't know, my darling. I don't know. I hope so.'

'Did someone take her?' she asked, solemnly looking up at me with wide eyes. I furiously fought back tears. How I wanted to reassure her that Chiddenford was still a safe place to live and she had nothing to worry about, that her dream was just that, a nightmare she could forget about by the time she'd finished breakfast.

'I don't know what happened, but I promise you –' I inhaled a lungful of air that burned my chest as it sank through my body '– I promise I won't let anything bad happen to you.'

I had no right to make such promises but I knew I would never take my eyes off my children again. I would never let them run through the trees where I couldn't see them or play hide and seek in the sand dunes where the grass was so high it devoured them. I would never trust anyone not to be lurking a breath away from me, ready to snatch my babies.

Later that morning I spoke to DCI Hayes who told me what I feared – that there was still no news. I pictured him and his team standing around their whiteboard, rubbing their chins, glancing at each other in the hope there was something they had missed. Surely the child couldn't have vanished without anyone seeing anything, they must have said. I wondered if they knew more than they were telling me, or were at least suspecting it. There had to be stats about these kinds of things, probabilities to determine what had most likely happened. Did they think Alice was already dead?

But he told me there were still no leads and couldn't even reassure me they were inching towards finding her.

The day before, Audrey had patiently listened as I clawed at the empty space between last seeing Alice and realising she wasn't there. I hoped that by dissecting it enough times something would come to me. If Aud went home and told her husband she couldn't bear to hear any more, then she didn't let on.

Karen and Gail had both called to see if there was anything they could do. Many friends had texted messages of support, a few asking if there was any news, and even mums from Molly and Jack's classes who I barely knew had found ways to tell me they were sorry about what had happened.

As much as I needed their support and was initially relieved that I wasn't being judged, I began to begrudge relaying the story just to feed their curiosities with first-hand details. Each time I closed the door or hung up the phone I felt as if someone had taken away another piece of me.

I'd even had a neighbour loitering on my doorstep, telling me, 'I couldn't imagine what I'd do in that situation.'

I tried to remain patient as I nodded along with her.

'Still, I suppose you have to be thankful it wasn't your own child.'

I looked at her in disbelief. 'What?'

'I mean, it's awful, obviously, but losing your own child – well isn't that worse?'

'No, it's not worse,' I cried. 'How can anything be worse than what's happened?'

'Oh no, I don't mean it isn't horrendous,' she blustered. 'I just think if it was one of yours then ... ' she trailed off, looking desperately over my shoulder. 'Where are your lovely ones anyway?'

'Thank you for coming by,' I said. 'But I really need to get back in.' I closed the door on her and pressed my back against it, shutting my eyes and silently screaming. I'd thanked her, for God's sake. What was wrong with me?

Was I so afraid of pushing people away that I was letting them eject their unwanted thoughts on to me? Was I scared of what they would say about me if I didn't?

Audrey came back to the house when I was making breakfast, at a point when we had temporarily fallen into chaotic normality, and when I opened the door I realised how it must have looked.

'Oh, Aud,' I blustered. 'I'm sorry, we were just trying to get breakfast sorted and the kids, well, you know what it's like.' I stepped aside to let her in, taking in the view of my hallway. Molly sat crying at the bottom of the stairs while Evie hovered in the doorway to the kitchen, dangling a sodden night nappy in one hand. The TV blared out from the playroom where Jack had turned up the volume to drown out his sisters.

'It's how it should be,' she said as she gave me a hug and carefully folded her cardigan on to the hallway table. 'I should have brought the boys round to sit with Jack. Anyway, you mustn't stop their lives going on as normal.'

'I know but—'

Audrey held up her hand to stop me. 'I'll make us both a coffee while you sort out whatever this is about.'

I smiled gratefully. 'I'll be through in a minute. Now, Molly, what's wrong?' I asked, crouching next to my daughter on the bottom step.

'Evie kicked me,' she sobbed.

'Evie? Is that true?'

'You forgot this,' Evie said, hurling the wet nappy across the hallway.

'Jesus, Evie, will you come and pick that up, please.'

'Can I have breakfast?'

'I said come and pick this up, Evie.' I pointed to the nappy, rising to my feet.

'I want Shreddies, not toast.'

'Evie,' I shouted. 'Just do as you're told. And come and tell me why you kicked Molly.'

'She kicked me first.'

'I didn't, Mummy, I promise,' Molly cried.

'God!' I clamped my hands over my ears. 'Will you stop arguing! What is wrong with you both? Do you really think any of your petty squabbles are important right now?'

Jack glanced over from the sofa in the playroom and then back to the TV. 'And will you turn down the volume, Jack?' I shouted. 'I can't hear myself think.'

'Why do you need to?' Molly asked.

'What?'

'Hear yourself think?'

I gripped on to the banister, my hand clenching round it. I knew I should laugh but somehow I couldn't. 'Don't talk back at me, Molly.'

Her bottom lip wobbled and then she flung her hands over her head, dramatically curling herself into a ball and crying.

'Come and have a coffee,' Audrey said, appearing in the kitchen doorway. 'Girls, why don't you go and sit with your brother and watch some TV? I'll bring you breakfast in there today.'

'Really?' Evie's eyes shone as she skipped into the playroom and eventually Molly unfurled herself and followed her in.

'Have you eaten?' Audrey asked, as we went through to the kitchen. The smell of coffee drifted from the pot. 'I'm making you toast if you haven't,' she said, popping two slices of bread into the toaster.

I shook my head. 'Thank you, but I'm not hungry.'

'You have to eat.'

'I will later.' I smiled at her gratefully and realised how good it was to have her here again, taking control. How we hadn't done this enough in the last couple of years, and had drifted apart since Tom and I hadn't been together. Audrey had been supportive throughout our separation but had always made it clear she thought we should stay together for the children, so I'd stopped confiding in her. Not like I did with Harriet.

We sat on stools at the island in silence. She had folded back the doors to the garden and a soft breeze blew in, the sun shining daggers of light across the stone tiles.

'So tell me more about last night,' Audrey asked after a while. I'd called her once Tom had left but only given the briefest details.

'It was awful.'

She nodded. 'How were they?'

I sighed, stretching my arms in front of me, my hands wrapped around the mug of coffee Aud had pushed in my direction. 'Brian more or less took over. He was the one asking all the questions and getting angry.'

'Really?' Audrey asked, a teaspoon of sugar hovering over her mug as she looked up at me.

I nodded. 'It frightened me. I know that's a daft thing to say given what he's going through. I suppose I should have expected it.'

'And Harriet?'

'Harriet,' I sighed, taking a sip of my coffee. 'You put sugar in mine?'

'I thought you could do with it.'

I frowned but took another sip anyway. 'Harriet very obviously didn't want to see me in the first place.'

'I thought she asked for you to go?' Audrey said.

'She did. The detective made a point of telling me she'd changed her mind and wanted me to go over. I don't know, maybe she changed it again, or possibly just seeing me was too much for her. Whatever it was, she couldn't bear to look at me.' I winced at the memory, still raw with its ability to slice through me as if it were happening now. Audrey sucked in a breath. 'What is it?' I asked.

'I just can't begin to put myself in her shoes,' she said softly. 'The first time she's ever left that little girl and then the unthinkable happens.'

'I know. And I was always encouraging her to let me have Alice.'

'She must be thinking she was right to be so bloody paranoid all along.'

'Aud, she wasn't paranoid.'

'Oh, she was. The poor woman is plagued by worries. She makes me nervous just talking to her.'

'She was never that bad,' I sighed. 'You just didn't know her, didn't want to know her.'

I could feel Aud staring at me but I couldn't bring myself to look at her. 'I never disliked Harriet,' she said. 'You know that. I just wondered why you two got so close. She's very different to us.'

I wouldn't get into this now. How Harriet genuinely wanted what was right for me and I could tell her anything. How she never judged me. But right now it was Audrey I needed, and I was so very grateful she was here.

'Harriet might not know it, but she'll want to see you again.'

'No.' I gave a short laugh as I shook my head. 'I'm the last person she needs and I can't blame her.'

'Charlotte.' Audrey leaned across the worktop. 'You can't give up trying. Tell me honestly who you think is going to get her through this?'

I sank my head into my hands. 'Brian? You could see how much he was trying to protect her.'

'She's going to need a friend as well as her husband.'

'I know,' I cried. 'Don't you think I realise I'm the only friend she has? And that that's what makes all of this so much worse? The guilt that I have because Harriet left Alice with me,' I sobbed, placing a hand over my heart. 'Me,' I repeated, balling my hand into a fist, this time slamming it hard against my chest. 'She'd never wanted to leave her before, you're right, but I was always telling her she should, and I know she has no one else, Aud, but what can I do about it when I'm the one who's done this to her in the first place?'

'Oh, Charlotte.' Audrey walked around the island and came to my side, folding her arms around me. 'I'm sorry, I'm so sorry. Maybe you're right and Brian will be what she needs,' she said, straightening up.

I raked my hands through my hair. 'I know you don't believe that but I really don't know what I can do when she doesn't want me in her house. Harriet isn't as weak as you think,' I said, when Audrey reached for the coffee pot and refilled her mug. I held a hand over my own and shook my head.

'I've never said weak. Fragile, maybe.'

'I felt worse after being in their house.'

'I'm not surprised.'

'Not just because it was so hard, but I felt this despair as I was driving home,' I said, my voice breaking at the memory. 'On the one hand they were both clawing at hope and desperate for me to tell them something that would give them an answer. But on the other hand it felt like there was no hope left. I walked out of there feeling like the worst had already happened.'

'That doesn't make any sense.'

'I know it doesn't.' I thought back to the dark oppres-
siveness of the living room and the way the walls had felt
like they were closing in on me. 'Oh God, Aud.' I buried
my head in my hands again. 'How's this going to end?'

'Alice is going to be found,' Audrey said, looking at me
over the rim of the mug.

'But what if she isn't?' I whispered.

'She will be.' Aud was resolute and I willed myself to
believe her.

'How was Tom?' Audrey asked me after we'd fallen into
a brief silence.

'He's ... Tom,' I said dismissively and then shook my
head. 'No, that's not fair. He's been very good, he just
doesn't always get it right.'

'He'll be trying his best,' Audrey said and I knew I
needed to change the subject.

'I want you to be honest with me. Would you leave your
children with me again?'

'Oh, for God's sake.'

'I need you to tell me the truth,' I insisted.

She rolled her eyes. 'You know I would.'

I didn't answer as I sipped my coffee.

'Charlotte,' she said, her voice firm, 'there are the friends
you trust with your children and the ones you don't. You
are definitely one I would. You know that.'

We had talked about it once at a barbecue at Audrey's.
She and I were both tipsy when Aud gestured towards

Kirsten, a neighbour of hers who was never less than fifteen minutes late picking her children up from school.

'I left the twins at hers the other day,' Audrey told me. 'When I went round to get them, her oldest, Bobby, was on the glass roof of the conservatory. He'd laid a mattress on the grass and was jumping on to it. Thankfully my two weren't being so stupid. Or maybe I just got there in time,' she laughed. 'I won't be leaving them with her again in a hurry. Even if my leg's falling off I'll wait for you to come round before I go to A & E.'

Audrey smiled now and said, 'I'd still wait for you first if I needed to go to hospital. If that's what you're thinking.'

'Thank you,' I murmured, though I wondered if she might be the only one.

Harriet

On Sunday morning Brian and Harriet sat in silence in the back of Angela's car as she drove them to the hotel where they were to make a public appeal. Harriet's stomach clenched in knots as they passed the familiar landmarks that blurred in a haze. She couldn't have told anyone how they got to the hotel if they'd asked her. None of it seemed real.

In the car park, Harriet looked out of the back window and saw the hotel was one of the generic boxes built away from the coast that always appeared to be filled with suited businessmen rather than holidaymakers.

Her door was opened and she stepped out, shivering, even though it wasn't remotely cold. Brian took her arm and with Angela on her other side she was led up the concrete steps and into the reception area.

There was nothing attractive about the orange bricks or the mass-produced paintings that hung behind the reception desk, and the air conditioning blasted through the clinical whitewashed conference room, making her wish she had worn something warmer.

The room was already filled with rows of people, chattering between themselves, oblivious to her and Brian. Angela pointed to the front and told her they would be sitting at the table where microphones were strategically placed and cameras facing.

Harriet stood rigidly in the doorway. 'I don't think I can do it,' she said in a whisper.

She felt Brian move closer, could smell a fresh waft of his aftershave. 'We can do this together,' he said, not taking his eyes off the front of the room as he began walking her past the rows of people who lulled into silence when they saw them approach.

A flash of light made Harriet startle as journalists began snapping photos of them before they'd even sat down. 'Come and sit over here,' Angela told her as she directed Harriet to a chair.

'Are you going to be next to me?' she asked.

Angela shook her head as she gestured for Brian to sit on Harriet's right. 'No, DCI Hayes will be,' she said and crouched down. 'You'll be fine,' she added quietly. 'Just remember what we spoke about earlier.'

Harriet nodded and glanced over at the young media officer who had come to the house that morning. Kerri had told Harriet she was there to advise them both about the appeal and confidently reeled through a list that Harriet was only half-listening to.

'We should find you something to wear,' Kerri had said, looking pointedly at Harriet who in turn waved her hand towards the wardrobe. Kerri could choose something and she'd wear whatever it was. Though now she felt exposed in the thin white blouse that clung to her skin and wished she hadn't been so vague earlier in her attempt to shut out what was happening.

The magnitude of the next hour was overwhelming, absorbing all her thoughts. Harriet knew exactly how important this appeal was. She'd been the one sitting at home watching Mason's parents last October and had seen the mother's raw grief seeping from every bone in her body. But then she'd listened to the journalists who picked apart the parents' gestures, twisting them and making suggestions. His father hadn't looked worried enough, according to one website. His eyes had shone bright with fear as far as Harriet saw but it didn't take long for the trolls to see him as aggressive. The mother was caught smiling at her baby when they left the news conference. Surely that meant she wasn't affected by her son's disappearance, one paper said.

People who knew nothing of Mason or his family wondered anyway, 'Do you think it was one of them?' How frightening that the media can turn on you in an instant. So Harriet knew exactly how important their appeal for

Alice was and knew it was about much more than looking for her daughter.

Brian fidgeted next to her as she watched the room. The journalists had started chattering amongst themselves again as they waited for someone to start. A burst of laughter arose from the back before the room descended into a guilty silence.

Brian continued to squirm in his chair as he tried to make himself more comfortable. His hands were splayed wide on the desk in front of him as if he were trying to ground himself. A night of no sleep, and his usually pristine stubble had turned into the clumsy start of a beard. The grey hairs near his mouth glinted pure white in the false light of the hotel. Her eyes drifted to his hair that tufted up on the top of his head and then down to his eyes, heavy from a night pacing the house. Despite everything he still looked effort-lessly handsome, she thought. The public would like that.

Harriet looked down at her blouse, one of its buttons straining slightly where it was too tight. She could feel herself sweating where the underwire of her bra cut into her and feared she might see a damp streak across her chest. Everyone watching would notice the difference between them. Brian had told her she looked beautiful as they all left the house that morning but she knew she didn't. They'd see he was well turned out but she had no idea what they'd make of her appearance.

How did Brian still look the same as when they first met? She'd overheard Charlotte talking about him to

Audrey once. Her friend had said she found Brian handsome but in a way that she'd easily get bored of, whereas Harriet just thought he was conventionally attractive.

In the bookshop in Edenbridge Harriet hadn't expected to meet the man she would marry eleven months later. Least of all the one browsing the fishing section. But when Brian asked her if she came there often, Harriet had laughed at his awkward line and was immediately drawn in by his large brown eyes and cheeky grin.

After their first date he walked her home, taking hold of her hand and smoothly manoeuvring around her until he was on the side of the kerb. He made her feel safe and she realised she'd been yearning for a man who would take care of her. Brian was rapidly filling the hole in her life her father had left.

'You are so beautiful, Harriet,' he told her under the street light outside her flat. 'I could shout from the rooftops about how lucky I feel.' He pretended he was going to leap on to a concrete bollard but she tugged him back, laughing, before he made a fool of himself. She had never met anyone before who was so effusive about her.

DCI Hayes introduced himself as the crowd settled. Brian's leg juddered up and down beside Harriet, knocking against her thigh, forcing his plastic seat into hers. She had never seen him so nervous.

One of his clammy hands reached for hers under the desk and she could feel its wetness on her palm. He took her hand and laid it on top of the table, clamped inside his. She wanted to prise it away and put it back into the comfort of her lap, out of sight, but she couldn't do that with everyone's eyes on them. Did you see the mum pull away from him? they'd say.

Instead she let his hand clutch hers tightly, burning into her skin until Brian eventually pulled away himself and placed his hands palms–down on the table. She half-expected to see a pool of sweat seep out from under them. DCI Hayes had introduced him now. It was time for Brian to speak, just as they'd agreed he would earlier.

'I'll do this, Harriet,' he'd said firmly as he speared a piece of bacon that Angela had cooked for them. She had pushed hers away. Even the smell of it made her feel sick. 'I will speak for the both of us so you don't have to worry about it.'

'Actually, it would be good to hear from Harriet too,' Kerri said.

'No, I'll do the talking,' Brian continued. 'It's what we've agreed.'

'Harriet?' Angela asked with a sideways glance at Kerri, who Harriet could see shaking her head.

'I don't know,' Harriet said honestly. 'I don't know if I can—'

'I don't think you can either,' Brian interrupted.

Harriet looked up at Angela who raised her eyebrows at Kerri. Did none of them think she was capable? That Brian

121

should be the one to appeal to the public? 'I still think she needs to say something,' Kerri had muttered.

Brian's voice now boomed into the room, making Harriet jump. 'Yesterday afternoon our beautiful daughter, Alice, disappeared.' He cleared his throat, straightening his tie with one hand. 'I'm sorry,' he said much quieter. 'This is very hard for me.' He glanced over at Hayes who nodded at him to continue.

'One minute she was having fun at a school fete and the next she vanished.' His voice was much calmer now as he carried on speaking and Harriet felt herself relax, ever so slightly, until he stumbled. 'Harriet, my wife, she's, er, well we ... ' Brian hesitated, looked down at the table and then back at the sea of faces. 'We are begging anyone who knows anything about what happened to Alice to come forward and tell the police. Anything. Please. Because we miss her so much.' His voice broke and he bowed his head again, shaking it from side to side. 'We want her back. We just want our little girl back.'

Harriet stared at him, willing him to carry on speaking. That couldn't be it. She had a lump the size of a football lodged in her throat but she knew she needed to say something, because as soon as Brian had left the kitchen earlier, Kerri had implored her to. 'You need to speak,' she said. 'It's so important they hear you too. As soon as Brian finishes you need to talk about Alice. Regardless of what he thinks is best,' she had added pointedly.

At the far end of the table Kerri was nodding at her. Harriet looked back at Brian, then at the crowd of strangers in front of her that were becoming uncomfortable in the silence, no doubt wondering if they could ask their questions yet.

'I want Alice back,' Harriet blurted, echoing her husband's words as a bolt of heat flashed through her body. She could feel tears running down her face in hot, damp streaks. She didn't know where they'd come from but now they were flowing furiously, her body heaving and jolting as she sobbed.

Brian looked at her in alarm and for a moment both of them froze until he eventually reached an arm around her shoulders and leaned across her, telling DCI Hayes they couldn't say any more.

'We are now open for questions,' Hayes announced, and the commotion of hands shooting into the air took the pressure off them as Brian's grip softened.

A tall man in the front row stood up and introduced himself then asked the detective the question they'd been told to expect. 'Are you linking Alice Hodder's disappearance to Mason Harbridge?'

'We've no reason as yet to suspect that the two cases are linked,' Hayes said, 'but of course we are looking into the possibility.'

'Have you got any other leads?' a female journalist piped up from the back row. She had shoulder-length bobbed hair and cold eyes that hid beneath layers of make-up. She didn't look at Harriet and seemed only interested in the detective. 'By the sound of it there's nothing solid.'

'There are a couple of lines of enquiry we're looking into but nothing we can divulge at present,' Hayes said.

Harriet's head snapped round. She knew nothing about other lines of enquiry. What weren't they telling her? But the questions moved on. This time a man at the far end of the room stood, introducing himself as Josh Gates who worked for the local newspaper, the *Dorset Eye*. 'Mrs Hodder, I wonder if you could tell me how you feel about the fact your friend was posting on Facebook instead of watching your daughter at the fete?'

'What?' Harriet said, barely audible. She felt winded, as if someone had come along and punched her in the stomach.

He held up his iPad as if to prove a point. 'At the precise time your daughter went missing she left comments on friends' posts and even wrote one of her own. Her attention was obviously elsewhere,' he went on. 'So, I just wondered how you felt about that, given she was supposed to be looking after your daughter.'

She felt Brian's body press forward, nudging against the table, certain he wanted to know more. Because if Charlotte had been on Facebook it was proof she wasn't watching Alice and was therefore a careless mother whose children ran feral. Just like he had said.

'I'm interested in what you think about your friend's actions, Mrs Hodder,' Josh Gates said.

'I, erm, I don't know anything about that,' she said hoarsely, tugging nervously at her blouse. Charlotte had admitted she'd looked at her phone, but this man's assertions made her distraction seem so much worse.

'If Mrs Reynolds was—' Brian started but DCI Hayes was already shutting the interview down, holding up his hand to stop the journalist and any more questions. Harriet wished he'd let Brian continue. She would have liked to know what her husband wanted to say.

They were shuffled out of the hotel and back into Angela's car where she told them it had gone as well as they could have hoped, but Harriet wasn't listening. Her head was spinning with what the last journalist had said, and now her window of opportunity to reach out to the world was over. Harriet didn't know if she was supposed to feel something, know if she had done enough even, but she just felt numb and exposed, and had no idea what would come next.

NOW

The air conditioning whirs slowly in the corner but it doesn't generate enough breeze to cool down the room, yet instead of taking my cardigan off I find myself wrapping it tighter around my body. I don't want DI Rawlings seeing the vibrant blotches of red on my chest: the unmistakable marks of nerves. Pulling the woollen belt around my waist, I hold its ends between my fingers, rubbing them the way I did with my comfort blanket as a child.

'Let's talk a little more about your friendship with Harriet,' the detective says. 'You said that even though you were close friends you didn't get together with your partners?'

I shake my head. 'Hardly ever. There was only one occasion I remember Brian coming to my house and that was when they came to a barbecue.' I don't offer any more. I barely spoke to Brian as I played host, skirting around groups of friends with offers of drinks and platters of kebabs. I didn't rest until everyone had eaten and by then Harriet and Brian had already left.

I wonder if DI Rawlings is sceptical we didn't do more together, because it is hard to read her. Her blank expression could be disbelief or dislike for me, I have no idea. But this was the case. Harriet and I met up during the day when we had the little ones, which suited us both. I had no need to integrate my new friend into the beginnings of my failing marriage and I liked that I had someone I could talk to who didn't know Tom. It meant she was solidly in my corner. With Harriet I could tell her how it was and I wasn't judged. I was listened to and sympathised with and on occasion I would make it a whole lot worse than it was just because it was nice having someone tell me they felt for me.

And yes, I admit I had no desire to spend time with Brian. I recoiled when Harriet told me that every night after Alice had gone to bed they would sit down together in the kitchen and discuss their days. How he would tell her the intricacies of his job in insurance and in return show much interest in her day with Alice. I couldn't tell you what Tom's job actually required him to do and I doubt he had any idea if I'd taken the children swimming in the last week or if it was months ago. Harriet and Brian's marriage always felt a little too twee for me.

'Yet you must have talked to each other about your home lives?' the detective asks. 'Isn't that what friends do?'

I bite my lip as I think about what I should say. Exhaustion hasn't just crept up on me, it's surging towards me like a tsunami, and I worry that soon I will say whatever I need to in order to finish this interview.

Rawlings's eyes look red; she must be tired too. Possibly she'd agree to me leaving. Or maybe she knows more than she's letting on and as soon as I show signs of failing to comply she'll arrest me and leave me no choice. In the end I decide it's not worth the risk.

'Of course. We talked about plenty of things,' I say.

'Like what?' Her words sound aggressive even if that's not her intention.

'Well, I talked about my marriage a lot. Even though Tom and I separated two years ago things hadn't been good for a while.'

I am sure she isn't interested in the state of my marriage but my flagging mind is drifting in and out of memories. When I see Harriet and me sitting on our usual bench in the park, the discussion that keeps invading my thoughts is the time I told her Tom and I were splitting up.

'Are you sure it's what you want?' Harriet had said. 'You can't try counselling or anything?'

'We have,' I told her. 'Well, once anyway. But I found out there's someone else. It's not an affair,' I added. 'At least not yet, but he's got close to someone, sending her messages; you know, ones that are inappropriate if you're married.'

I told Harriet that I'd asked Tom outright about the texts, my heart in my mouth, my body hot, desperate for him to tell me they were nothing. But Tom has always been too honest and the flush that engulfed his face forced him to stammer an apologetic explanation that, while nothing had happened, he had been flirting with someone else.

'How come you look so sad?' I joked to Harriet when the mood had darkened.

'I always thought Tom was a good man,' she replied.

'He is in many ways. Just not one I can be married to any more,' I smiled.

Harriet reached over and took hold of my hand. 'The children will be fine,' she said. 'They have two wonderful parents who love them and that makes them incredibly lucky. Besides, it's better to come from a broken home than live in one,' she said. 'Someone once told me that.'

I was conscious of the tears running down my face but I let them fall. Just to have her total support was all the strength I needed.

'Not many people have what you and Brian have,' I told Harriet. It was the first time I realised there were benefits to her type of marriage.

DI Rawlings is asking me if Harriet talked about her own marriage and I tell her she didn't.

Rawlings stares at me, waiting for me to continue. When I don't she suddenly says, 'So tell me about the times you met up with Brian on your own?'

I look up, sitting a little straighter. I hadn't been expecting her to ask that. I hadn't expected her to know. 'It was just the once,' I say eventually. 'Or twice,' I add when she continues to watch me carefully. 'It was only two times.'

'And what did he come to talk to you about?'

I take a deep breath and release it slowly. I don't know which time I should discuss. It's probably better to focus on the second. 'Brian came to my house two days ago,' I say. 'I told Angela Baker,' I add defensively. 'She's the liaison officer on the case … ' I drift off because of course she already knows this. She probably knows about every conversation I've had with Angela and DCI Hayes over the last two weeks.

'Tell us about the other time,' Rawlings says. 'When was that?'

My fingers reach out for my empty glass, twitching as I grab hold of it. My mouth is dry, I need to ask her for more water but surely she'll know I'm playing for time, most likely think I've got something to hide. 'Six months ago,' I tell her.

'And why did you meet up?'

'Brian came to see me because he said he was worried.'

'About what?' The detective leans forward and nods at me to continue.

'He said he was worried about Harriet.' I shrug. 'It was nothing much.' I rub the heel of my hand against my right eye and glance up at the clock again. 'Do you know how much longer you need me here?' I ask. My voice is hoarse.

'It would be helpful if we could carry on,' she says, cocking her head to one side. The room falls into an apprehensive silence.

Eventually I nod. 'Brian said he was worried that Harriet was getting things wrong and forgetting things.'

'Forgetting things?'

'Yes, like where she had been. It didn't seem to be anything major.' I give a thin smile but she doesn't smile back.

'So tell me what Brian said specifically.'

I chew the inside of my mouth until I bite too hard and can feel the metallic taste of blood.

'Specifically?' I release another deep breath that comes out as a sigh. 'He told me Harriet was suffering from postnatal depression. I thought it was ludicrous because, if all he was worried about was the fact Harriet was forgetting things he'd told her, he only had to speak to Tom. He would tell Brian I forget most things he says because I'm not listening half the time.'

I picture Brian standing in my back garden, running his hand across the oak table on the decking as he looked around, and I couldn't tell if he admired my garden or loathed it.

'I'm very worried about my wife,' he'd said. 'What I'm particularly worried about is that she puts Alice in danger. Yesterday she walked off and left Alice in the car on her own. She forgot she was in there.'

Brian stopped running his fingers along the wood and turned to look me in the eye and I instinctively took a step back.

'Harriet was so preoccupied with getting to the post office to renew her passport before it closed that she completely forgot about her daughter. Charlotte, anything could have happened to her,' he said. 'My little girl could have been taken.'

BEFORE

Harriet

'Can I help you with that?' Angela pointed to the dishes on the draining board, taking a tea towel off the oven handle. 'I always preferred drying up when I was forced to help in the kitchen as a child,' she smiled.

It was twenty-four hours since Alice had disappeared. Harriet had been trying to keep herself busy so she didn't have to think about how their appeal for her daughter had gone. 'I don't mind washing up; I've always liked looking out on to the garden while I'm doing it. I think I'd live outdoors if I could.'

'Really? Where would be your favourite place to live?'

Harriet paused. She liked that Angela was taking an interest in her, even though she understood what the detective's underlying reasons were. 'By the sea,' she said. 'When I was little I dreamed of living in a house at the edge of a beach. It had an open porch at the front where

133

I could sit and read and look at the water, and a wooden path that led through the dunes to the water's edge.'

'Wow.' Angela stopped and rested the towel on the draining board. 'That sounds wonderful.'

Harriet shrugged. 'I used to draw it in my mind. I have a picture of it that's crystal clear, and if I close my eyes I can see every bit of it. The shimmering water, the ripples on the sand, the gaps between the boardwalk I can look through. I would picture myself sitting in a chair on the porch and looking out at the sea and imagining.' Harriet smiled. 'I can imagine anything when I look at the sea.'

'I know what you mean,' Angela said. 'Though I love the forest too. So is that why you moved to Dorset, to live by the sea?'

'Supposedly.' Harriet quickly grabbed the scouring pad and begun scrubbing a pan. If she rubbed much harder, the enamel would start chipping, but she didn't relent. Brian had wanted boiled milk and it had left a white layer of skin on the bottom. It was easier to use the microwave but it wasn't a compromise Brian was prepared to make. He preferred it heated in a pan.

'So do you swim much?' Angela asked.

Harriet stopped scrubbing. She had momentarily lost her picture of the sea house and replaced it with the mundanity of Brian's milk. She'd almost forgotten they'd been talking about it. 'No,' Harriet replied after a beat. 'I can't swim.'

'Really?'

She knew this would surprise Angela. Who would want to live on the beach if you were afraid to go in the water?

'Tell me more about moving to Dorset then,' Angela persisted, but Harriet didn't know how to open up that can of worms. She wasn't sure that this was even the right time; after all she'd only known Angela since yesterday.

'You don't have to do this,' Harriet said instead, nodding at the mugs and plates that were slowly piling up on the draining board.

Angela shook her head and flicked out the tea towel. 'No, I want to help.' She picked up one of the mugs and started to dry again. 'Did you always live in Kent when you were a child?'

'Yes. I was born there. It's pretty – have you ever been?'

'Yes, I have an aunt who lives in Westerham.'

'I know it. It's lovely.'

'And it was just you and your mum, then? After your dad died?'

Harriet nodded. 'Yes, just me and Mum since I was five. It was all I ever knew.'

'That must have been hard,' Angela said. 'Your dad dying when you were still so young.'

'Yes.' Harriet paused. 'I do wish I'd had him in my life,' she said. 'Somehow I think I would have liked him a lot.'

Angela smiled sadly. 'And what about Brian's mother?' she asked. Harriet looked over as Angela casually put the tea towel down and started wiping a cloth across the draining board.

'I only met her once,' Harriet said. 'Brian took me to her house a month after we met. He was so excited, he said he wanted to show me off, but his mother had no interest in me. When I left the room I overheard him telling her that I was the girl he was going to marry and she laughed, told him marriage was a waste of time and then said he had to leave because she needed to get ready to go out to bingo. I never saw her again and as far as I know Brian hasn't either.'

'That's very sad.'

Harriet shrugged. 'My own mum was very different.' She gazed out of the window at the garden. 'We used to live in a flat that overlooked a park. We didn't have a garden. Mum hated that park. She said it was an accident waiting to happen. We saw a child fall off the monkey bars once and he lay at this angle that wasn't right at all.' Harriet cocked her head to one side and stuck out her arm to show how distorted the boy had looked. 'Mum raced down there, screaming for someone to call an ambulance, shouting, "Where the hell is this boy's mother?" Thankfully he was OK but whenever we walked anywhere near the park after that Mum grabbed my hand and sped past it. I don't think I ever went in it again.' Harriet stopped and looked up at Angela. 'She was a funny one, my mum. I was everything she had and I thought the world of her, but she didn't let me do a lot of things. She was always yelling at me to get down from walls that were only three bricks high in case I fell.' Harriet raised her eyebrows.

'She was worried about you. It's what mothers do.'

'It was more than that. She'd take my temperature every night just in case I was coming down with a fever. She was always the first mum at the school gate and even when I went to the secondary comp she walked me to the bus stop because it was supposedly on her way to the shops. No one needs to go to the shops at eight-thirty every morning.'

'Why did you let her then, Harriet?'

'Because I knew what it would do to her if I didn't. Like I said, I was all she had.'

'That's a lot to put on a child.'

'Maybe. Anyway, it meant I spent a lot more time in my bedroom than most kids and that's where I created my stories. These little alternative lives were in my head, like the house by the sea. Sometimes I used to dream I lived there with my whole imaginary family. Mum, Dad, and all my brothers and sisters. Crazy, isn't it?'

'Not at all. I had an imaginary sister. I'm one of four and the rest are boys. I was so desperate for a sister I made one up!'

'I was one of five in my head. We all used to sit around this big wooden table at Christmas and laugh and make fun of each other. It was chaotic but I always had someone to talk to if things got bad. It was totally different from reality. Some of the kids at school used to say I was mad. I sometimes forgot I was in public when I was talking to my family.' Harriet smiled sheepishly.

'You shouldn't underestimate imagination.'

'I didn't want Alice to be an only child,' Harriet said, immediately wishing she could take it back. What did she expect Angela to say to that? Harriet turned back to the washing-up and started scrubbing at the pan again. She'd probably said far too much anyway. Why had she even mentioned her imaginary family? 'What are you all thinking has happened to Alice?' she asked.

'I think the appeal will help us put together what happened,' Angela said carefully. 'It's going to make people think about who they saw at the fete, and hopefully bring them forward.'

'So you don't know anything yet, then?' Harriet asked. 'DCI Hayes said you had some things you were looking into. Things he couldn't divulge.'

'We don't have anything concrete,' Angela told her. 'I'm sorry.'

Harriet nodded and dropped the scouring pad and pan back into the sink. A patch of milk was clinging determinedly to the bottom of the pan but she could no longer be bothered.

'Harriet, I'm going to have to check into the station in a bit, but I'll come back again later. I'll be around as much as possible, but if there's anything else you need at all, you must speak to me. You know that, don't you? That's what I'm here for,' Angela said, her gaze resting on Harriet expectantly.

Harriet nodded. Angela had no idea how much she could talk about.

'We're doing everything we can to get Alice back soon,' she said. 'I promise you.'

'Angela?' Harriet looked up at the FLO's face. 'What that journalist said about Charlotte, you know, on Facebook when Alice disappeared. Is it true?'

'I believe so, but you shouldn't read too much into it. She may have been on it for mere seconds. Try not to think about that.'

Harriet turned and stared out of the window. 'I don't know what else to think about,' she said quietly.

When Angela returned to the Hodders' house later that day she had DCI Hayes in tow. They had news, they told Harriet and Brian. There had been a sighting at the fete. One of the mothers had seen an older man who looked suspicious, but she had apparently left the fete before she knew a little girl had disappeared. The grapevine hadn't reached her before she'd watched the appeal that morning.

'What do you mean, he looked suspicious?' Brian demanded, moving in between Harriet and the detective as if he was sheltering his wife from bad news.

'The woman says she didn't recognise this man and that he was on his own, wandering about at the start of the fete.' Hayes raised his eyebrows in a way that made Harriet think he didn't hold out much hope for the sighting. 'Anyway, she seemed to think there was something not quite right about the way he was walking around the field. We have an e-fit we'd like you both to look at.' Hayes held out a piece of paper that Brian took out of his hands before Harriet got a chance to see it.

Brian glanced at it briefly then handed it back to the detective, shaking his head. 'I don't recognise him,' he said.

'How about you, Harriet?'

Her hands trembled as she reached out and took the paper. She didn't want to look at it for fear of what she'd see. What if she recognised the face Brian had so resolutely rebuffed?

'Look at it closely, Harriet,' Brian urged her, and though he tried to sound calm she could sense his impatience that she wasn't.

Eventually she dropped her eyes to the page. She shook her head.

'Nothing at all?' the detective asked, though it seemed like this was the answer he'd been expecting and the whole 'sighting' had been a complete waste of his time.

Brian took it from Harriet and glanced at it again. 'Maybe? There's something oddly familiar about him, I suppose. How old did she say he was?'

'Her guess was late sixties,' Hayes told him. 'How do you mean, oddly familiar? Can you be a little more specific?'

'There's just something about him that looks like I might have seen him. But—' Brian shook his head. 'I can't place him.'

'And Harriet,' Hayes said, with the smallest hint of a sigh that he'd most likely not intended to let out. 'Definitely not?'

'Not at all. Sorry,' she said.

'Don't be sorry. It was a bit of a long shot. And I apologise for getting your hopes up too. Of course it doesn't mean we won't be looking into this more,' he said, flapping the paper in the air.

Harriet stood by the front door as Hayes left, feeling the welcome burst of air from outside as it touched her face. It would be so easy to follow him out of the house. Apart from the short drive to the hotel for the appeal that morning, she hadn't been out and the walls were closing in on her even tighter than usual. She felt trapped, like she was in a coffin and someone was hammering in the final nail. Now she had the overwhelming feeling that if she didn't run through the door that moment she might never be able to scratch her way out.

'I'm going for a walk to clear my head,' she called towards the kitchen where she could see Angela tidying mugs off the table. Brian appeared in the doorway, as if from nowhere. Harriet ignored him as she grabbed her cardigan off a coat hook and slipped on a pair of shoes that were neatly tucked into the corner beside the fishing rods that still hadn't been moved.

'I'll come with you, darling.' He was already reaching one arm across her for his jacket.

'No. Please. I just need to be on my own for a bit.' She didn't want him with her, step by step at her side, clutching her hand as he led her round the block. That wasn't her idea of getting out and being able to breathe.

'Harriet,' he held on to her arm like a child who wouldn't let go of his parent. 'If you go alone I'll worry about you. I'll feel awful if I'm left here not knowing where you are.'

How would she ever be able to escape now? With him looking at her, that forlorn expression hanging on his face. As soon as she stepped outside the house he would follow her, she wouldn't be able to stop him.

'Just let her go,' Angela said softly from behind, wiping her hands on a towel. Harriet released a deep breath that made Brian stare at her. 'It will do her good,' Angela continued, nodding at Brian, and as she gently took hold of his arm Harriet grabbed the chance to leave.

Brian remained rigid in the hallway. She felt him behind her but didn't dare look round. Instead she hurried down the path, her heart beating fast, expecting any moment he would break free.

'Like I said, I won't be long, I'll just walk round the block,' she called back, turning right out of the gate. She could have cried with relief as her legs carried her as fast as they could away from that house.

Charlotte

I couldn't face going into the office that week and my
manager quickly told me to take as long as I needed. How
long will I need? I'd thought, putting the phone down on
Monday morning. Two days had passed since Alice had
disappeared but it already felt like weeks. There was every
possibility that nothing would return to normal ever again.

For the next couple of days I twisted myself into knots
over what I could do to help. I walked up and down the roads
that surrounded the field in the hope I would see Alice, even
though I knew my search was futile – the area had been
meticulously covered in the hours after she disappeared.

I called DCI Hayes and offered to find money to help the
search.

'What for?' he asked me.

'I don't know, PR, any kind of publicity. I can get
whatever is needed,' I said, sure my stepfather would hand

it over unquestioningly without expecting a penny back. Funds had been set up for missing people before, appeals for contributions; surely the police would be grateful for the help. Hayes told me there was no need but I was getting desperate.

'What can I do, Aud?' I screamed down the phone. 'I have to do something. I can't sit around waiting for news.'

'I don't know,' she admitted. 'I think your priority has to be being there for Harriet.'

'But she won't see me.'

'Maybe ask Angela what you can do,' Audrey suggested, and I wondered if I could hear the tiredness in my friend's voice or if I was imagining it. I'd lost count of the number of times I had called her in the last few days.

'Yes, that's a good idea,' I said. 'I'm sorry, Aud.'

Instead I focused on chores that didn't require thinking, between taking Molly and Jack to school and picking them up again at the end of the day. I bought a new mop, a packet of dusters and spray for every surface and I cleaned my house from top to bottom. I scrubbed the back of cupboards, emptied, scoured and refilled the fridge, and scraped away remnants of stickers that were still stuck to the insides of new windows that had been installed two years ago. I sorted through the children's clothes and I bought Jack a new pair of pyjamas.

On Wednesday I bought fresh ingredients from the butcher and the grocer's. But by the time it came to cooking dinner, I was so tired with cleaning that I couldn't concentrate. As I stood by the hob and prepared the ingredients for lasagne, I found myself thinking about Alice, the investigation and what was in the press, and I ended up throwing it all into one pan and serving it as a pile of mush that the children refused to eat.

'This is really not nice, Mummy,' Molly told me, pushing her plate across the table.

'It's 'sgusting,' Evie added.

'I know it is,' I sighed. 'Don't eat it. I'll put a pizza in the oven.' I swept up their plates and tipped the food into the bin, trying hard not to acknowledge that everything I did was screaming out failure.

With my back to the children I tore into a pizza box and was only half-listening when Molly said, 'Mummy, Sophie said something horrible today.'

'Did she, darling, what was that?' I traced my finger over the back of the pizza box until I found the oven temperature.

'She said her mummy said she wasn't surprised you weren't watching Alice.'

I spun around, attempting to put the pizza on the counter, ignoring it when I missed and it dropped on to the floor. 'What did you say?'

'And she also said she wouldn't trust you to watch the cat. That's what Sophie told me today. I told her we don't even have a cat, and they don't either, but she said I was being stupid and that's not what she meant. What did she mean, Mummy?'

'Nothing.' I forced a smile. 'It sounds like Sophie's just being silly.'

'Sophie said that meant she won't be able to come here to play on her own again.'

My fingers felt tingly. It spread quickly into my arms and down my legs. Please tell me Karen didn't really say this, a small voice whispered inside me. Karen would call me up after the weekend to tell me she'd had another hellish couple of days because her mother-in-law had popped in again, uninvited. We'd laugh about it until we had tears rolling down our faces because she always made her stories so amusing.

But this wasn't the kind of thing a six-year-old would make up.

I picked the pizza off the floor, checked it wasn't covered in dust, and put it in the oven. 'I'm sure there's a mix-up,' I said, smiling at Molly. 'I'll speak to Karen and sort it out.'

'I want Sophie to come to tea again,' Molly said, hanging her head so I couldn't see her eyes.

'Of course she'll come again,' I said, the smile still plastered across my face. 'Now, you've got ten minutes to go and play and I'll call you back when dinner's ready,' I added, my voice far too high-pitched. 'Go on,' I urged, practically pushing her out of the room.

My hands shook as they reached for the island to steady myself as I sat down on a stool. I'd been doing fine hiding myself away, cleaning and scrubbing and filling my day with mindless chores. One stupid remark and I was falling apart again.

Karen had sent me flowers on Monday with a card that said she was thinking of me. They were on the windowsill – tulips, in a variety of colours because she knows I like them.

I reached for my mobile, my finger hovering over it. I wanted to hear Audrey tell me I was being stupid, that no one was talking about me. I wanted her to say that Sophie misconstrued it and it was all a misunderstanding. I wanted to laugh and put the phone down with relief that my friends weren't talking about me behind my back.

But on Wednesdays Aud went to rugby with her boys; she wouldn't answer so I pressed another button on the phone and waited for the dial tone. I'd promised I wouldn't do this, but I couldn't help myself.

'Hey,' Tom said when he picked up. 'Everything OK?'

'No.'

'Charlotte, what's happened? Is it Alice?'

'No, nothing like that.'

'You're crying. Slow down and tell me what it is.' And so I told him what Molly had said.

'Oh, Charlotte.'

The day we separated I swore I wouldn't rush back to Tom when things got hard. 'You make your bed, you lie in it,' my mother said when I told her we were splitting up. 'Your father left and tried coming back once and I was stupid enough to let him. And you know what happened then. Besides, the kids won't thank you if you chop and change your mind.'

But then again, my mother had never lost someone else's child.

'Call Karen,' Tom said.

'I can't.'

'Of course you can; she's your friend.'

'And say what? Do you not trust me any more?'

'Ask her what she said.'

'Tom, why do you have to make everything so simple? What if she tells me she did say it? What if she says she meant it?' I cried.

I knew I shouldn't have called him. There was no way I could ask Karen what she'd said. I'd sooner let the thoughts eat me up than confront her.

I stared at my phone, wondering what I should do. My mobile no longer felt like a lifeline between me and my friends. The initial flurry of messages I'd received in the aftermath of the fete had reduced dramatically. In fact it was pinging with alerts much less frequently than it had before the weekend and its silence was unsettling.

I clicked on WhatsApp again, something I'd been regularly doing in the previous few days, but there was nothing new since the fete. I scrolled up and down the various groups: Molly's class, Jack's class, book club … there were always messages waiting for me to read. Not a day passed without someone asking a question about homework or uniform or setting up a new group for a night out.

I pushed my phone away. I'd tried to ignore the thought that had begun to trouble me – the fear that new group chats had been set up without me, that my friends wanted to discuss things without involving me. But after what Molly had told me, I started to believe it *was* happening.

Since the appeal, when the journalist had pointed out that I'd been on Facebook when Alice went missing, I hadn't been able to look at the web page and even removed the app from my phone. Somehow I'd convinced myself that simply logging on would create a trigger for my activity to be monitored. As if someone was waiting for me so they could say, 'Hah, see. Here she is again, she can't keep off it.' I passed my theory by Audrey who told me it was ridiculous, but still I hadn't chanced it.

Once the children were in bed that night I knew I couldn't hold out any longer. I needed to face whatever was being said. I needed to know. I poured myself a large glass of wine, which I took up to bed, and with a deep breath, I opened up my Facebook page.

My pulse raced as I scrolled through posts about upcoming holidays and friends' high-achieving children. Furiously searching – for what, I didn't know. A post that stated what a dreadful mother I was? A high number of likes and shock-faced emojis attached to it?

The more I looked through, the more my heartbeat fell into an easier rhythm. I found nothing of the sort but then

I did come across a 'Help Find Alice' page that someone had started, asking others to share and post if they had any news.

It had been set up by one of the mums I barely knew, though at some point we had become Facebook friends. I stared at the profile picture of her and her two girls. If I didn't know her then Harriet wouldn't either, which made me wonder why she was pioneering this campaign. If anyone was going to do it, it should have been me.

I skimmed over the comments that others had left, but there were so many that I couldn't read them all. Many of them were messages of support and concern. Warnings to others not to let their children out of their sight when there was a monster loose on our streets. Prayers that had been copied and posted with attached personal messages of hope that Alice was found soon. Some chose to share their opinions on what had happened. Many thought it was most likely the same man who took Mason.

My name was mentioned a couple of times. People I didn't know relayed how sorry they felt for me.

'Just goes to show you can't take your eyes off your children for one minute,' they said.

'You shouldn't trust anyone, not even at a school fete.'

And, 'Don't know if it's worse to lose your own child or someone else's.'

I took a large swig of wine and placed the glass clumsily on my bedside table, almost knocking it over. I wanted to comment too. I had no idea what I'd say, but I wanted to let them know I was there, reading their thoughts, living, breathing, this hell they were talking about.

I closed my eyes, leaning back against the headboard, tears trickling out from beneath my lids. I could read between the lines; I knew they were all thinking the same thing – that it was my fault Alice was gone. They were careful with their words, but the sentiment was obvious: I was careless and I lost someone else's daughter.

I know that's what they meant because it was exactly what I would have thought if it were anyone else. It was what I thought about myself.

I should have stopped looking then and put my phone away, happy that I hadn't found anything vitriolic, but instead I sat upright and tapped Alice's name into the Google search bar. It was with a strange determination to punish myself that I knew I wouldn't give up until the damage was done, and it didn't take long to find what I was looking for.

I first found my name in a comments section of the *Dorset Eye* website beneath an article written by Josh Gates, the journalist from the appeal. His vindictive piece had attracted the attention of locals. Names I didn't know, some anonymous, all thrilled at the chance to let rip and confirm I must be an awful mother.

I should never have been allowed to look after someone else's child, apparently. Mine should be taken away from me because quite obviously they aren't safe. If I'd lost their child they wouldn't be able to help themselves, one said. What he would do, he didn't explicitly say, but the threat was clear.

I balled my fist into my mouth, gulping large breaths of air that I couldn't swallow down. These were people who lived near me. They came from Dorset, maybe even from my village, and they hated me. Every one of them hated me.

I slid down under my duvet, pulling it over my head. Screwing my eyes tight shut, I sobbed and screamed under the covers until I must have fallen asleep.

The following morning I bundled the children into the car for school, hiding my red, raw, swollen eyes behind sunglasses. After leaving Jack at the school gate and taking Molly to her classroom I was walking back across the playground with Evie when Gail called out to stop me. 'Hi, I'm glad I've caught you,' she said breathlessly as she struggled to keep up.

'Hi Gail, how are you?'

She flicked a long sleek black ponytail over her shoulder, pushing her own dark glasses on top of her head. After last night I was glad to have Gail search me out in the playground. I even felt guilty for the way I sometimes moaned about her. Gail wasn't so bad even if she could be high maintenance.

'Oh I'm fine, my lovely, I'm fine.'

'That's good.'

'I just wanted to catch you because I don't need you to take Rosie to ballet tonight.'

'Wh-what do you mean?' I stammered. 'I always take Rosie to ballet.'

'Oh, I know, but tonight she's getting a lift with Tilly's mum. She offered and you know – well, to be honest, I didn't know if you'd be going or not so I said that would be fine.' Gail flashed me a row of white teeth and took a step back, already preparing her exit.

'I'm still taking Molly,' I said. 'So it's not a problem for me to take Rosie too. And Tilly lives on the other side of the village.'

'Oh, well, thank you, Charlotte. But I might as well let her go with Tilly as I've agreed it.'

'Right,' I said. 'I see.'

'Well, I'll see you soon anyway,' Gail said, waving a hand in the air and turning on her heel.

'Gail!' I called after her before I had time to consider what I was about to say. 'Wait a minute.' I dragged Evie across the playground. 'Do you really think you can't trust me to take your daughter to ballet? You're worried I might come home without her?' My voice cracked as I spoke and I knew I was going too far.

'No! God no, my lovely, nothing like that,' she said, smiling that smile again that didn't reach her eyes. 'Like I said, I just didn't know if you'd be going or not.'

'You could have asked me,' I cried. 'That's all you needed to do. You could have just asked first.'

'Yes, I know; I realise that now of course. Silly me.' She gave a small, stupid laugh and I thought if I reached out I could slap the fake smile right off her face. I whisked Evie towards my car as quickly as her little legs would take her.

'She's a stupid bitch!' I cried down the phone to Audrey as soon as I got home. 'What are they all saying about me? And don't say nothing because I know they are.'

'Take no notice of Gail. She's narrow-minded and neurotic. She's bound to overreact.'

'You know that's not true, she's only saying what everyone else is thinking.' I told her what Karen had reportedly said via the children. 'Does everyone think I can't be trusted?'

'No. Of course not.'

'Then why does it feel like that?' I cried. 'I've seen the comments online, Aud. Have you read them? I have. Look at them. Read the article on the *Dorset Eye* website. No, better still,' I said, flicking up the internet, 'I'll send you the link.'

'Charlotte, you need to calm down. Whatever these comments are saying, they're just trolls. They're nasty people with small-town attitudes and nothing better to do. These are not the thoughts of anyone who matters, and you know that deep down.'

'But it's about me. It's personal. They're talking about *me*.' I slumped into a chair. 'So it doesn't matter what I know deep down because this is my life they're discussing.'

'I know, honey, I know,' she said calmly. 'But they aren't your friends. They aren't anyone who knows and loves you.'

'Except they are. It's Karen and Gail.'

'Who haven't said anything horrible about you,' Audrey said. 'They just act stupidly sometimes. They're putting their families first, and maybe they don't even know what to do for the best, but they'll regret it if they know they've hurt you.'

'Did they say anything about me before?' I asked. 'Was I judged before Alice went missing?'

'Charlotte,' Audrey sighed. 'No, of course they didn't. What happened to Alice could have happened to any one of us. It is horrific, but it didn't happen because of you or anything you did.'

'Then how come it feels like it did?' I said in a whisper.

Before hanging up Audrey reminded me about the school social the following Wednesday. 'You should come along.'

'It's another six days away,' I said. 'Anything could happen by then.' I didn't want to think what I meant by that but my hope was that Alice would be found. The thought of another week passing and still no news was unimaginable.

'Of course, and God hoping little Alice will be found safe and sound. But think of the social as a time for you to speak to the people you believe are talking about you and then you can put your mind at rest.'

'Maybe.'

'Seriously, Charlotte, you should.'

I promised Audrey I'd consider it but I knew I wouldn't go. I'd rather carry on hiding than face the mothers who'd be watching me with fascination. As soon as I put the phone down, it rang again. It was DCI Hayes asking if I would be in for the next hour. I told him I wasn't going anywhere and mindlessly watched CBeebies with Evie as I waited for him.

When he arrived I took him into the kitchen, making small talk as I poured a drink for Evie, who had followed me through, demanding a snack and asking if the policeman would play with her.

'No, Evie,' I said, handing her a packet of raisins and an apple. 'Go back to the other room and I'll be in soon.'

'Sorry,' I said to the detective once she was gone. 'Do you have kids?'

'Yes, I have two,' he said gravely. 'Mrs Reynolds, I have some news.'

'Oh?' The look on his face told me it wasn't going to be good.

'I'm afraid we've found a body.'

Harriet

'What does this mean?' Brian paraded back and forth in the small kitchen like a caged animal.

'We don't know,' Angela told them.

'But the body wasn't that far away?'

'No,' she said. 'Less than five miles from where he was taken.'

'And it's definitely Mason?' Brian asked.

'Yes, I'm afraid he's been identified.'

'That poor family,' Harriet cried. 'I can't even imagine how they're feeling. I can't even think—'

'Then don't,' Angela told her. 'There's still nothing that suggests what happened to Mason is linked to Alice.'

'So what did happen to him?' Brian demanded. 'How did he die? Was he killed straight away?' He had stopped pacing, his hands gripping the back of a chair as he pressed forward, leaning towards Angela.

'I understand you want to know all this, but I can't give you the details yet.'

'And I don't want to hear them.' Harriet put her hands over her ears.

Brian moved to his wife's side and carefully peeled her hands away from her head. 'And you don't need to, my love,' he said, kissing the back of them, his lips lingering on her skin, leaving moist patches when he pulled away. He slid into the chair beside her, still grasping her hands. 'You shouldn't have to be thinking about any of this,' he said.

He left her no option but to think about it, as he continued to ask Angela questions about Mason that she repeatedly told him she couldn't answer. Brian's grip remained tight. His face was close; she could feel puffs of his warm breath on her cheeks as he spoke. The scent of his day-old aftershave trickled up her nose and into her throat each time she breathed in.

Eventually Harriet extracted herself, making the excuse that she needed the bathroom.

She didn't know what finding Mason's body meant, but her heart broke for his parents. They had no hope now – all they had was a finality that didn't make anything better. She wanted to write and tell them how sorry she was for them, and that she understood how their lives must have shattered. Only she didn't understand. Because Harriet still had hope. So instead she wrote down her thoughts in the little Moleskine notebook that she kept hidden under a floorboard in her bedroom, and wished they were getting comfort elsewhere.

More comfort than Harriet was getting. She and Brian swept like ghosts around the house that now groaned with loneliness. He would reach out to touch her, utter words in her ear, but they weren't comforting. Each step she took on the wooden staircase echoed eerily back at her. In the hallway the Ikea lamp no longer cast any warmth, just a long menacing shadow along the floorboards.

The living room looked as if it had been swept clean of any trace of Alice. Harriet's fingers itched to grab hold of the plastic toy boxes so perfectly stacked in a corner and upturn them, making it look like her daughter was still there. Had she been the one to hastily tidy them away once Alice had gone to bed last Friday night, or was it Brian who'd meticulously set things to order, restoring the room to a child-free zone?

But Harriet knew she couldn't start throwing Alice's toys round the house. She could imagine what Brian would say if she did. It would give him another reason to convince her she should be taking the medication she knew didn't exist.

At times she would just sit on Alice's bed, running her hand across the pink duvet embroidered with birds, still ruffled from her daughter's last sleep. Harriet would look for the indent in the pillow where Alice's head had last lain, imagining her blonde hair splayed around her in a fan, but the image was rapidly vanishing.

Now there was just Hippo on the bed, where she had carefully placed him after finding him wedged down the side of Alice's car seat. It broke Harriet's heart into two clean pieces to think of Alice without the grey hippo that had always gone everywhere with her.

Over the week the sense of Alice in the little girl's bedroom diminished until Harriet was left wondering what was her imagination and what was real. It was so frightening that she started writing everything down in her book again.

Eventually she entered the bedroom less and less but the thought of Alice somewhere else, sleeping in a place she couldn't imagine, opening her eyes and not being able to see her string of butterflies hanging in the window, was slowly killing Harriet.

One week had passed since Alice had vanished. It was Saturday morning and her disappearance was still hot news. A handful of journalists continued to hang around outside their gate now that Mason's body had been found and there was more interest than before.

Harriet still read everything she could, however painful. Often she would lock herself in the bathroom with Brian's iPad and scour websites to see what people were saying. Then she would delete the search history. Brian wouldn't understand her need that had turned into an obsession. He would only point out how unhealthy it was.

Maybe he was right. She didn't need strangers voicing their opinions about her and Brian. It was Angela whose opinion counted; she was the person living Harriet's hell with her, yet she was giving little away.

Harriet liked having Angela in her life. In very different circumstances she thought they could be friends. She wondered what Angela was feeding back to her bosses at the station. It was her job to watch and cast judgements on their tiny family, so she must have opinions. What did she make of them, dancing around each other like two strangers trapped in a prison of their own misery? Angela had eaten with them, waited while they slept, seen them at their worst. What was Brian telling her when Harriet wasn't in the room?

When Angela left that evening, Brian launched upon Harriet. 'I'm not the only one who's worried about you,' he said, shuffling far too close to her on the sofa, the smell of stale coffee drifting off his breath.

'What do you mean?'

'Other people have noticed too,' he said. 'I'm only telling you this for your own sake.'

'What are you talking about, Brian?'

He sighed, rubbing his hands up and down his jeans. 'When you went out for a walk the other day, Angela specifically told you she didn't want you going out on your own, but you ignored her and went anyway. Why are you doing this to me, Harriet?'

'Angela never said that,' Harriet said, slowly shaking her head as she thought back.

'Yes, she did, my love.' Brian turned around to face her, furrowing his brow and cocking his head to one side as he studied her. His eyes drifted to her hairline and he reached out a hand to gently push a few stray strands away. 'You said you needed to go out for a little walk but Angela told you it wasn't a good idea and asked you to stay in the house. Yet you were insistent. Even when she told you it wasn't safe,' he said, his hand remaining on her scalp.

Harriet stared at her husband.

'I just need to understand why you're doing this to me,' he said.

'I'm not doing anything to you. Angela didn't tell me I shouldn't go out,' she repeated.

'Oh, Harriet, you don't remember, do you?' he said, inching nearer still. He took hold of her arms, rubbing his thumbs across the fleshy skin above her elbows. 'I knew this would be the case,' he continued.

'Brian, I know Angela didn't say that to me. I would have remembered. If she had told me not to go out, I wouldn't have.'

'Oh, Harriet.' He shook his head. 'Do you have any idea how hard this is for me? I'm trying to deal with Alice and I can't worry about you too.' He gripped her a little harder. 'There are things you choose to forget.'

When Harriet didn't answer he carried on, 'We'll go back to the doctor. I'll make an appointment for Monday morning.'

'I don't need to see a doctor.' She would be firm over this. She would not have a doctor brought in again.

With one last squeeze he let go of her arms and stood up, pacing over to the window. Brian's head hung low. She watched his shoulders heave slowly. Up, down, up, down.

When she could bear the tension no longer she said, 'Fine. I'm sorry. I believe you. I remember it now; I know what you're saying about Angela is right. So I don't need to see a doctor again, Brian.'

'That's good, my love,' he said, turning back and smiling at her, his dark, hooded eyes reflecting the light of the evening sun. 'I knew you would remember in the end.'

NOW

It is clear DI Rawlings has decided she doesn't like me as she looks at me with scrutinising eyes that frown under her thinly plucked eyebrows. I am not the kind of mum she would want to be friends with, though I doubt she has children of her own.

She is interested in the differences between Harriet and me. Not the glaringly obvious ones like money and houses, but the little nuances that separate us.

'You were happy to share everything about your life,' she comments. 'But Harriet didn't do the same with you?'

She already knows the answers to most of her questions. I'm sure her intent is to point out my shortcomings.

'I don't share everything,' I say in defence. 'Many parts of my life are private.'

'But you talked about your upbringing and the intricacies of your marriage.'

'With Harriet, yes,' I say. 'But Harriet is a friend; it's what friends do.'

165

'Yet Harriet didn't open up to you in the same way?'

'Look, I don't really know what you're getting at.' I don't mean to snap, and wonder if I have overstepped the mark.

'Don't you, Charlotte?'

'Harriet told me what she wanted to. I can't force someone to talk about their home life if they don't want to,' I reply.

'Or maybe you didn't try,' she says and leans back in her seat as if satisfied with her trump card.

My fingers stop fidgeting with my belt and instead clench tightly until I can't stand the pressure. I know she thinks I wasn't a good friend to Harriet, that I took more than I gave, but her judgement angers me. She has comfortably positioned herself on Harriet's side, if there are sides to be taken. Before I even walked in this room she'd probably made her mind up.

'I'm going to have to take another break if you want me to answer more questions,' I say sharply.

'Of course, of course. Take as long as you need.' She gestures to the door but doesn't smile and again I wonder if I should tell her I'm not prepared to stay any longer.

Once I get out into the fresh air of the courtyard I call Tom. 'How are the children?' I ask before he has the chance to speak. 'Are they asleep?'

'Of course,' he says. He sounds drowsy himself, as if I have woken him up, but if I have I don't particularly care.

'What about Molly?' I say. 'Is she OK? Has her temperature gone down?'

'I think so,' he says. 'She's fast asleep, though.'

'Go and check on her,' I tell him. 'If she feels hot, the thermometer's in the bathroom.'

'Charlotte, I know where the thermometer's kept,' he says. 'Are you sure you're all right?'

'I'm fine. It's turning into a long night. It's taking longer than I thought it would.'

'You're still at the station?' He sounds surprised. 'I thought you'd be on your way home by now.'

'I'm sure I won't be much longer. Obviously they have a lot they need to get straight,' I say.

'But they're not, you know, suspecting you of anything?' he asks cagily. 'I mean, they don't think you've done anything wrong, do they?'

'No,' I feign a laugh. 'Of course not. Like I told you earlier, I'm here to help them, that's all. It's better I get it done now and then hopefully they won't need to speak to me again.'

'Yeah, of course. It just feels like you've been there a really long time.'

'I have, Tom, it's been nearly four hours,' I say, glancing at my watch.

'Right.' I can see he's trying to figure out what is really going on, wondering if there is anything I'm not telling him. But then Tom thinks I tell him everything. Just as the clever detective pointed out – people like me tell everyone what's going on in their lives.

'And is there any other news?' he asks. 'You know – about—'

'No,' I say as I rest my head against the wall. 'No, not that I've been told.' I don't know if they would tell me anyway.

'OK, well look after yourself.' I guess he's ready to go back to sleep. 'Call me when you're out.'

'I will. Thank you.' I hope he won't ask me what for but I'm grateful he is there for me, caring for me in a way I no longer expect anyone else to.

Not long after Molly was born I remember Tom saying something to me that hadn't had much resonance at the time. 'You'll always be the mother of my children,' he told me. 'Things have changed; there's almost another dimension between us. Whatever happens, I'll never stop caring for you.'

I had brushed him off then but now I know he meant it and it makes the space between me and my family stretch unbearably further apart.

When I hang up I head back into the station, my heart feeling as heavy as my legs as I drag myself to the vending machine to get another coffee. As I wait for the cup to fill I catch sight of DI Rawlings at the far end of the corridor, ushering someone in through the front door. As the DI steps to one side and the bright lights flood the entrance, I realise she's speaking to Hayes, who must have just arrived. And while I should be relieved to see a familiar face I can't help feeling my heart sink a little lower.

BEFORE

Harriet

On Sunday morning, eight days after Alice's disappearance, Harriet woke at six a.m. and walked out of the house. She had checked first to make sure Brian was still sleeping. He was, which was no surprise as he'd been scratching around downstairs for most of the night, coming to bed in the early hours of the morning.

She'd noticed his habits and sleeping patterns had changed in the last week. The previous day he'd taken himself fishing but only an hour had passed before he returned to the house to be with Harriet. And while she'd always been the first to bed, Brian usually followed shortly after. But during the past week Harriet had lain in bed alone, barely sleeping while Brian stayed up until two or three a.m., prowling around beneath her. What he was doing she had no idea.

Harriet crept down the stairs, slipped on the shoes that were tucked under the coat pegs and carefully opened the front door and closed it behind her so she wouldn't wake her sleeping husband. She was grateful there were no journalists awaiting her this early as she took a deep breath of the morning air and climbed into her car.

As she drove along the nearest stretch of coastline, she glanced out at the cliffs. They were high and jagged with sheer drops to the sea below that would crash into the rocks when the wind picked up. The unlit road could be dangerous at night and there had been a few occasions when a speeding car had driven over the edge. A dented barrier ran parallel to the road, a sobering reminder in the daylight.

Harriet drove for another five minutes until she reached a sharp turn where she pulled off and headed down a stony track to a car park.

She loved it here. The beach itself was tiny and very pebbly. Alice always complained that she didn't like walking over the stones to the sea because they hurt her feet, but Harriet thought it was beautiful. The water was as clear as glass and she could sit at the edge and wiggle her toes while Alice filled up her bucket with stones.

Harriet opened the boot, pulled out a small bag from under the picnic blanket and walked to the sea. It looked so peaceful, she thought, as she pulled off her dress and laid it on the stones. Fiddling with the straps of her red swimming costume she walked into the water, one tentative step at a time, keeping her eyes on the horizon. The cold didn't bother her. It numbed her and she needed not to be able to feel anything, even just for a moment.

With each pull of the tide, the water gradually built up over her body, as inch by inch it devoured her. It crept up her thighs and lapped around her waist, slowly edging up to her armpits until the rest of her was submerged. Harriet plunged her head under and held it there as long as she could before she needed air. The release was instant. She felt anaesthetised and it was a glorious sensation, but one that never lasted long enough.

Soon Harriet was swimming, further out till she had to tread water to stay afloat and keep her blood circulating. Each time she sank her head under, only the basic desire to survive brought her back up again.

Despite telling Angela she couldn't swim, there was actually a time when Harriet swam in the sea every week of the year. Christie, her friend from university, had got her into it. Harriet loved the euphoria she felt when she let the water consume her. Nothing compared to that moment of pure bliss when she became part of nature and it a part of her.

Then one day she stopped. It was six weeks into her wonderful new relationship with Brian. He had surprised her, turning up at her door with a large picnic hamper, and even more when he drove thirty miles to take her to the beach.

'I know it's your favourite place,' he said and she felt herself falling even deeper. She remembered praying nothing would jeopardise their relationship. No one had ever made her feel so special.

On the sand Brian laid out a checked blanket and they talked and laughed and fed each other strawberries.

'Doesn't it look inviting,' she said, nodding towards the water as they held hands and wandered to its edge, paddling as the waves lapped around their feet. The tide pulled out, further than before, and sent the water swishing back to them rapidly and much more forcefully. Harriet shrieked with childish delight but Brian had leaped back, a look of ridiculous panic on his face.

'I'm going to sit on the rug,' he said and turned on his heel, leaving her no choice but to follow.

Back on the safety of the picnic blanket, Brian's face was flushed with embarrassment as he admitted that not only could he not swim, he also had a fear of water. She begged him to open up to her but the more she pushed the more he withdrew until he eventually snapped, 'It's not something I like to talk about. But something happened to me as a child and I'd rather not think too hard about it.'

He looked away and Harriet didn't say anything, just reached out to him, touching his leg. Brian flinched and said quietly, 'My mother wasn't that attentive. She thought it didn't matter if I went into the sea on my own when I was six years old. Didn't even notice I'd been dragged under the water till some stranger shouted out to her.'

'Oh, Brian,' Harriet said. 'I'm so sorry.'

'It's really not a problem,' he said with a sudden change of tone and began packing up the unfinished picnic. Harriet knew she needed to do something. The day was turning sour and she could already feel Brian slipping away from her. With an overwhelming sense of pity and fear that she might lose him for good, Harriet told him the first thing that came into her head, which was that she couldn't swim either.

Brian turned to her and stopped packing away the food. He cupped her face in his hands, and with a serious look told her, 'I'm now absolutely certain that we're right for each other.' He seemed so grateful for her little white lie and she immediately felt their closeness again. At the time she didn't think about its consequences – that while they were together she would never be able to go into the sea. But then she was so in love with Brian it seemed such an easy thing to give up.

Harriet had lived with her lie ever since. She'd lost touch with many of her friends, including Christie, not long into her relationship with Brian, so there was no threat of him finding out the truth by accident. The subject rarely came up now, but if it did Harriet had simply got used to telling people she couldn't swim.

That Sunday morning Harriet drove home and was back in the house by seven-forty a.m. Brian was still asleep so she crept into the bathroom, burying her wet costume at the bottom of the laundry basket where he'd never find it. The smell of salt water was hard to hide and, as she let the warm water of the shower cascade over her body, she wondered what Brian would actually do if he found out.

'All I ask is that you're truthful with me, Harriet. It's not too much to ask for, is it?' He always begged her for honesty. As if there were much honesty in their marriage.

The following morning Harriet's phone pinged with the alert of an unexpected text.

'Everything OK?' Angela asked as Harriet stared at the message.

'Yes. I've just heard from an old friend.'

'Oh?'

It was a surprise to her too. 'It's funny,' Harriet said, 'I was only thinking about my university friends yesterday and now one of them has texted me.'

'What does it say?' Angela asked as she filled a bucket with water. She'd offered to clean the kitchen floor, though it looked spotless to Harriet.

She read the text aloud. *'I don't know if this is still your number but I saw you on the news. I want you to know I'm thinking of you. Let me know if there's anything I can do.'* Harriet looked up. 'It's from my friend, Jane. She was one of my best friends at uni. She, Christie and I did everything together.'

'That's nice that she's got in touch with you.'

'Yes, it is. I haven't seen her for ages. Well, neither of them, actually.'

'Why's that? Did you just drift apart?' Angela turned off the tap and heaved the bucket on to the floor. Harriet wondered if she was expected to help clean, but it was the last thing she wanted to do.

'No,' she said. Angela paused expectantly, the mop poised in the air. 'Well, maybe we did; I don't remember exactly what happened,' she said, absently running a finger over the phone. Of course she remembered every detail.

'I liked Jane and Christie a lot. I never had many friends at school; I wasn't one of the popular girls and I guess it didn't help that my mum kept me so—' She waved a hand in the air. 'What's the word I'm looking for?'

'You mean, the way she was so protective over you?' Angela asked.

'Yes. She didn't let me out of her sight really. It's hard to make friends when your mum is always hovering nearby.'

Angela dipped her head away before Harriet caught her expression. Did Angela think she was becoming her own mother? It was painfully clear there were more similarities than Harriet would have liked.

'Jane was like me,' she went on. 'Studious and sensible. Others probably thought we were boring.' She smiled at the memory. 'Christie was wilder, though. Not into clubbing or anything like that, but she was more adventurous. She had this crazy, curly, red hair. It was her who got me into—' Harriet stopped abruptly and fiddled with her top. How easily she'd nearly revealed the truth. It went to show how little she talked about her old friends. 'Christie loved travelling. When we left uni she went backpacking; she wanted me to go with her.'

'But you didn't?'

Harriet shook her head. 'I've never even been abroad,' she smiled sadly. 'Can you believe it? I've never had a passport.'

Angela dipped the mop into the bucket, splashing water over its edge. She looked up at Harriet. 'Really?'

Harriet could see Angela was shocked, but surely it wasn't that unusual.

'You really don't need to do that.' Harriet pointed at the floor. 'It's not that dirty.'

'I just wanted to be helpful,' Angela smiled. 'So do you miss your friends?'

'I didn't think so, but hearing from Jane now ... ' Harriet trailed off.

'Then text her back and tell her how nice it is to hear from her and say you'd like to speak. It's not too late to get back in touch, Harriet. Good friends will be there, no matter how much time has passed.'

'Only I don't think I was all that kind to her,' Harriet said softly.

'What happened?' Angela asked, genuinely surprised.

'It was a couple of months after I'd started seeing Brian. Jane used to invite me to stay at her flat but the invitation never openly extended to him. I didn't mind because it was nice seeing her on my own, but Brian didn't like it. He said if she was such a good friend then she wouldn't be trying to keep me away from him.' Harriet remembered how upset he was. She'd told him over and over that she was sure he'd be welcome too but Brian blankly refused to listen.

'The thing is, I don't think Jane was too keen, but she was too nice to say it. Only Brian wouldn't let it drop. He'd say to me, "She doesn't like the fact you have a boyfriend, Harriet. Girls like her can't stand it when their friends are happier than them."'

'*Schadenfreude*, my love,' he would say to her. 'You must have heard of it. It's completely obvious Jane is jealous of you and will only be happy if you are miserable.'

Of course Harriet had heard of it, but that wasn't Jane. Jane had raced out of her exam when she found out Harriet's mum had died, scooping her up from the floor of the hospital corridor where she'd still been curled up in a ball half an hour later. She'd stood by her side at her mum's funeral, and when Harriet went on stage to accept a Promising Student award, it was Jane who sat in the allocated family seats, loudly whooping for her best friend.

'I took Brian's side and asked Jane if she was jealous of me. She said I was crazy, and I tried telling Brian he'd got it wrong. But he said, "Of course she's saying that, she's completely manipulating you."' Harriet took a breath. 'I believed him,' she said, with a thin smile. 'No, actually I never believed him, I just chose him.'

'Oh, Harriet,' Angela sighed. 'I'm sure Jane will forgive whatever happened in the past. She obviously cares enough about you to get in touch, and besides,' she said, resting the mop against the sink and reaching out to take Harriet's hand, 'I think you could do with a friend right now.'

'I don't deserve her.' She withdrew from Angela and began fiddling with cups in the sink.

'Do you keep in touch with anyone else from your past, from the school where you worked in Kent?' Angela asked.

Harriet shook her head, thinking of Tina. The reason they had moved to Dorset. 'No. Everyone else disappeared from my life too,' she said flatly.

Angela opened her mouth as if she were about to speak, but before she had the chance her mobile rang. 'It's Hayes,' she said, gesturing towards the hallway. 'I'll take it through there.' She answered the phone as she left the kitchen. 'What the hell do you mean?' she said quietly, disappearing into the living room and closing the door behind her.

Harriet stepped forward. Angela's voice was muffled but she could just make out what she was saying.

'Who? Brian? But why would he do that? No, you're right,' Angela sighed. 'This changes things a lot.'

Charlotte

When the doorbell rang on Monday morning, I'd been lost in thought. None of us expected a whole week would come and go with no news of Alice. I had dropped the children at school, Evie at nursery, and phoned the office to explain I still couldn't face going in, and as was frequently the case my mind wandered to thoughts of Harriet and Brian.

When the bell blasted a second time, I answered the door to a man who looked vaguely familiar. He had a goatee and eyes that bulged under a fringe that hung slightly too long.

'Charlotte Reynolds? I'm Josh Gates,' he said, holding out a hand, a gaudy, gold signet ring glistening on his little finger. I shook it tentatively. 'How are you today?' he asked, in the irritatingly confident manner of a salesperson. I told him I was fine.

'I'm with the *Dorset Eye*.'

'Oh.' Now I knew where I'd seen him. He was the journalist at the appeal who'd accused me of being on Facebook when Alice disappeared. The one who'd subsequently written a piece in the paper. 'I have nothing to say,' I told him and started closing the door but as quick as a flash Josh's foot stopped it. 'Please,' I said, 'can you move your foot?'

'I wondered if you'd like to tell your side of the story? Make sure people know the truth?'

'I told you I don't have anything to say. Now please get your foot off my doorstep.' I pushed the door again but it wouldn't budge.

'Actually, I don't mean about this case. I mean the other story, Charlotte.'

'What other one? What are you talking about?'

'Beautiful place you have here,' he said, peering over my shoulder. 'Must be worth a fair bit. Maybe I could come in so we can chat inside?'

'I asked you what you're talking about,' I said through gritted teeth.

'Well, I've heard this isn't the first time you've lost a child.'

'What?'

'And that one time your little boy, Jack, went missing.'

'I don't, I—' I shook my head. In the corner of my mind, I saw a flash of Jack and the memory of the time Josh was talking about. I saw the only person who knew what I'd done, and I saw tiny pieces of my loosely-held-together world falling apart.

'Apparently he went off one afternoon and you didn't realise he was gone?' He raised his eyebrows in dramatic shock.

'Who have you been speaking to?' I cried, though of course I already knew who it must be. I just couldn't believe Harriet would do it.

'So it's true?'

'Get off my property,' I hissed and kicked Josh's foot out of the door, slamming it shut. 'Get away from my house,' I screamed. 'I'm calling the police now.'

'I can always speak to the newsagent who found him if you'd rather?' Josh shouted back.

'Just piss off!' I cried. 'Leave me alone.' I slumped back against the front door, sliding down it, burying my head in my hands. The hallway spun around me, bringing with it waves of nausea. Why was everyone so interested in me? They should be focusing on the monster who had taken Alice but instead their attention was on me. Why was everyone so keen to make sure I was the one to blame?

It was three years ago when Jack went missing. I'd walked home from the shops with the children, Molly asleep in the double buggy, her baby sister next to her screaming all the way, while Jack scooted a few metres ahead. As soon as I let us into the house, I needed to feed Evie before she woke Molly up.

'I hope you're not going to be this demanding forever,' I murmured, lifting Evie out.

I pushed the pram into the hallway and settled Evie on my lap in the living room. Jack was quiet and I assumed he was playing with his new set of trains.

With Evie latched on, silence filled the house. I rested my head on the back of the sofa, closed my eyes, and let the tears of exhaustion trickle down my cheeks. My body ached with tiredness and it didn't take long for me to drift off to sleep while Evie fed.

When I woke with a start, Evie's eyes were fluttering closed in the early stages of sleep. I didn't want to disturb her but I called out quietly to Jack anyway. He didn't answer, but then he didn't always, so I lay my head back and shut my eyes again.

When the phone rang I ignored it. I didn't want to move and I was loath to transfer Evie to the buggy where Molly was still sleeping. When it rang off and immediately started ringing again, I carefully manoeuvred Evie on to the sofa and got up to answer it. As soon as I walked into the hallway the first thing I noticed was that the front door was wide open.

'Jack, where are you?' I called out. I was sure I'd closed it behind me. Evie started crying again. I could see her squirming on the sofa that I knew I really shouldn't have left her on, but Jack was still not answering.

'Jack?' I checked my watch. We'd been home for over half an hour. 'Jack?' His name caught in my throat as I sprinted up the stairs, looking into each of the rooms. 'If you're hiding you need to come out right now.'

The phone rang once more and when it stopped it began again. It must have been the fifth time when I picked it up and cried, 'Yes?' into the receiver, only to hear the calm voice of Mr Hadlow from the corner shop telling me Jack was at his counter. Someone walking past had found him outside.

'Why did you never tell me that?' Audrey asked when she turned up fifteen minutes after Josh Gates had left. I was still sitting on the hallway floor when she arrived.

'I didn't tell Tom either.'

I couldn't tell my husband because it would have confirmed I was failing. I couldn't tell my mother, who would have reminded me three children was more than I could handle, and I didn't tell Audrey because she would have assured me 'these things happen' but I would have still seen the shock on her face. Audrey locks the front door behind her; she doesn't leave car doors wide open all night by mistake. She doesn't lose her sunglasses case or her watch or her children and Audrey would never ever lose someone else's child.

'But you told Harriet?'

'Is that the important bit right now?' I said, though I did feel guilty. I couldn't tell her I'd confided in another friend because I wanted to tell someone who didn't judge me. Not when I was well aware Aud was the only friend not judging me right now.

'Yes and no,' Aud said. 'She's obviously talked to this horrible Gates character.'

'I only told her to make her feel better about herself,' I admitted.

'How?'

'She was panicking about something utterly unimportant, like forgetting to pack a spare nappy for Alice. I don't even remember what it was. It was a year after I'd lost Jack anyway. I wanted her to realise that mums aren't perfect, even the ones she seemed to think were.' We both knew Harriet put me on a pedestal. 'I told her to make her feel better and made her promise not to tell a soul.'

'Well she's done that all right.'

'I said, "Don't even tell Brian," and she said, "Oh God, no, I would never tell Brian," so I didn't worry about it going any further.'

'That's an odd thing to say.'

'What is?'

'"God, no, I would never tell Brian."'

'Maybe.'

'I'd never say that about David.'

'Oh, Aud,' I sighed. 'Does it really matter?'

'No, it probably doesn't,' Audrey said. 'But I still think it's odd.'

'What am I going to do?' I asked, burying my head in my hands. 'Harriet must really hate me to speak to that journalist.' Telling him this story did nothing but back up what he'd already implied about me at the appeal. That I was irresponsible and couldn't be trusted. 'I can't believe she's done it,' I said. 'I know she must be hurting, but this – it just doesn't feel right.'

NOW

'Why do you think Harriet went to the press?' DI Rawlings asks.

'I don't know that she did any more,' I say. My eyes are sore from rubbing them. I ache for the luxury of being able to place a cold pack on them, but all I can do is try to stop touching the tender skin.

'So she must have told someone?' The detective is relentless. 'Even though you asked her not to. That must have made you angry?'

'Angry?' I could laugh at the woman who quite obviously has no clue. 'No, it didn't make me angry. In some ways I thought she had every right to tell that journalist or her husband or whoever she wanted.' I sigh. 'I think it was Brian. I believe Harriet told him at some point and he was the one who spoke to Josh Gates.'

'Why do you think that?'

'Because of what he said when he came to see me on Wednesday night, two days ago,' I say with bite. I take a breath and then add, a little more calmly, 'I'm struggling to see how this is relevant. What happened when Jack was young has got nothing to do with any of this.'

'We are just trying to build up a picture,' she says and presses her lips into a perfect heart.

I look away and sit back, resisting the urge to fold my arms. She knows she's getting to me and I have to be careful, but to say I am exhausted is an understatement.

'Let's talk about the call you received this morning,' she says. 'Friday morning, thirteen days after you'd last spoken to her. It must have been a shock?'

'It was.'

'What were you doing when she phoned?'

'I was supposed to be meeting DCI Hayes. He'd asked me to go to the station but then the school called me to say Molly was ill. So I was going to collect her first.'

'And the call from Harriet was totally unexpected?'

'Yes.'

'How did she sound?'

'Frightened. Desperate,' I say, remembering the sound of her voice with unnerving clarity.

'And why do you think she called you?'

'Probably because I was the first person she thought of.'

'After what had happened, she still turned to you? Why would she do that?' Rawlings asks.

'I don't know,' I say, my voice rising a notch. 'She was afraid. Most likely it's because Harriet has no one else to call.'

'And so as soon as she called you, you went to help her?' the detective asks, raising her eyes as she waits for me to respond.

'Well, no,' I say. 'Like I said I had to pick up my daughter from school.'

'So your close friend calls you, frightened and desperate, and for a while you did – nothing?'

'Not nothing. I had my daughter to look after—'

'But you didn't call the police?'

'No.'

'Or tell anyone else?'

'No.'

'Despite how desperate Harriet sounded?'

I nod silently.

'Then what I don't understand is why the delay in doing anything, Charlotte?' she asks. 'Why did you sit around for what – an hour, more even – before deciding what to do?'

My mouth is dry, regardless of how many times I swallow. I lean forward in my chair, my hands beneath me. My heart is painful, it is beating so hard, and all the while she doesn't take her eyes off me.

But I cannot tell her the truth.

'Charlotte?' she is prompting me. I wipe my hairline, edged with a thin streak of sweat. I have to say something but the harder I try the faster words escape me. My voice is low and hoarse when I finally whisper, 'I'd like to take another break, please.'

BEFORE

Harriet

DCI Hayes arrived ten minutes after Angela had hung up and Brian quickly ushered him into the back garden. 'Let's not worry my wife further,' he snapped at the detective. 'She's dealing with enough at the moment.'

Harriet watched them from the window. Both men had their backs to her; Angela stood mutely at their side. She knew that if it was anything serious they'd have taken Brian to the station, but she was still desperate to hear what they were talking to him about. What had he done to make the detective come round so quickly?

When Brian eventually came back into the house, Angela and Hayes stayed talking in the garden. He slammed the door and banged his fists on the table, snapping his head up when he noticed Harriet hovering.

'Why were they questioning you?' She continued to watch the detective through the window.

'They weren't questioning me,' Brian replied curtly. 'They had questions, yes, but they weren't questioning me.' He hesitated as if he was thinking about what to say next. 'Are you hungry?'

'No, I'm not hungry,' she said.

His body softened as he removed his balled fists from the table. 'You haven't eaten anything all morning. I'll make you some toast.'

'Brian, I don't want toast.'

'I'll put some honey on it for you.' He began trawling through the jars in the cupboard until he found a pot of honey at the back. He knew she didn't like honey. It was only him who ate it.

Harriet took a deep breath. 'Why won't you tell me what they wanted to talk to you about?' She hated begging yet it scared her that Brian knew something about Alice that she didn't.

'Harriet.' Brian slammed the jar hard on the counter behind him. 'I am going to have something to eat. As I have just told you, I will tell you everything after I've eaten. But please, will you listen to me for once and accept what I've said instead of trying to manipulate everything? You must see what you're doing to me.'

The scream started in her gut, shooting up through her body like a bullet, as it often did. If she opened her mouth she wouldn't be able to stop it from coming out and filling the room with all the anguish inside her. She knew too well that if she screamed Brian would win, calling in

Angela and the detective to tell them his wife seemed to be suffering a breakdown.

Brian wouldn't tell her what had happened in the garden until he was ready. Not until he had played with the situation a little more. Maybe not until she left the room wondering if a conversation with the detective had even taken place by the sandpit.

Resigned, Harriet squeezed her eyes shut to push back the threat of tears until the smell of toast wafted under her nose. 'Eat up,' he smiled, waving a piece in front of her that was slathered in honey.

'I'm not hungry.'

'Then why did you just ask me to make this for you?' he snapped, and threw the toast into the sink.

Once DCI Hayes had left, Angela came into the kitchen and found Harriet sitting at the table with her head in her hands.

'I'm trying to get my wife to eat something,' Brian said. When Harriet looked up at him he flashed her a smile.

'What were you talking about in the garden?' Harriet didn't care who answered as long as one of them did.

'Have you not said anything, Brian?' Angela asked.

'Oh, Harriet.' Brian shook his head and swept across the room towards her. Kneeling down beside her, he took her face between his hands, gently brushing her hair as he spoke. 'Of course I've told her, Angela,' he said, without taking his eyes off his wife. 'I've just been through it all with her while you were both outside. Have you forgotten already, my love?

'I told Harriet it would be sorted and it's nothing for her to worry about. Because I don't want her worrying any more.' He looked worried himself as he pushed up from the floor.

'Are you OK, Harriet, you do look a bit pale?' Angela asked her.

'You haven't told me anything, Brian,' she said. 'So will one of you please tell me what's going on?'

Brian took a deep breath and nodded. 'Of course I'll go through it all again if that will help,' he said with feigned patience. 'The detective wanted to know why my alibi had fallen through.'

'Your alibi's fallen through?' Harriet repeated.

'Yes. Ken Harris,' he said, rubbing her shoulders. 'You know what he's like. You've said yourself the man forgets what day it is half the time.' Brian paused. 'Well, now he seems to think that he can't actually remember seeing me the day Alice went missing.'

'I've never even met Ken Harris,' Harriet said slowly, watching Brian carefully for a reaction. When he didn't give one she went on. 'So what does that mean, that he can't remember seeing you?'

'Nothing. Please don't look at me like that, Harriet. You know I'm telling the truth. I wouldn't lie about where I was.'

Harriet chewed on her lip, unsure what to say, as Brian leaned in closer. 'Harriet, I'm not lying, you know that, don't you?' She could hear the desperation in his voice, feel the tremble in his hands, and see the beseeching way his eyes flickered over her. Harriet looked at Angela, who gave her nothing.

'I don't know what to believe any more, do I, Brian?' she said quietly.

Ten minutes later, while Brian was still in the kitchen with Angela, Harriet crouched beside her bed and peeled back the corner of the carpet. She reached under the loose floorboard for her notebook, tucked it beneath her top and crept into the bathroom, carefully stepping over Brian's iPad that had strangely been left charging on the landing.

She locked the door and sat on the closed toilet, opening up the thick, deep-grey Moleskine notebook that she had treated herself to on a trip to Wareham. Turning to the next clean sheet of paper, Harriet pressed it flat with the heel of her hand. Then she pulled out a silver pen and started to write.

In meticulous detail she wrote down what had just happened. What Brian actually said to her while Angela and the detective were in the garden, her husband's promise to tell her eventually, his intent on forcing her to eat toast and honey. Then how he calmly told Angela he'd already relayed the story of his lack of an alibi to her. When she'd finished,

Harriet read through her notes and the discrepancies between what Brian said and what he tried to make her believe until she was confident she knew the truth.

Before she closed the book she flicked through the pages that came before, ones that had become a lifeline to her since she started writing. The eighteenth of May 2016 was her first entry, almost twelve months ago.

The rest of the world might think she was losing her mind. Brian might be trying to prove she was. But at least she'd found a small way of gripping on to reality.

That evening, while Harriet ran herself a bath, she thought how Brian had been unnervingly calm earlier on. He seemed unfazed by the fact his alibi had fallen through as he skittered around the house, tidying shelves, offering cups of tea, and casually flicking through an old copy of the *Angler*.

She had run the bath water so hot, it almost scalded her as she placed a foot in to test it, but Harriet couldn't stand baths that turned cold soon after she'd got in. As the bubbles soaked around her neck she closed her eyes and felt herself drifting into the state where she was almost falling asleep when there was a shriek.

She jolted upright to find Brian standing in the doorway as her phone, attached to its charger, slipped off the side of the bath and into the water. Harriet screamed and jumped out of the bath in horror, then stood naked on the mat.

'What were you doing?' Brian yelled.

She stared at him wide-eyed, her shivering body dripping water into a puddle around her feet. 'I didn't do anything,' she said. She'd never felt so exposed as she did then, the thought of lying naked in the bath while Brian had crept in.

He took a towel off the radiator and wrapped it around her so tightly that she couldn't move her arms. 'You can kill yourself doing something stupid like that.'

'But I didn't. My phone wasn't even upstairs. I wasn't charging it, I'd never bring it into the bathroom.' She tried to untangle herself from the towel but with every movement he swaddled her tighter.

'So tell me what it's doing here,' he said. 'Oh, my goodness.' Brian pulled her against him as they heard Angela racing up the stairs.

'What's happened?' she asked, looking from one to the other.

'Thankfully there's no harm done,' Brian said, as his eyes wandered into the bath where the phone lay sadly at the bottom of the water, its lead still attached and snaking out of the door on to the landing. 'Please just give me a minute to get my wife dressed,' he said and Angela nodded, silently backing out of the room.

'You were lucky I got there in time,' he said, loud enough that Angela would hear. 'I saw the phone plugged in and pulled it out of the socket before I found you in the bath.'

'I didn't do it, Brian,' she said as he led her on to the landing where Angela hovered at the top of the stairs.

'It was an accident,' he said and she could have sworn she saw him furrowing his brow at Angela. 'Thankfully everyone's fine.'

'I saw your iPad charging. It wasn't my phone.' Harriet looked over her shoulder but there was no sign of Brian's iPad. 'It wasn't me,' she mouthed at Angela, whose eyes flicked to the plug that had been pulled out of the socket just as Brian had said.

'If I hadn't been here,' he said as they disappeared into the bedroom, 'you'd be dead, my love.'

Harriet

It was Wednesday, eleven days after Alice's disappearance, and Harriet knew she had to get out of the house again. She called to Brian and Angela that they needed milk from the shop, but before she got to the front door Brian appeared at her side. Where he had sprung from this time she wasn't sure, but he was making a habit of skulking around corners then pouncing on her.

'But we don't need any more milk, my love,' he said. 'We only bought some last night.'

'No, it's all gone,' she assured him, standing her ground. 'You can check if you like.'

Brian's tongue whipped out, licking his bottom lip as he was about to protest, when Angela called from the kitchen. They both turned to see her shaking an empty plastic bottle. 'Actually we do need some,' she said and, while Brian was looking the other way, Harriet took the chance to slip out.

She didn't turn back as she hurried down the path, which meant she didn't notice him still waiting on the doorstep, watching her. When she returned half an hour later he was still standing in the open doorway. Had he been there the whole time? She couldn't care less, she thought, as she tried to push past him. All she needed was to get in so she could lie down because all of a sudden she was feeling dreadful.

'And how was your walk?' He didn't budge as he held her on the doorstep, his eyes crawling over her face as he waited for an answer.

'I was just getting milk,' she muttered. Her hands were trembling and, amidst the hot flushes that ran through her, Harriet felt surprisingly cold. She hoped she'd be able to pass it off as coming down with something – Brian was already looking at her strangely.

'Are you OK?' he said, eventually stepping back so she could get into the hallway. 'You look very pale.' He reached out and took the milk from her.

'I don't feel well.'

'Are you sick? You look as if you're going to be. I hope nothing's happened while you've been out?' His smile vanished.

'No,' she whispered, 'nothing's happened; I just really don't feel well and I need to lie down.' She slipped off her shoes and pushed them into the corner of the hallway with her foot.

'OK, let's get you up to bed. I'll come and lie down with you.'

Harriet took hold of the banister. 'No,' she said. 'I'll go on my own.' She started to walk up the stairs when he grabbed her arm and stopped her.

'Everything OK?' Angela asked, stepping out into the hallway. Her handbag was slung over her shoulder and a cardigan draped over her arm. 'You don't look well, Harriet.'

'She's not,' Brian said. 'But I'm taking care of her. Aren't I, my love?'

'Can I get you anything before I go?'

'No,' Brian said. 'We're fine. I can get my wife what she needs. Thank you, Angela,' he added as an afterthought, or maybe because Brian was never one to forget his manners.

All Harriet wanted was to be left alone, but as she climbed the stairs Brian was right behind her. When she got to the bedroom she asked him for a glass of water just so he reluctantly had to go down again. Curling up on top of the covers, Harriet found that every time she tried closing her eyes they sprang open again. The swirling patterns on the wallpaper danced in front of her until they blurred into one large fuzzy shape.

Harriet knew every inch of those walls by heart. Every change of colour in the paper, all the bits that didn't quite match. She had loved it when she'd picked it out, her tummy swollen with her baby, wondering if they were having a girl or a boy. Brian was adamant he wanted a son. An heir, someone just like him, he was always saying and in turn Harriet found herself praying they'd be blessed with a girl.

Now Harriet hated the wallpaper. Its patterns made her feel even more nauseous until she thought she actually would be sick. She pushed herself up and held a hand over her mouth, waiting for the feeling to pass.

How happy she had been when she was expecting Alice. What a lifetime ago that felt like, wandering the aisles of Mothercare, promising herself she would always protect her baby. She could never have foreseen this. The terror of not knowing where her daughter was and whether she was safe coursed through her veins until it paralysed her. And for a moment, Harriet didn't register that something wasn't quite right in their bedroom even though she was staring directly at it.

When she finally refocused her eyes, the silver frame on her dressing table eventually became clear. 'Oh my God.' Harriet shuffled to the end of the bed and reached out to pick it up. The day Brian had bought her the frame three years ago, he had put a photo of her and Alice in it. He had taken the picture on a beach in Devon and given it to Harriet as a present. It was a beautiful picture of her with her baby girl, their cheeks pressed against each other's, Alice's wide eyes bright blue as they reflected the light. Her yellow-dotted sun hat skewed at an angle on top of her head, tufts of baby-blonde hair poking out beneath it.

But now Harriet found herself looking at a very different picture. It was a photo of their wedding day, one she'd never liked because her eyes were half-closed and she was looking away from Brian while he stared intently at her. 'Look at you,' the inexperienced but cheap photographer had laughed. 'You adore her.'

'Of course I do, she's my wife,' Brian said.

'Yes, and she's not even looking back at you.' The young man laughed at what he thought was a very comical situation.

Brian's head snapped up to look at Harriet. 'Well, she is a lot more beautiful than me,' he smiled.

When the photographer had finished Harriet forced herself to drink the lukewarm champagne. 'Why would you do that to me?' Brian leaned in close as he spoke into her ear.

'Do what?' Harriet was genuinely baffled.

'Try and make me look a fool on our wedding day. That boy is laughing at me, no doubt telling everyone my new wife doesn't even want to look at me while I can't take my eyes off you.'

'Don't be silly, Brian, of course I was looking at you,' she said. 'I just saw that waiter spill red wine down this man's shirt.' Harriet giggled. 'He was so flustered trying to mop it up as—'

'Well,' he spat, taking her hand as he led her off towards the dining tables. 'Isn't that just wonderful.'

When he slipped into bed beside her that night, Brian left a cold space between them. 'You didn't take your eyes off him all evening.'

'Who?' Harriet turned towards her new husband.

'The waiter, of course. You embarrassed me on purpose, Harriet.'

'What do you mean? I wasn't looking at him,' she pleaded. He had caught her attention a couple of times because he was so incompetent but that was all. Did it look like she was staring too much, though? she wondered with a pang of guilt.

'You spoilt the day for me. How do you think you made me feel on our wedding day when you kept looking at another man?'

'I wasn't looking at him. Not like that. Brian, I'm sorry, I didn't mean to hurt you. What you think happened just isn't true.'

'You think I'm lying? That I'm making things up? I know what I saw.'

'No, I don't think you're lying but—'

'You made me look like an idiot,' he snapped, his face flushing with rage. 'So don't start trying to pretend this is my fault.'

'Brian, I'm sorry.' Harriet couldn't believe she'd hurt him so badly. How stupid she had been. She reached over to touch her husband, moving closer, hoping that as it was their wedding night he could forgive her. He wasn't a big drinker so maybe he'd had a little too much. But then she didn't remember him having any alcohol after the champagne on the terrace. 'Come here,' she murmured softly. She would make him forget whatever he was working himself up over.

But Brian rolled away and she was left looking at the back of his broad shoulders, rising and dipping with his sharp breaths.

Harriet lay and stared at the hotel ceiling, tears sliding down her cheeks that their wedding night had come to this. It was none of the things she had hoped for. She had never felt so alone.

'I'm sorry,' Harriet whispered to her husband's back. 'I'm so sorry, I never meant to hurt you.' She knew he was still awake but he didn't answer.

'I've been wondering why you swapped the photo.' Brian's voice made her jump. 'Did you not like the one I took of you and Alice?' He stood in the doorway with a tumbler of water that he carefully placed on the bedside table. His eyes never left Harriet's.

'You know I didn't swap it,' she said, letting the frame drop on to the bed beside her.

Brian leaned forward and picked it up. 'And you know I don't like this picture.'

'I didn't change the photo, Brian,' she said again, noticing the muscles twitching in his jaw.

'So she's gone,' he said, waving the frame in front of her.

'What are you saying?' Harriet shifted nervously on the bed. 'Brian, you're scaring me.'

'Am I?' he said, getting closer until she could feel his breath on her cheek. 'My love, I wouldn't do that.' He reached out and took a tendril of her hair, stroking it between his fingers. 'You must be getting confused again.' And with that Brian let go of her hair, and walked out of the bedroom.

Charlotte

By Wednesday evening Audrey had persuaded me I should attend the school social, though when Tom arrived to look after the children I was already regretting asking him to come over for something I really didn't want to go to.

I'd fallen into a routine of making pleasantries at the school gate, keeping my eyes hidden behind sunglasses, my head down and scurrying away again before anyone could stop me. I stopped returning messages and became completely reliant on Audrey acting as a go-between, thanking friends for whatever thoughts they were passing on to me.

Aud removed Facebook from my phone again. She told me I was banned from reading anything online. I knew if I did I'd find myself talking to her about what I'd read and then she'd most likely fulfil her promise to take away my phone. Strangely I began finding it relatively easy to hide away from the world. What I didn't know wasn't hurting me.

But withdrawing had made the thought of the social even more terrifying. I was only going because of Audrey's insistence that it would be good for me and my desire not to let her down after everything she'd done.

'I thought you said it was starting five minutes ago,' Tom said, tapping his watch. 'It's already eight-fifty.' He found me rummaging through the children's school bags. I'd already laid out their uniforms and washed up the water bottles – jobs I'd usually leave till morning. 'Just go,' he said, practically pushing me out of the front door.

'When did the light stop working?' I muttered when the outside lamp didn't automatically come on.

'I'll have a look at it,' Tom said, peering up before sighing, 'Oh, I can hear Evie. I thought you said she was asleep. I'll see you later.' He closed the door behind him, leaving me standing in the semi-dark driveway. As I walked towards my car a flicker of movement stopped me in my tracks and Brian's face suddenly appeared above the corner of the privet.

'Brian, you made me jump,' I said, wondering how long he had been watching me. He didn't answer. 'Do you, erm, want to come in?'

'No,' he said blankly. 'I want you to come to my car.' When I didn't move he added, 'I don't think you have the luxury of refusing me that, do you?'

I jangled the keys nervously in the palm of my hand, looking up at the house in the hope that Tom might be at a window, but there was no sign of him. Reluctantly I nodded and followed Brian to the silver Honda parked a few houses up. He held the passenger door open, and as I climbed in the smell of dead fish wafted from the boot and into my nostrils.

Our cul-de-sac was quiet and eerily still. The click of the doors locking was loud and sharp in the silence as Brian twisted to face me.

His mouth twitched at the corners and, tilting his head to one side, he spoke slowly. 'Tell me what you know.'

'What I know about what?' I asked.

'Tell me what you know about my wife.'

I fidgeted uneasily. 'Why are we talking about Harriet?'

'I do everything for her; she's my world,' he continued. 'I always have. But she doesn't treat me the same, though I assume you know that. She must tell you everything.'

'No, actually Harriet doesn't say anything to me,' I said.

'It breaks me. She breaks me. Do you know that? Yes, of course you do. You're her best friend,' he laughed. 'Despite what you say, you must know everything.'

Brian's behaviour was as disturbing as his appearance. His hair stuck out wildly in different directions, as if he'd grabbed it with both hands and ruffled it vigorously. His eyes were dark and heavy as they bore into me. I'd never seen Brian anything less than pristine and despite the situation I knew something else was wrong.

'Did she tell you she doesn't love me?' he went on.

I shuffled forward uncomfortably in my seat. 'Harriet loves you,' I said. As much as I didn't want to confront his anger about Alice, I still thought it would be preferable to whatever this was about. 'Whatever is happening right now, you can't start doubting that.'

'I know you were close, Charlotte. Why else would you tell her about losing your son?'

'What?'

'Make a habit of it, don't you? Losing children. Almost like it comes easy to you.'

'Brian—' The air in the car was getting unbearably close. 'Can I open the door? Or even just the window?'

Brian ignored me as he slammed the palm of his hand against the steering wheel and turned to stare out of the windscreen. 'Mothers like you should pay for what you do,' he said. 'But you don't,' he carried on. 'You never do.'

'I need to go,' I said, my voice shaking. 'I want you to unlock the door now, Brian.'

'I'll make sure they write their story about you,' he said. 'I'll make sure it's out there.'

I wondered if I should scream, whether anyone would hear me if I did. The air was getting closer and I could feel my breaths quickening yet the only thing stopping me from hammering on the windscreen was the thought that this was nothing less than I deserved.

'Tell me what she's told you,' he yelled. 'What you know.'

'I don't know what you want me to say,' I pleaded. Harriet had never uttered a word against her husband. 'Harriet's only ever had good things to say about you—'

'You know I've always liked you, Charlotte,' he said, interrupting me with a sudden change of conversation. His words sounded lighter and softer as he arched himself forward. 'Of course I'm glad she has you as a friend but I need you to be honest with me.'

'Brian, what are you talking about?'

'I'm sure you can make her see sense,' he said. 'Anyway, I need to go now.'

'Brian, I don't understand what you're—' I stopped as he stretched across me to open the door, giving it a shove so it swung open.

'I'm sure you do, Charlotte,' he said. 'I'm positive you understand very well what I'm talking about. Now please get out.'

I stared at him incredulously as I backed out of the car. He pulled the door shut behind me, started the engine and hastily drove away. All thoughts of the school social had vanished; it was with relief that I made my way back to the house.

I had no idea what had just happened. Whether he and Harriet had had an argument; if this was Brian's way of taking it out on me. Wasn't it all any father would do in his situation? I didn't stop to think Harriet was in any danger because, despite his behaviour that evening, I still didn't think Brian was to blame. His words were nothing compared to what the trolls had said they would do to me, after all. I should have expected much worse.

NOW

'Do I have to go over the facts?' DI Rawlings says. 'We have a missing person and someone died tonight.'

'I know.' I press my fingers into my closed eyes, squeezing them shut. 'I know.'

'And we still aren't getting to the truth,' she goes on.

'I'm telling you what I know,' I snap.

'Are you?' She sits back in her chair and stares at me.

'Yes,' I plead, though even I know I don't sound sincere.

Harriet never told me what was going on in her marriage. Yet, as much as I try to believe it was because she didn't want me to know, I can't ignore the feeling I didn't look hard enough.

Maybe that's what the detective saw the moment I walked into the room. That right from the start of our friendship I was wrapped up in my own life. Isn't that what the mums like us are like? The gaggle of women who take over the playground with our raucous laughter, acting like the school owes us something for being there?

I saw that in some of them over the days after the school fete, the way they ushered their kids away from me, afraid if I came too near that one of their children would disappear as well. Not all of them. Not Aud, of course. But it made me realise how fragile the strings were that tied the rest of us together. How some friendships are built on so little they can fall apart at the slightest strain.

But I wasn't like them, I wanted to plead with Rawlings. I still feel the urge to persuade her that I wasn't and that is why I was drawn to Harriet.

Harriet reminded me of the person I wanted to be, the one I still was in my heart. Harriet didn't kiss the air or gush over handbags like they alone would solve Third World problems. I could tell Harriet anything and I knew she cared.

She could have told me anything too. Only she didn't.

'But you didn't see any clues?' the detective persists.

Now I look back there were possibly many clues but I tell the detective I didn't. Yet as I sit here in the whitewashed room, with the tape recorder still whirring and my mind dissolving, I remember a particular time when Harriet and I sat on our usual bench in the park.

Evie was a baby and finally asleep in the pram and, while I wouldn't be able to rest completely with the threat of her waking any moment, I'd closed my eyes and was revelling in the peace when Harriet's voice rang out from behind me. I felt my stomach sink. I didn't think we'd arranged to meet.

When I opened my eyes I saw Alice toddling off to the sandpit where Molly was filling a bucket. Harriet had stripped off her cardigan and pulled a lunch box out and I remember thinking it looked like she was there to stay. 'What are your plans today?' I asked her. 'Are you and Alice off anywhere nice?'

'No, nothing special. I have to go back to the shops later.'

'What, on a lovely day like this?' I said.

'Yes, I bought this jumper for Brian and I need to return it.' Harriet reached into her bag and grabbed a handful of the top.

'Tom had one like this,' I murmured, running my hand over the soft wool. 'What's wrong with it? Doesn't Brian like it?'

'Oh I think he probably does. I just got the wrong one. He said he'd asked me for red.' Harriet raised her eyes and shrugged her shoulders. 'I could have sworn he said green.'

I sighed and folded the top. They were hardly two colours you could mix up and I felt myself getting irritated by Harriet's mistake. My patience was almost on empty and in those times her scattiness annoyed me.

'I could do with going shopping,' I said. 'We should go one day, blow some money and treat ourselves.' When Harriet didn't answer I realised my tactlessness and flustered, 'I mean, I'd like to treat you to something. You'd be doing me a favour just by coming. I'll dump Evie on my mum for the day.'

'Yes, maybe.'

I looked at Harriet who was waving at Alice, holding up a packet of raisins to her daughter while she played obliviously in the sandpit. Nearby a mother was raising her voice at her young son, her finger wagging an inch from his face as the little boy started sobbing.

'He didn't even do anything wrong,' Harriet said. 'I was watching him. He only wanted another go on the swing.'

The mother shouted louder; the little boy slunk backwards. She raised her hand and the next moment she'd slapped him across the back of his legs and marched him through the park.

'We should say something,' Harriet gasped.

'Don't get involved,' I said quickly, placing a hand on Harriet's arm.

'But he's in a dreadful state.'

'I know, and it's horrible, but no one will thank you for saying anything,' I said. 'About this shopping trip,' I added, desperate to avoid confrontation with the mother who was by now at the gate. She had hard features that looked like she was permanently angry and I knew who'd come off worse if Harriet got into it with her. 'When shall we go?'

I opened up Harriet's bag and was about to put the jumper back in when I noticed a necklace glistening at the bottom. 'Harriet, I haven't seen this before.' I pulled out the chain, holding its delicate gold-leaf pendant in the palm of my hand. 'It's beautiful.'

'My necklace,' Harriet gasped and grabbed the chain from me. 'Where did you – where was it?'

'It was just lying in your bag. It's gorgeous.' It really was, and I couldn't remember ever seeing Harriet wear it.

'I thought I'd lost it.' Harriet stared at it suspiciously, turning the leaf over in her fingers. 'I thought—' She shook her head and didn't finish the sentence. 'It was my mum's. I know it was in my jewellery box. I don't wear it because it's so precious. But then it was gone and I looked everywhere.'

'Well you have it now.'

'But I searched the house.' Harriet's voice dropped as she continued to marvel at the pendant, and I stared at her, wondering if she was talking to it or to me. 'I don't get it. How could it even be in my handbag?' she said in little more than a whisper.

'Does it really matter if you've found it?' I sighed, fearing I might have snapped at Harriet as I closed my eyes again. I could hear Aud's voice as clear as if she were sat on the bench between us. 'Charlotte, I'm sure your friend is very sweet but she looks like she's away with the fairies half the time.'

I remember turning to look at Harriet who was then staring at a point in the distance, past Alice, past the trees that lined the park. Her lips twitched, deep in thought. I had lost Harriet completely and Evie was stirring and I knew any minute she'd start screaming, and I felt the rise of irritation spreading inside me like fire.

*

'When you ask me if there were any signs,' I tell DI Rawlings, 'it's that bloody memory that comes into my head, and I think that if that's all I had to go on then did I really miss anything?'

When she doesn't answer me, my body burns with the sheer frustration that we are going round and round in circles and somehow continue to end up in the same spot every time.

My arms feel like jelly as they hang limply by my sides. My back slumps as I reach forward and my hands fall on to the table. 'Please,' I say, 'I need to go home. I want to go now.'

Yet what I do know is that, if I had sensed what was going on behind Harriet's closed doors, I could have helped. I would never have convinced her to leave her daughter with me, persuading her Alice would be safe. I knew, more than many, how controlling some fathers and husbands can be because my own dad was like it. Harriet understood that, yet still she didn't confide in me. She didn't trust in me to help her.

And Brian knew so much more than she gave him credit for.

BEFORE

Harriet

On Thursday morning, twelve days after Alice went missing, Harriet woke knowing that, like it or not, everything was about to change. She was relieved that on that day Angela wasn't getting to the house until four p.m.

She watched Brian cautiously as he moved around like a ticking time bomb. He hadn't uttered one word since he'd walked out of the bedroom the night before, leaving her staring at their wedding photo. But she could see he was still wired by the way he flittered about.

Above her, the floorboards of the bathroom creaked. It was already late morning and Brian still wasn't dressed. There had been plenty of times when she had sat like this at her kitchen table with her hands wrapped around a cold mug of tea waiting for her husband to appear, though never so late in the day. She didn't know what to expect as her mind raced through thoughts of the previous night, trying to figure out if she'd done something wrong. Harriet had become reliant on Brian reminding her.

Over the years memories had faded into a dark recess in her mind until she had no way of gripping on to them again. She knew how hard it was for Brian because he told her often enough. Her husband's support had never wavered, though. Brian would always be there for her.

He told her that often enough too.

He promised her that.

Threatened it.

At first Harriet didn't want to believe she had problems with her memory, but Brian was insistent. He first took her to a private doctor two years ago, to a practice on the other side of Chiddenford. Harriet sat mutely as her husband described her problems, the many mistakes she made, how concerned he was for his wife's and daughter's safety.

'I didn't have an issue as a child,' she told the doctor when he asked if she knew when it had started.

'Well it often comes on in adulthood,' Brian had said sharply.

Like the day I met you? Harriet now wondered.

The not knowing was frightening. Believing so adamantly in one thing but then having the one person she loved and trusted tell her the reverse was true. Harriet once found herself standing in the middle of a supermarket, frantically trying to remember if Brian preferred biscuits covered in milk chocolate or dark.

'I've told you so many times, Harriet,' he said, as she handed him the packet of milk chocolate digestives later that evening. 'It's the dark ones I prefer.'

The next time she went to the supermarket Harriet rolled his words around and around on her tongue. 'Dark chocolate, dark. Remember it's dark, Alice.'

They stood in the biscuit aisle, her fingers trembling as they hovered over the dark ones. 'Alice, what did I say?'

'Dark.' Her daughter nodded as Harriet cautiously put them in the basket.

When they got home and she laid one out next to his mug Brian picked up his biscuit and turned it over in his hands as if he had never seen anything like it. Then he looked up at Harriet and said, 'Oh my love, come here. You've done it again, haven't you? It's the milk chocolate I prefer.'

Harriet was losing her mind. By then she was certain of it. She feared she would ultimately lose everything.

'You will lose Alice one day,' he would often tell her.

He was right about that. Now she had lost her daughter.

The creaking above her stopped and Harriet froze as she listened for his footsteps down the stairs. Of course by now she knew she wasn't losing her mind any more. She was well aware it was Brian trying to convince her she was. She had become sure of that over the last twelve months, since the day she started writing in her notebook.

Though it was also fair to say she had done something crazy.

When he came into the kitchen he stood by the table and looked at her, though still he didn't speak. 'Is everything OK?' she asked as calmly as she could.

'I need to go out. I need to speak to someone,' he said, though he didn't move.

'Who?'

Brian gave a small shake of his head. He seemed uncertain about leaving her in the house, which made her wonder what was so important that he would go anyway. 'Remember, Angela is coming round soon.'

'Yes. I know.'

'She'll be here in half an hour so there's no time for you to go anywhere.'

Harriet nodded. The clock behind Brian showed it was nearly midday. Angela wouldn't be here for another four hours.

'Twelve-thirty, Harriet. That's what time she's arriving,' he persisted as if goading her to contradict him, but Harriet just nodded again. Eventually Brian tutted and walked out of the kitchen. 'I won't be long,' he called as he let himself out the front door.

It crossed her mind Brian was going to see Ken Harris, who'd withdrawn his alibi, but she couldn't think about either of them right now. Wherever he was off to it was the least of her problems. Harriet needed a clear head to work out what she was going to do next, because she only had four hours until Angela arrived and even less time before her husband returned.

Closing her eyes, she pressed her fingertips against her eyelids. 'Think, Harriet.'

The past twelve months flickered like a movie in the darkness of her eyelids. The realisation that Brian had created a life she and Alice couldn't escape from, the appearance of the ghost from her past, the sheer desperation that made it seem like her plan was a good idea.

Harriet knew it was dangerous to leave, but Alice was her priority. It was always about Alice. It was Harriet's fault her daughter had disappeared twelve days ago because she was the one who had planned it. Every meticulous detail of making Alice vanish from the fete was so they could escape from him.

But everything had changed in the last twenty-four hours and now Harriet didn't actually know where Alice was. And if she didn't get out of there right now and find her daughter, there was a very real chance she would lose her mind, and possibly her daughter, for good.

Harriet's story

Wednesday 18 May 2016

I fear I might do something bad.

Brian came home from work last night and rushed straight up the stairs. He was frantic. 'Why did you leave Alice in the bath on her own?'

'I didn't,' I said, shocked. 'I'd never do that.'

He looked at me in that way he does, head leaning to one side, gaze rolling over me. It always puts me on a back foot because I know it means I have done something that I can't remember.

'So why has she just told me you did? Alice wouldn't lie.'

He's right. We both know she wouldn't.

'I'm worried, Harriet.' He drew in a deep breath, squeezing his mouth so his chin wrinkled up like a walnut. 'If this carries on Alice will get hurt.'

'I didn't leave her for a moment,' I said. I pictured myself in the bathroom, sitting on the footstool, leaning over the bath and running my hand under the tap as it splashed out more hot water. I'd filled a jug and tipped it down Alice's back, making her squeal with delight, then twisted round to get her a clean towel from the radiator, holding it up to wrap around her as she stepped out of the bath. I remember it all. I didn't leave the room. Yet if Alice says I did …

Already there's a problem with the memory. It always starts in the middle. A small black hole appears that slowly spreads outwards like spilt ink until there is a gaping blankness in the picture that I can no longer fill in.

'Alice is a little frightened, my love, but she'll be OK.'

When Brian keeps talking at me the hole spreads quicker. I wonder if he knows this. 'Hey, Harriet, don't cry.' He wiped away my tears with his thumbs.

'I'd never do anything to hurt her,' I sobbed.

'I know you wouldn't,' he said softly. 'I know. But all it would take is for her to slip under the water and—' He shakes his head. 'Alice would be dead.'

I screamed at Brian not to say that, clamping my hands over my ears. I would never let that happen.

But what if I had?

I told Brian we would go back and see the doctor again. I am to call him today and make an appointment. He will write more notes on me, pen it in black and white that my daughter is not safe alone with me.

Maybe she isn't. All night I couldn't sleep because every time I closed my eyes I saw Alice disappearing under the water. Beside me Brian lay peacefully still, his breath deep and content with his spotless conscience.

There are plenty of things I forget but never before has it put my daughter in danger. This morning I asked Alice, 'Do you remember your bath last night?'

'Yes.' She looked at me oddly, but then it was an odd question.

'Tell me about it,' I said, tickling her in the ribs until she giggled. 'Did you enjoy it?'

Alice shrugged. 'It was OK.'

'Did I leave you on your own?' I asked her. 'Because if I did, Mummy is very sorry. I should never do that.'

'No,' she said. 'You never leave me on my own.'

'That's good.' My heart was beating hard. 'You must always tell me off if I do. Maybe you told Daddy something about your bath?'

'No.' She giggled again, this time a little nervously. 'Daddy didn't see me last night because I was hiding behind the sofa.'

'Really? He didn't speak to you when he came in?'

Alice shook her head. 'I stayed there until he came upstairs to talk to you.' She looked away. 'Mummy, did I do something wrong?'

'No, Alice, you didn't at all.' A splinter of daylight shone through the window, making me look up. 'Actually, I don't think either of us did.'

I must remember to ask Alice why she was hiding behind the sofa. It seems an odd thing for her to do.

Harriet

The day I left Alice with Charlotte I knew that if everything went to plan my friend would not be bringing her home. On the drive to her house I couldn't take my eyes off Alice through the rear-view mirror. I wanted to soak up every part of her because I didn't know how long it would be until I saw her again.

Under her left arm Alice clutched Hippo tightly. Her head bent towards him and every so often her right thumb slipped towards her mouth until she realised what she was doing and pulled it away again. We had talked about how sucking thumbs wasn't good for her teeth. At some point between home and reaching Charlotte's house, Hippo slipped out of her grip and fell between her seat and the door. I didn't notice she wasn't holding him as I led her up Charlotte's driveway.

I rang the doorbell and looked up at the bedroom window where the curtains were still closed. I'd been looking for signs that I shouldn't go ahead. Anything to tell me that, even though I had got this far, my plan was ludicrous and wouldn't work. If Charlotte had forgotten she was having Alice, I thought, pressing the doorbell again, then that would be a sign. I couldn't do this without Charlotte.

Alice sank into my side and I pulled her tighter against me. Each time I inhaled my breaths felt sharp, like they were stabbing the inside of my chest. 'You'll be safe, Alice,' I murmured for my benefit as much as hers. I was doing this to keep us both safe.

When Charlotte appeared, still in her pyjamas, my heart plummeted with dread that it was all going to go wrong. I considered telling her I'd changed my mind and was coming to the fete with them. She wouldn't bat an eyelid. She probably expected me to back out of leaving Alice anyway.

Charlotte gabbled away, unconscious of Evie yelling in the background as Alice sank deeper into me. But if I pulled out now what would we do? I had been through it so many times. There were no other options.

I bent down and told Alice yet again that she would be safe. I must have looked so jumpy to Charlotte but she tried to brush over it, telling me they would all have fun and how exciting it was that I was doing a course in bookkeeping.

I knew she didn't believe that. Neither of us did. Being crammed in a hotel on a course for the day was nothing more than an alibi. It was also an explanation Brian would fall for when he'd demand to know why I hadn't told him I was leaving Alice with someone else. The police would find the red demands he'd hidden from me in his bedside drawer. They'd hopefully see the bundle of itemised receipts I'd always needed to produce for Brian that were neatly folded under his pants. No one could question I was only trying to help. What they hopefully wouldn't find was the rainy-day money I'd squirrelled away in a box, buried under a conifer next to the sandpit.

Eventually I let go of Alice and walked away. I didn't turn back. I couldn't let either of them see the tears that flowed down my face, leaking into my mouth. It was the bravest thing I had ever done but I'd never felt so frightened.

At one p.m. on Thursday afternoon, twelve days after the fete and three hours before Angela was due, I left the house with the bare essentials, which were little more than a small amount of cash, Alice's Hippo, a toothbrush, and my notebook. I still hoped I wouldn't have to make the four-hour journey to find my daughter because I knew how much I was risking by leaving the house. I hoped I would track them down before I got out of Dorset. My phone wasn't working, thanks to it sinking to the bottom of the bath, so I was reliant on stopping at payphones.

I prayed my next call would be answered. I refused to dwell on the fact it had already been twenty-four hours since I'd started trying to get hold of him, and what that might mean.

My hands trembled against the wheel as I drove. In my rear-view mirror Hippo smiled back at me from Alice's car seat. She would be over the moon to get him back, but I didn't know if I could leave him with her. Would Angela notice he was missing?

'Shit.' I thumped my hands against the steering wheel, stinging the flesh. This was all going horribly wrong. Whatever I did from now on there would be too many consequences and if I couldn't get hold of him soon my head wouldn't be straight enough to think clearly.

After thirty minutes I was almost on the outskirts of Dorset when I spotted a payphone on a side street and pulled over. As I dialled the pay-as-you-go number I had memorised, I knew that if there was no response I would need to drive all the way to Cornwall to find the cottage I had only ever seen pictures of.

The ringtone filled my ear but it rang and rang until eventually it abruptly stopped. 'Oh God, where are you?' I cried. None of this was right. He'd told me with such certainty he would always answer my calls and I believed him.

It was too late to ask myself why I'd trusted him. I had only known him six months. I had known Brian double that before I married him and look how wrong I'd been about him.

'You stupid woman.' I slumped down the side of the phone box, balling my fists and hitting my forehead with the heels of my hands.

The plan to escape Brian had once seemed so certain in my head that, even though I knew many things could go wrong, I never expected this. Now it was hanging together by loose pieces of disconnected thread and, as I squeezed my eyes tightly shut, I knew that not only could my daughter be absolutely anywhere, it was all my fault.

Monday 4 July 2016

Brian has been given a bonus at work. 'A well-overdue payment,' he beamed. I thought it was embarrassing that he'd never been shown any gratitude for his commitment before, but Brian was easily satisfied with the news he shared with me this weekend.

This morning he announced he wanted to give me a little something so I could treat Alice and myself at the shops. 'Brian, that's more than a little something,' I gasped, watching him count out twenty-pound notes and slide them into a long, white envelope.

'There's three hundred pounds in here, Harriet.' He winked at me as he licked the envelope and sealed it. 'You can get whatever it is you fancy. I'm going to leave this up here.' He indicated the top of the fridge. 'Will you go shopping today?'

'Of course.' I was almost jumping up and down like a little kid. I'd get myself something and then let Alice choose a new outfit and we'd even go to the toyshop. Maybe all we needed was for Brian to be given a boost of confidence at work and things might get better.

I kissed him goodbye and left him to finish his coffee while I got Alice up and dressed. By the time we came downstairs, Brian had left for work.

'We're going to go shopping today,' I said. 'Would you like to get yourself a new dress?'

'Like Molly's?'

'Yes, like Molly's. Or anything else you see that you like.' I reached on the top of the fridge for the envelope and tucked it carefully into the inside pocket of my handbag. In it there was more cash than I'd ever had on me and I kept a hand pressed protectively over my bag as we walked through the shopping centre.

At the counter of the first store I laid out two jumpers I liked for myself and a red dress Alice hadn't been able to keep her hands off. 'Can I show this to Molly later?' she asked, stroking the birds embroidered onto its top. It was a little big on her but the rate she was growing I knew it would soon fit her and it really was beautiful.

I reached in my bag for the envelope. 'She'll be at school,' I said. 'But maybe we can show Evie?' I ran my fingers under the seal and reached inside. 'Oh. That can't be right.'

'Is there a problem?' the girl behind the counter asked.

Yes, there was a problem. Instead of the three hundred pounds I had watched Brian count out there was now only a ten-pound note.

'I'm sorry,' I flustered, picking up Alice's hand. 'I'll need to come back.' I turned and pulled Alice towards the doors.

'Mummy?' Her little feet ran behind me in my haste to get out of the store. 'Does that mean I can't have the skirt?'

As soon as we were outside the shop I crouched down beside her and took her hands in my own. 'Silly Mummy forgot the money.' I smiled at her. 'But I promise you,' I said, pressing her hands against my heart, 'I promise you that one day I will definitely come back and get you that skirt.'

Monday 8 August 2016

I told Brian it would be hard to make nice meals every night with my allowance cut right back.

'You'll just have to be a little more creative, my love.' He smiled at me and ruffled my hair.

'Why do we have to budget?' I pulled away and flattened my hair back down. 'I thought things were better at work?'

'Oh, don't use that word "budget".' He screwed up his nose and sighed deeply. 'We don't have money issues, Harriet. You know why I'm doing this. I need to learn to trust you again.'

I bit the inside of my lip. I would not rise to him. 'I just need more than this to survive,' I said patiently. 'Alice needs new shoes and—'

'Harriet,' he snapped. 'Can you really expect me to hand over cash to you? You remember that time, don't you? I don't have to spell it out. You lost three hundred pounds.'

'I didn't lose it. The money wasn't in the envelope.'

'Oh, please, let's not go through all this again,' he sighed. 'Money doesn't disappear. Just keep itemised receipts for everything and if Alice needs new shoes then we can both take her on Saturday. OK?

'OK, Harriet?' he said when I didn't answer. 'It will be nice for us to have a family trip out together. As soon as I get back from fishing you can be ready to go and I will buy Alice her new shoes.' He reached out and ruffled my hair again. 'There, you see? All sorted.'

Harriet

I sat in my car, staring blankly at the unfamiliar road ahead, my handbag clutched tightly on my lap as I considered if I had any other options. There was no choice. I had to find the remote hideaway where we had planned for Alice to be taken.

From now on I would have to pay for what little I needed in cash, but I was still praying it wouldn't be long before I knew Alice was safe and I could figure out what came next.

Fear was driving me on to Cornwall but I was also filled with dread at what I'd left behind, and that the longer I was away the worse it would be.

Was Brian back at the house already?

I imagined his face when he came home and found me gone. For a while he would presume I had popped out, but how long until he realised I should have been back? How long before he alerted Angela to the fact I'd disappeared?

Until he urged them to believe I was as unhinged as he'd been making out and they should track me down immediately?

I put my handbag on the seat next to me and started the engine. I couldn't waste any more time – I needed to get as far as I could as quickly as possible.

As soon as I saw the flashing lights of the police car parked outside my house the day of the fete, I knew my plan had been carried through and Alice was gone. Brian had already been told the news that his daughter had disappeared and soon they would tell me. I couldn't back out now, I kept thinking as I watched them from inside my car.

Brian had dragged me out of the car and up the garden path, his fishing rods clanking like boat masts in the wind. For a very short moment my heart went out to him. Despite everything he had done, I wondered if he deserved to think his daughter had been taken.

'Alice is missing.' His words screamed out into the still air. My legs were pulled from under me as I fell on to the ground like my body had been taken along with her. That's when it really smacked me that in that precise moment I had no clue where my daughter was. I could pinpoint on a map where she should be, but even as I imagined it, every road and motorway between us stretched interminably until I feared I might have lost her forever.

Had I made a mistake? What if someone else had taken her at the fete? How would I know if she was in a car accident? I screamed out Alice's name, clawing my finger-nails into the concrete until I was taken inside and forced to endure her last known movements.

When Angela suggested it would be a good idea to talk to Charlotte I knew she could be my downfall – I'd want to tell her everything. As adamantly as I refused, Brian was insistent and eventually I caved in. But as soon as my friend stepped inside my living room I couldn't bear to look at her. I wanted to freeze time around us so I could crawl across the floor and whisper in her ear, 'I know where Alice is. This isn't your fault. I'm sorry for what I'm putting you through but I'm doing this for her.' As fear and guilt dripped from Charlotte's words, I realised how stupid I'd been to convince myself she would one day understand why I'd done what I had.

Before then I'd satisfied myself that it was only a matter of time before my daughter reappeared and Charlotte could move on with her life. Her abundance of friends would get her through the short term and no one would blame her. In fact I not only thought they wouldn't blame Charlotte, I believed they'd feel sorry for her. How dreadful she must feel, they would say. Their hearts would go out to her. It could have happened to anyone.

What I didn't anticipate was that Charlotte would be posting on Facebook the moment my daughter was taken. That a journalist would pick that up and twist it until she looked nothing more than careless and inattentive and ultimately as responsible as whoever had my daughter. To make it worse, every news report on Alice attracted comments from strangers lashing out at Charlotte, making out she was a bad mother. Everyone was focused on her failings and I couldn't bear to imagine how she was coping. Yet still I continued to reassure myself that as soon as Alice was back everyone would forgive and forget.

But deep down I knew what I'd done to her. Because seeing Charlotte in my living room, trying to piece together how she could have lost my daughter, my broken heart fractured into more pieces. She would never get over it.

Later Brian paced the living room, loading every ounce of blame on to Charlotte, skilfully dodging it himself as always. Of course he could justifiably wipe his hands clean on this one, though it never stopped him when he couldn't. This is your doing, Brian, I thought, watching him prowl the room, smacking a fist into the palm of his other hand when Angela wasn't watching. If you hadn't made it so impossible for me to leave, I would never have resorted to this.

It was ironic that the reason I'd never confided in Charlotte about my husband was because I didn't want to lose her, when I knew now that I would anyway. When she came to the house that night, it was clear there was already too much separating us to be able to claw it back.

I'd had another friend once. After Jane and Christie and before Charlotte I worked with a girl in Kent called Tina who was a receptionist at my school.

Sometimes Tina and I would slip out and have lunch at the local bakery. She was in her early thirties and lived alone in a one-bed purpose-built flat with two cats she wasn't supposed to own. She was always intrigued by married life and how it didn't seem to make people as happy as they should be.

'I'm happy,' I'd told her during one lunch.

Tina had snorted, wiping a serviette roughly across her nose, making me wonder how it didn't catch the tiny stud that sparkled when she moved. She took a large bite out of her prawn sandwich. 'No, you're not,' she said as sauce dripped on to her plate.

'Of course I am.' I'd been married a year and had a husband who was forever telling me he loved me and how beautiful I was, how I was the only thing in his life worth living for. We had just enough money to get by and I enjoyed my part-time job at the school, even if I wasn't making the best use of my education. How could it be possible that I wasn't happy?

'Really?' She opened her eyes wide. 'Can you hand on heart say everything's great?'

I fidgeted in my seat and looked down at my own untouched sandwich. Brian might not be the person I thought I'd end up with and maybe I didn't always feel like I got things right. It was true I managed to upset him quite regularly. Only the night before he'd questioned why I never showed him much affection.

'Why don't we ever see Brian?' she persisted. 'He turns up to collect you but he never comes out. Nor do you, much.'

'I do,' I protested. I couldn't tell her Brian couldn't stand her brash sense of humour or how her loudness grated on him. 'In fact, I'm coming to the end-of-term drinks on Friday,' I announced suddenly, knowing I'd get away with it because Brian was, unusually, away overnight at a conference.

That Friday evening, as Tina downed her sixth glass of Pinot Grigio, she slurred at me, 'Brian has a weird hold over you.'

I brushed her off though her words stayed with me, and a few months later when Brian and I had a row, I ended up walking out of our flat and staying at hers.

'I can't believe what I've just done,' I told her. I was shaking. I'd never stood up to him before. Brian wanted me to cut my hours at school but for once I wouldn't agree. I loved my work and had even just been offered the chance of going for a promotion. 'Mrs Mayer's job,' I explained to Tina.

'What's the problem with that?' she asked. 'And you should totally go for it. You could do that job with your eyes shut.'

That was what I'd thought, only Brian wanted me home more.

Tina choked on her wine, managing to spit a mouthful back into her glass. 'You're kidding, right?'

I wasn't. He told me I should be more of a homemaker than a career woman and asked me if I wanted our marriage to work because if I did I was going the wrong way about it.

But as Tina continued to vilify Brian I found myself drawing away from her, unable to defend my husband but increasingly anxious to do so. He was still Brian, the man I loved, and I didn't agree he was as controlling as she said. I needed to believe he was only worried for my sake because, if I didn't think that, then what else was wrong with our marriage?

By the time Brian turned up at Tina's door, I was ready to run back into his arms and tell him I loved him. I wouldn't go for the promotion, I assured him, but I stood my ground: I wasn't prepared to give up any hours.

I tried ignoring how much he continued to obsess over Tina and how she'd influenced me so easily. How unhappy I'd made him putting my friends and my so-called career first. At the time I was just pleased I'd stood up for myself, though deep down I knew he felt betrayed.

What I never expected was for three weeks later, when I was back at school after the Easter holidays, Brian to pick me up and tell me we weren't going home to our flat any more. 'Surprise! I've bought you your dream, Harriet,' he said, clapping his hands.

'You've what?' I laughed. 'What are you talking about?'

'We are moving, my love,' he said, straight-faced and carefully monitoring my reaction. 'Everything is packed already so you don't need to worry about a thing.'

'No,' I giggled nervously. 'But I like our flat,' I told him, watching his face fall. 'You're having me on, Brian,' I added cautiously.

'No, I am not. I've bought us a house by the sea in Dorset. We are starting again. A new life,' he said, a little more despondently than the conversation had started.

'But—' I began. 'You mean you've sold our flat and bought a new house? You can't have.' But I knew that was exactly what he had done and because it was all in his name he didn't need me to approve it. 'But why?'

Brian looked at me carefully. 'It's just going to be me and you, Harriet,' he said. 'You can't tell me that isn't what you want?'

It took a long time for me to understand how threatened Brian felt. How close someone had come to seeing him for the man he was. Someone who, in his eyes, was turning me against him. I stood up to him. I refused to let my job go. It was Tina's fault: it couldn't have possibly been my decision.

Other friends had been more easily disposed of but one of the reasons Brian disliked Tina was because she was so dogged. When Brian moved us to Dorset he knew he couldn't let that happen again. He needed another way to ensure I wouldn't slip away from him. Having his daughter wasn't enough. He needed me to believe that without him

I wouldn't survive. And he would do this by eating away at me until I doubted my own sanity. How could I leave when I was so reliant on Brian? When I had no money of my own to live on? How could I leave when he'd set it up so he could effortlessly prove I couldn't be trusted to look after my daughter and that she could be taken from me so easily?

As I pressed on towards Cornwall, I ignored the unsettling feeling Brian might have been right. If I could be trusted, I would know where Alice was right now. Instead I was heading to a place I'd only ever seen on the internet.

'It's dirt-cheap,' he had told me, pointing to the holiday cottage on the rental website. 'It's tucked away on a lane that's pretty much deserted. There are only three cottages and no one bothers you. No one even goes down there.'

I shuddered at the pictures of the mismatched furniture and the old-fashioned stand-alone units in the kitchen. The garden at the back was long and much larger than Alice was used to, but it was also overgrown and untidy and I couldn't imagine what she would have made of it when she was taken there from the fete.

But wasn't it also perfect? I had thought at the time. We needed a hideaway where no one would notice the little girl and the man appear one Saturday afternoon, before they were aware the country was searching for them. A place where no one would consider looking for her.

Only now all the things I had convinced myself were good about it made me feel sick. The secluded shack of a cottage was more of a threat than a safe house and I was still over three hours away from getting to it.

NOW

'Is there any news?' I beg.

I know so little of what is happening. All I know for sure is that Charlotte is being questioned in another room, somewhere along the corridor by the detective who turned up at the beach. But this isn't the news I am after.

DI Lowry shakes his head and tells me no. Behind his small circular wire-rimmed glasses and his light ginger stubble, his face is the epitome of blankness. It has been since he introduced himself when I was brought into the station, his short legs scurrying up the corridor as I followed quickly behind.

I am desperate to leave so I can get back out there and find out for myself what is happening. I am sure the detective is keeping something from me. Maybe he thinks that by keeping me in the dark he can manipulate me to his advantage, use my fear to break me down.

I peer at the clock and then at the door, dismissing a crazed yearning to jump out of my seat and run towards it.

Is it locked? I am certain it isn't. Can I run out? I've not been arrested, after all. Lowry has told me I'm here to help with his enquiries and he is stepping around me like I might snap at any moment. Of course I could physically walk out but what would I do then? Where would I go? If I did that I'm sure they would haul me back in handcuffs. So even though I want to run, I know it's impossible.

I gaze towards the wall on my right and wonder if Charlotte is on the other side of it. She could be saying anything and I have no right to ask her not to. I lost that luxury the day of the fete.

'Are you OK, Harriet?' DI Lowry asks.

'Sorry?' I look up at him and he nods at my wrist. I hadn't noticed I'd been rubbing it. I pull my hand away. The skin is red but the searing pain has subsided and in its place is left a dull throb.

'I think it's OK,' I say, though no one has checked, but right now my wrist is the least of my problems.

He is still watching me, glancing at my wrist. He looks concerned as he strokes a thumb against his stubble, before he checks himself and glances down at his pad. Now he is moving on and is interested in my friendship with Charlotte. I tell him she was always a good friend to me.

'Charlotte knew I didn't know anyone in Dorset,' I say. 'She made me feel welcome.' I was grateful for that, more than I would have ever let on. It had taken me three months to find a part-time job and settle in at St Mary's Primary School and still I had no one I could call a friend.

I'd seen Charlotte in the playground huddled in her group of mums. She stood out more than the others, with her long blonde hair always swishing behind her in a ponytail, her skinny jeans, expensive clothes and selection of sparkly flip-flops. I couldn't take my eyes off Charlotte, though for no other reason than she attracted me like a moth to a light.

I would go into school in the mornings and look out for what she was wearing. I used to pull my own tangled mat of hair back into a ponytail and see if I could look like her.

Charlotte was the picture you stick on the fridge: the one that reminds you there's something to aim for. For me she epitomised everything I wanted in life: freedom and the ability to make choices without repercussion.

'Charlotte introduced me to her group of friends but, to be honest, I didn't have much in common with the rest of them,' I say.

'But you did with Charlotte?'

'Surprisingly, yes. We were both raised by our mums. We lost father figures in our lives from an early age. There was an understanding between us, because of that, that not everyone gets.'

DI Lowry looks at me quizzically, but I won't go into it. Instead I say, 'It just meant we had something in common. Something we could talk about,' I add, even though I was never the one to talk.

I tell him more about our friendship, the hours we spent chatting on the bench in the park.

'Your friendship sounds a little –' DI Lowry waves a hand in the air as he searches for the right word '– one-sided.'

I look up at him.

'Don't you think?' he says, tapping his pen lightly against the desk.

'One-sided? No, I think she wanted it too.'

'Absolutely, Harriet. I meant it seems like she needed you a lot more than you did her.'

I smile thinly because he could not have been more wrong.

'Or maybe I have the wrong impression, but it sounds like you were there for Charlotte a lot more than she was for you.'

That might be true, but only because I made it that way.

'Do you think on some level she knows this now?' he asks, and his words sound shrill as they ring across the desk. I know what he is getting at but he doesn't say it outright.

'It wasn't a matter of either of us needing each other,' I lie, because surely that was the essence of our friendship.

'But why didn't you ever share anything with her, Harriet?' he asks. 'Were you afraid she wouldn't believe you?'

No, that wasn't it.

At first I was afraid I didn't believe myself and then I was afraid I would lose her. But I was also scared of what would happen, how far Brian would go. He had dispensed of Jane easily because I had let him. He had moved our whole life because of Tina, but with Charlotte I couldn't take the risk because I had Alice to think of too.

250

Wednesday 5 October 2016

'Harriet is getting worse,' Brian told the doctor today. 'When I came home yesterday I found out she'd locked herself in a cupboard for most of the afternoon.' He raised his eyes.

'Oh?' The doctor looked at me from under his bushy eyebrows. I might have mentioned my fear of small spaces once. 'How did you cope with that, Harriet?'

'The poor thing is claustrophobic,' Brian said. 'She can't even lock toilet doors. We once had to walk up thirteen flights of stairs because she wouldn't get in the lift.'

'And where was Alice – was she with you?' the doctor asked me.

'She was there,' Brian interjected again, shaking his head. 'The little mite must have been going out of her mind with you in that cupboard. The worrying thing is, Dr Sawyer, I explicitly told my wife yesterday morning not to go anywhere near it because the lock was faulty.'

I closed my eyes.

'Harriet?' the doctor asked.

What was the point in answering? Brian would only contradict me. I shrugged my shoulders and said I couldn't remember. But I can. I remember all of it.

'I think my wife needs some more tablets,' Brian said. Still I didn't bother saying anything. It's easier to go along with him. If I do that he has nothing to argue with me about. I would take the bloody tablets and flush them down the loo.

The day before

I woke with a burst of relief when I realised Brian had left the house without waking me because I could start my day without having to look at my husband. Never mind it was raining heavily outside. Alice and I would stay in and watch TV and play games.

'What are you looking for?' I asked Alice when I found her in the living room with the plastic boxes upturned and her toys scattered over the floor. I would need to tidy them before Brian came home.

'The game with rockets,' she said.

'I know the one. With the aliens and the spaceships?' I crouched down next to her and together we looked through her toys but she was right. Neither the rocket game, nor any of her other board games, were there. 'That's odd,' I said. 'Did we move them somewhere?'

'No.' Alice shook her head.

'No, I don't think we did. Didn't we play with it yesterday?' I asked, now in the habit of checking everything with her.

'Yes,' she said and then laughed. 'I won five times!'

'Oh my goodness, you're right. You're absolutely right. And we put it back in here, didn't we?' I tapped one of the plastic crates.

'Yes.' She nodded again.

'Then that's very odd.' I stood up. 'The only place I can think of is the downstairs cupboard. Hold on a minute. Mummy will go and have a look.'

I rarely use the downstairs cupboard, but it's the only other place to store anything in this small house. I held the door open with my foot and pulled the light cord but the light didn't come on. 'Damn,' I muttered under my breath, knowing the box of spare bulbs was at the back of the cupboard. I squinted in the darkness and could just about make out a stack of board games shoved on to a shelf at the far end. Edging closer, my heel still against the door, I leant in to grab the rocket game but couldn't quite reach. I shuffled a little more, and as I touched the box my foot slipped and I fell forward, just as the door slammed shut behind me.

I screamed out in the pitch-black. But with one hand on the game I straightened up and felt my way back to the door. It wouldn't open. I shoved at it, pushing as hard as I could, but the door remained jammed. My heart hammered inside me as I shoved and shoved, banging on the door, though what use was that when it was only Alice and me in the house?

'Mummy!' I heard a whimper the other side of the door. 'Where are you?'

'Alice, darling! Silly Mummy is stuck inside the cupboard.' I tried my best to keep the fear from my words but I was scared stiff. 'Can you try and pull the door from the outside?'

I felt the door give a little as she pulled but still it didn't open. 'Turn the handle,' I said.

'I can't do it,' she sobbed.

'Oh Alice, don't cry. Mummy will be fine; we just need to find a way out. OK, stand back,' I told her. 'Are you away from the door?'

'Yes,' she squeaked.

I shoved against it with everything I had but still it wouldn't move.

'OK. Alice, what I'm going to ask you to do is a really big thing. Do you think you can go into the back garden and climb on to your big flowerpot? Lean over the fence to Mr Potter's house and call for help.'

'No,' she cried. 'I'm too scared.'

'I know but you need to. OK? You have to do this for me. Please be a big, brave girl and go and see if you can get his attention.'

Mr Potter climbed over the fence to get into our back garden, and came into the house with Alice. When he tugged and twisted the handle and eventually got me out of the cupboard, I sank into his chest and sobbed, pulling Alice towards me too.

'How long were you in there for?' he asked.

'It felt like hours.'

'Well, the lock's jammed somehow.' He gave it another tug and the whole thing came off in his hand. 'Lucky that didn't happen a minute ago; you might have been in there a lot longer.'

'Thank you so much,' I said.

'Not a problem.'

'While you're here, do you think you can wait while I get the spare light bulbs – that one must have blown already,' I said.

'I doubt it,' he said, nodding up at the ceiling. 'There isn't even one in there.'

'That can't be! I changed it just a few days ago.' I shook my head, though of course realisation was dawning on me.

BEFORE

Harriet

It was around six months before that fete that I understood how deeply Brian had me under his control, but by then I also knew there was little I could do about it. Not if I wanted any chance of keeping Alice.

One morning last autumn I took Alice to the park in Chiddenford in a haze of despair. He had fooled everyone. Mostly me, but he'd managed to drag everyone else into his version of reality too. What chance did I stand against him? The crazy wife who put their child in danger. Who would believe me if I told them my truth?

Charlotte was already at the park and I slipped on to the bench alongside her, watching Evie run around with a bubble wand clutched in her tiny hand. Alice stood by my side, hesitant to join in until she was ready. Charlotte babbled on about her sister's wedding and, as I often did, I lost myself in the wonderful mundanity of her problems until she said, 'There's still no news of that little boy, Mason.'

'I know. The parents must feel awful. You just can't imagine what they're going through, can you?' I shuddered and both our eyes followed Evie a little closer as she ran around the park. 'I haven't read much about it,' I admitted. Even though his disappearance was headline news, every time I thought of the little boy vanishing I felt sick.

'Hmm. I know this is a dreadful thing to say, but do you think the parents are involved?'

'No. Not at all,' I gasped. 'Why, do you?'

'I don't think so but that's what some people are saying. I read this article online listing all these weird reasons the case doesn't stack up and it makes you think, doesn't it?'

'No. I don't think it's them,' I said. 'I don't believe for one minute it is.'

Charlotte sighed. 'No, I don't either,' she agreed. 'But isn't it awful that it gets so twisted by the media? His family's lives have been invaded. They can't do anything without the world watching them; it must be so hard.' She fiddled with a scarf that lay across her lap. 'But then I suppose if they do have anything to hide they won't be able to for long.'

That night I read everything I could about the Mason Harbridge case – the boy who vanished out of sight from a park. It was an interesting thought: how someone can disappear completely. And Charlotte was right: the eyes of the world are on those left behind. Mason's parents couldn't put a foot out of place without someone picking up on it.

If they stripped back the walls that Brian had so skilfully built around us, what would they see? How long could he deceive everyone? Press poking into our lives, police trawling our house: living with us, watching every moment, hearing every lie that came out of his mouth.

All I needed was for everyone to see what I saw. Then Alice and I could escape him. And Alice wouldn't have to disappear for long. Just until the world recognised the monster I lived with.

After all, how clever is Brian, really?

Charlotte's throwaway comment about the Harbridge family never left me and a few weeks after, in late November, I first saw a chance of turning the idea into reality.

I was cleaning the house one rainy Monday morning when the doorbell rang. I smiled at Alice who was painting at the kitchen table and, with a duster in one hand, answered the door to find a man standing on my doorstep. He looked as shocked as I must have done when he saw me, and with one hand gripped on to the doorframe he leaned slightly forward as if he were about to speak.

My eyes skimmed over his face. I shook my head nervously, took a step back. I didn't recognise all of him, but his large green eyes were so familiar.

'Harriet,' he eventually said. It wasn't a question.

'No,' I muttered, still shaking my head. 'It can't be you.' I looked up and down the road but there was no one around, then back to him as he awkwardly scuffed his feet.

He dropped his gaze to the ground, leaving me to stare at the patch where his white hair was thinning.

'What—' I said in a low breath. There were too many questions running through my mind. What are you doing here? Is there bad news? How did you find me? Are you really who I think you are?

'Do you think I could, erm, come in?'

I shook my head again. I couldn't let him in. What would I tell Alice?

'I don't need to stay long. I would just like the chance to talk to you.'

I eventually opened the door wider and directed him through to the kitchen, telling Alice that if she watched TV in the living room we could make a cake that afternoon.

She didn't need telling twice and, as soon as Alice was out of the room, I gestured for the man to sit down while I stood against the kitchen sink and said, 'Everyone thinks you're dead.'

'You didn't believe I'd died, then?' My father, Les, played with his hands, twisting a wedding band around and around. I watched those hands closely, trying to remember them picking me up as a child or playing a game with me, but nothing came to mind.

'No, I knew the truth,' I said quietly. What I did remember was the first time I heard my mum tell someone in a shop that my father was dead. I'd looked at her in shock, wondering when it could have happened, but Mum gave a small shake of her head and even at such a young age I quickly understood she wasn't telling the truth. It was another of her fabrications.

'So Daddy's not dead?' I asked her later when we were on our own.

'No, he's not,' Mum said, flapping about a large sheet that she was desperately trying to fold. In the end she rolled it into a ball and stuffed it into the airing cupboard. 'But he is gone and it will be a lot easier for Mummy if we tell people he is.'

I hadn't liked the sound of it, but I went along with her because she was my mum. There was no one else I could turn to, to ask if what we were doing was right. It certainly didn't feel it, but I absorbed her lie and at some point over the years it became easier telling people he'd died than facing up to the fact my mother had deliberately created such a dreadful story. By the time I met Brian I didn't even consider another version.

As I grew older I understood Mum well enough to know she wouldn't have coped with the looks of pity, neighbours talking behind her back, asking questions and wondering what it was that finally drove my father away. Or maybe what took him so long. I don't know if Mum blamed herself for his departure – outwardly she blamed him – but she would have assumed everyone else thought it was her fault.

All I was left with was a memory of him from an old crumpled photograph. Our faces pressed together with wide smiles as he held me in his arms, both sharing an ice cream with a flake stuck out of the top.

Now I searched his face for the features I recalled. They were there, but hidden under skin that puffed in layers on his cheeks. The bright-green eyes were watery now and drooped under his white eyebrows. The years had taken away the one picture I had in my head and replaced it with this old man who looked so lost and out of place in my kitchen. Years I would never get back, I thought, as I turned away from him sharply and fussed with the kettle, filling it with water so my face didn't betray me.

His sudden appearance had brought a rush of unexpected emotion that I hadn't even realised I'd been ignoring. Had I actually missed him? 'How did you find me?' I asked eventually. Not why? I didn't know if I was ready to hear the answer to that yet.

'I found you on that Facebook first, about a year ago.' He had a gentle lull to his voice. 'You were there under your maiden name and it said you worked at St Mary's School in Chiddenford.' I had set up a page once to keep updated on school news when I worked there but had never added a post or even bothered updating my details when I left.

'Bit of a funny story after that,' he went on. 'I have a cousin who lives down here. He knows the area well, told me where the village was.' He paused.

'Yes?' I prompted.

'One day I thought I'd come down and have a look around. I didn't really think I had any chance of seeing you but I happened to be walking past a park just round the corner from the school and—' He paused. 'I recognised you straight away. I never forgot your face. You had your little girl with you. She looks just like you,' he said, glancing up at me and smiling. 'The image of you back then.'

'So you saw me and then what?' I said harshly.

'Then I followed you,' he said, dropping his eyes to the table.

'You followed me?'

'I know, I know, it was an awful thing to do, I just – well, I should have come and talked to you but I didn't have the courage,' he said. 'I dithered for ages until you got up and started walking away and I didn't want to blow it. I wasn't sure what I wanted to say and—' He laughed. 'Now I'm here I fear I'm still not doing a very good job.'

I dipped a teabag into the cup and poured in a splash of milk, then turned back to him. My dad fidgeted uncomfortably at the table. Had he come to tell me he was dying? I wondered. Would that matter to me?

'It's a shock for you, I know that,' he said. 'Seeing me on your doorstep.'

'I think there was a part of me that always imagined it might happen one day.'

'I hope I haven't upset you?' He looked up at me with a glimmer of expectation as he tried to meet my gaze but he couldn't hold it for long.

'I'm more intrigued than anything,' I said flatly, trying to sound distant. Often I had looked at Brian and thought children are better off without their fathers, but mine had never given me the chance to find out.

I handed him the tea and he wrapped his large hands around the mug, pulling it towards him and studying the ripples of liquid inside. 'I'm sorry,' he said simply.

'What are you actually sorry for?' I asked him, my back pressed firmly against the sink as I clutched my own mug tightly. A sudden desperate need to hear his apology surprised me.

'For the way it happened,' he said. 'For not seeing you again.'

'I don't really know what happened,' I admitted, watching him, wondering what it would have been like to have had a father around. If my life would have taken a different path and whether I'd have wanted it to anyway. The quiet hum of CBeebies filtered through the wall and I knew that no, despite it all, I wouldn't have changed a thing. 'Obviously Mum told me her version.'

'It didn't happen quickly,' he said. 'It was never a light decision for me. When I first met your mum she was a beautiful young woman.' His eyes sparkled at the memory.

'Full of energy and plans and I fell for her head over heels. We didn't have much money but we were happy for a long time. Over the years I began noticing she had a lot of demons bothering her, troubles I wasn't very good at handling. She worried about everything. Hated me leaving the house, convinced I wasn't coming back. Every night she made me get out of bed at least three times to check the locks. Always on at me over some concern about something or other. I started drinking a lot.' My father paused and nodded. 'My way of blocking it out. One day I realised I wasn't living any more, I was surviving, and I didn't want to do it any longer.'

I pulled out a chair and sat down opposite him.

'I was suffocating, Harriet,' he said. 'Being in that house with her was too much. But I don't expect you to understand what I mean.'

I didn't answer but I must have made a sound because he looked up at me and said, 'I'm sorry. Of course you understand. You would have seen the way she was. I realise I don't know how it was for you after I left.'

'Mum was fine,' I said, and for the first time I considered I had been suffocated by someone my whole life. 'She was who she was and I loved her for it.'

'She loved you very much too. More than anything else in her world so there was no doubt in my mind you'd be fine after I left, that you'd be better off with her. I'd never have considered taking that away from her.'

'But surely you didn't need to make that choice?' I said sharply. 'You didn't need to get out of my life completely.'

'I could have fought,' he said solemnly. 'It would have been one hell of a fight, though. I'd met someone else, you see. Marilyn. She was this light, she saved me from—' He paused. 'Well, from many things really.'

'So you chose Marilyn over me?'

'It wasn't like that. Your mum knew about Marilyn and made it very clear that if I didn't leave her I wasn't welcome in your life. I begged her, pleaded that she didn't need to stop me seeing you, but there was no moving her. If I'd stayed, it would have ended me, Harriet. Like I told you, I was already drinking too heavily and it was only with Marilyn's help I finally stopped.

'I tried to visit,' he went on. 'But your mum wouldn't even let me in the door. It was the seventies; there weren't support groups for dads back then. Then a week or so later I found out she'd told everyone I'd died. I didn't come back after that. Part of me thought it would be for the best.' Les shook his head. 'I didn't want to make things harder for you, with people wondering why your mother had lied to them. I'm sorry, Harriet. If I could turn back time—'

'Then you probably wouldn't do anything differently,' I said. 'Are you and Marilyn still together?'

'She died six months ago but yes, we were.' His eyes watered and I found myself reaching across the table and taking hold of his hand, feeling his rough fingers curling around my own. It may not be how I would do it but could I honestly blame him for needing to get away?

'I'm sorry,' I said.

'So how was it after I left?' he asked.

'Well, I wished Mum wouldn't hover over me as much as she did but I never lacked love. Why have you come looking for me now?'

'It was something I'd talked about for a long time. Marilyn kept prodding me to do it – she was the one who told me to try Facebook – but I never had the nerve. Then she passed away and now everything in life looks different. I'm an old man with no one left. I don't deserve to have you back in my life, but I wanted the chance to see you again. And see your little girl, of course.'

'Alice.'

'That's a pretty name. How old is she?'

'She's just turned four.'

My father nodded. 'I promised myself that whatever you wanted from me, I would do it. If you tell me to get lost then I'll go.' He gave me a sad smile. 'I just had to know for sure. I don't want any more regrets.' He looked at me expectantly, but I didn't answer.

Eventually he pushed away from the table and told me he should probably be going. I didn't stop him because I didn't want to risk Brian arriving back, however unlikely it was, to find my father in our kitchen. But when my dad asked if he could see me again and spend some time with Alice, I agreed because I had nothing to lose. I wanted to find out more about him and he wanted to get to know us. And whether I liked it or not, there were similarities between us.

We arranged to meet the following week in a cafe in Bridport and I led him to my front door and said, 'My husband thinks you're dead.'

'Oh?' He looked shocked. 'You told him that?'

I nodded. 'I told everyone that,' I said. 'And I don't think I should tell him otherwise for now.' He looked at me quizzically but I didn't add any more. 'So it's better we keep this between us,' I went on. 'I'd rather no one else knows you are here.'

'Apart from my cousin.' He gave a small smile.

'Oh, right.' I'd forgotten he'd mentioned a cousin.

'But you don't need to worry about him. He's practically a hermit,' my father said.

'Well please don't mention any more to him.'

'Of course I won't if that's what you want.' He smiled. 'But you may be surprised; if you tell your husband about me you might find he's a lot more understanding than you're giving him credit for.'

I shook my head. No, Brian would not be understanding in the slightest.

Tuesday 8 November 2016

'You're both soaked through.' Brian grabbed two towels from the airing cupboard and ordered me to take off my clothes. 'What were you thinking, Harriet?'

'I didn't think the weather was that bad,' I said, wrapping my arms tighter around the damp shirt that clung to my body. I hadn't expected the clouds to open. I hadn't taken umbrellas and our raincoats were packed at the bottom of the suitcase.

'You were inches from the edge of the train platform,' he hissed into my ear. 'Do you have any idea what went through my mind when I saw you?' I turned my head away from him as he peeled my arms apart and shoved a towel against my chest. 'You need to get undressed.'

'I will.' A sob balled in the back of my throat. I wished he would leave the bathroom. I didn't like the way he was watching me, waiting for me to take my clothes off.

Brian began unbuttoning my shirt, exposing an old greying bra that bagged over my breasts. I recoiled from his touch, which made him suddenly stop. 'Do you do this on purpose, Harriet? When I've done everything for you, this is how you treat me?

'You were leaving me, taking my daughter with you. Did you see how Alice was shivering when I got there? Her little body was drenched. Harriet, how do you expect me to live without you?' He took hold of my arms and pressed his thumbs into my skin.

'I can't do this any more,' I cried.

'Do what?'

'Live like this.'

'And how do you suppose you can live without me, Harriet?'

I didn't have the answer to that. When I'd packed up a case and taken Alice to the station, telling her we were going on holiday, I hadn't thought through what we would do. Not long term. All I knew was that we needed to get away from Brian.

'I found you. I'll always find you. You do know that, my love, don't you?' He took a step back. 'I can't shake the image of you both standing so close to the edge. I wondered what you were about to do. I doubt you even knew what you might do next, did you? Of course I'll need to talk to the doctor about this and see what he suggests, though I'd hate him to say you need a stay in a hospital, but—' Brian tapped a finger against his lip.

'I see you turning into your mother, Harriet. That's what worries me.'

'You can't put me in a hospital,' I cried. Brian looked at me pityingly and then walked out of the bathroom knowing he held all the power.

Harriet

In the aftermath of Christmas, as Charlotte became embroiled in the planning of her sister's wedding, I found myself increasingly reliant on my father.

We met up in various places over Dorset, each time somewhere different. With him living in Southampton he wasn't so close that Brian would ever bump into him, but he was near enough to see us for a day. I hid our meet-ups from Brian, always arranging them when he was at work. Seeing Les was an escape from the downward spiral of life at home and I began to enjoy watching his blossoming relationship with Alice.

There were times when I was resentful, particularly when he would run away from the waves with a squealing Alice or make her cars out of sand.

'Why didn't you try harder?' I asked, when he insisted on buying us ice creams in the middle of January. I had missed out on so many moments like this. I'd been fine not knowing what I hadn't had, but now that he was back in my life it opened up a hole I hadn't realised was there.

Then I would see Alice curl up on his lap like a contented cat, in awe of his card tricks, and I wondered if it really mattered what had happened in the past. It was more important that I didn't let it ruin the future. Alice had a grandfather in her life now, and one she doted on. And secretly I was excited at the thought of having my dad again.

Les felt like a world away from my real life and I began telling him snippets about the man I had married, certain he would never meet Brian. It was good to finally share the truth with someone, and even better when that person was my father. Eventually I told him how Brian had led me to believe I was crazy.

'I can assure you, you are not crazy,' he said.

'He drops it into conversations that I'm like Mum.'

'He never even knew your mother,' my dad said angrily. We were sipping hot chocolates in the cafe of a National Trust house watching Alice play outside. 'And she wasn't crazy. She just had a lot of anxieties.'

I didn't tell him Mum and I were more similar than I would have liked, but it was what I was thinking.

'Besides,' he said, 'being like her is not a bad thing. She was a very good mother and in her own way she always put you first.'

I dropped my head so he couldn't see the tears that had sprung into my eyes. 'I can't see a way out,' I said.

'There's always a way out.'

'I have no money. Not a penny of my own. I don't even have my own bank account. If I walked out I wouldn't be able to buy Alice and me our next meal.'

'Well, I can help,' he offered.

'Thank you, but with what? You've already told me your state pension barely gets you through the week.' He didn't have his own house and was still in the rented flat he and Marilyn had lived in for years.

'So you need to go to the police,' he persisted.

'And say what? I have no scars to show them,' I said, rolling up my sleeves. 'No bruises. I've no way of proving he's abusing me.'

'But somehow you just need to get away, take Alice and—'

'I've tried,' I cried. 'Brian finds me. He's done it before. Somehow he manages to track me down and haul me home, and I know he'll take Alice away from me. He'll prove I'm crazy, that's the beauty of what he does,' I said sarcastically. 'Brian has it all worked out.'

'You really think he wants to take her from you?' my dad asked. 'I don't have the impression he has much of a relationship with Alice.'

I watched Alice pick up a leaf and carefully tuck it into her pocket. 'He loves her,' I said. But I also saw the way their conversations looked awkward, that he didn't always know how to talk to her. That, when the three of us were together, Brian often hung on the edge like an outsider. Surely he must have noticed that too? 'I have no doubt he'd make sure she was taken from me,' I said. 'If he thought it was what he had to do.'

'Let me help,' my father pleaded. 'At least come and stay with me while you work things out. You can both have my bed and I'll sleep on the sofa. Let me do this for you and Alice, please.' He took hold of my hand and squeezed it tightly. 'I want to.'

'But everyone thinks you're dead,' I cried. 'Don't you see? If I suddenly announce I'm off to stay with my dead father, who I've been seeing for the last few months, Brian will have a ball. I write "mother and father deceased" on forms. My best friend thinks you died when I was five. If they find out I've been lying to them all this time, Brian will be shouting from the rooftops that this is exactly what he means.'

'But there's got to be something I can do for you,' my father said.

'Maybe there is one way.' I took a deep breath and told him about the Harbridge family and the idea Charlotte had put into my head.

'You want me to abduct Alice?' He was clearly aghast at the idea.

'Shhh.' I looked around but the cafe had emptied. 'Let's go outside.' We grabbed our coats and went out, waving at Alice, who was still busy stuffing her pockets with leaves and twigs that she'd make into something later. 'It would only be temporary, and you're not abducting her. You'd be keeping her in a safe house for me while I figure out a way of exposing Brian.'

'No, Harriet. I don't like it one bit.'

'No one will suspect you because you don't exist,' I went on.

'No.' He shook his head. 'Too many things can go wrong. The police won't see it that way.'

'If anything went wrong I'd tell them it was all my idea,' I promised him.

'It's ridiculous. You'd go to prison. Have you even thought of that?'

'Yes,' I lied. I hadn't thought of much more than getting away from my husband.

'And how do you suppose it ends, Harriet? What are you planning? That you'll run away with Alice and live abroad?'

'No.' I'd thought about that, but I couldn't contemplate us living the rest of our lives hiding. In some ways it would be no better than what we had now. 'No,' I said again, carefully. 'What I've been thinking is that, when the time is right, you leave her somewhere. Somewhere safe where there are people and you could tell her to call the police.' I spoke with as much conviction as I could. We both needed to believe it was a plausible outcome. 'By then you'll have gained her trust and she'll know not to say it was you. All anyone will have is her description of the man who took her. She's four, they'd expect inconsistencies, they wouldn't expect her to know exactly where she'd been.'

'Yes, she's four,' my father said. 'You're entrusting a four-year-old to carry this lie. It's so not right, I can't believe I'm hearing it.'

'Alice trusts me. And you,' I replied. 'She's bright, she'd understand if we told her this was the only way to be safe.'

'Oh, Harriet,' my dad sighed, shaking his head. 'This isn't the way.'

'Do it for me,' I pleaded, ignoring him. 'If nothing more, then because you owe me this.'

'Don't put that on me.'

'But that's what you said. The first time I met you, you told me that whatever I wanted you to do you'd do it. This is what I want,' I said. 'You can either walk away or be in our lives,' I tried as a last-ditch attempt.

He walked away.

I had lost my only hope of a future and my dad. He still turned up at the museum where we'd arranged to meet the following week as planned, but there was a distance between us. We reverted to being more like the strangers we'd been two months ago than the father and daughter we'd become.

Over the following weeks the gap widened. The only times I saw flashes of the father I'd grown to care so deeply about were when I watched him playing with Alice. He'd throw her into the air and spin her round and tickle her on the ground until she begged him to stop because she was laughing too hard. Only in those times did he look like he'd almost forgotten what I'd asked of him.

One Wednesday in mid-March we took a ferry to Brownsea, an island in nearby Poole Harbour. I sat on a log while my dad took Alice to show her the peacocks, but when they came back he had a grave look on his face. 'We need to talk.' He joined me on the log as I continued to watch Alice running across the grass. 'If you're adamant it's the only way, I'll do it.'

'Are you serious?' I gasped.

'There are many things we need to sort out.'

'Yes. Yes of course.' I leaned towards him and wrapped my arms around his waist, though I felt him stiffen. 'Are you sure about this?' I asked, pulling back.

'For what it's worth I think it's very risky, Harriet. Many things could go wrong.' He took my hands and peeled them away from him. 'And if anything bad happens, I need you to promise me something.'

'OK?'

'It's me who takes the blame. Not you.'

'No way. I can't let that happen.'

'That's one of my conditions,' he said firmly. 'It's up to you to ensure no one knows you had anything to do with it. I won't let Alice be taken away from you.'

'But—'

'I mean it,' he said. 'If you can't promise me that, we don't go ahead.'

'How would I ever be able to do that?' I asked him. 'Alice will say she knows you and then it'll be clear I've been meeting you for months.'

'I'll come up with something,' he said. 'But for now it's best we don't see each other again.'

I gaped at him. 'Why can't we?'

'We can't risk anyone remembering us together while we work out what to do. But I'm deadly serious, Harriet. You need to promise me you'll never let anyone think you had anything to do with this if it all goes wrong.'

I stared at my father whose eyes hadn't once strayed from Alice. 'OK,' I said in a whisper. 'I promise.'

He nodded.

'What made you change your mind?' I asked him.

'I just did,' he said shortly.

'Dad? What is it?' I followed his eyeline to where Alice played, running after an unsuspecting peacock. 'Has Alice said something to you?'

He squirmed beside me, not taking his eyes off my daughter.

'If she's said something, please tell me.'

'I've said I'll do this, Harriet, so let's just focus on what we do now.'

Right from the moment we agreed to this plan I knew there were many 'what ifs'. I was well aware everything could fall apart at the slightest crack but by then I was desperate.

I picked out parts that needed slotting together and forced them into place. I ran my fingers over the points where something could go horribly wrong and I knew I was taking a leap of faith, but faith was all I had to hold on to.

'I trusted you, Dad,' I said aloud as I drove on towards Cornwall, hands trembling against the wheel. 'I trusted you.'

But then, deep down, didn't I still?

Yet, if I did, all I was left with was the unsettling worry that something must have happened to them to stop him from answering my calls.

Harriet

Four days after Alice was taken I first called the pay-as-you-go mobile my dad had bought, as we'd agreed. I told Angela and Brian I needed to get some fresh air and stopped at a payphone three streets away to make the call. My hand was shaking as I tapped in the numbers, praying I'd remembered them in the right order.

As soon as my dad said, 'Hello,' four days of tension flooded out of my body.

'Is she OK?'

'Yes, she's fine. She's asking after you, but she's OK.'

'Oh, thank God,' I breathed. 'Can I speak to her?'

'She's in the garden but I don't think it's right that you do anyway. She's more settled today.'

I tried to imagine Alice through the pictures of the house I'd seen on the internet. It was my dad's idea to take her to Elderberry Cottage, a holiday home in the tiny village of

West Aldell in Cornwall. He and Marilyn had stayed there twice and we were both comfortable that he knew the area. He assured me that previously they had never been bothered, that during both stays they'd barely seen anyone around, at least no one who took any interest in them.

'But she's OK?' I asked him again. 'She's well?'

'Alice is doing fine. I've told her it's a little holiday. She thinks you've not been feeling well, like we said.'

'And how was she at the fete? She wasn't frightened?'

'No. She was surprised and confused, but I told her what we agreed, that you asked me to look after her, and that Charlotte knew. Then she was just worried about you, but once I assured her it was nothing serious—' My dad broke off. I felt our deception cutting through my skin and I knew he did too.

'It's so good to speak to you, Dad,' I said.

'Right.' He sounded flat.

'Dad? You sound strange, what is it?'

'It's nothing, Harriet.'

'Tell me. What's the problem?'

I heard his intake of breath. 'Where do I start? You're all over the news. Alice is too. Her picture is everywhere. I worry about leaving the cottage in case someone sees her.'

'I know, but it's not going to be for long,' I said, sounding more determined than I felt. 'You have to do this now, we can't turn back.'

'I know that. But it doesn't feel right any more. Hell, what am I saying – it never did.'

'You're scaring me,' I said, pressing my hand against the glass of the phone box.

'I am scared,' he said in a whisper. 'And I have a very bad feeling this isn't going to work out the way we want it to. Listen, we need to keep these calls short. Just let me get on with it here and we'll keep our heads down.'

'OK, but I'll call you again next Wednesday as agreed.'

'Fine.'

'Keep her safe, Dad. Don't take her anywhere.'

'We have to go out sometimes.'

'Well, nowhere anyone sees you.'

My dad sighed. 'We go to the beach but that's all. Like I told you, it's deserted most of the time and the cottage has a fishing boat I can borrow so I'm going to take her out on that.'

'OK, but be careful. Alice hasn't been in a boat before,' I said, thinking that at least no one was likely to spot them in the middle of the sea. 'Thank you, Dad. You know I couldn't do this without you.'

I hung up the phone, the tension already creeping its way back inside. It was a relief to know Alice was safe but what if my father couldn't hold out?

I'd go through the motions until I'd arranged to call him again. Just to hear him tell me they were both OK was all I needed to get me through. If I'd known then that when I called the following Wednesday he wouldn't answer, I would have driven to the cottage to get my daughter back straight away.

*

I had just passed the halfway mark on my journey to Cornwall when a warning light flashed on the dashboard. The car started to slow and, as much as I pressed my foot on the accelerator, I could feel it losing power until it stuttered to a stop three hundred metres from a petrol station. Grateful for its proximity, I asked the assistant if he knew a number for an emergency call-out and waited in the stark light of the convenience shop for an hour until help arrived.

The mechanic advised he would have to tow me to a local garage, adding that of course no one would be able to look at my car until the following morning.

'I can't wait until then,' I cried.

The mechanic shrugged as he wiped his hands on an oily cloth and closed the bonnet. 'I'm afraid you don't have much choice. No one will be there tonight.'

'What do I do?' I couldn't leave my car there and I certainly couldn't turn back.

'Well, if you want to come with me while I tow the car to the garage I can take you on to my brother's B&B?' he suggested. 'I'll call him now and make sure they've got a room, but I'm sure they will,' he added softly, eyeing the tears cascading down my cheeks. 'Thursday night, so he won't be busy, and he's very cheap. He'll take you to get your car in the morning.'

It was the only realistic option. We left my car on the forecourt of a garage where the mechanic posted a note with his brother's number on it through the door. Then he drove on a further two miles through narrow country lanes to the shabby B&B, which was nothing more than a house with a handwritten 'Vacancies' sign stuck to its latticed bay window.

As darkness crept in, the idea of being so isolated without a phone made me physically tremble. 'It'll be warm inside,' the mechanic said, mistaking my fear for cold as he pressed the doorbell.

I could never explain to him that this was so much more than the inconvenience of a faulty car. I had no idea what I'd walked away from and even less what I was walking into, and the thought of being trapped midway between the two was terrifying.

Charlotte

On Thursday evening Charlotte stood at her bedroom window and watched Angela step out of her car, gazing up at the house opposite with its 'For Sale' board attached to the gatepost. She knew what Angela would be thinking. There were a few coveted roads in Chiddenford and this was one of them. The pretty cul-de-sacs with their beautiful houses sat on plots much more generous than in other parts of the village. Eventually Angela turned away and walked towards Charlotte's drive.

Charlotte smiled warmly as she opened the door and tried to gauge the expression on the detective's face. 'The kids are still playing out in the garden. I should get them ready for bed but it's such a nice evening.' She looked at her watch. It was already seven p.m. 'Can I get you a drink?'

'Just water would be lovely, thank you,' Angela said as she stepped into the hallway. 'Wow, this is amazing.'

'Thank you.' Charlotte gave a small smile. Everyone commented on her grand hallway and usually she was proud of it. But it seemed so lacking in importance now.

'So, how can I help you?' Charlotte asked, leading Angela through to the kitchen where she filled a tumbler with water and handed it to her. 'Please sit down.' She gestured to a bar stool and Angela perched on it, resting her glass on the island in front of her, continuing to gape at the expanse of Charlotte's kitchen.

'Have you heard anything from Harriet?' Angela asked, taking a sip of water and carefully placing the glass down.

'No, not since I went to her house after the fete. Why do you ask?'

'I just wondered if she's come to see you, or spoken to you,' Angela said.

Charlotte shook her head. 'I haven't heard from her once.'

'Only she isn't at the house,' Angela went on. 'I arranged to be there at four this afternoon. Harriet's never not been in, especially when she knows I'm coming.'

Charlotte pulled out a stool for herself on the other side of the island. There was obviously more bothering Angela than Harriet not being at home. The thought of her visitor the previous night was beginning to set off alarm bells.

'Brian was here last night,' she said.

'Brian?' Angela looked surprised.

Charlotte shuddered at the memory of him waiting for her the other side of her front hedge. 'He was outside my house when I was going out. He wanted to speak to me in his car. He wouldn't come into the house, I don't know why.'

'So what did he want?' Angela asked, pressing forward on her stool.

'That's the strange thing. All he kept talking about was Harriet and how much he loved her. He wanted to know if she ever talked to me about their marriage, which she never did. It was an odd conversation.'

Angela looked as confused as Charlotte felt. 'Did you get the hint they'd had an argument?'

'I wondered that but he didn't say as much. He was just a bit –' Charlotte gestured a hand in the air '– weird. I assumed it was the stress of Alice and everything – but, like I said, it was Harriet he was talking about, not Alice.'

Angela sat back and reached into her handbag beside her, pulling out a notepad.

'Has something else happened?' Charlotte asked, trying to see what the detective was writing but unable to make anything out.

Angela looked up at her. 'Nothing in particular. But the house was a little disrupted when I got there this afternoon.'

'How do you mean, disrupted?' That didn't sound good. Harriet's home was always so neat and organised.

'It was a mess; things had been disturbed,' Angela said, pen poised in the air. 'When I looked through the living-room window I could see all of Alice's toys strewn across the carpet.'

Charlotte shivered at the thought. 'What did Brian say?' she asked. 'How did he explain it?' She'd always thought she was the one who liked it so tidy. Harriet never seemed to mind a bit of a mess; you only had to look in her handbag to see that. But still there was no way Harriet would have thrown Alice's toys around.

'That's the strange thing,' Angela said. 'He's not there either. There's no sign of Harriet or Brian and I have no idea where either of them have gone.'

NOW

The detective wants to know why I didn't tell anyone where I was going when I walked out of my house yesterday. Twelve days after my daughter had disappeared, why did I get up and drive off without telling my husband or Angela or my best friend, who is currently sitting in another room being questioned by his colleague?

I tell him the same story over and over but each time I do he asks me again, only he frames the question slightly differently in the hope he might catch me out. I fear he soon will.

Eventually DI Lowry suggests a 'comfort break'. I think I hear him sighing.

'Is there any more news yet?' I ask as I'm leaving the room. 'Could you find out for me, please?' I cannot bring myself to say the words.

'I will, Harriet,' he says, and for a moment I see a fleeting look in his eyes that resembles compassion. He hesitates by the door as if about to tell me something. I hold my breath, but in the end he says nothing.

There is news. There is something he isn't sharing.

DI Lowry heads one way up the corridor and I turn off in the other direction towards the toilets. It is thirteen days since I have been with Alice. Before the fete, not thirteen hours had passed when I hadn't been able to look at her face and hold her in my arms. That's what tears me apart the most: not being able to touch her.

The air in the corridor becomes so thin it's hard to breathe. I reach for the wall to steady myself as a sharp pain splits across my forehead. The bright lights flicker and dim, and my vision narrows. I haven't eaten since breakfast, though they offered me a biscuit an hour ago. I should have forced it down, but I couldn't, and now I regret it as I feel the ache of my empty stomach.

The thought of staying here a moment longer is almost unbearable. With one hand on the wall I feel my way along, a few more paces, until I reach the toilet door. Pushing it open I reach for the basin, clasping on to its cool, white enamel with both hands.

Eventually I pull my head up and focus on my reflection until I become clear. In some ways it seems like only yesterday that I'd slunk out of my course and was staring at myself in the hotel mirror, waiting for news that my plan was under way. In others, it's a lifetime ago.

I turn on the cold tap and drench my hands, splashing water over my face until the sharp pain recedes. I have no choice but to pull myself together. No choice but to stick to my story, whatever Lowry isn't telling me.

BEFORE

Harriet

By eight-thirty the following morning I had been told that the garage owner had called and that my car would hopefully be ready in two hours. Finally, things were turning in my favour. By lunchtime I would be in Cornwall.

I wolfed down a plate of greasy eggs and undercooked bacon made by the brother of the kindly call-out man, paying him twenty pounds for the hard bed and well-meant breakfast, and accepted his offer of a lift to the garage where I waited for my car that was ready as promised. By ten-thirty I was back on the road.

On the A30 I continued heading west. With the sun trying to break through the clouds I turned the radio up a notch and allowed my thoughts to oscillate between what lay ahead and what was behind me.

Best case, I would find Alice safe and, if I did, I would turn around and go straight back to Dorset. During the night I'd decided I would tell Brian and Angela that I'd needed to get away from the house. That I needed one night on my own away from the prying eyes and invasive questions, where nobody knew me or my story. I'd tell them I drove without thinking about where I was heading and would give them the name of the B&B owner who could vouch for me. I didn't know if they would believe me but it was all I had.

With the rest of the journey passing without mishap, I soon approached the tiny village of West Aldell, where the familiar, unnerving surge of dread resurfaced. I had no idea what I was walking into: whether my daughter would be there; if anything had happened to them.

I turned off the main road and drove down the winding lane that eventually led to a short row of clapboard-fronted shops and cafes. Passing the White Horse pub, I slowed down so I wouldn't miss the right turn that meant I'd otherwise end up at the beach.

This lane was even narrower and lined with hedges on either side. It climbed a steep hill, twisting to the left. There were two unloved houses on the right before I finally spotted a sign for Elderberry Cottage. The wooden name was stuck to a post and jammed at an angle into the hedgerow at its front. I assumed that if I carried on, I'd wind up at a dead end at the top of the cliff as my dad had told me.

It was twelve-thirty p.m. when I finally pulled up alongside the hedge opposite the cottage, wincing at the scratch of its branches against the side of the car. There was little space to park without jutting into the centre of the lane.

So this was it. Sadly, it looked exactly like it had on the website. My dad was right about West Aldell; it did look idyllic but I still had no idea what he and Marilyn had seen in Elderberry Cottage and certainly not what had possessed them to come back a second time.

I didn't bother checking the deserted lane for oncoming cars as I crossed over. A gate hung limply on one hinge leading on to a cobbled path, overgrown grass peeking through its cracks. On the front door a bell dangled dubiously on a wire. I took a deep breath and knocked.

'Please be in, Dad,' I muttered. 'Please God, let Alice be here.'

I knocked again, louder this time. Still nothing. To my right a net curtain partially hid the living room behind it, but I could make out the red velvet armchair and faded brown two-seater sofa I'd seen on the website. The cottage looked like it had been caught in a time trap. I imagined a thin veil of dust coating the china figurines that were lined up on the mantelpiece like a row of soldiers.

I banged on the door again until my hand felt bruised. My heart echoed back with each thump I made on the peeling green wood. How had I allowed her out of my sight? Yes, she was with her grandfather, but she'd only known him six months. I barely knew him at all.

'Where are you, Dad?' I cried at the closed door, pressing my forehead against it in despair. 'Where's Alice?'

When I pulled away I noticed the side gate was ajar. It led to the back of the house, weaving through tubs of plants that stood sorrowfully on a slab of concrete. Through the glass panel of a shabby blue door I could see the kitchen, with mugs left on the table, a few bowls stacked in the sink.

Trying the handle of the back door, it turned easily, swinging open, and I tentatively stepped inside. 'Dad?' I called out. 'Alice?' The only response was the loud ticking of a grandfather clock.

My legs felt like liquid as I drifted through the house, one step at a time, climbing the staircase, its floorboards creaking beneath me. I called their names again as I reached the top. Now the clock's ticking was much fainter.

They weren't here; I was certain of that. But had they been? Were they here this morning?

I glanced into a bedroom with a double bed neatly made, a purple eiderdown quilt tucked over the top. Next to it was a small box room, half the size of Alice's at home. A single bed had a green blanket laid carefully over its end. Had Alice slept here?

My hand shook as I reached out to touch the sheet, frightened I'd find no evidence beneath it that she'd been here. One tug ripped the covers back. 'Oh God.' I held a hand over my mouth as the other touched the corner of the fabric that peeked out from under the pillow. Slowly I pulled the pillow away to find a neatly folded nightie, dotted with pretty pink owls and a frilled hem. I pressed it against my face, breathing it in. There may have been the faintest scent of Alice, but I couldn't be sure I wasn't imagining it.

Exhilarated by that small find, I went over to the chest and pulled out its drawers one by one. Balled socks, a new pack of girls' pants, a couple of T-shirts. Then, in the last one, Alice's red dress and placed next to it her little blue shoes with their pinpricked stars.

I let out a cry as a wave of nausea rushed over me. Of course this was a good thing, I told myself. It meant she'd been here. My dad had at least brought her here as he'd promised. And he had bought her a pretty nightie and new clothes. I had to take comfort in these things, I thought, grabbing a handful of shells from the pile on the dresser. And now I was convinced I knew where to find them. My dad had taken Alice to the beach.

Racing down the stairs, I went back through the kitchen and out the door, leaving it unlocked like I'd found it in case they didn't have a key. I ran down the lane until it came to an abrupt stop at the top of the cliff. Only then did I pause and inhale deep lungfuls of air.

Over the edge of the cliff was a sheer drop. Below me waves rolled in, their white foam washing up on the sand before being dragged out again. The tide was out, revealing a small slip of beach, and while it wasn't windy it looked like there was a strong current.

I stepped back before I lost my balance and started down the steep, grassy path that wound down the cliff to my left. Intermittent stone steps had been laid in places where the ground was rough and I needed to carefully find my footing. It was the type of walk Alice would love.

At the bottom the path joined the main lane that ran through the village. Opposite was a small, deserted car park and to the right a slipway led on to the beach, which looked wider than it had from the top though I wondered how much of it would disappear once the tide came in.

It was almost empty, as my father had said, apart from a little boy playing with a fishing net at the furthest edge of the cove, watched by a couple who were engrossed in animated conversation.

I looked one way, then the other. Had I really expected them to be here? Seeing the box of shells in the cottage had made me certain I'd find Alice and my dad on the beach. Only they weren't.

My feet circled and circled as I refused to accept that they weren't here. Everything started to spin and I fell to the sand in a heap of desperate tears. A sound escaped but I couldn't be sure it had come from me.

'Are you OK?' A voice drifted towards me but I ignored it as I dug my hands deeper into the sand. Never had I felt so frightened or alone.

'Excuse me?' The wind carried the words over.

Go away.

Thoughts swarmed my head like locusts until they turned the sky black.

'Do you think we should call a doctor?' The voice was approaching. Nearer and nearer.

I buried my head into my knees.

Go away. Go away. Go away.

'Do you need help?' A hand touched my side, making me sit up. The light from the sun was harsh and I was forced to shield it away with my hands.

'I'm fine.' I pushed myself on to my knees, my legs trembling as I forced myself to stand. 'Thank you,' I said, brushing the sand from my jeans.

'Can we get anything for you?' the woman asked. A man was right behind her, the little boy with his fishing net trailing reluctantly behind.

'No, I'm OK,' I said. 'Maybe I had too much to drink last night.' I attempted a smile. The woman nodded but didn't smile back and eventually she allowed the man to take her arm and called the boy to follow as they walked away.

I waited until they had disappeared and then retraced my steps quickly back up the slipway, past the car park and up the cliff path. Tears raced down my cheeks until I was sobbing great gulps of air that made me double over in pain. When I reached the top I looked out to sea, mouthing my daughter's name.

What could I do? Alice was now genuinely missing but there was no one I could tell. The police would say, 'We know she's missing, Harriet, she disappeared nearly two weeks ago from Dorset.'

'Alice!' I cried quietly. 'Baby, where are you?' I ran back to the cottage on unsteady legs, letting myself in through the back door again. 'Dad? Alice?' I screamed into the cold, silent air as I collapsed on to a wooden chair in the kitchen. 'Where have you gone?'

Charlotte

On Friday at lunchtime Charlotte placed the phone face down on the kitchen table having ended the call from school. Molly was sick and asking to come home. She had professed to have tummy ache before school that morning but Molly occasionally did that if there was a chance of not going in. Usually it turned out to be nothing.

She told the receptionist she'd get there shortly but it scuppered her plans. Evie was in nursery and Charlotte was supposed to be meeting DCI Hayes at the police station in fifteen minutes. He had called her earlier asking her to come in 'for a chat', admitting that neither Harriet nor Brian had returned home all night.

'I don't know any more than I told Angela,' she said. 'But of course I'll come in if you think I can help.'

'I wouldn't be asking you if I didn't,' the detective said.

Charlotte hung up. His sarcasm grated and it made her wonder if he thought she was lying and she knew where Harriet and Brian were. Now she was going to have to call him en route to the school and explain that not only would she be late, Molly would be with her too. She could picture his exasperated face when she gave him the news.

Charlotte grabbed the car keys and picked up her handbag. Rifling through it to check she had her purse, she was just about to leave the house when her mobile rang from the bottom of her bag, flashing with a number she didn't recognise.

'Hello?' Charlotte cradled the phone between her ear and shoulder as she fiddled to close the zip on her bag. It was forever jamming and she knew if she tugged it much harder the whole thing would snap.

'Charlotte?'

She froze. 'Harriet? Is that you?'

'I need your help,' her friend cried.

'Thank God you're OK. Where are you? Has something happened? Where's Brian? Why didn't you go home last night?' Her questions tumbled out.

'Charlotte, I need your help,' Harriet whispered.

Charlotte dropped her bag and pressed the phone closer to her ear. Wherever Harriet was, it was difficult to hear her. 'Harriet, what's happened? Is Brian with you?'

'Brian?' There was a short pause. 'No, Brian's not with me.' Another pause and then, 'I don't know what to do.'

'Oh God,' Charlotte muttered and all she could envisage was that Harriet was planning something stupid. 'OK, tell me where you are and I'll come and meet you. Are you nearby? I can be there—' Charlotte hesitated. She had already committed to be in two different places but Harriet had to come first. She would call the school and ask them to keep Molly a while longer. No, she would call Tom. He would have to leave work and collect her. 'I can come over straight away, Harriet. Are you back at home or can you get there?'

'No. I'm not there.'

'So tell me where you are. I'll come and meet you, wherever it is,' Charlotte said.

'I'm in Cornwall.'

'Cornwall? What the hell are you doing in Cornwall?'

'I never meant to hurt anyone.'

Charlotte's grip tightened around her phone. 'What have you done?' she asked slowly.

'I had to do it and I don't expect you to forgive me but she's gone, Charlotte. I'm so scared. I don't know where she's gone.' Harriet let out another sob.

'Slow down. Just try and tell me what's going on.'

'I had to get Alice away from him, Charlotte, I had to. But it's gone wrong and I don't know where she is.'

'What are you saying?' Charlotte's fingers were beginning to feel numb, she was clenching the phone so hard. What exactly was Harriet trying to tell her?

'I had to get Alice away.'

'No.' Charlotte stared towards her spiral staircase. 'No,' she said again, shaking her head. 'Did you ... did you have something to do with it?' With her spare hand she reached out for the hallway table, which shuddered under the strength of her hold.

'I had to,' Harriet begged through her sobs. 'I had to get away from him. But it was never meant to be like this.'

'No. This doesn't make sense. You're lying to me, Harriet.'

'I'm not lying and I'm sorry. I'm so sorry but I don't know where Alice is any more. I did, but she isn't here and I can't find her ... ' Harriet's voice trailed off.

'But you made me believe she was abducted. You made me think a stranger had grabbed her.'

'I'm sorry,' Harriet cried, but Charlotte wasn't listening.

'You made me think it was all my fault, that I wasn't looking after her, but all along you did this?' she spat. 'I don't believe it. I can't believe it.'

'I know,' Harriet said. 'I know everything you're saying is true and I'm so sorry but right now that's not important.'

'Not important?' Charlotte let out a shallow laugh. 'Are you kidding me? Of course it's important. What actually happened to her? I was accused of not watching her, Harriet,' she cried. 'Jesus, how could you do that? What kind of mother would kidnap her own child?'

'I had no choice,' Harriet pleaded.

'Of course you had a choice,' she screamed. 'No one abducts their own child.'

Harriet was silent.

'You must have known how guilty I'd feel,' Charlotte went on. 'Surely you've seen what everyone's been saying about me; you can't ignore it. How could you have done this?'

'Charlotte, please, I will explain it all to you, but I really need you—'

'Tell me what happened,' Charlotte said, cutting her off. Her body was shaking with rage. 'Where is she?'

'I don't know,' Harriet sobbed. 'That's just it; she's supposed to be here but she isn't.'

Charlotte pressed the heel of her hand against her forehead. She couldn't believe what Harriet was telling her; it was unthinkable that her friend had done this.

'He was supposed to answer my calls but he didn't,' Harriet continued. 'And that was two days ago and now I'm here and there's no sign of either of them.'

'He? Who is he? The person who took her? I'm assuming you weren't at the fete.' She tried to force herself into a state of calm so she could piece together the story that had so many holes in it.

Silence.

'Who took her?' she asked again, her voice rising.

'My father.'

'But he's dead,' Charlotte said, incredulous.

'No,' Harriet said quietly. 'He was never dead.'

'What?' Charlotte choked the word out. 'But you told me he died. Right at the beginning. In fact the first time we met you told me your dad was dead and I felt awful because I'd been going on about mine walking out on us.'

'I always thought of him as dead because that's what my mum used to tell everyone, but actually he left us. I hadn't seen him in over thirty years but he turned up one day last November.'

'This is crazy,' Charlotte cried. 'Why would you lie to me about something like that? Have you any idea how this sounds?' Charlotte was trembling again and she had to sit down. Her balled fist gripped tightly in her lap. 'This is—' She broke off. 'Has anything you've ever told me been the truth, Harriet? Do you even know what that word means?' she shouted.

'Please,' Harriet begged. 'I know how it all sounds, I do.'

'And he's taken Alice?' Charlotte went on. 'I can't even get my head round this.'

'I know it doesn't make any sense.'

'You don't trust anyone with Alice,' Charlotte said. 'Why did you trust him? Why did you do this, Harriet?'

'We weren't safe,' Harriet cried. 'I had to get us away from Brian and he made it impossible for me to leave him.'

'Brian? What do you mean, you weren't safe?'

'I was desperate, Charlotte. He tricked everyone. He would have taken Alice from me.'

Charlotte recalled the first time Brian had turned up on her doorstep when he was worried about Harriet's state of mind and Alice's safety. She'd disregarded it completely. But what if Brian was right? Just because Harriet didn't behave how Charlotte supposed someone would with postnatal depression, it didn't mean she wasn't capable of doing something stupid.

'Then how come you never told me?' she asked carefully.

'I was too ashamed,' Harriet said. 'He was making out I was crazy and for a long time I thought he was right.'

Yet you've just kidnapped your own daughter, Charlotte thought, remembering Brian telling her he was worried because Harriet had left Alice in the car and forgotten all about her.

'You have to believe me.'

Charlotte pressed the back of her head against the wall behind her. How could Harriet expect her to believe her?

'I'm frightened,' she said. 'I've got no one else I can ask and I'm sorry but, please, you have to help me find Alice.'

Harriet's fear sounded genuine but Charlotte didn't have any idea what she should do. She listened as Harriet told her about her dad not answering her calls and the empty cottage where Alice should be.

'But they could be anywhere. How long have you waited?' Charlotte couldn't believe she was already trying to placate her friend, but the pain in Harriet's voice was very real.

'I know something's not right,' Harriet said. 'I can feel it.'

'You need to call the police, Harriet. There's nothing I can do.'

'I can't,' Harriet cried. 'If I call them I have to admit this is all my doing. If I do—' She paused. 'I could go to prison.

Brian would have custody of Alice and that can't happen, Charlotte. You have to understand I cannot let him have my daughter.'

'What are you asking me to do?'

'Come here. Help me find her.'

'Seriously—' Charlotte gave a short laugh. She couldn't get embroiled in Harriet's plan any further. The very idea of driving to Cornwall to aid her friend in a fake abduction was ridiculous.

'I'm in a place called West Aldell,' Harriet was telling her and began reeling off the address of Elderberry Cottage. 'I've been to the beach but I'll wait at the cottage for you.'

'No, Harriet. You need to tell someone who can help you and it's not me.'

'There is only you!' Harriet sounded almost hysterical at the other end of the line. 'Charlotte, I know you don't know whether to believe me or not, but you have to know by now that I would do anything for Alice.'

'Please don't ask this of me,' Charlotte said. There was silence and for a moment she thought Harriet had hung up. 'Harriet? Are you listening to me?'

'I can't not ask,' she whispered. 'If I don't, then it's over.'

Charlotte

Charlotte pulled out of the drive and to the end of the cul-de-sac. Her shoulders ached with tension. She'd have thought the weight of her own responsibility would have shifted now that she knew it wasn't her fault, but if anything it was worse.

She couldn't get her head round the degree to which her friend had betrayed her. Her life had been tugged apart; everything she thought she knew about herself had shattered. Her friends didn't trust her; she didn't trust herself any longer. Charlotte's happy existence had been ripped at the seams and it was all Harriet's doing.

She had only ever been a good friend to Harriet, taking her under her wing when Harriet needed it most. And this is what she did in return?

Everything deep inside Charlotte told her to call DCI Hayes. She needed to extract herself from the mess she'd already been unwittingly caught up in. As soon as they knew the truth Charlotte's name would be cleared. And it was all Harriet deserved.

Charlotte pulled up at red lights and waited for them to turn green, slamming her hand hard against the steering wheel. She was already fifteen minutes late picking up Molly but hopefully her daughter wasn't as ill as the school had made out.

She pressed the telephone button in her car, ready to redial Hayes's number, playing out the conversation in her head. He'd suck in his breath loudly as he listened to her tell him it was Harriet who had abducted her own daughter. Then he would badger her with questions she didn't have answers to while signalling for a force to raid the cottage in Cornwall. Charlotte shuddered. She could picture Harriet waiting for her at the window but instead of seeing her friend would watch as a police car drew up, officers marching to the door, ready to handcuff her and drag her to the station.

There had been a case recently where a father had escaped to Spain with his son. He'd pleaded that the mother had abandoned her child and he was taking him back to his own country to live with his parents. Regardless, the dad was sent down for seven years. Her heart went out to him when she saw a picture of the mother. She didn't seem remotely bothered by what her son had been through.

Charlotte tapped on the steering wheel as she waited for a mother and daughter to cross. The telephone option on the dashboard flashed off when she hadn't used it. Her chest tightened as she took deep breaths. She knew that as soon as she told DCI Hayes the truth Harriet's life would be over.

Was that what she deserved?

On the crossing in front of her the little girl stopped, letting go of her mum's hand to pick up a grey teddy she had dropped. The mother turned and scooped her daughter into her arms, kissing her on the head as she carried her the rest of the way over the road. Images of Harriet with Alice filled Charlotte's head.

She could hear her friend's voice begging her to believe her about Brian.

He was acting so oddly two days earlier when he'd turned up at her house; his focus on Harriet rather than his daughter had concerned her.

But could he really be the man Harriet described? Capable of such hidden abuse, bad enough to make her stage such an elaborate plan.

And then there was the story Brian told when he'd visited months earlier. When he'd calmly explained how Harriet had left Alice in the car while she renewed her passport at the post office.

Charlotte shuffled forward in her seat, rolling her shoulders. There was something niggling her, she thought, as she absently watched the mother and her little girl. Something in the corner of her mind, a fragment of conversation that felt important. Only she couldn't quite reach it.

*

Charlotte checked for traffic wardens as she stopped on the zigzag lines outside the school. She didn't expect to see any at this time of day, but it wouldn't be the first time she was caught out.

'I'm sorry, I got held up,' Charlotte said as she ran into the office. Molly sat on a plastic chair at the far side of the room with a bowl on her lap and a teaching assistant's arm hung loosely around her shoulder. Her face was washed white apart from the skin under her eyes that in contrast made her look like a panda.

'Oh Molly.' Charlotte had obviously ignored how unwell she was that morning in her rush to get out of the house. Her daughter fell into her arms, crying louder as she did so. Charlotte hugged her tight and then, holding her at arm's length, looked into her face and wiped a stray tendril of hair away from Molly's eyes. 'Come on, let's get you home.'

'She hasn't been sick,' the teaching assistant said, 'but she feels very hot. You can take this with you,' she added, handing her the empty bowl.

Charlotte placed a hand against Molly's forehead, and agreed she was very hot to the touch. 'Is there anything going round?'

'Not that I know of.'

'I think I should call the doctor,' she said. She'd usually have left it twenty-four hours but Charlotte was leaving nothing to chance any more. Not where the children were concerned. Picking Molly up she carried her back to the car, snuggling into her daughter's warm hair. She couldn't leave her like this.

On the way home Charlotte rang the doctor's surgery and a nurse had returned the call by the time she pulled into the driveway. 'Just a bug, I expect. Give her some Calpol and get her to rest but keep an eye on her,' the nurse told her. 'If she gets worse, call back.'

In the living room Charlotte laid Molly on the sofa, covering her with a crocheted blanket, and stretched out on the other one so she could watch over her for a bit while deciding what to do about Harriet. But no sooner had she lain down than her mobile started ringing.

'Charlotte? It's Angela Baker.'

'Oh, Angela, hello.' She'd completely forgotten to cancel her appointment with DCI Hayes. 'I'm sorry. I meant to call and say I wouldn't be able to come in after all.' She looked over at Molly. 'My daughter's sick.'

'I'm sorry, I hope it's nothing too serious?'

Molly was sleeping soundly already; in fact some colour had already returned to her cheeks. 'No, I think she'll be OK. I just need to keep an eye on her,' Charlotte said, realising she'd have to get back to the school and nursery soon to pick up the others. Maybe Audrey could collect them.

'Well, I hope she's better soon. I'll let DCI Hayes know you can't make it, but he'll probably want to call you.'

'Of course.' Charlotte's heart was beating so loudly she wondered how Angela couldn't hear. She knew if she was going to say anything about Harriet, this was the time to do it. Any later and she'd be—

'So can I arrange another time for you to speak to him? Maybe he could come to your house if you aren't able to leave your daughter?' Angela was saying, interrupting her thoughts.

She needed to tell her now. If she ended the phone call without admitting what she knew she'd be withholding evidence.

Yet there was still that thought niggling at her. Something wasn't right and if she let them take Harriet away then what would happen to Alice? What if her friend was telling the truth?

'That's fine,' Charlotte said, her heart banging so hard it almost burned through her skin. 'I'll be able to come in later.'

'OK. Thanks. Before I go, have you ever heard of a friend of Harriet's, a Tina?' Angela asked. 'Harriet knew her in Kent.'

'I don't think so.'

Angela didn't answer, and Charlotte couldn't help herself asking, 'Has she heard from Harriet? Do you think she knows where she is?'

'Possibly. She may have gone back to Kent. Somehow I don't think she's gone too far.'

'Really?'

'She won't have fled the country anyway,' Angela said.

The memory she'd been trying to grip on to felt closer. 'Why not?' she asked, but in that moment she already knew the answer.

'Harriet's never had a passport,' she murmured at the same time as Angela spoke the words.

Harriet

I waited at the cottage as I'd told Charlotte I would, though I didn't know whether she would come. Five years I've had to confide in my only friend and I didn't, so I doubted I'd got across what I needed to in five minutes. I didn't know if she believed me – I couldn't blame her if she went straight to the police – but I had no choice but to wait.

Had I made another grave mistake by calling her? My plan was already so feebly held together. I had proved that by the frantic way I was ripping it apart. I was becoming my own undoing and, now that I had reached out to Charlotte, I might well have given her the rope that would hang me.

But I hadn't known where else to turn. I needed help and the only person I hoped I could trust was possibly the one I should have confided in at the outset.

Will you come, Charlotte?

The minutes ticked by on the grandfather clock as rhythmically as the metronome that sat on my music teacher's piano at school. Back then it had lulled me into a trance when I'd waste large chunks of lessons staring out of the window, dreaming of a different life. Now, with each sharp tick, a fraction more hope evaporated.

Tick. You still don't know where Alice is.

Tock. The longer you wait, the worse it will be.

I fidgeted impatiently in the armchair by the window. I got up and paced the floorboards in the kitchen. I went upstairs and looked out of the front window on to the lifeless lane below. Everything remained morbidly still. Even the branches of the trees were immobile, captured in a moment of time.

How long would I wait? Hours? Days? There would come a point when I needed to do more than scratching about the inside of an empty cottage. When I needed to call the police myself.

What would be the tipping point?

I stood at the window, my hands splayed against the net curtains as they pressed against the glass. My heart burned with the crushing realisation that whatever happened now Alice would undoubtedly be taken from me, but all I wanted was to see her. I would risk everything to know my daughter was safe.

'Come back, Alice,' I called into the silent room and, as if in response to my plea, a shard of sunlight pierced through the window and flickered on to the patterned carpet. In a moment of clarity, I knew I had to take back control and consider what I would say if the police arrived or it got to the point I needed to call them.

Searching in my bag for my notebook downstairs, I took out the Elderberry Cottage business card I kept in the back pocket. I turned it over and stared at the blank space. Then I grabbed a pen from a jar on the mantelpiece and sat back in the armchair, chewing on the end of the pen as I thought. Carefully, in an impression of my father's loopy scrawl, I wrote a short note on the back of the card.

It was crude and doubtfully sufficient, but as I read over it I figured it was better than nothing. I tucked it into the back pocket of my jeans as the grandfather clock chimed six.

If Charlotte had walked out of her door the moment we'd hung up, she could be here by now. I set myself deadlines. I would go back to the payphone and call Charlotte again if she wasn't here by seven.

I would call the police and tell them everything if my father and Alice hadn't returned by eight.

At half past six I peered out of the window again but the same quiet, motionless scene lay outside. The little lane lined with hedgerows, the tall trees dappled by the sun. I wished something looked different just so I could see there was still life out there.

My stomach grumbled with hunger, reminding me I hadn't eaten since breakfast, so I searched the kitchen cupboards. There were a few tins and a loaf of bread, a half-eaten packet of crackers, and a variety box of cereal with three boxes missing.

I ran my fingers over the cereals trying to work out which ones had been eaten. Had Alice had a packet that morning? When was the last time she'd been in the house? It could have been days ago, I thought, with a surge of sickness rising through my stomach and up into my throat. I slammed the cupboard door shut just as there was a loud rap on the front door.

Automatically I froze. It felt too good to be true that it could be Charlotte. But if it wasn't her, who was it? The police?

Slowly I crept towards the front door, peering through its obscured window, but not even a shadow flickered behind it.

I opened the door a crack and looked out, pulling it open wider. With a plummeting sense of disappointment, I realised there was no one there and that deep down I had thought it would be my friend. Closing my eyes to stem the threat of tears, I felt a heavy sense of despair. I should never have expected Charlotte to come.

I began pushing the door shut when I felt the slightest puff of breath against the back of my neck. The hairs on my arms pricked up; goosebumps splattered across my bare skin.

Someone was behind me.

I felt him. I smelled the woody scent of his aftershave. He was inside the house, standing in the hallway, his breath blowing against my neck. I would have screamed if the sound hadn't frozen in my mouth.

'Hello, Harriet,' Brian murmured, his mouth so close against my ear I could almost feel the brush of his lips.

My hand shook violently against the knob of the door as his arm reached over my shoulder to gently close it. 'Surprise,' he whispered.

Slowly I turned around. Brian's face was almost pressed against mine, skewed into a smirk though it couldn't hide the anger in his empty eyes.

'Brian? What—' I tried stepping away from him but there was nowhere for me to go as he'd trapped me against the front door. He must have gone down the side of the house and crept in through the back.

'What am I doing here?' he asked, with his head cocked to one side. 'Is that what you want to know? But where did you think I would be, Harriet?' He held out a hand and took a lock of my hair within it, winding it slowly around his fingers as he stroked it with his thumb.

I shook my head with the slightest of movements. My heart pounded, reverberating in my ears. He must have been able to hear it too.

'Maybe I should be asking what you're doing here, don't you think?' he said. He tugged on my hair and even though it wasn't hard I could feel its pull on my scalp. 'Not found Alice yet?' He gave me a smile that knifed through my chest.

'Where is she?' I exhaled the question in one tight breath.

'What a funny question.' Brian's eyes travelled up to the top of my head as he tenderly stroked my hair. 'And how do you suppose I would know what's happened to my daughter?'

'What have you done to her, Brian?' I cried. 'Where's Alice? Please, you're scaring me.'

'I'm scaring you?' he snarled. His face contorted into the pained shape I had seen so many times. Every one of my questions was angering him more.

I wanted to turn away but I resisted the urge, keeping my eyes on him. 'If you've done something to her—'

'You'll what?' he snapped. 'Because the funny thing is, you're the one who's done something to her, aren't you, Harriet?' With a sharp tug on my hair Brian twisted my neck down with it. The pain shot through my shoulders and up into my head. 'Letting me believe my daughter was kidnapped.'

'Is she safe?' I pleaded. 'Just tell me she's safe.' His aggression shocked me, not least because Brian was never physical – but then I had never seen him this enraged before.

'Oh, isn't she here?' he said, arching his eyebrows, leaning back and casually looking around him.

'Please, Brian—'

'Shut up, Harriet.' He took his other hand off the door and pressed his palm flat against my mouth. 'Stop your questions. Don't you think I have a few of my own?'

The sound of my breath was unbearably loud as I was forced to breathe through my nose. I didn't know how long

I'd have to endure his torment before he'd tell me what had happened to my daughter. Or how he had found me.

When he removed his hand Brian gently took hold of my bottom lip, squeezing it between two fingers. 'And stop biting your lip,' he said. 'You'll make it bleed.' He rubbed his finger across it and then let go of me with both hands and casually strode off, sitting down on the sofa.

He knew I wouldn't run because he had things I wanted to hear and, as always, Brian was in control. He knew I would follow and sit opposite him in the armchair.

'I never thought you had it in you, Harriet,' he said. 'You took Alice and made me believe the worst.' He shook his head, making the light reflect the moisture in his eyes. 'Why did you do that to me? I was nothing but a good husband to you.'

When I didn't answer, he carried on. 'Only it wasn't just you, was it? It was your daddy. Come back from the dead.'

'How did you—' I stopped. 'Where's Alice?' I said again. What did it matter how he knew so much; finding out what he had done to my daughter was more important.

'What did I ever do to make you hate me so much, Harriet?'

'You ruined my life,' I said, turning my head so he couldn't see the tears in my eyes. 'You manipulated me and made me think I was going mad. You told me you'd take Alice away from me.' I couldn't let him get away with it any more. Not if he'd done something to her.

'No, Harriet. I never did,' he said firmly. 'I would never do that.'

'You're doing it now,' I murmured. 'Please just tell me where she is.'

'I said if you ever left me I would find you, and look –' he gestured about himself '– I have.' He forced a smile that made him seem incredibly pleased with himself as he clasped his hands together between his knees. 'I won't let you go, Harriet. I can't ever let you leave me. I love you. I love you both too much for that.'

'No. You don't love me, Brian,' I said.

'You, you think you're so clever,' he snapped, his hands unclasping and waving in the air. 'Trying to get one over on me. Well, look about you, my love. You're not really, are you? Because I've foiled your plan and look where you are now. Sitting in this godforsaken cottage with no clue what's happened to your daughter.

'Did you hope I'd get arrested for it?' he went on. I shook my head as he snorted. 'But you will now, won't you, Harriet? They'll lock you up for what you've done. I could have told you your stupid idea would never work.'

'Where's Alice?' I asked him again. I knew by now I had no chance of fighting for my own freedom.

'Don't you want to know how I found them?' Brian said, still ignoring me. 'Your notebook. A little bit stupid,' he continued, pinching his fingers together to emphasise the word 'little', 'to write so many things in there.'

But I hadn't ever written my plan in the notebook. I had only kept a diary of the things Brian told me and the way I believed them.

'I have to say, I'm quite surprised you allowed him to bring her here.' He screwed his nose up as he looked around the living room. Then he turned and smiled at me, 'Ah, you're wondering how I found the book, aren't you?'

Of course I wanted to know, but I needed to see my daughter first. 'Just tell me what you've done to her. Tell me you haven't hurt them.'

'You see, no one knows you like I do, Harriet. Since Alice went missing, there's been something about your behaviour that didn't quite fit. It was more than Alice, you were acting strangely, but I couldn't put my finger on it. Then two days ago I saw you pouring a pint of milk down the sink before telling me we'd run out and you needed to buy more.'

I slumped back into the chair. Brian was always watching, loitering in the last place I expected to find him.

'I followed you. I waited until you'd turned the corner at the end of the road and I came after you. When you went into the phone box and came out again ten seconds later I knew you couldn't have made the call you wanted, so as soon as you'd disappeared I went in after you and hit the redial button.'

My fists clenched tightly at my sides. How could I have been so stupid? I played back the memory in my head, but knew I'd been so intent on calling my father I would never have noticed Brian following me.

'He answered thinking it was you. "Hello, Harriet,"' Brian said with a snarl, failing to imitate my dad's voice, '"I'm sorry I didn't pick up but Alice was hanging upside down on a tree at the end of the garden." When I said nothing, he spoke again, a lot more nervously this time. "Harriet, is that you?"' Brian laughed and shook his head. 'Eventually he hung up and when I called back he didn't answer. So that, my love, is how I found out you knew where your daughter was.'

'What makes you think it was my dad?' I said.

He chuckled. 'Are you going to pretend it wasn't? Alice was calling out in the background. I knew it was her, but I couldn't work out what she was saying at first. Then I played it over and over in my head until I was convinced she was calling out "Grandpa".'

I held a hand over my mouth to stop myself from crying. My need to see my daughter was so desperate.

'It made me think that whoever had her was some sick old man trying to make her believe he was her grandfather, because supposedly she doesn't have a real one, does she, Harriet?' Brian spat. 'My own father is dead and apparently so is yours,' he went on. 'But then I wondered, what if yours wasn't? After all, you never went into much detail about him. Always clammed up when you mentioned his dying. I'd no clue what had finished him off. And the more I thought about it, the more it made sense that he could still be alive.' Brian paused. 'Anyway, I did a quick online search and found there was every possibility of it because there was no record of his death.

'I knew I wouldn't get the truth out of you so I watched you even closer. You don't always know when I'm watching you, do you? When you came back with your milk you protested you felt ill and asked me to get you a glass of water, which I kindly did. But when I left the room, after you accused me of swapping the photo of Alice, I didn't go downstairs like you thought. I waited a while to see what you did next, how deep your deception ran.'

'God!' I cried. 'My deception?'

'I saw you fussing around down the side of the bed, moving your bedside table, then pulling out a notebook. You'd hidden it under a floorboard, hadn't you, Harriet? I found it when I looked there later. When you were downstairs I pulled it out for myself and read everything you'd ever written in there. I knew then for certain your dad was alive and it was clear you wanted to get away from me.

'I found the card for the cottage and called the number. I told the woman a friend of mine, Les Matthews, had recommended me the place and do you know what she said, Harriet? She said, "How funny. Les is staying in the cottage at the moment." That's your dad's name, isn't it, Harriet? See,' he tapped the side of his head with his finger, leaning in closely, his teeth bared in a smile, 'I remember the things you did tell me. The ones you didn't lie about.' He leaned back, savouring his words.

'I went to see your good friend that night,' Brian said, in a sudden change of conversation.

'Charlotte?' I asked, stunned.

'I thought she must be involved too, but the poor cow doesn't have a clue what you've done, does she?'

Brian carried on. 'I paid a visit to my old fishing buddy yesterday too, Ken Harris. What happened there, Harriet? Your dad manage to have a word with him and get him to withdraw his alibi, did he?'

'No,' I said. 'No, my dad knows nothing about any of your fishing buddies.'

'No, well, the man's a drunk anyway,' he said eventually. 'Doesn't have a clue who he sees and who he doesn't. The good news is he's making another statement for me. They'll soon know I was there after all that day, though after this it won't really matter, will it, my love? Very soon everyone will know this is all down to you.'

He stood up and paced over to me, taking hold of my wrists and pulling me up too. 'How could you have done this to me, Harriet? I have always loved you, only that was never enough for you, was it?'

The sound of a car stopping outside the house made us both jump. Was it my dad and Alice? Or Charlotte?

Brian grabbed my arms and pushed me against the wall, out of sight of the window so I couldn't see out. He arched his back to peer out, his eyes flicking back and forth. 'Are you expecting anyone? I can see a woman in the car.'

It had to be Charlotte. She had come for me, only now I regretted making that call, involving her further, and I wished there was some way I could stop her coming any closer. If Brian saw her he'd never believe she had nothing to do with Alice.

I shook my head, though he would know I was lying. Brian always knew everything, that was clear enough now.

He pursed his lips. With a jerk he reached behind himself and grabbed my handbag, which was sitting in full view on top of the side table. He pressed it into my chest, forcing me to take hold of it. Then, with one finger against my mouth, he leaned in close to my ear and told me not to make a sound while we waited for the inevitable knock.

The loud rap on the door still surprised me. Silence. Then another knock. I waited for her to walk away when all of a sudden a key was pushed into the lock. Brian's face froze in panic as he gripped on to my arm, his fingers pinching hard into my flesh.

It wasn't Charlotte. It must have been the owner of the cottage. In seconds Brian was pulling me through the kitchen and out the back of the house. Behind us the front door opened, but by then we were already making our way down the side path towards the gate.

Brian wouldn't stop running as he turned right on to the path and headed towards the clifftop. I yelped in pain as he raced down the hill, tugging on my wrist and making it burn. Each time I begged him to let go of me, his grasp tightened. When we reached the cliff edge he stopped.

The air was getting colder, the light beginning to fade. 'Brian, tell me where she is,' I cried.

'I'll do better than that,' he sneered, his fingernails piercing my skin where he was clutching so hard. The wind picked up from the sea and carried his words towards me. 'I'll show you.'

But as he stared out at the ocean I recognised the same flash of fear I'd seen that day he'd taken me for a picnic on the beach. I followed his gaze. The waves were choppy, encroaching on to the sand as the tide came in. Brian hated even looking at the water.

'You're scaring me. Where are they?' I said.

With a shaking finger he pointed towards the horizon. I followed his finger, looking out to sea.

'Where are they, Brian?' I shouted. The feeling of helplessness was almost drowning me by then.

'Out there,' he replied, and nodded towards the open water.

Friday 21 April 2017

When I spoke to my dad on the phone today he finally told me what Alice said to him on Brownsea Island when they were looking at the peacocks. He didn't have to tell me much more – I now fully understood why he'd changed his mind about what I'd asked of him.

'I'm not a liar.' Alice had started the conversation.

'Goodness me, no,' my dad said. 'Whatever gave you that idea?'

'Daddy says I make things up because I like to make him cross. I don't,' she said. 'I don't make things up.'

'Tell me what he says you've done,' my dad demanded.

Alice told him about an incident with an ice cream that I had all but forgotten. On New Year's Day Brian drove Alice and me to the New Forest. Alice hadn't wanted to go, she preferred playing on the beach, but Brian was adamant we would walk in the woods. I had noticed by then how he liked to make the plans for the three of us almost as if he was marking his place in the family.

I was walking ahead with Alice when I slipped into a rabbit hole and twisted my ankle. Brian muttered in my ear that I had done it on purpose. I told him it wasn't the case but despite his annoyance I needed to go back to the car and rest it.

Alice didn't want to leave me because she didn't like that I was hurt, but regardless Brian dragged her over to the river to make her look at the fishes. I watched through my side mirror for a bit as she agitatedly prodded the water with a stick. Eventually I looked away, the pain in my ankle making me close my eyes and rest my head against the seat.

Fifteen minutes later they came back to the car and I could see Alice's eyes were red from crying. I asked her what was wrong and Brian told me she was upset because she couldn't have an ice cream from the van that was parked up the road.

'Oh, it's too cold for ice cream,' I smiled. My ankle was hurting and I was desperate to get home.

But Alice gave my dad her version of the story, which went more like this:

'If you look a bit happier I'll get you an ice cream from that van.' Her daddy pointed up the road.

'Can I have a whippy?'

'Yes, with a flake too,' he promised.

They watched the fish and Alice made a brave show of being dragged away from her mummy when all she wanted to do was ask me if my foot was any better. 'Can we get my ice cream now?' she'd said when she was eventually allowed to go back to the car.

'Ice cream? It's too cold for that.'

'But you said I could have one.'

'No, Alice, I never said that.'

'Yes you did,' her voice would have cracked. 'You said I could have a whippy with a flake—'

'Alice,' her daddy snapped. 'Stop making things up. No one likes a liar.'

'But—'

'You're ungrateful,' he said, taking hold of her arm and leading her, tear-streaked, back to the car. 'Do you want me to tell your mother you're turning into a liar?' he asked. 'Or shall we just keep this between ourselves and not upset her?'

'Grandpa, he says Mummy makes things up too and that I lie for her, and he doesn't like it,' Alice had said on Brownsea Island. 'He says I make him hurt. Can I tell you a secret?'

'Alice, my darling, you can tell me absolutely anything,' my dad replied.

'If I hide behind the sofa he can't find me, then he can't get cross with me because I haven't said anything wrong.'

Surely, whatever happens, I am doing the right thing for all of us?

Harriet

'I don't understand,' I shouted to Brian. 'What do you mean, they're out in the water? What have you done to them?'

Brian continued to stare out to sea from the edge of the cliff. 'I haven't done anything to them,' he said eventually.

'Then what's going on?' My voice shook as I took a step nearer. I wanted to grab him and shake him, scream at Brian to tell me where Alice and my dad were. But I also knew I would get nothing from him if I did. It took every ounce of strength I had to restrain myself.

'They went out in a fishing boat. I watched them get in it. Just before you turned up this morning,' he said, facing me. 'I followed them down to the beach and he took a boat that was tied up on a jetty by the rocks down there.' I looked in the direction he was pointing but the rocks were high in places and from where we stood I couldn't make out the jetty, let alone see if there was a boat tied up to it.

'You must have missed them by ten minutes,' he said. 'I saw you running down to the beach and watched you from behind the rocks. You didn't see me, but then you weren't looking for me, were you, Harriet?'

I stared at Brian, wondering what he expected me to say. Of course I wasn't looking for him.

'You were looking for Alice,' he said frankly and it crossed my mind, not for the first time, that my husband was jealous. 'And your father, of course,' he added flatly.

My dad had told me about the fishing boat; he must have decided to go out with Alice but that was hours ago now.

'The old man seemed very determined as he headed down there,' Brian was saying. His jaw tensed. 'Holding on to my daughter's hand as if he had every right to. It made me sick.'

I turned back to the beach. The sky had clouded over now and even though the rocks were still clear I knew there would only be another hour of daylight before the sun disappeared. Surely they would be back before it was dark? 'I still don't understand any of this,' I said. 'You're telling me you watched them this morning. That you followed them to the beach and you let him take her in a boat and did nothing to stop them?'

'I've been watching the house all night, Harriet,' Brian said calmly. 'I got home yesterday and found you gone. When you still weren't back two hours later I had a feeling you were on your way to find them. But when I got here last night there was no sign of you.' He turned to me, expecting me to tell him where I'd been, but I didn't answer. 'I saw him, though. Clear as day through the window, sitting in that armchair. I sat in my car and waited for you. All night I waited but you didn't show up. I was beginning to think I'd got it wrong.'

'If you knew Alice was in the house, how could you just sit there watching it?'

'Like I'm telling you, Harriet,' he snapped. 'I was waiting for you.'

I stared at him, incredulous.

'Do close your mouth, Harriet,' he said. 'I could see Alice was safe this morning. There was no need for me to rush in. Not when I was still certain you would be along soon. And here you are.' He reached out to stroke a hand through my hair. 'You came in the end.'

I pulled out of his way. He hadn't seen his daughter in two weeks, he'd believed she'd been abducted for the most part, and yet once he knew where she was he was happy to let her wait until he got what he wanted: me.

'I knew she was OK,' he growled, as if guessing my thoughts. 'If she was in any danger I would have got her, so don't try and make out I'm not a good father.'

'Oh my God,' I muttered under my breath. Brian stepped closer and took hold of my wrist. I winced as pain shot through it and up my arm from where he'd grabbed me when we ran out of the house.

'You weren't there, Harriet,' he said, his words ice-cold as his eyes flashed brightly. 'And I need you to realise you can't take our daughter away. You have to know you can't leave me, Harriet.'

When Brian let go of my arm I rubbed the tender spot as I flexed it up and down. Who knew what damage he had done? An X-ray might show me that, but it would never tell the real story. The one that lay deep beneath the skin where the scars are invisible.

Brian began walking along the clifftop, towards the path that led down to the beach. 'I don't know why you let them get in the boat,' I shouted as I followed him. He ignored me but I knew it would have been his fear of the water that stopped him going any further. 'So what did you do when they'd gone? Why didn't you come looking for me?'

'I waited for them to come back,' he called behind him. 'I didn't think they'd be long.' Brian started making his way down the path and I stayed close behind. He stopped and turned back to me. 'Over five hours I waited before I came back to the house and saw you. They shouldn't have been gone that long, should they, Harriet?' he said, his eyes drifting over my face as if he wanted to see my panic.

I shook my head. 'No,' I said quietly, 'they shouldn't.' I had no idea what my dad thought he was doing. All I knew was this morning she was safe and all I could hope was that he was looking after her like I believed he would be.

'So what happens now?' Brian asked. 'We go home one big happy family?'

'Yes,' I told him. 'We can do that.' Whether he was serious or not, I'd take the bait. 'We can, Brian,' I said again. 'We need to talk about what we do next.'

I'd do whatever I had to do to make sure Alice was never out of my sight again. I'd stay with Brian forever if it meant he wouldn't tell the police.

He laughed softly. 'You really think I believe that? That you'll walk straight back into our life together? Jesus, Harriet. How stupid do you think I am?' His dead eyes bored through my pupils, into my head where he could always see everything that was going on. And then he turned on his heel and began down the path again.

Finally we reached the bottom and arrived at the lane. Brian strode off towards the slipway that led to the beach. The tide had come in and was now covering nearly all of the sand. I wondered if it could come in further still. I'd been to coves like this and seen the sea wash straight over the rocks, hitting the walls beyond when it was stormy.

To our left the rocks stretched ahead of us but they were clearer now and as soon as we started down the slipway we could both see the jetty and a little fishing boat that must have been there all along.

'Is that it?' I cried. My legs felt like jelly as Brian grabbed my wrist again and began pulling me towards the rocks. 'Brian, is that the boat?' I believed it must be by the way he hauled me towards it. I strained to see past him and could just make out the outline of a figure in the boat.

As desperate as I was to see Alice, it was still a struggle to keep up with him, but then the nearer we got the more visible the figure became until I was certain it was my father.

'Dad!' I cried, clambering over the rocks towards him. He looked up as he stepped out of the little fishing boat that bobbed on the water, glancing at Brian and then turning to me, his face dropping in shock.

'Where's Alice?' I shouted when I could see no sign of her. Brian's grip on my arm tightly squeezed my flesh. 'Where is she?' Panic coursed through me, my legs buckling beneath me. We had reached my dad now and it was clear Alice wasn't in the boat.

'Alice is fine.' My dad stepped forward as we reached him. 'Harriet,' he assured me, 'she is fine.'

'Where is she?' I shouted again. 'She's not with you so what have you done to her?'

'Harriet, I haven't done anything.' His eyes sought Brian out and then flicked nervously back to me.

'Dad, will you just tell me where she is,' I said urgently. The need to hold her in my arms and know she was safe had become unbearable.

'He's been here all night,' my dad said to me, his eyes wide with fear. I felt Brian tense at my side. So my father had seen him. He'd have known Brian was watching the house. No wonder he looked so frightened; he must have been worrying all night about what Brian would do. But that could all wait. Right then I needed to see my daughter.

'Alice!' I cried out and when my dad turned to his left I followed his gaze towards a bundle of blankets on the rocks. I stepped forward but Brian, still holding on to my arm, yanked me back. Reminding me he was there.

'She's sleeping,' my dad said as the bundle stirred. 'I took her out for the day because I didn't know what else to do. It's been a long day and she fell asleep so I just laid her there while I finished up on the boat.'

'Alice!' I called out again, trying to pull away from Brian whose hold remained resolutely tight on my arm. I turned to tell him to get off me, noticing the way Brian glared at my father. He wasn't even looking in our daughter's direction.

'Mummy!' a voice came from behind me and, when I looked back, Alice was sat upright and pushing herself to her feet.

'Alice, oh my baby.' I held out my arm as far as I could reach but already Brian had pulled me back again, sidestepping around me, until he was between me and my dad and my little girl who was now carefully picking her way over the rocks towards us.

'Let me get to her,' I cried, but Brian wouldn't budge.

I watched her finding her footing in bright-pink wellington boots that I'd never seen before. In my desperation to touch her and hold on to her I tried to wrench away from Brian but lost my footing and stumbled.

'Mummy!' she called out again, panic rising in her voice.

'I'm OK,' I called back. 'Mummy's OK.' I was but the searing pain shot through my wrist once more.

I needed to hug her, tell her I would never leave her again, but I also knew there was no way Brian would let me get to her right now, and I had to go carefully. He held too many cards in his hand and could still make sure I lost everything.

Beside him my dad glanced nervously between me and Brian. He was rooted rigidly to the spot. Brian began edging towards him. Still he didn't look at Alice.

'Dad, you should go,' I said.

But my father didn't move. 'He was here all night,' he said again. 'Just watching.' He sucked in a breath and held it tightly.

'Please,' I urged. 'Just go.' He was never going to win any fight with Brian, who continued to stare coldly at my dad.

When Dad eventually took a step back he said to me, 'I meant what I said, Harriet. My one condition – you remember that, don't you?'

I nodded, praying he'd walk away, when his footing faltered on the rocks and I saw a flash of the fragile, old man he'd become since I'd last seen him. My heart fractured at the sight of him trying to stop himself from falling over. Automatically I held out my free hand to steady him but, before I could reach, Brian pushed me back and lurched towards my father.

I stumbled back on the rocks again. Alice's cries filled the cold air. Brian continued to ignore his daughter as he grabbed for my dad, clasping his hands around his neck.

'No!' I cried out as Alice screamed louder. 'Let go of him, Brian.'

But Brian wasn't listening. Amid Alice's screams and my own yelling I couldn't tell if Brian was saying anything to him or not as he shoved him backwards. All I could see was the terror in my dad's eyes as Brian lunged for him and propelled him to the rocks.

'Leave him alone,' I cried. 'This isn't his fault. Please. He's an old man, Brian.'

My dad steadied himself but Brian held out a hand to block me from getting to him or Alice. I was helpless as I watched my father place his hands carefully in front of him, trying to get back up. Alice stood shaking and crying, 'Mummy, make him stop.'

But Brian wouldn't stop. I knew that. His back formed a solid wall between us and he had shut us all out.

Slowly my dad pushed himself unsteadily on to his knees and eventually to his feet, holding his hands up in surrender as he struggled to catch his breath.

'Brian!' I begged. 'Please don't do anything to hurt him.' I tried pulling Brian away but he thrust his arm backwards and pounced once more, catching my dad off guard as he sank his thumbs into my father's neck.

Horrified, I watched the fear in my father's glassy eyes and the skin on his thin neck rippling around Brian's fingers where they dug into his throat. 'Don't do anything stupid,' I sobbed. 'Please. We can all just go home.'

'You must know that can never happen now,' Brian roared, and with one last push he flung my dad to the rocks with such force that I heard the back of his head crack.

There was a moment of pure silence before the air was filled with screams. By then I could no longer tell whose they were: mine, Alice's – they blended together and rose deafeningly above us.

There was no sound from my dad who lay motionless as Brian swiftly turned away from him and back to me. His breaths were deep and quick, his eyes so dark they were almost black. Every muscle in his body was tight and I knew he was still ready for a fight. I could see how much he wanted to hurt me for what I had done.

Alice had now lulled into a whimper. I too had stopped shouting and the beach was eerily silent once more except for the rhythmic lap of the waves as they hit the rocks.

Brian's eyes didn't leave me. They devoured me, absorbed me. I could see his mind working overtime, wondering how he had lost me and what he would do about it. Then he seized hold of my injured arm and began dragging me towards the jetty. I called to him to stop. I reached for Alice as he swept me past her but I couldn't touch her.

'Brian, what are you doing?' I looked back at my little girl, her lips quivering in fright as she stood frozen to the spot.

He ignored me as he continued to push me towards the boat, though he paused when he reached it and I caught his flicker of indecision. Surely he wasn't planning on getting in? What could be going through his mind to make him put his greatest fear to one side? It was a terrifying thought.

'Brian, stop this,' I said urgently. 'We can't leave Alice. You don't want to get in that boat.'

But Brian knew he had lost control and somehow he needed to claw it back, even if he wasn't sure how. He shoved me into the bottom of the boat. 'Alice will be fine,' he muttered.

I scrabbled to get back out but Brian pushed me into the corner. 'We can't leave her here,' I cried. 'And my dad needs help. Brian, you've got to stop.' My father lay motionless on the rocks. Alice had inched towards him.

'Brian, stop!' I tried hauling myself up, grabbing on to his shirt, gripping handfuls of the cotton and crumpling it into balls.

He ripped his shirt away from me and with one hand untied the rope that held the boat to the jetty then turned on the engine, which burred into action. Winded, I pulled myself up and lurched towards the side of the boat but now he had hold of my ankles and, as much as I tried to lever myself forward, his strength overpowered me.

Slowly we started to move away from the rocks. Alice's arms hung limply by her sides, her little pink boots pointing inwards, her mouth open wide – and in that moment I had never hated him more. Never before had I such an intense desire to hurt my husband.

With everything I had in me I prepared to swing round and push Brian away, when I saw a figure running down the slipway. Briefly halted in my tracks I watched the figure running closer until I could make out the long grey cardigan and the skinny jeans, the ponytail swishing behind.

Charlotte?

My breath caught in my throat, relief washing over me as the woman I now knew must be Charlotte turned in Alice's direction. My hesitation meant we were drifting further away from the shore. If she was calling out I couldn't hear her, yet Alice must have because she'd looked away from the boat and had started carefully climbing towards her.

I pressed a hand over my mouth to stifle my sobs. At least my daughter was safe. And they'd call an ambulance for my dad, who as far as I could tell was still not moving.

Brian's hold on my ankles loosened. I glanced behind me and watched him staring out towards the horizon, presumably unknowing that Charlotte was there. If I acted quickly I could escape his grip and jump out and swim back to the rocks. The water was shallow and it wasn't far. In minutes I'd be back with my daughter.

But Charlotte was there now. And I knew that if I did leave him he'd follow and make sure it was over for me. I wouldn't ever get away with what I'd done.

Trapped in a moment of indecision, we continued drifting out to sea. Each wave we bobbed over made the boat wobble, which in turn caused Brian to grab hold of the edge.

Back on the beach Charlotte and Alice's silhouettes were fading into the distance. The light was dimming too now.

Soon it would disappear completely. Already the sea was turning an inky black.

I considered that one way or another it was all over for me. Likely I would pay for what I'd done and I figured that if there was any slim chance of staying out of prison then maybe I shouldn't leave Brian again.

And as I contemplated the idea of staying in the boat I reminded myself that I surely had the upper hand on the sea. Because I could swim. And he couldn't.

Charlotte

Charlotte wrapped herself tighter around Alice to keep the little girl warm. For two weeks she had felt responsible for Alice's disappearance and now here she was holding her in her arms, breathing in her smell as Alice's head nestled into her chest. The relief was so intense Charlotte had to force herself to keep from sobbing. Alice was frightened and Charlotte knew how much she needed to keep it together for her, yet it was getting increasingly hard.

'Where's Mummy gone?' Alice asked again. 'When's she coming back?'

'Soon,' Charlotte told her. 'I promise you she'll be back soon.' She didn't want to think about what was happening out on that tiny boat or where Brian was taking them. She looked down at the little girl whose body shivered against hers and pulled her closer. When she looked up again the boat had disappeared completely.

'Is Grandpa going to be OK?' Alice asked.

Two paramedics now crouched on the rocks ahead of them. She couldn't see Les beyond. 'They're doing everything they can,' she whispered into Alice's hair. She had to admit it didn't look good.

Ten minutes earlier Charlotte had arrived at Elderberry Cottage and was met by a woman who looked as confused as she felt. 'Oh hello, I was looking for a friend but maybe I've got the wrong address.' Charlotte leaned back to see if there was a house name, but she was sure the weathered sign at the front read 'Elderberry'.

'Who is it you're looking for?' the woman asked. Behind her heavy, dark fringe and thick-rimmed glasses Charlotte could barely see her eyes. 'I own the cottage but I have a guest staying here at the moment.'

'Erm,' she stumbled. She had no idea what Harriet's father was called and knew she shouldn't risk getting into conversation about him.

'I've got a Les Matthews here – is that who you want?'

'Yes,' she said cautiously. 'This is Elderberry Cottage?'

'That's right. He wasn't here when I turned up earlier. I only came by because Glenda called and told me there was someone funny lurking around last night. Glenda lives in the house on the corner.' The woman pointed up the lane in the direction from which Charlotte had come. 'She's nearly ninety.'

'Oh. Right.'

'We don't get lurkers. No one comes up here. I told Glenda it would be nothing but I promised her I'd check anyway. To be honest, I don't think she likes me renting the cottage out. She'd rather have someone permanent living here, but what can you do?'

'I don't know,' Charlotte said.

'That's why I always feel like I have to come and check these things out whenever she calls me but—'

'I'm really sorry to be rude,' Charlotte interrupted, 'but I do need to find my friend. Can you tell me how I can get to the beach?'

'The beach?' The woman looked at her watch. 'It's gone half eight; no one will be down there this time of night.'

'I'd like to check, as he's not at the cottage. Can I get down that way?' She pointed towards the clifftop.

The woman shook her head. 'No. It's far too dangerous to use the path at night. You won't be able to see where you're stepping. You're best going back down the lane and through the village by car if you really want to be going to the beach. But the tide will be in, mind. There won't be much of it left.'

Charlotte thanked her. She would have preferred to get back into the car and drive home. Darkness was encroaching and the lanes weren't lit, but she knew she'd never forgive herself if she didn't at least look for Harriet on the beach.

She turned the car round in the narrow lane, careful not to hit the woman's Land Rover that was haphazardly parked in front of her, and drove back the way she'd come, turning right into the village and following the signs to the beach.

As soon as Charlotte saw Alice standing on the rocks she realised it was her, but relief soon passed when she noticed the fishing boat with the two figures in it, slowly drifting out to sea.

She climbed on to the rocks, yelling out Alice's name. The little girl turned round, tears streaming down her cheeks. 'Alice, it's me, Charlotte. Come this way.'

Gradually Alice took small steps towards her until Charlotte reached her and pulled her into her arms.

'Daddy took Mummy into the boat,' Alice cried. 'And he hurt Grandpa. He threw him down on the rocks,' she sobbed as she pointed a finger towards where he lay.

'Jesus,' Charlotte exclaimed when she saw him. She took a step towards the body but didn't want to get too close with Alice gripping her tightly. Reaching into her pocket, Charlotte pulled out her phone and dialled 999. 'Ambulance and police,' she said urgently, when the call was answered.

The police and paramedics turned up and, once they'd obtained brief details from Charlotte, called the coastguard. It hadn't crossed her mind to ask for them too and she berated herself, hoping they would get there fast because already the light was taking with it her last dregs of hope that Harriet would be OK.

Charlotte talked to Alice to drown out the noise of the two police officers and their radios, hovering nearby.

'When the lifeboat gets here it'll go straight to find your mummy and bring her back,' she said. As Alice hadn't mentioned her dad, Charlotte didn't either. 'Now, tell me about what you did in Cornwall.' She tried keeping their minds occupied though her own kept drifting to Harriet.

She'd told the police Harriet couldn't swim. Had shouted it to them as they made their call to the coastguard. Alice had looked up at Charlotte strangely and she'd told the little girl not to worry, that her mummy would be fine. She should never have said anything in front of her.

But Alice had continued to look at her, puzzling over something.

'What is it?' she'd asked. But Alice had shrugged and didn't answer so she didn't pursue it.

'I don't want Grandpa to die.' Alice's voice now was so small she could barely hear it. Charlotte couldn't get the picture of his body out of her head, skewed at an angle it definitely shouldn't have been in.

She looked over at the paramedics and wondered what was happening; then at the policemen, who'd question her shortly. And when they did, she'd have no choice but to tell them the truth.

Harriet

Brian's face was screwed tight as he steered the boat into the darkness of the sea. I thought it was rage that drove him on, but each time he turned I caught glimpses of his eyes that were now no more than dead, black holes.

There was nothing left of him. An empty carcass of the man I met, the one I'd allowed to control me since. Brian knew he'd lost me but this meant he had nothing left to lose.

My poor, tragic husband. So coiled up in his own world where there was no room for anything but me. Not even Alice. His own daughter came nowhere close to the so-called love he had for me. I'd seen that tonight more than ever before.

I needed to at least try and talk him down from whatever he was planning. Though I doubted even he knew what that was.

'Brian,' I said gently, arching my back as I bent my knees beneath me. 'I don't think you want to hurt me, you love me too much for that.'

'Love?' He laughed softly. His shoulders tensed as his right hand curled around the edge of the boat. 'There's no love left,' he said quietly, his focus fixed on the fading horizon ahead of us.

'What are you planning to do?'

'Shut up, Harriet.' His body tightened, his hand gripped harder on to the side.

'I know you don't want to lose me,' I said. After all, he'd had his chance to call the police at any point over the last twenty-four hours. Brian could have already ensured I'd pay for what I'd done; he could have had me locked up and away from Alice, just like he was always telling me.

Only I knew now he wouldn't have done that. He didn't want Alice without me. Taking my daughter away was never more than a threat to ensure I stayed with him.

I wasn't sure he'd throw me out of the boat and save himself but I was beginning to wonder if he planned for us both to go. As I looked back at the shore, I could no longer make out any figures but, as the blue lights arced in the sky, I knew help must have arrived. It was a relief that my dad would be taken care of, though I was also aware the police would be questioning Charlotte. They'd know what I'd done by now.

I slumped back against the side of the boat. Was it all over? I couldn't let it be. I had to find strength from somewhere.

'Brian,' I started, 'we need to go back for Alice.'

'I told you to stop talking,' he snapped.

'I know you love her,' I went on. Not in the way you'd want your child to be loved but still I was certain he didn't want to hurt her. 'Imagine how scared she must be.'

'I said shut up.' He swung around to face me. The boat tipped to one side, rooting Brian to the spot, and I saw his fear again – the precariousness of balancing on the water he so dreaded. 'Don't say another word,' he hissed, slowly turning back towards the horizon.

I didn't speak. Instead I crawled deeper into the bottom of the boat and watched him closely, imagining the sensation our situation had caused. The franticness of the officers and paramedics on the beach, the questioning, putting it all together. In contrast, it was entirely peaceful out at sea. By then the sun had slipped away and, other than the intermittent blue lights, it was getting harder to see.

We continued to drift further away into nothing. I no longer looked back at the beach. I told myself a lifeboat would soon be on its way. Shortly it would race down the slipway and into the water, gathering speed as it approached us. Would they reach us in time?

I hugged my arms tightly around myself. Now the sun had disappeared it felt so much colder. I buried my head into my knees, biting a finger to stop my teeth from chattering.

What if it didn't reach us? What if one hadn't even been called? There was no way of knowing for sure. My life hung in Brian's hands, as it always had, and as renewed fear bled through me I knew that somehow I had to take back control. I couldn't give up. What kind of mother would that make me?

I shuffled my legs beneath me, pulling my finger out of my mouth where my teeth had been clamping down harder than I realised.

I couldn't trust Brian. I was sure he didn't trust himself any longer and if I let him continue dragging us out into the black sea he would win. I had to stop him once and for all. But did that really mean I had no other choice than the thought that had begun rooting itself in the corner of my mind?

Quietly I pushed myself off the bottom of the boat and, still crouching, on to my feet. I had the upper hand, I reminded myself. Brian couldn't swim and he didn't know I could. I repeated the words inside my head until they drowned out the part of me that knew what I was thinking was preposterous.

My heart pounded heavily as I rocked on to the balls of my feet. As soon as I stood I would have to lunge forward quickly and catch him off guard but I feared my legs wouldn't move me fast enough. Even as my mind formulated my next steps, I still couldn't believe I was capable of what I was about to do.

Taking a deep breath, I pushed myself up and leapt towards Brian, my hands grabbing on to his shirt. The boat rocked and Brian whipped around, his own hands reaching for my arms to steady himself.

'What are you—' he began to scream, and with every bit of strength left in me I pushed him backwards towards the edge of the boat.

I knew that, whatever happened, Brian would keep his promise that he would never let me go. If he went over the side, I would too.

His eyes flicked between me and the water beneath us that stretched for eternity. I filled my head with thoughts of Alice waiting for me. Brian's would be filled with the dread of falling into the icy darkness that lay no more than an arm's stretch away, and with that image I thrust forward, and together Brian and I toppled into the water.

The sea was ice cold, stinging my skin the moment I hit it. With every breath I took, pain shot through my chest. Brian's eyes widened as he followed, his arms still grappling to keep hold of me. As he opened his mouth to scream he bobbed under the surface, his mouth filling with water before he rose back up, choking and spewing it out.

I saw the horror burn its way deeper inside him as he struggled to hold on to me. He knew he would go under again, and was prepared to take me with him, but his hands shook on my arms and already I felt them loosening.

It was a bittersweet moment as my husband thrashed wildly, his limbs flailing uselessly, as I kicked my legs as strongly as I could to tread water.

Still holding on to me, when Brian submerged he pulled me down too. I had already inhaled a deep breath but he somehow managed to tighten his grip again and his frantic kicking took us deeper.

I needed air and, as I pushed us both back up to the surface, I wondered how many times I could allow him to take me down again.

The beam of a flashlight curved in the sky above us, closer than the lights from the beach. It had to be a lifeboat and, when Brian's panicked eyes followed my gaze, searching for signs of help, it hit me how someone who might have been so prepared for us both to die looked like he wanted nothing more than to live.

I had the power, I told myself again. He had none any longer.

I felt a fleeting pity for my husband. There were two things he'd been so scared of all his life: being left to drown and losing me. In some ways it felt like his life was coming full circle.

He didn't deserve to die.

Did he?

The lights were getting closer. The lifeguards would be with us soon.

My heart raced and I looked into his eyes. Cold. Dark. I fell for those eyes once, had thought them powerful and protective, but I had seen them too many times in the years since controlling me. Making me his.

Drawing up my legs as much as I could, I drove them into him, feeling his thighs against my feet as I pushed him away. His hands slid off my arms, his eyes searching mine. His arms thrashed above his head.

Did he realise I could swim? I wondered.

As Brian sank under the surface I waited a few seconds, all the time knowing I could dive under and save him if I wanted.

The tide was slowly dragging me away from him. I counted to five but Brian didn't reappear. Frightened, I swam forward to where the ripple of water spread in swelling circles.

The lifeboat was nearby now; its light swept across the sea catching me in its beam.

Then finally I lay on my back and pushed myself away from Brian. They would pick me up in a moment. By then it would be hard to tell where he was.

Harriet

'Where's your husband?' The lifeguards were understand-ably concerned that they couldn't see any sign of him. I gestured vaguely into the water. I was struggling to breathe; the icy coldness had hit me hard and pain was spreading rapidly through my body.

'Over—' I tried, but it was hard getting the words out. The moment I'd been pulled out of the sea my body started going into shock. I closed my eyes until their voices hovered above me in jumbled whispers. Adrenaline coursed through me but just for a moment I wanted to blank everything out.

The voices made decisions. They would take me back to the beach, they finally agreed; another lifeboat was already on its way. 'Don't worry,' one assured me, close against my ear. 'We'll find him.'

I wanted to tell them not to bother. Brian couldn't swim. He'd be long gone by now. He only felt safe dragging us both out to sea because he didn't think I could swim either. But my breath came short and sharp and I chose to save it.

In minutes we were on the beach, a policewoman helping me out of the boat, wrapping me in a foil blanket. A paramedic ran towards us as emergency lights still lit up the sky like fireworks. Eventually my shaking body began to absorb the warmth and my head started to clear.

'Where's my daughter?'

'She's taken care of,' the paramedic told me, ushering me behind her to the far edge of the beach where an ambulance waited, brightly lit, two or three people milling around it. 'Can you tell me your name?'

I screwed my eyes up until Alice came into focus, sitting in the back of the ambulance. Charlotte was at her side, one arm around her shoulder, while a man in a green uniform crouched in front. His hand waved some kind of instrument at Alice. I imagined I heard her laugh, which made me smile.

'Do you know your name?' the paramedic asked again, slower and louder this time as if I might not understand. Her fingers pressed into my wrist as they searched for a pulse.

'Harriet Hodder.'

The commotion had by now attracted a small handful of onlookers who stood together in a huddle at the top of the slipway, pointing and nodding and drawing their own conclusions about the drama unfolding on the beach. We must have been an exciting addition to their otherwise boring evenings.

'I need to see Alice,' I said.

'And you will in a minute, but we need to make sure you're OK first.' The paramedic fussed around me. 'Do you know what day it is, Harriet?'

'It's Friday. I haven't seen my daughter in thirteen days.'

'I understand, Harriet,' she said to me. 'And you will soon.' She released her grip on my wrist and carefully laid my hand down at my side. The sand was damp beneath me. 'Open your mouth, please,' she asked. I obliged, allowing her to look in then take my temperature until eventually I pushed her away and begged her to let me see my daughter.

The paramedic looked up at the policewoman who stood beside us, silently deliberating for what felt like an eternity. 'OK,' she said finally, though she seemed unsure.

The two women then took an arm each and helped me over to the ambulance. My legs shook as they carried much of my weight. I was weak from lack of food and drink, from the coldness of the sea and the energy I'd used keeping myself afloat.

Alice cried out to me when she saw me coming, pushing herself off the seat.

'Sweetheart!' My voice broke as I pulled away from the women's hands and stumbled the last few metres to Alice, wrapping my arms around her as I sobbed into her hair. The relief of being able to hold her again consumed me. Every other thought ebbed away and in that moment

I didn't consider what had happened to my husband, or what the future held for us. It was enough just to be back with my daughter.

When I finally looked up I caught Charlotte's eye. She was still sitting in the back of the ambulance, contorted forward, anxiously balling the hem of her cardigan in her lap. Tears welled in my eyes at the sight of her. I opened my mouth to speak; I needed to thank her, but surrounded by people what could I say? Charlotte nodded, a small movement of her head, but her expression was pained as she watched me.

A paramedic told me he still needed to check me over but I assured him I was fine, and as soon as he went around the side of the ambulance I turned to Charlotte. 'Thank you,' I said at the same time as she spoke.

'Brian?' she said. 'Is he – what's happened?'

I looked out to sea and shook my head. 'I, erm, they're still searching for him. I think they—' I broke off and bent down towards Alice. 'Are you OK, sweetheart?' I couldn't bear to imagine how much she was taking in.

Charlotte stood up and gestured to the seat. 'Let's lie her down,' she said. 'I think she'd have fallen asleep if she hadn't been waiting for you.' She pulled a rough woollen blanket off the seat and, as I picked Alice up and laid her down, Charlotte draped it over her. Crouching down on the floor beside Alice, I stroked her hair.

'They're going to want to talk to you,' Charlotte said quietly.

I nodded, still watching my baby. Already her eyelids were fluttering. It wouldn't be long until she drifted off; she was obviously exhausted.

'Harriet,' Charlotte said, this time more urgently. 'The police will want to speak to you any moment.'

'I know,' I said, standing so that I was face to face with her. 'What have you told them? Why do they think you're here?'

'They haven't spoken to me yet, but they will and I don't know what—'

'Just say I asked you to come here because I was scared. Say you knew nothing more,' I told her, thinking quickly. 'That way there's nothing that links you. Where's my dad?' I said. 'Is he OK? Is he conscious?'

Charlotte began scratching her wrist until bright-red streaks appeared. I grabbed hold of her hand and held it still. 'He is OK?' I asked again.

'He was unconscious when the paramedics got here,' she said. 'I'm so sorry, Harriet, I know this isn't what you need to hear. He didn't make it. I'm so sorry but—'

'No.' I shook my head manically. 'No, that can't be true.'

'He wasn't in a good way, but he wouldn't have known what was happening or been in any pain and the paramedics did everything they could—'

'No,' I cried out, clamping my hands over my ears so I couldn't hear what she was saying. If I didn't hear it, it might not be true. Just as I'd believed when I'd seen my mum's empty hospital bed.

My father couldn't be dead. Not when I had so much I needed to say to him.

'Harriet.' Charlotte was taking hold of my hands, prising them away from my ears. 'You need to be careful,' she whispered urgently. 'There's too many people nearby.'

'But I haven't told him I'm sorry,' I sobbed. 'He'll never know.'

He'd never know that if I could turn back time I would in a heartbeat and I'd go back to the day he walked into my life again. And this time I would never have asked what I did of him. I would never have put him in a position where he couldn't say no.

Grief balled in the pit of my stomach, expanding with every tight breath I inhaled. Not my dad. Not the man who'd risked his life for me and Alice. This was all my fault and now it was too late and there was nothing I could do to make any of it better. 'He only took her to keep us safe.'

'Harriet!' Charlotte said. 'You can't do this. Someone will be watching.'

I knew what she was telling me. The police would be monitoring my every action. I wasn't supposed to show remorse for the man who had taken my child. But I couldn't help myself. Bile rose into my mouth so quickly, so forcefully, that, before I could stop myself, I threw up outside the back doors of the ambulance.

Charlotte's arms were around me, stroking my hair, making me sit down on the seat next to Alice who had thankfully fallen asleep already. How much I wanted to lie down with her, have sleep take me away too. Turn this into nothing more than a bad dream.

'You cannot break down. He took your daughter, remember,' she said so quietly only I could hear.

'But it's all my fault,' I whimpered. She knew that, of course, but still she continued to stroke my hair and tell me I needed to pull myself together.

Yet the pain wrenched at my insides, tugging them apart, scrunching them back together again haphazardly until they felt like they weren't a part of me. A searing heat spread through me like fire until I could feel nothing else.

I couldn't let them think my father was responsible. Not now he was dead. I lifted my head up, surveying the sight around me. Taking in the chaos, the panic, the pain. Everyone was only here because of me.

'How can I live with myself if I don't tell the truth?' I murmured.

'Harriet, look,' Charlotte snapped, turning my head to the left. Alice was curled up in the shape of a peanut. Her breaths slow and deep. Oblivious – as she should be. 'How can you live with yourself if you do?'

I couldn't understand how, after everything I'd done to her, Charlotte was trying to protect me but I never got the chance to ask her why. Or indeed whether she would be prepared to lie for me. At that moment a police officer appeared at the back of the ambulance, introducing herself as DI Rawlings, and while she murmured condolences for nothing specific she went on to ask both Charlotte and me to accompany her to the station where she and her colleague would like to ask some questions. Another officer would stay with Alice, she assured me as she led me to the car waiting at the top of the slipway. I never got the chance to tell Charlotte how sorry I was before she was led in for questioning. And I never got the chance to ask how far she was prepared to go.

NOW

From the moment my dad agreed to what I'd asked of him, I'd always known there was every possibility I'd one day find myself lying to the police. I tried convincing myself he would get away with hiding Alice for me and did my best not to think about the many ways it could go wrong but I knew, of course I knew, how easily it could.

Sometimes I imagined myself in a police interview room – my only idea of them conjured from TV dramas – and I'd be sticking to my story, persuading the investigating officers I had nothing to do with my daughter's disappearance.

What I never considered was that I'd also be lying about murdering my husband.

Was it murder? I left him to die but I didn't actually kill him. Is there a difference? My fingers tap nervously on the table as I wait for DI Lowry to come back into the room. I wonder what the detective was called away for and suspect there must be news of Brian.

Maybe he isn't even dead, I think, my fingers pausing as the door swings open. I move my hands to my lap so Lowry can't see them twitching. Lowry doesn't look at me as he slides back on to his chair and switches the tape recorder on, well-rehearsed lines rolling off his tongue as he announces the interview has recommenced.

I have already told the detective how my husband abused me for years, that he dragged me on to the boat tonight against my will, leaving my daughter alone on the beach. I've told him Charlotte will vouch for this as she found Alice on the rocks.

'What I don't understand, Harriet,' he is saying, 'is why you never thought to mention your dad was actually alive when Alice first went missing.'

I look at him, silenced briefly, because I expected him to continue questioning me about Brian. If Lowry feels uncomfortable speaking about my father like this, now that he is dead, he doesn't show it. But to me his words are fired into the room like bullets, loud and sharp, echoing around my head.

I tell him the truth about my mother's lie, that my husband thought him dead, and add that I never considered contradicting Brian when he spoke to the policewoman after the fete. And when the detective wants to know if I've seen my dad since he left, in the last thirty-four years, I admit he turned up at my door six months ago.

Lowry raises an eyebrow and settles back in his seat, letting my admission linger between us. It isn't the answer he expected. 'Now I really don't understand why you didn't think to mention him,' he says. He is either excited or nervous by the turn his questioning is taking – he certainly didn't think I would so readily admit I'd seen him again, but I have no choice. Alice will tell them she knows him.

'Harriet,' he says, pressing closer to the tape machine. 'Did you know your father had taken your daughter from the fete thirteen days ago?'

I close my eyes and bow my head, inhaling a deep breath, slowly and deliberately.

'Harriet?'

My father made me promise him I'd deny my involvement. Betraying him feels so much more unforgivable now. 'No. I didn't know anything about it,' I say, Charlotte's words reverberating in my head: how could I live with myself if I didn't lie?

DI Lowry crosses his arms and leans back further into his chair, cocking his head to one side as his eyes bore into me.

In the twenty-minute journey from the beach to the police station I'd stitched together a fragile story made from fragments of truths, creating another version of reality that I needed to believe. I may have learned to make up stories when I was younger but it was thanks to Brian that I'd acquired the gullibility to believe anything.

I take another sip of water, swallowing it down loudly, and remind the detective what my husband was like and how scared I was of how he'd react.

'Right. Your husband,' he says flatly. 'Who no one else knew was abusive.'

I ignore his tone. 'My father was the first person I confided in.'

The detective glances at my wrist. I have been rubbing it again; a wide red circle has banded my arm. 'It wasn't physical.' I stop rubbing and gesture with my wrist. 'Though he did grab me tonight. But no, what he did throughout our marriage felt much worse,' I say.

'So what did your father say when you told him?'

I tell Lowry my dad tried persuading me to leave Brian but that Brian had made it impossible. And then I tell him the story my dad came up with when he said he couldn't see me any more. That he'd said he'd moved to France and he was sorry he couldn't do more to help and I tell the detective that I didn't see him again until tonight.

Lowry is still incredulous that I mentioned none of this to the police thirteen days ago. That surely I would have suspected my father could have taken Alice from the fete.

'If I could turn back the clock I would have said something,' I say. 'Of course I wish I had now. I haven't seen my daughter in two weeks.' Tears trickle down my face at the thought of Alice and how desperately I need to be with her again. I wipe them away with the sleeve of my T-shirt. I would change everything if I knew I could save my dad.

'Are you sure there's no news?' I ask him again. 'Has Brian been found?'

*

DI Rawlings folds her hands, one on top of the other, on the table in front of her. Her shoulders are taut, rolled forward; her forehead now has a permanent crease along the length of it. She can't hide her frustration, as much as she tries to.

'I'm sorry, I just don't buy that you didn't know anything about Brian.'

'Christ!' Charlotte falls back into her chair and looks away from the detective.

'What's the matter, Charlotte?' Rawlings's interest is piqued.

'I just can't believe we are still going over and over the same thing. I didn't know,' she says through gritted teeth. 'Harriet never told me about her husband's abuse. I didn't know Harriet as well as I thought I did, I realise that now,' she snaps. 'I don't know why you're trying to make me feel worse about it than I already do.'

Somewhere along the line tiredness has bled into exhaustion. But her heart is thumping, adrenaline feeding her veins, and the more DI Rawlings accuses her, the more Charlotte wants to shout, 'Just bring it on.'

'I'm not trying to make you feel bad,' the detective says, her face still void of emotion. 'I just want to get to the truth.'

'I've been telling you the truth,' Charlotte cries, feeling the blood rush to the surface of her skin. 'And maybe I should have looked harder but the fact is –' she falters '– the fact is if you don't want someone to know, they won't.'

The detective pulls back, her eyebrows pinched, seemingly amused by Charlotte's outburst.

Charlotte's chair screeches across the hard floor as she pushes herself up. She rips open her cardigan and pulls up her T-shirt with one hand, lowering the waistband of her jeans with the other. 'This,' she says, pointing to the puckered red scar on the side of her stomach, 'is what I didn't want anyone to know.'

She lets her T-shirt fall and uses her hand to wipe the tears until they smear across her face. Tom was the only person who knew the truth: that one night her dad's temper led to him ripping the hot iron off the ironing board, out of the socket, catching Charlotte as he swung it around in anger. It might have been an accident but still she never wanted anyone else to know.

'And they never did,' she cries, slumping back into the chair. 'They never did. So don't you dare make out this is my fault.'

'Harriet, I know this has been a distressing night for you but I will tell you if there is any news.' DI Lowry looks up sharply when we are interrupted by another knock on the door. An officer pokes her head around and calls him out of the room again. 'Bloody hell,' he mutters. 'Two minutes,' he snaps, glancing at me.

When he returns he takes his seat and clears his throat, sitting slightly more forward in his chair as his elbows reach out to find the table. 'Let's continue,' he says firmly.

'What's happened?' I ask.

They have found Brian. I know they have. He is still alive and telling them what I did to him.

'Mrs Hodder, I'm the one asking the questions,' he says as he shifts awkwardly in his chair and clasps his fingers together. 'What made you come to Cornwall?'

Another deep breath. Another lump to swallow down. 'I got a note,' I lie. 'It came through the letterbox three days ago.' I lean forward and from my back pocket I pull out the Elderberry Cottage business card I'd written on that afternoon, glancing at it one last time before I push it across the table.

Lowry looks at it and reads it aloud. *'I'm sorry, Harriet, but I'm doing this for you. You're both in danger if you stay.'* He turns the note over and reads out the address. 'So you get this and decide to come to Cornwall and find Elderberry Cottage?'

I nod.

'Without even thinking to mention this to anyone?' He flaps the card in the air. 'Not even the FLO who was practically living in your house at the time?'

'I just needed to get to my daughter,' I say quietly. 'I wasn't scared of my father, I believed Alice was safe, and I was worried that if I told anyone else then something would go wrong.'

Though I'm well aware of how very wrong everything is going.

'How much longer will I be here?' I ask him, draining the last of my water and letting him refill my glass.

Lowry glances at the fat watch on his wrist but doesn't answer me.

'Have you found Brian?' I ask.

He hesitates. 'No, Mrs Hodder,' he says after a beat. 'We haven't found your husband.'

'Oh—' I sink back, trying to make sense of how the news makes me feel. I was convinced they had.

Is he dead? He must be.

Lowry is asking me more questions about Brian and what he did to me, in the same tone that suggests he doesn't believe my story, when all of a sudden a thought hits me.

'My diary,' I say, jolting upright. 'It's in my handbag. I left it—'

Where is my diary? I had taken my bag to the beach because Brian shoved it at me when we were at the cottage. 'I dropped it somewhere.' I shake my head, I can't remember. I must have dropped it when I saw my dad. Maybe it's still on the rocks. Or maybe it's been swallowed up by the sea.

'Perhaps you'd like to take a break, Charlotte?' Rawlings seems keen; she doesn't know where to look.

Charlotte never meant for an outburst. She nods and, once outside the room, turns left and heads for the toilets. The detective walks off in the opposite direction.

When Charlotte emerges from the toilets five minutes later she spots DCI Hayes at the front door, with DI

Rawlings and a man she doesn't recognise. She ducks into a doorway out of sight, where she can only just make out the voices further down the corridor.

'How's it going?' Hayes is asking. 'Progress?'

'I don't know about progress.' Charlotte hears DI Rawlings's voice. 'But I don't think we'll get any more out of Charlotte Reynolds.'

'And Harriet Hodder's convinced the husband's going to turn up,' another voice pipes up. Charlotte leans forward and takes a better look at the short man with wire-rimmed glasses. She wonders if he's the detective who's been questioning Harriet. 'It's rattling her.'

'Rattling her?' Angela suddenly joins them in the doorway and Charlotte pulls back before one of them spots her. 'Do tell me what that's supposed to mean, DI Lowry?'

'Well I believe he'd have a very different story to tell us. One she doesn't want us hearing.'

'Oh, dear God,' Angela cries. 'Are you kidding me? Harriet Hodder is scared. That woman's been abused by him for years. Of course she's rattled.'

'If it's true,' Lowry says. 'We only have her word for it and I'm not sure I believe her version of what happened on the boat.'

'Well, this makes for interesting reading,' Angela snaps. 'She's been writing this diary for the last year.' She falls silent and for a moment all Charlotte can hear is the blood swishing in her ears.

'Yet you didn't pick up on it?' Lowry asks. 'You were in that house almost living with them and you didn't see that side of Brian Hodder?'

Silence again. Charlotte can imagine what Angela must be thinking. None of us did, she wants to tell her. None of us saw it.

'I didn't,' Angela says eventually. 'You're right. At the time I didn't see what he was doing, but look in this notebook. What he did is subtle. Brian Hodder was a clever, manipulative man.'

'Well, whatever happened on that boat, we might never know the truth.' Lowry says.

'Angela?' DCI Hayes speaks her name. Charlotte leans forward again, chancing another glance at the four detectives. Angela is looking the other way. 'Is there something else?' Hayes says.

'Angela?' he asks her again when she doesn't respond.

'No,' she says firmly and looks back at the others. 'Nothing else.' Though Charlotte's sure there is something on Angela's mind.

'Do I need a solicitor?' I ask when Lowry comes back. He has been gone over ten minutes and it's felt like a lifetime, waiting for him, wondering what he'll decide to do next, whether he's going to charge me. My chest is burning with heat and I scratch at the thin cotton of my T-shirt until I feel my skin sting. 'Am I under arrest?'

'No,' he says, though I don't believe he's happy with the outcome.

'Then I can go?'

He nods slowly and watches me warily, as he says, 'Yes. Though we will need to speak to you again. And we'll need to talk to your daughter in the morning.'

I can't believe what I'm hearing. I can go? Does that mean they believe me, or at least have no evidence? Does that mean Charlotte has lied for me?

'There's someone here for you.' Lowry's voice is low and I look up to see Angela in the doorway. I push my chair back and fall into her arms as she wraps them around me and walks me out of the room.

'I'm really free to leave?' I say to her, my words no more than a whisper.

'Yes, you are.' She smiles as she manoeuvres me down the corridor and towards the reception area at the front of the station. 'I'm taking you to a safe house for the night. Alice is already there,' she says as she opens the main door. 'She was fast asleep when I left her.'

Outside the chill of the night air hits me. When we're alone in the car park, Angela turns and says, 'Your bag was found at the beach. I've read your diary, Harriet. Why didn't you tell me what Brian was doing?'

I stare ahead of me. It was my plan for Angela to know what my husband was really like; I needed everyone to see what Brian was doing. 'I wanted to,' I say. 'But I wasn't sure you'd believe me. You had to see him doing it with your own eyes.'

I feel Angela tense and I can't be sure if it's because she fell for Brian's lies too or whether she's still not certain if she can trust me.

'He's very clever,' I say. 'I'd hoped with a bit more time you'd have seen what he was doing. I've no doubt you would have, it's just that things went wrong before then.'

'Did you plug your phone in?' she asks. 'The day it fell into the bath? You were adamant it wasn't you, but Brian was so—' She brushes a hand through the air.

'Convincing?' I finish for her. 'No, I didn't. That was him.'

Angela leads me to the taxi that is waiting at the far side of the car park. 'He killed my father,' I say. 'He attacked him, completely unprovoked.' After everything that has happened I still feel numb. Grief has rooted itself inside me, a part of me now, and it terrifies me that somehow I just need to accept it.

'I'm sorry, Harriet,' she says. She takes hold of my arm. 'I'm very sorry about your dad.'

'I know what everyone will be thinking of him but what he did was out of love for me and Alice.' It breaks my heart to be uttering these words. I have a feeling I will be saying them a lot in the future but I suspect it will fall on deaf ears.

'You know you'll be questioned again, don't you?' Angela says. 'DI Lowry will want to ask you more about what happened on the boat.'

I nod. 'He told me that.'

'It's just – just make sure your story's clear, Harriet.'

I glance at her, questioningly. 'I don't understand.'

'He'll want to dissect what happened at sea between you and Brian.' She pauses as we reach the taxi, resting a hand against its door but not opening it. 'I know you said you couldn't swim,' she says, 'only I did see some things.'

'What do you mean?'

'I saw your swimming costume at the bottom of the laundry basket once,' she says, shaking her head as she goes on. 'Don't answer,' she adds. 'I don't need to know any more.' Angela's eyes drift to my stomach and my hand that is rubbing it in circles. 'I missed that, though, didn't I?' she says.

My breath catches and I look down at my feet.

'How many weeks?' she asks gently.

'Seven,' I mumble. 'There was one night.' I feel the need to explain the time to her. The reason I slept with my husband when the act itself had become such a blessed rarity. I wanted nothing to upset Brian so close to the fete and feared a refusal could have triggered doubts that everything was normal. 'How did you guess?' I ask. 'There haven't been any signs yet.' I haven't felt sick, and so far this pregnancy has been so different to Alice's that often I forget I'm pregnant or wonder whether I still am.

'A bit of a long shot but there was something in your last diary entry. You wrote, "Surely I am doing the right thing for all of us." It's a small detail but it stuck out because you'd have usually written both of you. And you haven't stopped rubbing your tummy tonight,' she adds. 'I was looking for it, though.'

I found out about the baby a week before the fete and, as much as I've tried putting the fact I'm carrying his child to the back of my mind, I knew the timing meant I had to go through with the plan. As soon as Brian knew I was pregnant I would have no chance of escaping him. Especially if it is the son he always dreamed of, the one he always hoped might turn out just like him. I take a deep breath to swallow down the thought as Angela opens the car door for me. I begin to climb in when I spot a figure waiting by the far wall.

'Actually, can you hold on for just a moment,' I say. 'There's someone I need to speak to.'

Charlotte's pale face is lit against the dark sky by the harsh white light flooding the front of the station. Underneath her eyes the skin is red and smudged with make-up. She blinks rapidly as she looks at me and then away and neither of us know what to say but I know I have to find something. 'I can't begin to say how sorry I am; I should never have done what I did.'

'No,' she says plainly. 'You shouldn't.'

Angela is watching us and I angle myself so she can't see my face. 'Thank you. I didn't deserve you coming to Cornwall. I shouldn't have asked—' I stop because even to me my words sound hollow.

'You should have always known I'd have done anything for you. You could have told me what was happening. I was your friend, Harriet. It's what friends do,' she says, her voice tired.

I don't even know what to say. She's right.

'For the last two weeks I've been blamed for losing Alice,' she goes on. 'I blamed myself too. And tonight I've had to listen to them blaming me.' She gestures towards the police station. 'For hours they've been asking me why I didn't know my best friend was in trouble, why I didn't act as soon as you called me this morning, and I couldn't tell them, could I?' She shakes her head and looks away, her eyes glistening wet. 'This evening I still felt guilty, can you believe that? I felt guilty that I hadn't been a good enough friend to you.'

'No. Don't ever say that, you've been the best—'

'Don't,' Charlotte stops me. 'I can't hear it. I just want to get back to my family.'

'I'm so sorry,' I say, reaching out for her, but she moves her arm away before I can touch it.

'I can't forgive what you've done, Harriet,' she replies.

'I understand,' I say, and I do. I truly do, but I can't help thinking this is exactly what Brian would have wanted.

ONE YEAR LATER

Audrey pours a large measure of red wine into Charlotte's glass, cradling her own, as yet untouched. Charlotte waits but she knows Aud has no intention of speaking first.

'I don't know what happened.' Charlotte rubs the stem of the glass between her thumb and finger.

'This isn't the first time,' Aud says. 'You made an excuse to leave Gail's two weeks ago and obviously didn't want to be at book club. But tonight you drove off before you even made it through the door.' Audrey sighs, reaching over the table for Charlotte's hands. 'Talk to me.'

Charlotte takes a large gulp of wine and puts the glass back down on the coffee table, too heavily. *Well, Audrey, here's the thing. I feel like I'm on the brink of a breakdown.*

'There's this black cloud hanging over me,' she says eventually. 'I can't shake it.'

'It's been a year now.' Audrey's tone is a little softer.

'I know, and I realise I should have moved on, but I can't.'

Audrey looks at her quizzically. Charlotte can't expect her to understand when she doesn't know the truth. 'You still feel responsible,' Aud says.

'I don't.' *Not for what happened to Alice anyway.*

'Then I don't get it. You don't like coming out any more. I watch you in the playground and your head's somewhere else completely. Charlotte, look at you. You look permanently panicked. And you've lost weight too,' she says. 'Too much.'

Charlotte picks her glass up, swilling the red liquid around until she almost spills some. It's true, a lot of her clothes hang off her now.

'Talk to me,' Audrey says again.

'You know when everyone found out Alice had been taken by her grandfather?' Charlotte says. 'Within twenty-four hours every one of the people I'd felt had shunned me turned up on my doorstep, each of them telling me how wonderful it was that Alice had been found and how relieved I must be.'

'But you were.'

'Of course I was relieved she was safe but only days before they'd all distanced themselves in some way from me, pulling their kids away from mine. But then they all got a neat resolution, which meant they could brush over what had happened and pretend like it never did. I felt like they were forgiving me.'

'You're losing me.' Aud shakes her head.

'Their forgiveness meant they thought I was guilty in the first place. And they'd been happy to victimise my children because of it too.'

Audrey looks down at her glass but doesn't answer. They both know there's truth in what Charlotte says.

'None of them apologised because they didn't want to acknowledge that they'd acted badly towards me. And I never confronted them. I just let it go.' Charlotte shrugs. 'The elephant in the room is always there, though. The other day Gail started talking about that TV drama, *The Missing*, and I was genuinely interested but then she just suddenly stopped, and looked at me, and it felt like the air had frozen. Someone changed the subject and we were all talking about hairdressers or some other crap and I thought, it's always going to be like this, isn't it?'

'If this is what's eating you up you should tell them how you feel,' Aud says. 'You can't expect them to understand if you don't.'

'Oh, I don't know,' Charlotte sighs. What would be the point anyway? She couldn't tell them everything. She couldn't tell anyone that.

'Is that what this is really about?' Audrey asks. 'There's nothing else on your mind?'

Charlotte leans her head against the back of the sofa. She's often come close to telling Audrey the whole truth, but she's always stopped herself. She wonders how Aud would react if she knew Harriet had set her up and that Charlotte then perjured herself to save the same friend.

Maybe talking to Audrey would help lift the black cloud because recently it's been drawing so close she expects one day to wake up and find it's smothered her completely. It's not easy pretending life has returned to normal.

Yet there are no grey shades with Aud. She'd undoubtedly tell her to go to the police and tell them the truth. Harriet would be arrested and tried, Alice would be taken from her, and what would those same people say then? What kind of friend would that make Charlotte?

No. She made her decision a year ago and she needs to learn to live with it.

'I'm thinking of going to see Harriet,' Charlotte says.

'Good. I never understood why you lost touch, especially when she was so keen to see you.'

'Well, she moved away—'

'Oh, don't give me that again,' Aud says. 'You pulled away from her before she moved back to Kent. You haven't even seen the new baby. Is that why you're going now?'

'That's part of it,' Charlotte says. She doesn't add that the bigger part is to get things off her chest. To ask Harriet about something that's been bothering her since that night on the beach. 'If I go next week, could you have the children?' she asks.

A warm puff of air explodes into Harriet's kitchen as she opens the oven door. She leans in and jabs a knife into the sponges. They look done but she hesitates, her head practically inside the oven, as she decides whether to take them out or give it another five minutes. In the end she closes the door and glances at the clock, stretching her back and rubbing her stomach. It feels knotted. A feeling that comes and goes but it's tighter today, which isn't surprising when Charlotte is due in one hour.

Harriet picks up the baby monitor and holds it to her ear. She can hear a faint murmuring, a heart-warming sound. As she places the monitor back on the windowsill her gaze drifts to the garden where Alice is wandering alongside the small flower bed with a watering can. The letting agent told her the garden was a good size for ground-floor flats in the area, especially so close to the school. The moment she saw the flat she said she'd take it. After the other fifteen, Harriet knew she'd struck gold and wished the agent had shown her this one first.

Moving back to Kent had been an easy decision. They couldn't stay where they were in a house filled with memories where Brian still lingered in every corner. Each morning when Harriet woke the first thing she imagined was her husband lying in the bed beside her. And then the last memory she had of him, in the sea, would flood her thoughts and equally that wasn't a good way to start the day.

There was nothing left for Harriet in Dorset. Nowhere she could take Alice without crushing reminders of what she'd lost. Once she'd stood in the cafe of a National Trust house and felt the world evaporating as the memory of talking to her father in that very same room blinded her. When Alice pulled at her sleeve Harriet looked about her and realised she was crying. A couple were staring at her from their corner table.

In that moment she understood they needed a fresh start, a chance to make new memories rather than reliving raw and painful ones every day. The flat in the tall Victorian semi around the corner from Alice's new school became the perfect base.

Harriet takes a deep breath as a waft of smoke fills the air. 'Oh no,' she mutters, pulling the oven door open. The sponges have crusted around the edges, dark-brown circles that she knows without touching will be crispy and hard. She throws the cake pans on the side and fights back tears.

'Mummy, what's that smell?' Alice comes into the kitchen, her nose screwed up as she drops the empty watering can on the floor.

'I've burnt the cake.'

Alice totters over and peers at the two sponges. 'They'll still taste nice, Mummy.'

Harriet smiles and ruffles her daughter's hair. 'What are you doing in the garden?'

'Watering Grandpa's rose,' she says, matter-of-factly.

'Good girl.' She pauses. 'Have you watered your daddy's too?'

Alice nods and Harriet changes the subject, asking if she'd like a drink. She has no idea if she's doing the right thing when it comes to talking to Alice about Brian. Counsellors advise her not to ignore him, to make sure Alice knows she can talk about her father, ask questions whenever she wants. But she often wonders if it does either of them any good.

Harriet hadn't wanted to get Brian a rose bush. In the garden centre, she'd originally only picked out one with the intention of planting it for her dad. It wasn't until they were at the cash desk when the thought hit her that Alice should have one for her own father. 'Let's go and choose one for Daddy too, shall we?' she said, and Alice followed her back through the store at least three paces behind. Harriet pointed out pretty bushes until eventually Alice agreed to one.

At first Harriet would pick a bud and put it in a bud glass on the windowsill. She told Alice that sometimes they were from Grandpa's bush and sometimes Daddy's but over time she couldn't bear having anything of Brian's in the house and stopped picking flowers from his.

It's only a plant, she would tell herself. But it wasn't. It was a constant reminder that he was out there watching her and one day she feared she'd end up ripping the damned bush out of the ground.

'Do you want to take this outside?' Harriet fills a tumbler of water and hands it to Alice. She still needs to tidy the kitchen and change her clothes and lay out the new napkins with the cake she'd bought as a back-up. Make it all nice.

She hasn't spoken to Charlotte since telling her there would be no trial. By then this was no surprise but the confirmation was still a relief. Harriet understood there was no evidence of her connection. No proof that anyone but her father was involved, whether others believed it or not.

So she ended up letting him take the blame, just as he made her promise to if it all went wrong. And how wrong it went, she thinks, her eyes filling as they are drawn to his rose bush again.

Her dad was only in her life for six months but he managed to change everything. She takes a deep breath and looks about her, reminding herself as she often does that he gave her all this. Freedom: it was all she ever wanted.

Over the last year Harriet has told him many times how sorry she is. She whispers it at night as she curls up in bed and the tears flow down her cheeks. She longs for one more day with him so she could relive all the magic he brought into their lives. They would build sandcastles and eat ice cream when it was cold, and they would laugh. Laugh until it felt greater than any pain.

Harriet presses her hand against the windowpane, covering the view of the rose. She can feel the hole in her heart stretching, tugging, until she forces herself to tear away. She needs to think about the day ahead. Charlotte will be here soon. Her stomach flutters and she allows herself to feel a little excited as she pulls a cloth out and begins to wipe down the surfaces.

Charlotte squeezes the teabag against the inside of the paper cup with a plastic spoon. Fields roll past outside the train window. The carriage was empty until they pulled into the last station where a handful of passengers shuffled in. Now there are at least a dozen of them, including a couple who sit at the far end of the carriage and keep drawing her attention.

The girl looks barely seventeen. She's sitting next to the window and stares glumly out of it. Her boyfriend, who is at least ten years her senior, kicks a battered purple suitcase with a restless foot. Each time his foot bangs against it the girl flinches. Behind his scruffy beard and dark eyebrows there are steely grey eyes that flick around the carriage as if he's expecting or looking for trouble.

Charlotte feels the plastic spoon snap between her fingers and glances down, surprised to find she's broken it in half. She forces herself to turn away from the couple and think about what she plans to say to Harriet. There are many things she's tried ignoring that won't stop haunting her.

At first Charlotte was relieved when Harriet moved back to Kent. She wouldn't have to look over her shoulder every time she went to the park. Not that she ever went to that particular one any more. But then, as the weeks passed, relief turned to anger, which settled in her gut and began to grow. She was angry with Harriet. So full of rage.

The papers called Harriet's story 'tragic' and labelled her brave. Charlotte swallowed down the lies she read, that stuck in her throat, and all the while her rage grew and grew. What made it worse was that she couldn't release it. Instead she had to sit back and accept she'd played a part in turning Harriet into the victim.

Some mornings Charlotte yanked back the curtains, wanting to open the windows and scream. Let the world know that it was her who should have their pity and admiration. Not Harriet. Where were the stories about Charlotte? What had happened to the people who attacked her in the press? None of them retracted their slurs. No one seemed interested in what became of the friend, but then maybe she should be grateful they'd stopped talking about her. And that that awful Josh Gates's story about Jack had never been published.

Yet keeping quiet is suffocating. It feels like it's quite literally drowning her. After Harriet moved Charlotte started imagining the life her old friend is now living: what her house is like, if Harriet's cut her hair, if she has a circle of friends who've accepted what happened to her. She's wondered about it to the extent that she actually hates Harriet for running away and setting up a new life for herself, while meanwhile Charlotte's been sinking lower and lower into her own despair.

She can't move past the fact that she lied to the police, but there's also something else. And if what Alice told her is true then Charlotte needs to know what she's been covering up.

Charlotte sips her tea and checks her watch as they pull into another station. Hers is the next stop, and they're due to arrive in twelve minutes. The train pulls away again and she texts Audrey to check on the children, looking up as the boyfriend at the end of the carriage raises his voice. He calls his girlfriend a stupid bitch and slams his fist on the table in front of them and now she is crying, her shoulders heaving and tears streaming down her face in black streaks from her smudged mascara. The other passengers keep their heads down or stare out of windows except for a lady in her eighties who watches them, shocked by their public display of anger and hysteria. Now he is close up in the young girl's face making her recoil with each word he speaks.

Charlotte pushes herself out of her seat. There was a time when she would have stayed out of other people's business but she can't allow this behaviour. As she strides down the carriage she can feel the nervous glances of the other passengers who likely think she's mad for getting involved. But as soon as she reaches the couple Charlotte stops short. The man has hold of his girlfriend's face but now he's kissing her on the nose and telling her he's sorry and how much he loves her. Choking back her sobs with laughter, she tells him she loves him too. Both of them are oblivious to Charlotte hovering in front of them, about to step in.

She could carry on walking and pretend she was going to the toilet but she can't be bothered with that charade and instead turns on her heel and makes her way back to her seat. An arm reaches out, stopping her in her tracks, and Charlotte looks at the old woman who says, 'You did a good thing there, love. You were the only one prepared to step in.'

Charlotte turns back to the couple. 'I don't think the girl realises she needs help.' She feels angry that he's treating her like this. That girl is someone's daughter and she knows she'd want someone to step in if it were Molly or Evie.

'No,' the old woman says. 'But she will do one day.'

'Maybe I should go back and say something.'

'I wouldn't,' the lady says. 'You don't always know when you're doing more harm than good. If she's not ready for help then neither of them will thank you.'

Harriet's ground-floor flat is easy to find. It's at the end of a pleasant street, where just around the corner there's a small row of quaint shops and across the road a wide expanse of green park with a pavilion and a pond and a children's playground.

Charlotte hovers on the pavement outside. Suddenly the thought of seeing Harriet is far too overwhelming and she needs to force herself up the short path to the front door, ring the bell and wait without running. Her heart is beating hard and she wonders if she might throw up when Harriet opens the door.

Harriet is wearing a long blue dress with a white cardigan over the top of it. Her hair has been cut short and coloured a much richer brown. Her mouth that sparkles with gloss breaks into a small smile as she steps aside to let Charlotte in. Charlotte mumbles a thank you as she passes and is walking through to the kitchen when Alice rushes in, armed with a handful of flowers that she thrusts into Charlotte's hand.

'Oh, goodness,' she says as she bends down to the little girl. 'Thank you.' The tears surprise her. She didn't expect to be so emotional at the sight of Alice who's even taller than Molly now. Her hair has been plaited down the back and tied with a huge yellow ribbon. She is chattering about the garden, something about a rose bush, and now about the new baby who sleeps in a cot next to Mummy's bed, and is asking if Charlotte would like to see her bedroom because she's hung her butterflies in the window.

'I'd love to, maybe a little later?' Charlotte says, straightening up. Alice won't stop talking, excitedly telling her all about school, and now she is pulling a drawing off the fridge that she brings over.

'That's my picture of the school rabbit,' Alice says. 'It's a real one.'

Harriet is drifting around them, filling the kettle and sliding a cake on to a plate that she puts on the small round table sitting snugly in the corner of the room. A pile of muslins are neatly folded on its edge and baby bottles are lined up in a row behind the sink. Charlotte wonders where the baby is as Alice carries on chattering to her.

'I go to big school,' Alice smiles proudly. 'I go every morning five times a week.' She holds up five fingers.

'That's very good counting. Do you like it at your big school?'

Alice nods eagerly. 'The rabbit is called Cottontail and we can hold her at break time and yesterday it was my turn to feed her but do you know you're not supposed to feed them too many carrots?'

'I didn't know that.'

'It's because they have sugar and they can give the rabbits bad teeth. My teacher said that in assembly.'

'You're a bright little button.' Charlotte smiles at her.

'She is,' Harriet says as she comes to stand next to her daughter, resting her hand on Alice's head. 'She doesn't forget a thing,' she adds but in a way that suggests this isn't necessarily a good thing. 'Alice, why don't you take a piece of cake and watch some TV?' As soon as she passes Alice a plate, the girl is out of the room.

'She seems very happy.' Charlotte watches her go.

Harriet nods. 'I hope so. But then you don't always know for sure, do you? Please, have a piece.' Harriet hands her a plate. Charlotte takes it and sits down on one of the seats Harriet is gesturing towards.

'George is asleep,' Harriet says, frowning as she nervously checks her watch. 'He's already been down two hours. He'll probably wake soon.' Charlotte remembers those days like they were yesterday – she can't tell if Harriet's desperate for George to wake up or desperate for him not to. 'I was pleased to hear from you,' Harriet goes on. 'But now you're here I have a feeling this isn't a friendly visit.' She tries to laugh but it is a nervy sound that comes out.

'No, maybe not,' Charlotte admits. 'I'm struggling.'

Harriet nods. 'Because of what you said to the police?'

'That's part of it.'

'Do you think you did the wrong thing?' Harriet's gaze drifts away as she prods a slice of cake with a small fork, sending tiny crumbs flying across the plate.

Charlotte sighs. 'I never thought I was capable of what I did. It makes me feel guilty. And afraid. I'm afraid that one day it will all catch up with me.'

'That can't happen now,' Harriet says.

'No, maybe not, but it doesn't stop me thinking it. I don't even know who I am any more.'

'What do you mean? You're still the same person.'

'No. I'm not,' Charlotte replies flatly. 'I'm not the same person at all. I do things now that are so out of character,' she says. Tom wouldn't believe her if she told him how she'd almost interfered in that couple's argument. 'I'm so far from that person and it scares me because I liked the old me.'

'But what's actually changed?' Harriet asks. 'Your life's still the same. You have the same group of friends and live in your lovely house with your amazing kids. What's so different?'

Charlotte lays her hands flat on the table and fiddles with the corner of a paper napkin. She imagines Harriet buying them especially for her visit and feels a flash of pity for such a futile effort. 'Everything is different, Harriet. None of it is real. It feels like everything I do is a lie and I can't talk to anyone about it. My best friend doesn't even know what I've done.' She doesn't mean to but she finds herself emphasising the words 'best friend'.

'You want to tell Audrey. Is that what this is about?'

'Yes, I'd love to tell Audrey, but that's not what this is about. It's about me feeling so angry all the time. I have this rage inside me that has nowhere to go,' Charlotte says, holding a hand against her stomach. 'Can you imagine how that feels?'

'Of course I can. I felt exactly the same when I was told my dad was dead. I felt that way for most of my marriage.'

Charlotte looks down. She knows how upset Harriet was about her father but that wasn't why she's come here and she refuses to be pulled into Harriet's world today. 'I'm sorry about your dad,' she says. 'But you need to tell me what to do with this anger.' She can feel the heat bubbling inside her. 'I'm angry with you, Harriet,' she says bluntly. 'I'm angry that you seem to have moved on and set up such a nice life for yourself.'

Harriet glances around the room with its tiny window and minimal cupboards, the gas hob with its rings that look dirty no matter how much she scrubs them.

'You have the life you always wanted,' Charlotte says.

'The life I always wanted? What do you imagine my life is?'

'I don't know,' Charlotte admits. 'But you've started again and meanwhile I'm left—' She isn't sure how to finish the sentence.

'You're left what?' Harriet asks.

Charlotte sighs. 'I don't know. Dealing with it all.'

'You think I'm not?' Harriet says. 'Every day I expect to see Brian turn up on the doorstep. I open the door and imagine him standing there, that look in his eyes, his head hanging to one side, and I can hear him as clear as day: "Hello, Harriet. Surprise."'

'That's not going to happen.'

'His body was never found,' Harriet says. 'So it might be unlikely but it's not impossible. The years of dreading him coming home, fearing I'd done something wrong or said the wrong thing. Wondering what I was going to be quizzed about next – none of that leaves me. I don't know if it ever will.'

'Are you telling me that, after everything that's happened, it's no better?' Charlotte asks.

'Of course it's better. But it doesn't turn magically wonderful. I'm happy once I've reassured myself he's not going to walk in the door any moment. Then I breathe again and I go back to living my life with the children. But I'm still dealing with it. And I doubt I have the kind of life you think I lead.' Harriet smiles sadly. 'I don't do much with it but it's fine. It's what we need right now and that's what matters. Alice needs to feel safe. They both do.'

Harriet places her fork carefully on the plate. 'There's not a day passes that I don't look back and wish I could change what happened. But at the time I was so desperate,

I didn't know what else to do. I was living in a trap that Brian created and honestly couldn't see any way of escaping him.'

'But why didn't you ever tell me?'

'It took me a long time to realise what he was doing,' Harriet says. 'By then I felt like he'd convinced everyone around us that I was crazy. When I started writing my notebook I was already wondering if I was myself. I didn't—' She stops.

'You didn't trust me?'

'No, maybe not,' she admits. 'But only because I was so frightened. I didn't trust anyone. I believed him when he said he'd have Alice taken from me and I thought that if I'd fallen for it for years then how could I expect you not to. Can you honestly say you would have taken my word over his?'

'Of course I would,' Charlotte says, but Harriet hears the beat, the moment's pause that's just a fraction too long.

'Do you regret what you said to the police?'

Charlotte looks down at her untouched cake. 'No. Actually I don't,' she admits. 'Because I don't think the alternative was a better option. But there's something else—' Her heart is beating hard. She isn't even sure she wants to hear the answer any more. 'I know you can swim, Harriet. Alice told me when we were on the beach. She said you used to take her swimming but that it was a big secret. She actually told me so I wouldn't worry about you in that boat.'

Harriet continues to look at Charlotte and gives a barely perceptible nod. Her hand is shaking as it grips the fork again.

'What happened to Brian?' Charlotte says as a cry erupts from above them. 'Did you – did it happen on purpose?'

Harriet looks up to the ceiling but doesn't move. The cry stops and she glances back at Charlotte, eyes wide in shock, and now Charlotte really doesn't want to hear her answer.

The crying starts again, this time in a persistent wail, and Harriet pushes her chair back and hurries out of the kitchen. Charlotte slumps back in her seat. She shouldn't have asked.

When she comes back Harriet is holding her baby, tightly swaddled, against her chest and when she sits down she gently peels the blanket away and moves forward so Charlotte can get a better look.

Baby George has a head of dark hair and tiny features and when he opens his brown eyes Charlotte sees the resemblance immediately. The baby is the image of Brian. She hopes she hasn't shown a reaction as she runs a hand over his soft hair but for a moment she can't breathe. 'He's lovely,' she says eventually, because of course he is, whether he looks like his dad or not.

Harriet presses her lips against her son's head and continues to watch Charlotte, who in turn is wondering if Harriet can see the similarities or whether she only sees her son. She prays it's the latter.

'The first time I felt protective over George was when I was on that boat with Brian,' Harriet says. 'Before then I'd tried to ignore the fact I was pregnant. I couldn't imagine bringing another child into our family the way it was.'

Charlotte keeps looking at George as she strokes his tiny head.

'Brian had started controlling Alice too,' Harriet says. 'I couldn't let him do any more damage.'

'I shouldn't have said anything—' Charlotte starts but Harriet interrupts her.

'Tell me what I should have done,' she says softly. 'He could have killed me. He would have taken me from Alice and once he knew he had a son—' She pauses and closes her eyes as she nestles deeper against her son's head. 'Children are our priority, aren't they?'

Charlotte shuffles nervously in her chair, looks towards the door, then back at Harriet and her precious baby.

'Tell me what you would have done, Charlotte?' Harriet murmurs.

'I really don't know,' she says honestly. She'd never have been able to consider that she could be capable of murder, but then being a mother can make you go to extraordinary lengths.

'I know I've asked so much of you already and I have no right to ask any more.' Harriet shakes her head as tears escape from the corners of her eyes. 'But I beg you—'

'Don't,' Charlotte says. Her heart feels as if it's in her mouth. 'You don't have to ask, I'm not going to say anything.'

'Thank you,' Harriet whispers. 'Oh God, thank you.'

*

'Mummy, I'm hungry!' Alice runs into the room and falls against her mum dramatically, dropping a kiss on to her baby brother's head. 'Can I have another piece of cake?'

'No,' Harriet smiles, rubbing her daughter's tummy. 'You'll spoil your tea. Will you stay?' she asks Charlotte.

'Thank you, but I need to get going.' Charlotte pushes her chair back and gets up from the table. She's booked a hotel for the night so she doesn't have to go straight home but for now she needs to be on her own.

'Did you know that when you told me you and Tom were splitting up, I was envious of you?' Harriet says as she gets up too and waits for Charlotte to gather her bag and the flowers Alice had given her. 'I know it sounds mad but it summed up everything I wanted. I was also sad because I knew Tom was a good man but you weren't happy and you did something about it. I craved having the ability to make a choice and live with it.'

'I've started a gardening course,' Harriet goes on.

'Really?'

She nods. 'One evening a week. I have an elderly neighbour who comes to sit with the children. You gave us this security,' she says. 'And I'm sorry for the way I did it, I really am. It was wrong on so many levels but I won't ever stop paying for it.'

Harriet steps aside and follows Charlotte into the hallway. 'I'm glad you came,' she says. 'I miss you.'

Charlotte stops at the door, as Harriet reaches past her to open it. 'I know you're sorry,' she says. 'I do know that.'

It would be so easy to tell Harriet she forgives her. Maybe one day she will, but for today she feels – well, a little bit lighter, she supposes. A little bit more like she can go home to those amazing kids she has and give them a big hug. Tell Aud she wants to dress up and go out for a few drinks, and, sod it, she'll even call Tom and say thank you. Because, even though they didn't make a very good husband and wife, he's been a wonderful friend to her over the last year. She is lucky, she realises. She's always been one of the lucky ones and she doesn't need more than what she's got.

Charlotte bends down when Alice runs into the hallway behind them, allowing the little girl to come crashing into her legs for a hug.

'Alice is doing fine,' she says quietly to Harriet when she pulls herself up. 'She's doing absolutely fine.'

Harriet nods, biting her lip, willing the tears not to start again, though she knows they will anyway.

'Bye, Harriet,' Charlotte says eventually and steps off the doorstep.

'Charlotte,' Harriet calls out. She wants to ask her friend not to go but she knows she doesn't have the right. 'Take care of yourself,' she says.

Harriet watches Charlotte walk away, knowing she has no choice but to let her go. Just like she did with Jane. When Charlotte disappears around the corner she closes the door, thinking it's unlikely she'll hear from her again, but hoping that one day she might.

She can't imagine how Charlotte thought she could be living the life of Riley but then she supposes no one can really understand.

I see Brian watching me from the bottom of the garden, Charlotte.

I see him every time I look into my son's eyes.

Whenever the phone rings I expect someone to tell me Brian's alive, found washed up on some beach.

My father's dead and it's all my fault.

Some nights she wakes up drenched in sweat and reminds herself that, apart from her children, she has lost everyone who has ever been important to her. She tells herself that for some reason she must deserve it and hates herself for what she's done.

Then Harriet creeps into her daughter's bedroom and sees Alice, her blonde hair fanned around her on the pillow, an innocent smile on her lips, and knows in a heartbeat that she'd do it all again if she had to.

And now there is George too. Whose little fingers grab on to her hand, wrapping tightly around her, letting her know she is his world and nothing else is important to him.

She took his father away before Brian knew he'd have the son he always wanted – the boy he hoped would turn out like him – and now she can only hope she's saved her son in time. That there's nothing more in George than his father's brown eyes, but only time will tell her that for sure.

403

'Mummy?'

Harriet is still standing by the front door when she feels a hand on her arm. She looks down at Alice.

'What's for tea?'

'Oh honey, I don't know. What would you like?'

'Pizza. Have you been crying?'

Harriet rubs her sleeve across her face and smiles at Alice. 'Mummy's fine,' she says. 'Didn't we have pizza yesterday?'

Alice looks at her in the way she does when she knows something isn't right. 'Grandpa let me have pizza every day at the cottage,' she says quietly. 'Are you happy sad?'

'Yes,' Harriet laughs. 'I'm very happy to have such a wonderful daughter.' She crouches down and pulls Alice into her. 'I'll make you a sandwich in a minute.'

'And ice cream too? Grandpa also let me have ice cream every day.' Alice pulls her head away. 'You're making my hair wet, Mummy.'

'I'm sorry!' She laughs through her tears as she tickles her daughter. She hopes Alice won't ever stop talking about the two weeks she spent with her precious grandpa.

'Mummy, can we paint a picture?' Alice asks. 'Can we paint a big seaside to go in my room?'

'My darling,' she says. 'You can do absolutely anything you want to do.'

ACKNOWLEDGEMENTS

When I began writing this book I had no idea how it would end, whether it would be any good or even if I'd finish it. I just knew I wanted to write it and if no one else liked it, well then I suppose I would have started something new. It's been a three-year journey and one that's had a few bumps along the way, but it's thanks to many people that I've been able to reach this point. I know without doubt I wouldn't have succeeded without them.

I can clearly remember the day Harriet and Charlotte's story started as a seed of an idea. Holly Walbridge, that was down to you. Thank you for endlessly listening during trips to the park as I made you think dark thoughts about how it would feel if your children went missing. I hope I haven't scarred you!

The idea then turned into a first draft and I owe huge thanks to Chris Bradford, who let me quiz him about all things police related, and for directing me towards an alternative – much better – ending than the one I'd originally written. Chris, your knowledge is immeasurable, and any mistakes are entirely my own.

I am very lucky to have such amazing friends who not only read early copies of my book but also read subsequent ones, and under very tight deadlines! Donna Cross and Deborah Dorman, you're the best. Thank you for reading so quickly and for your invaluable feedback. And as ever, Lucy Emery and Becci Holland, who read early copies and who are always there with support. To all my other friends and family who have shown a huge interest in what I am doing – it means so much to be asked how the book is going and to see your genuine excitement when there is good news.

To my wonderful group of writers who have become lifelong friends: you picked me up when things weren't going so well and celebrated with me when they were. Cath Bennetto, Alexandra Clare, Alice Clark-Platts, Grace Coleman, Elin Daniels, Moyette Gibbons, Dawn Goodwin and Julietta Henderson – writing would not be the same without you all.

Then along came Nelle. You picked my book off the slush pile and told me we were going to work hard and, yes, we certainly did! It took a year of rewrites until I finally heard you utter those magical words – *your book is ready to fly*. Nelle Andrew, I would not be allowed enough pages to harp on about how fantastic you are. I could not have wished for a bigger champion. Thank you so much for believing in me and for taking me on this incredible journey. And big thanks also to the wider team at PFD including my wonderful step-agent Marilia Savvides, and the fantastic rights teams: Alexandra Cliff, Jonathan Sissons, Zoe Sharples and Laura Otal. You have all worked so hard to make this a success.

When we did let my book finally fly I was fortunate that two incredible editors fell in love with it. Emily Griffin at Cornerstone and Marla Daniels at Gallery in the US – I am thrilled to be working with you both. Your observations and direction are spot on and between you, you have taken the story to another level. Also at Cornerstone many thanks to Clare Kelly, Emina McCarthy and Natalia Cacciatore. You have all been so enthusiastic and determined to make this a success.

Finally to my wonderful family. Mum, ever since I was eight you have been telling me I can write and you have never stopped supporting me since. I have never lacked love or encouragement. Whatever choices I have made you have always remained unconditionally by my side and these are things that matter the most. I know how proud you are, and I know how proud Dad would have been too.

My husband John – I probably wouldn't have taken the time to 'see if I could write a book' five years ago if it weren't for you. Your belief in me has not once wavered and I needed this more than I've probably ever told you. Thank you for reading the book nearly as many times as me and for your editorial input. I'm always telling you that you know too much but in this instance I appreciate it! You make me laugh every day and you are the kindest man I could wish to have met. Thank you for being you.

And my beautiful Bethany and Joseph. My proudest achievements ever. You have turned my world upside down and I love you for it. My own words don't do justice to how much I adore you and so I have stolen yours: Bethany, I love you to Pluto and back infinity times and Joseph, I love you more than infinity more times than the universe. Always follow your dreams, my little ones.

**Read and loved *Now You See Her*?
Tell Heidi what you thought.**

Are you #TeamHarriet
or #TeamCharlotte?

#NOWYOUSEEHER

If you enjoyed NOW YOU SEE HER, read
on for an extract of Heidi Perks'
compulsive new novel...

COME
BACK
FOR
ME

Coming summer 2019

EVERGREEN ISLAND

SEPTEMBER 1993

We left in a storm. The sea was rising in sharp clumps of angry waves, rain hitting my feet like bullets. Dad must have known we shouldn't be making the crossing to the mainland, yet he stood on the boat, one hand frantically flapping for one of us to reach out and take it. The hood of his red mac had whipped off his head, the rain plastering his hair to his scalp. He yelled over the wind for us to get in, but we wouldn't move from the end of the jetty.

The boat rocked violently as it tugged at the rope that kept it tethered to the dock, and I noticed Dad's other hand gripping tighter to the steel railing of the steps. 'Get in, Stella,' he shouted.

Thunder cracked overhead and the sky lit up with magnificent streaks of light. Behind me our house flashed bright between the silhouettes of our tall pines, making it look like something from a horror film. I pushed my hands deeper inside my raincoat, clutching Grey Bear harder to my chest. I didn't want to leave the only home I had ever known, but I had never seen my dad so determined. His jaw was set in a flat line, his teeth bared. It wasn't like him to be so persistent, so unrelenting, and I found myself shrinking further back.

'I'm not going anywhere,' Bonnie screamed from beside me. 'We'll all die if we do.' My sister held her hood tightly against her head but I could just make out the haunting paleness of her face in the moonlight. Bonnie had yearned to leave the island for years but this wasn't the way she wanted to go.

'We will not die and we need to go,' Dad yelled back. He turned to me and added a little softer, 'I promise you. It's fine. We'll be safe.' Dad owned the small ferry that he was demanding we board, and he'd run the thirty-minute crossing between Evergreen and Poole harbour every day for the last sixteen years. If anyone could take us to the mainland safely, it was him, but we'd never dared attempt a crossing in weather like this before. Mum wouldn't usually let us out of the house when it was this bad.

'Why can't we wait till morning?' Bonnie was begging.

I stared at the water, its white foam bubbling and spitting in rage. 'Because –' Dad shouted. 'God, will you both just *get in*?' He flapped his hand again, his gaze drifting over my shoulder to where Mum was coming down the jetty. Her head was low, arms tucked inside a plastic poncho as she trailed a suitcase behind her.

'Where's Danny?' he yelled as another flash of lightning lit up the sky, making both Bonnie and me jump. I counted, too quickly, only reaching two before thunder roared overhead. The storm was creeping closer. My brother trailed behind Mum, shrouded in a shapeless black coat that hung over his bulky body, reaching the ground.

Bonnie started shouting again, gesturing at the sea as it rose and dipped, higher and lower than I'd ever seen it go. Another loud crack filled the air and I yelped as the branch of one of the pines fell to the ground beside me. I jumped out of its way as the wind carelessly tossed it along the jetty.

For a brief moment, Dad stopped yelling and stared at the branch. My tears were already bleeding into the rainwater that soaked my face, but my heart broke every time I thought of leaving my beloved island. All I wished was for Dad to realise that whatever we were doing, it wasn't worth it.

'I do think we should wait, David.' Mum's voice was high-pitched, her eyes wide as she looked from him to the water. 'It wouldn't hurt to stay another night. We could leave first thing ... '

We held a collective breath as we waited for Dad to answer. He took his eyes off the broken tree and glared back at her. 'No, Maria. We go *now*.'

'I don't understand,' I cried. Dad was the easy-going parent. The one who allowed another half hour of play or a chocolate digestive even if we'd just brushed our teeth.

'Mum?' I cried, turning to face her. Why wasn't she doing more to stop him? Mum understood more than anyone how much this island was a part of me, that I wouldn't be able to survive without it. She loved Evergreen as much as I did.

She stared back at me, the fear I'd seen only moments ago replaced by a blankness. 'Mum—' my voice trembled as I waited for her to demand we go back to the house, but instead she placed a hand against my back and started moving me towards the steps of the boat. I hesitated at the bottom, but she pushed harder until I eventually had no choice but to get on, ignoring Dad's outstretched hand as I scurried to one of the few benches that sat undercover.

Danny silently followed, sitting behind me, turning his back to stare out of the window. He wouldn't look at any of us, though there was nothing unusual in that.

'I don't want to go,' I cried, searching each of their faces in turn. Only Bonnie looked at me as she settled beside me. Her legs shook against mine and I couldn't remember a time when we had been so close.

Removing the hood of my coat, I looked back at the island through the scratched glass of the boat where the rain still lashed against it. I could have drawn a line right through my heart where it was splitting in two.

Tears continued to trickle down my cheeks as the wind rocked the boat heavily to one side, making Bonnie yelp. I reached out my hands to steady myself, letting go of Grey Bear. Maybe Bonnie was right and we wouldn't make it to the mainland, but for some reason Dad was determined to try. Maybe I no longer particularly cared if the sea swallowed me up.

At eleven I wasn't prepared to accept our parents' hurried reasons for leaving the island. I couldn't believe that this was for good and I couldn't understand one bit why they were dragging us away in the middle of a storm. 'Will we come back?' I whispered to my sister.

Bonnie's hand shook as it reached for mine under my mac. 'No,' she said, 'I don't think we ever will.'

NOW

My clients sit on the sofa opposite me. Her arms are crossed tightly in front of her chest; he is leaning forward, his hands clasped between his widely stretched legs. I could easily fit in the gap between this couple, and in each of their sessions they are moving further apart.

Her jaw is so tense I can almost see it pulsing as she stares at me. I'm surprised she hasn't cried today – she has in every other session. Her husband keeps glancing over at her but she won't look at him. Each time he does, his eyebrows twitch as if he's either wondering where it all went so wrong or what he should do about it.

'I don't know what more to say,' he mumbles and she laughs and shakes her head, mouthing something so quietly I can't work out what it is. 'I'm sorry,' he continues.

'God!' she cries and looks up to the ceiling. Her determination is so resolute I can see her willing the tears not to fall.

I hate this time of the session but already the minute hand has ticked past six. Tanya will be waiting for me to leave so she can close up behind me. Looking after reception means she is always the last one out of the door.

'I'm afraid—' I start but my client interrupts me as she pulls herself out of the chair and grabs the cardigan that hangs limply on the arm.

'I know,' she says. 'Our time is up.'

'I'm sorry,' I say. 'Before you go, is there anything else you want to mention?' I don't like leaving them like this. I would take them both to the pub and let them carry on talking if it was etiquette.

'I think he's said enough today, don't you?'

Her husband chews on the corner of his lip but doesn't look up at her as he stands, turning the other way to reach for his jacket.

'Do you ever wish you'd never asked a question in the first place?' she says quietly as she follows me to the door.

'Do *you*?' I ask her.

She moves her head but it is so slight I can't tell if it is a nod. 'I can't not know it now, can I?'

I shake my head. No, she has to face the fact her husband once slept with someone else. I consider telling her to come back and see me on her own but already she is talking to Tanya, fixing a date for them both the following week.

When they've left, I lock up my room and wander over to the desk, where Tanya is pushing her thick glasses higher up her nose and tapping furiously on her keyboard. She doesn't look up until I'm almost on top of her. 'I'm off then,' I say. 'Sorry I was a little late.'

The phone rings and she checks the line before answering, 'Stella Harvey's office.' I still feel a tingle of pleasure every time I hear her say those words. As she explains the pricing structure of my family counselling sessions I wonder, not for the first time, how much I could save if I didn't have to pay a share of Tanya's salary. I'd had little choice when I'd rented the room with the others in the building. Next to me is a physio and further down the corridor a chiropodist and a reiki healer, but none of us work full time and I don't believe we really need a receptionist.

Tanya hangs up and turns back to her keyboard. A few more taps and she closes down the computer. 'Prospective clients,' she tells me. 'A young couple having problems with their daughter. They're going to call back next week.'

'Thanks,' I say. 'Are you up to anything nice this weekend?'

'Mike and I are visiting his parents. What about you?'

'I'm having lunch at my sister's tomorrow,' I tell her.

'And how is Bonnie?' She raises her eyebrows.

I laugh. 'She's fine. Her husband's away this weekend,' I say, though I'm not sure why I mentioned it. I don't even know whether this means Bonnie will be happier or more pissed off.

Tanya nods, her lips pressed into a thin line, and I imagine her thinking back to the one and only time she met my sister. I know she wasn't keen but I stopped bothering to defend Bonnie long ago. At some point I got past caring what anyone else thought or feeling the need to explain that, with so little family left, I can't be blamed for wanting to cling to her.

Besides, no one has ever been able to understand our relationship. Not even I could explain all the intricacies that tie us together. In most ways we are polar opposites. But I'd made an unspoken promise soon after Danny left that I would always be there for my sister. That was when I began to wonder if it wasn't all Bonnie's fault she was the way she was.

Mum used to whisper to me at night sometimes. When she thought I was sleeping she'd creep into my room, pulling the duvet back over me where I'd kicked it off. I'd liked her kneeling on the floor beside me, her warm breath on my face, the smell of her perfume washing over me, which lingered long after she'd left the room.

'My everything, Stella,' she would whisper as she would gently stroke my hair. 'You're all the babies I ever need.'

I always used to wonder if that left no room for Bonnie.

Tanya and I leave the offices together. She turns left as I cross over towards the park, a cut through on my twenty-minute walk home, past the cathedral and to my flat that sits just on the outskirts of Winchester.

I like the walk home, even in January when the only light is from the street lamps and the cold air bites at my skin. It gives me a chance to mull over my client list for the following week and, as I always do on a Friday, vow to invest more time in building up my business.

Making a decision to set up on my own as a family counsellor hadn't been done on a whim. I was never one of those children who'd decided early on what job they would do. When I was young I thought I'd most likely end up drawing pictures for books just because my best friend, Jill, wanted to be an author, despite not having an artistic bone in my body. Even after A-levels, I still had no idea and it took ten unhappy years in recruitment and a satisfying redundancy package for me to make the break.

It was eleven months ago that I signed up for the training and obligatory counselling I had to undertake myself before I could counsel others. My trainer had underlined the importance of the latter early on. Carrying childhood scars or unresolved issues from previous relationships could make my advice biased.

I'd tried to decline the opportunity but it was clear this wasn't something I was going to get out of, and I knew if I pushed much harder I would raise suspicion. I was sure they'd think it highly unusual that I didn't want to dig into my own family dynamics. But I had filed away most parts of my life into a neat little box and hidden it deep. We were very good at that as a family. I had learnt from the best, even if it did go against everything I expected from my clients.

'So why are you interested in family counselling?' was the first question I'd been asked in my introductory session.

I told her how lucky I'd been growing up. That I'd had very loving parents and my upbringing on the island of Evergreen had been idyllic. I said I was interested in familial relationships and always thought I had an ability to listen and help. I told her the truth to a point. The point where we left the island. Or maybe just before that.

My trainer had been keen to know more about Evergreen, as most people are. 'And only one hundred people lived there?' she'd asked me, stunned.

I nodded. 'Just over. I knew all of them and they all knew me.' I told her how wonderful it was as she gaped back at me. 'I honestly loved it,' I laughed. I knew some people thought it was claustrophobic but there was nowhere else on earth I had wanted to be.

'And you didn't find it too remote?' Another popular question because even though the ferry only took thirty minutes, you couldn't see Evergreen from the Dorset coast.

'I didn't,' I told her. My sister, however, hated the fact that in the winter months my dad's ferry ran only once a day. But then my sister had hated all the things that had made me love it. I had smiled, careful not to let cracks show.

I knew the trainer would soon be digging her fingers into the end of our last summer on the island and the years after we'd left. She would want to know what triggered my family to break down, and I wouldn't be able to tell her. Every one of us had held secrets too close and because we'd never spoken about them, they'd cracked us apart in the end.

I wanted to help other families talk because that's where we went wrong, only I wasn't going to tell her that. Instead I breezed through what happened to us after we left, highlighting only the bare facts.

I try to banish the memories of the few sessions I'd endured, as a drop of rain splats on my head. Soon I need to dive undercover of the nearest shop before I'm drenched. I must have left my umbrella at work, I realise, as I meander towards the wine shelves of the convenience store, choosing a seven-pound bottle of Sauvignon Blanc while waiting for the worst of the rain to pass.

Back at my flat I pour a glass and sit by the window in the kitchen watching the rain that is now steadily drumming against the pane. Despite having little to do this weekend and regardless of the fact I don't work a usual five-day week, I still get that Friday feeling and have got into a comfortable routine: once I have finished this glass I'll make a curry, then have another drink with Marco in his flat above mine while ignoring his pleas to join him clubbing.

As it is, I don't get back to my own flat until just before ten, but I'm not ready to go to bed. Instead I pull a blanket over me and snuggle down on the sofa, flicking on the TV, then grabbing a magazine from the coffee table and idly thumbing through.

The news comes on and I glance up. A reporter is standing outside a house, a large umbrella held over her while the wind whips her ponytail from side to side. My eyes drift to the ticker tape along the bottom of the TV screen and then back again to her. I don't recognise any of the details behind her at first and am about to turn back to the magazine when something catches my attention.

They've caught it at a funny angle, and you'd barely stop to look at it, but there's a distinctive window on the top floor, circular with obscured glass. I inch forward on the sofa and grab the remote again, turning up the volume so I can hear what the reporter is saying over the hammering that's beginning to beat in my ears.

It's funny that I didn't recognise it immediately when every detail is etched on the inside of my eyelids. When all I need to do is call up my memory and I can paint a picture of a thousand pixels in intricate detail. But then it doesn't look the same. Not entirely.

The other windowsills are painted a deep teal and now the camera is panning out so I can see more of the house. There are colonial-style white fascia boards and a conservatory at the front. It doesn't look like my home any longer. Yet unmistakably it is. The white picket fence that runs along the left-hand side is still there. Dad had put that up one summer to separate our garden from the path that runs alongside it. On the right, tall pines still drape the length of the garden.

I feel my pulse racing quicker and I try to ignore it to focus on her words. 'Clearly the whole island is in shock,' she says.

I look back at the ticker tape reeling its breaking news, the words '... *Island last night'* roll out of sight to the left of the screen and a new headline about Syria follows.

'And as yet the police aren't able to release any more details?' This comes from a woman in the studio but the screen is still filled with the view of my house and garden, panning out further still and exposing a white police tent that is flanked by officers. It has been erected on the right at the rear of the property, tucked neatly in between the house and the trees that separate the garden from the woods beyond.

'Not yet, but the forensics teams have been working here all day,' the reporter says.

I look back at the tape. *'Body found on Evergreen Island last night,'* it now reads in full. I scrunch my hands up tightly, willing the blood to rush through them and stop the numbness from spreading up my arms.

A body has been found on the island. And even though no one has said it outright, it's clear it's been buried in the garden of my old house.